Praise for

One Part Angel

"Enchanting . . . Readers will keep reading." —*Publishers Weekly*

"Quietly inspirational, quirkily humorous, Shaffner's feel-good sequel to *In the Land of Second Chances* firmly launches what promises to be an uproarious and uplifting series." —*Booklist*

"George Shaffner . . . continues his delightful explorations of small-town life." —*Seattle Post-Intelligencer*

Praise for

In the Land of Second Chances

"If you've been charmed by Jimmy Stewart and the small-town miracles of *It's a Wonderful Life,* treat yourself to this unusual little novel full of hope, humor, and singular characters." —*Parade*

"*Chances* morphs from *Fried Green Tomatoes* into a wisecracking *It's a Wonderful Life.*" —*Entertainment Weekly*

"A winsome fable." —*Kirkus Reviews* (starred review)

"An accessible, engaging story peppered with characters who are eccentric, conflicted, tragic, and humorous." —*Seattle Post-Intelligencer*

"Just what the doctor ordered." —*Detroit Free Press*

"A folksy, wise, and gently amusing look at the importance of living life to the fullest and not only trusting in chance, but embracing uncertainty as the spice of life." —*Rocky Mountain News*

ALSO BY GEORGE SHAFFNER

In the Land of Second Chances
The Arithmetic of Life and Death

One Part Angel

One Part Angel

a novel

George Shaffner

BALLANTINE BOOKS ∎ NEW YORK

2007 Ballantine Books Trade Paperback Edition

Copyright © 2006 by George Shaffner
Reading group guide copyright © 2007 by Random House, Inc.

Published in the United States by Ballantine Books, an imprint of The Random House Publishing Group, a division of Random House, Inc., New York.

BALLANTINE and colophon are registered trademarks of Random House, Inc. READER'S CIRCLE and colophon are trademarks of Random House, Inc.

Originally published in hardcover by Algonquin Books of Chapel Hill, a division of Workman Publishing, Chapel Hill, North Carolina, and in Canada by Thomas Allen & Son Limited in 2006.

ISBN 978-0-345-48499-4

Library of Congress Cataloging-in-Publication Data

Shaffner, George.
    One part angel : a novel / by George Shaffner.
      p. cm.
    ISBN 978-0-345-48499-4
      1. Nebraska—Fiction.   2. City and town life—Fiction.   3. Female
friendship—Fiction.   4. Bed and breakfast accommodations—Fiction.
5. Traveling sales personnel—Fiction.   6. Life change events—Fiction.
7. Psychological fiction.   I. Title.
PS3619.H345O54 2006
813'.6—dc22   2005054577

Printed in the United States of America

www.thereaderscircle.com

9 8 7 6 5 4 3 2 1

Design by Anne Winslow

For Annie and Bill

With thanks to Kathy Atchison, Jane Dystel, Antonia Fusco, Miriam Goderich, Amy Johnson, Grace, and the kids.

One Part Angel

Chapter 1

Back in the Soup

YOU MAY REMEMBER ME; my name is Wilma Porter. I own the Come Again Bed and Breakfast, which is the last B & B in Ebb, Nebraska, and the only one in Rutherford B. Hayes County that is recommended by nine Internet directories. Some time ago, I wrote to you about our local troubles and how they were fixed by an unusual lodger of mine, a man named Vernon L. Moore. Well, a lot has changed since he left, meaning we're right back in the soup.

On the second Saturday of last September, the Bold Cut Beauty Salon was vandalized and set afire by three young men in ski masks. Loretta Parsons, the owner of the salon, Ebb's sole resident black person and my best friend, was beaten into a coma, which broke my heart, and that's not all. Before she lost consciousness, Loretta managed to say a few words to Dot Hrnicek, our county sheriff, about the sweater of one of her assailants. A fiber underneath one of Lo's fingernails subsequently revealed the identity of its owner: none other than Matthew Breck, my grandson. Did I tell you that my heart was broken?

The next thing we knew, Matt was sitting in the county jail awaiting sentencing for two counts of attempted murder, one count of first-degree arson, and a long list of lesser offenses that added up to 150 years in prison—if Loretta lived. Then "Hail Mary" Wade, the county attorney, offered him a plea bargain, but only if he would name his two accomplices.

As I live and breathe, Matt wouldn't do it. Hail Mary couldn't convince him to spill the beans; Dottie couldn't either. He wouldn't say word one to his mama or me. Clem Tucker, who is the richest man in southeast Nebraska and my Fiancé in Perpetuity, hired a big-time criminal lawyer from Chicago, but even he couldn't get through to that boy. Meanwhile, his mama was sobbing herself to sleep every night, Loretta was not getting any better, and two of her assailants were running free, which frightened everybody.

Loretta used to call our town the Last Oasis of Nice, but we were in deep, deep trouble and there was nowhere else to turn, so I got down on my knees and asked the Lord to send Vernon Moore back to help us one more time. I'm still not sure I believe what happened next. I didn't bear witness to every pot he stirred myself but, with the help of the Quilting Circle network, my fiancé, and a few of my men friends—plus a peek or two at some police transcripts—I finally managed to piece it all together.

You'll have to come to your own conclusions.

Chapter 2

Large Talk

I HAVE A BIG BRASS knocker on my front door that must weigh five pounds. My daughter Mona says it can be heard in Kansas. I was sound asleep when it smacked my door two times—*wham, wham.* I rolled over and checked the clock. It was five forty-five on Monday morning, which made me surly. Even in the country, right-minded folk don't go around beating on other people's doors before dawn.

I hadn't decided whether I would answer when I heard the knocker again—*wham, wham*—and that settled the matter. I hauled myself up, adjusted my hair in the mirror, and hoped to God that my slept-in-the-barn countenance didn't frighten my untimely caller to death.

Standing right there on my porch, bathed in the glow of a single, predawn porch light, was none other than Vernon L. Moore. The sun wasn't even up, but he was clean-shaven, his hair was combed, and he was dressed in one of those thousand-dollar suits of his. It was a black pinstriped, double-breasted affair and there was hardly a wrinkle in it. If I hadn't known better, I would've thought that 007's whiter-haired brother had come to visit my B & B.

Words failed me. I know what you're thinking, but it wasn't the first time.

Mr. Moore looked down at me with those crystalline blue eyes of his and said, "Is there room at the inn?"

Well, what's a girl supposed to do? I grabbed him around the neck and gave him a big smushy kiss on the cheek. After that, I stepped back and exclaimed, "You get into my house right now, Vernon Moore! Where have you been?"

He tried to answer, but I wasn't done. "One minute you were here; the next minute you were gone. You didn't write; you didn't call. Where did you go for so long? Couldn't you have stopped by to see Loretta? And me?"

I suppose a woman ought to allow a man to talk after she's asked him sixteen questions in a row. I almost did, but I gave him a big hug instead and asked, "Where are your bags?"

He pointed toward his car, a white, flat-roofed Chrysler parked in the little lot under the grand old oak tree just beyond my porte-cochere. Even in the dim light from my porch, it looked shiny and brand new. Before I could say boo about it, he remarked, "It's wonderful to see you again, Wilma. You're more beautiful than ever."

That's what he said, and I looked like I'd just been rolled across the rodeo floor. I couldn't have been any uglier if I had alfalfa shoots sticking out of my hair.

"Do you have room for an old salesman?" he repeated.

"If I didn't," I replied, "I'd heave my own kin out the back door. You're on the second floor in the same room you had before. It's all made up, fresh sheets and all, and there's a radio and an ironing board already in it. Why don't you take your bags up and change into something more countrified? Meanwhile, I'll make you some tea and a waffle. How would that be?"

"That would be perfect, Wilma."

My eyes followed him as he turned and walked back to his car. He still had nice buns, which reminded me of the last time I had watched him walk away. I stopped myself right there because I was afraid that I was assuming too much. For all I knew at the time, his arrival was just a coincidence: he had come back to Ebb to see Loretta at last, but he had no idea what had happened.

I left the door open and went back to my kitchen in the rear of the house. It's commercial grade, you know. I could cook for a regiment and feed them in my dining room. Everything about the Come Again is big, including the six bedrooms and five bathrooms on the second floor. Clara Tucker Booth Yune, Hayes County's most famous recluse, occupies the entire third floor all by herself.

I was just finishing up the waffle batter when Mr. Moore came down the back stairs wearing jeans, a collarless white shirt, and running shoes; still slim and trim and straight as a rail. If you saw him from the shoulders down, you might mistake him for a military man. From the neck up, he looked like a middle-aged gentleman who'd beaten life's hardships into fond memories. The lines on his face crinkled when he laughed, his eyes twinkled like the stars on a cloudless night, and he had a smile that could stop a bar fight.

By now, you might be wondering if I had once had designs on Vernon Moore myself, but that was never the case. Not really, anyway. At the end of his last and only visit to Ebb, he was snared by Loretta Parsons, my best friend, but she couldn't hold him. Lo never could hold a man, but I wonder if any woman could keep a bridle on Vernon L. Moore.

He took a deep breath and said, "It's a delight to be back, Wilma. Of all the places I've visited over the years, this feels most like home. It must be you."

Before I could reply, he sat down in his usual spot at my kitchen table, just like he'd been sitting there every day since Elvis died. He added, "You have to tell me everything that's happened since my last visit, starting with Loretta. How is she?"

Well, that was all it took. I started sobbing like a schoolgirl. A two-time mother, four-time grandmother, battle-savvy divorcée, business-woman, and founder of the infamous Quilting Circle ought to be able to do better than that, but I couldn't. The next thing I knew, Mr. Moore was taking me in his arms. I just put my head on his shoulder and bawled—a long, doleful, shuddering bawl—until my tear ducts ran out of ammunition. His shoulder must have been soaking wet but I didn't notice. I was thinking about my best friend, my grandson, my daughter, and my poor, pitiful self.

I was about to reach for a Kleenex in my apron, but Mr. Moore beat me to the punch and handed me a white cotton hanky that he had in his left rear pocket. I blew my nose right there in front of him and said, "I'm so sorry, Mr. Moore. I'll wash it before I return it to you."

"Don't give it a second thought. It's a gift."

I looked down at the handkerchief. It had the initials WRP mono-grammed in navy blue on one corner. My middle name is Ruth. How did he know that? I started to protest but he said, "It was made in Cambodia. Please keep it."

"Thank you," I replied, still mystified. With Mr. Moore, it was best to let things go sometimes. You never knew if you were going to get a one-word retort, a sales pitch, or a sermonette. I blew my nose again and added, "Your tea is steeping and I have some freshly sliced bacon and crumbled pecan for your waffle. How would that be?"

"Better than perfect."

I turned around to wash my hands in the sink.

Most folks like to say they aren't good at small talk. I can't say that; I'm very good at small talk. It's the large talk I have trouble with. I knew it was time for me to tell Mr. Moore about Loretta's sad state but I had no idea where to begin. I turned around and said, "Can I tell you all the news after breakfast? I could use the time to organize my thoughts."

"That would be fine, Wilma. I'm in no hurry."

While we ate, we talked about the weather. Next to football, it's the most reliable topic in Nebraska. I thought about telling Mr. Moore about Clem Tucker and the Big Buyback, too, but I decided to put it off. That was closer to large talk than small.

After breakfast was over, I cleared the table and sat back down. "Okay," I said. "I'm ready to fill you in. If I start to blubber again, would you do me a favor and pour a bucketful of cold water over my head?"

"The news can wait, really."

"No it can't. If you're going to help us, we have to get a move on."

"Then you better tell me everything, starting with Loretta."

I could feel my eyes welling up, so I took Mr. Moore's hanky out of my pocket. It felt damp and cold, like it was used, so I decided to cut to the chase. "She's in a coma in the county hospital. Nobody knows if she'll ever come out of it."

I was afraid that Mr. Moore would get all emotional when I told him the news—fighting mad or terribly sad or something like that. I cried for days and days myself. Loretta wasn't only my best friend, she was my keel. When ill winds blew in the Porter household, she was the one who kept me from falling over. Now I fall over all the time.

Mr. Moore must've had his own keel. He said evenly, "I stopped by the hospital on my way in this morning."

I ought to have known better by then, but my chin fell to my belly button the moment Mr. Moore mentioned that he had already seen Loretta. "You did? How did you know?"

"I can't explain, Wilma. All I can say is that I know very little, too little. How did Loretta get hurt? Give me the details, please."

I turned away; I so wanted to beat around the bush. Without looking back, I said, "It's not the how you need to know, Mr. Moore. It's the who. It was Matt. Matt and two others."

"Matthew Breck? Your grandson? How? Why?"

I started to well up again but I gritted my teeth. "Sometime in the wee hours after the Homecoming Dance over at the high school, Matt and two of his friends went to the Bold Cut. They smashed up the salon with a baseball bat and threw red paint all over everything. Loretta came downstairs when she heard the ruckus, so they beat her up and threw red paint on her, too. When they were done, they set the place on fire.

"The fire trucks got there in minutes but the main floor was burned out, and the smoke and water ruined Loretta's upstairs apartment, including some of her antique furniture and most of her book collection. If she knew, it would break her heart."

"The things can be replaced. What happened to Loretta?"

"Those boys beat her to the verge, Mr. Moore. She had broken ribs, a punctured lung, a broken forearm, and bleeding inside her cranium. The doctors cut a little hole in her skull to reduce the pressure, but it was too late. She had already lapsed into the coma." I glanced at the pink baby monitor on the wall and added, "There's something else, Mr. . . ."

"Matt didn't act alone. Who were the other two?"

"That's what everybody wants to know, but he won't name them."

"Hmmm. They were probably people he knew. What can you tell me about his friends?"

I took a deep breath. "Not very much. Matt was a popular boy at school: good-looking; a fine athlete; a committed underachiever; a smoker; everything teenagers seem to admire nowadays. At the beginning of the school year, he even fell in with two boys from some kind of religious sect on the other side of the county."

Mr. Moore leaned forward. "A sect or a cult?"

"I don't know what they call themselves. According to Matt, they spend six days farming and Sundays in church. They believe in strict interpretation of the scriptures, word-for-word, and that anybody who doesn't is going straight to hell."

"I see. Is there a name for this group?"

"There is and it's a name and a half. They call it the Divine Temple of the Everlasting God Almighty."

"That is a mouthful. What else can you tell me about these people?"

"The women are dour and barely polite. They wear homemade, ankle-length dresses with cotton bibs, simple shoes, and white bonnets. The men dress up like cowboys: blue jeans, boots, cowboy hats, thick belts with silver buckles. Unlike the women, they're a smiley bunch."

"I take it that they come to town from time to time?"

"The men come in every couple of weeks or so, usually to visit the bank or the Corn Palace. We hardly ever see their women."

The Corn Palace is a pre–World War II Quonset hut with a saloon-like storefront on the far end of Main. It's been Ebb's chief watering hole since before I was born, and it's still the place where men get together in these parts. They have a dart board, a shuffleboard, and two pool tables over there, plus a half dozen TVs stuck high up on the walls that play nothing but ESPN from opening 'til closing time. They even have sawdust and peanut shells on the floor. A lot of the old-timers sit around there all day and play pinochle or pitch for money. They don't play for much, but a retired man needs a reason to brag every once in a while.

The Corn Palace also serves the best burgers and the finest fried clams in the county, bar none. Even I go there for lunch sometimes, but I don't go in expecting a salad. Except for the beer on St. Patrick's Day, half a dill pickle is about the only green fare you'll ever see.

"Did the men from this sect ever stop at the Bold Cut?"

"They used to, but they quit going months ago. Loretta mentioned it to me herself."

"Why?"

"She told me she refused to serve their leader, a man named Reverend Gault. I guess he didn't like Loretta's attitude. Some men don't. Anyway, they never went back after that." I added, "You seem to be awful interested in the Divine Temple, Mr. Moore. Dottie was, too. Do you think they were involved?"

"I have no idea whether they were or not, Wilma. Zealots interest me, that's all; especially religious zealots. Did Matt's association with these people affect his behavior?"

"We were on the alert but it didn't seem to make any difference at all. He kept right on smoking and getting into trouble at school, just like always. Up until the very day of the Bold Cut incident, he was just a sulky, mopey, teenaged kid with a melon-sized burr under his saddle."

"Imagine that. An angry, disaffected teenager. As I recall, his parents separated a few years ago. Could that have been the burr?"

I cleared my throat. "Matt was always a sullen boy, but I think it was the last straw. He had a heck of a time accepting the divorce. He had a hard time changing schools, too. His mama and I did everything we could to help him. So did his teachers, but it didn't seem to do a speck of good."

Mr. Moore was silent for a moment, and then said, "Sometimes, the people who need help the most are the ones who want it the least. Where is Matt now?"

"He's in the county jail awaiting sentencing."

"Are any of his friends from the Divine Temple on the suspect list?"

"I'm sure they are, but there wasn't any proof. Dot was spitting fire. She would've charged three sheep if she had found fleece at the scene. I know it for sure."

Mr. Moore stood up. "I need to take a walk," he said. "You might want to check on Laverne. She may be awake by now."

He was gone from my kitchen before I could get the knot out of my tongue.

I have never been completely certain that Loretta captured Mr. Moore's heart, but she definitely captured his body. He was in Ebb for only a week, but that was long enough for him to father Laverne, and then he disappeared. Loretta was never able to contact him with the news. As far as I know, nobody else did either, which raises a question: How did he know that she had given birth to his child? And that raises another question: If he knew, why didn't he come back sooner, a lot sooner?

Lo never expected him back, bless her heart. She said Laverne was a gift, not an obligation, and her choice, not Mr. Moore's—except during her labor, which was an exhausting, painful affair. She said things about Mr. Moore in the final hour that I have never heard any woman say about any man, alive or dead.

Laverne Parsons was a scrawny little thing at birth, all knees and elbows, but she is my godchild now, and the prettiest little girl in the county. She has huge, amber-colored eyes with long, curly lashes, black, silky hair, and beautiful, milk-chocolate-colored skin. Her second birthday is two months away, but she is just discovering the power of words. She calls both Mona and me "mee-maw" and all cats and dogs are named "kitty." If Laverne doesn't have a word for what she wants, she points and says "mine," and she expects you to hop to it, too.

The most interesting thing about Laverne is the way she looks at the world. She can sit in a high chair at Starbucks for an hour straight without ever getting cranky or saying word one. She just watches the people of Ebb go by, and she never cries. I have never seen her shed a tear.

Of course, Mona and I are raising her now, just as if she was our very own—maybe even more so; we feel so bad for Loretta. Even Mark pitches in. He's Matt's younger brother and Ebb's next tycoon.

Mr. Moore didn't get back to the Come Again until almost nine a.m. By then, Mark had gone to school and Mona was over at the Bold Cut supervising the restoration of the salon. When he came into my kitchen, Laverne was sitting in her high chair eating banana slices and Cheerios. Well, that's nearly what she was doing. Most of her baby teeth were in so she could chew the Cheerios just fine, but she preferred to squish the banana on her tray.

Mr. Moore went straight to her side, knelt down, and said, "Hello, sweetheart. I thought I was your father, but you're much too pretty for that. I couldn't be the father of any girl who's as beautiful as you are."

Laverne smiled at Mr. Moore and said, "Juice?" Then she smeared banana across his forehead. They were officially introduced.

He talked to her for a while after that. I washed the dishes and tried not to listen to what was said. When I was done, he asked, "Can we go for a walk?"

"What about Loretta?" I asked.

"I'll see her later today, but I'd like to get to know my daughter a little first. Will you come along?"

"Are you sure you want me to, Mr. Moore? I don't want to get in the way."

"You won't, Wilma. Besides, I sense that you have more to tell me."

"Isn't that a fact?" I replied.

Chapter 3

....

One Foot in Front of the Other

CALL ME OLD-FASHIONED, but I don't like to wear pants. I might if I had the hips of a teenaged girl, but I'm heavier now. Thirty years of child rearing and leftovers will do that to you. Like many of my sex, most of the extra poundage has been deposited in my derriere. That's why I wear dresses, floral ones mostly. I wear hose when I go out too, even during the daytime. I know they don't match my running shoes the way they should, but they tighten and tone my legs.

Mr. Moore jumped up from the wooden bench under my porte-cochere when I wheeled Laverne through the door in her stroller. It was cloudy and chilly outside, so I had dressed her in a little red and white Care Bears outfit, with a white sweater, a white, crocheted hat, and little white footies.

"We're ready to boogie," I said. "Where would you like to go?"

"Can we head down to Main Street toward Millet's?"

Millet's is the last department store in three counties. Mr. Moore saved it when he last came to town, plain and simple. If he hadn't, there'd be a Wal-Mart in a ravine fifteen miles away and downtown Ebb would be as dead as the Roman Empire. Mr. Moore saved the owner, too, a real popular man in these parts named Calvin Millet, although the cost was high. A year ago, Calvin hired Bebe Palouse, which rhymes with "canoes," to run the store. Thanks to her, it's a much better place for women to shop, but the men probably don't like it as much because the store no longer carries handguns or chewing tobacco. Some progress is good.

As we started down my driveway, Mr. Moore asked, "How is Mona?"

Mona is my eldest daughter and Matt's divorced mother. At the mention of her name, I took a deep breath. "She's doing her best, Mr. Moore. She goes to see Matt at the county jail every single day and she takes care of his brother Mark. When she can, she helps me with Laverne, and she is supervising the reconstruction of Lo's salon."

"How is she dealing with Matt's incarceration?"

"She's doing what you and I are doing right now, Mr. Moore; she's putting one foot in front of the other. There can't be any closure until Matt is sent off to jail and we know what's going to happen to Loretta. Until then, I'm afraid we'll all be stuck on a treadmill just like the one Clara has upstairs. We may be putting one foot in front of the other, but we're really standing still."

Clara Tucker Booth Yune is the strangest woman in the state. She lives on the third floor of the Come Again, where she spends her time exercising, watching movies from the 1940s—Clark Gable is her latest favorite—and playing gin rummy with my grandson Mark. Except when Mr. Moore was here, she hasn't said a single word other than "yes" or "no" in ten years.

Mr. Moore asked, "How is Clara?"

"That woman hasn't changed a whit. She's as skinny as a reed. She still wears leotards mostly and keeps her hair in a ponytail. If there was a cheerleading job at the university for a mute, sixty-year-old recluse, Clara would be a lock."

"How are she and Clem getting along these days?"

Clem Tucker is the owner of the local bank and the richest man in southeast Nebraska by a country mile. He could buy or sell half the state any time he wanted to, which keeps the townsfolk of Ebb constantly on edge. They never know what he's going to do next. I don't either and I've been engaged to the man for upwards of two years.

"They're the same as always, Mr. Moore. Clara tries to give her money away from time to time; Clem tries to stop her. He's been upstairs to see her a few times lately, though. That's unusual. It's not like they could be talking."

"And how about you and Clem?" Mr. Moore asked. "I had a suspicion that you two might be getting back together."

We turned the corner as I was about to answer, and there, walking half a dozen dogs of various varieties without a leash, was none other than Lulu Tiller. Lulu is a tall, redheaded divorcée who likes to wear jodhpurs and boots. She made some sort of signal with her hands and the dogs stopped dead and sat down. Before I could say a word of introduction, she said, "Hello, Wilma, and welcome, Mr. Moore. A few of us had a feeling you'd be back some day."

"Mr. Moore, this is Lulu Tiller. She's the town veterinarian and Queen Bee of the Quilting Circle. You probably don't remember, but I introduced you two on almost this exact same spot a little over two years ago."

Laverne pointed at one of the dogs, a big German shepherd, and exclaimed, "Kitty!"

"Of course I remember," Mr. Moore replied. He shook Lulu's hand

and continued, "I've never been able to convince Wilma, but would you call me Vernon? It's a pleasure to see you again."

"The pleasure is mine, Vernon. Did you know that you've become famous in the Circle since you left?"

I've never told you much about the Quilting Circle, but I suppose I have to now. Years ago, Lulu, yours truly, and a few other women decided to form a club with two goals. The first was to make sure that every child in Ebb was warm at night. The second was to make Ebb the nicest place on earth to live, which meant keeping a harness on Clem Tucker more than anything else. Today, there are two hundred women in the Quilting Circle and no men. Nearly half of us are grandmas and two-thirds of us are divorcées. To be truthful, not every woman in the Circle makes quilts, but most everybody sews: My specialty is classic American patchwork quilts; Mona and Lily Park Pickett make beautiful, long-flowing Hawaiian quilts; Lulu Tiller hooks rugs and does needlepoint; Dottie knits; and Loretta embroiders the most exquisite pillow cases you can imagine.

When we aren't sewing, we work on various community projects and manage our political agenda. Almost every prominent woman in the county is in the Quilting Circle, including the county supervisor, the county prosecutor, the county sheriff, the superintendent of schools, the county assessor, and the owners of more than half the stores in Ebb. The main exception is Clem's sister, Clara. I guess recluses don't make good joiners, but we have enough clout to give Clem a fair fight anyway. He doesn't always fight fair to be sure, but we can usually keep him on the straight and narrow when we need to. The only time we couldn't, Mr. Moore came to town and saved our bacon.

He said, "I don't know what I could've possibly done to become famous. I was only here for a few days."

"It's no mystery," Lulu replied. "Some folks say you saved the town. I say you gave us hope when we needed it." She shifted her eyes to me and said, "I take it you've already told him about Loretta and Matt."

"I have," I answered.

Lulu is a fine person, but she has a persistent problem: she's a veterinarian who's allergic to animal dander. Doc Wiley changes her medication all the time because it never seems to work right. Lulu is always itching; and she never feels as if she shouldn't scratch, no matter where it is or she is.

She must've gotten an itch under her panty line because she started to scratch her bottom as she said, "Except for the odd drunk husband, we women have always felt safe in Ebb, Mr. Moore. But ever since the attack on poor Loretta, we've been like lambs ravaged by wolves. Half of us can't get to sleep at night and the other half are buying handguns. I can't speak for Wilma, but I don't want to live in a town where fifty percent of my friends are dead tired and the rest are armed to the gills. We need your help again."

"I'll do what I can, Ms. Tiller."

"Good." Lulu stopped scratching, thank God, and then she looked at me and added, "How about Clem? Have you told Mr. Moore about his latest adventure? He should know about that, too."

"I haven't," I answered sheepishly, as if I'd forgotten a footnote in a book report.

"Don't put it off, Wilma. You know he won't be here for long."

With that, Lulu gave the dogs another secret signal and they all jumped up at once and started wagging their tails. We said our goodbyes and off they went in single file. Laverne waved and said "bye-bye" as they cantered by her stroller, one by one.

Mr. Moore hunkered down and waved with her, then he said to me, "As I remember, we aren't far from Starbucks. How about a mocha?"

Chapter 4

....

The First Shoe

BACK WHEN WE STARTED the Quilting Circle, Ebb was a picture of rural flight. The stores were rundown, the streets were nearly empty, and weed-infested lots dotted Main Street. Since then, we've gotten everyone in the county to work together to restore the downtown area. Today, Ebb looks like what Hannibal, Missouri, could've been 150 years ago, except for the carts and the horse poop, of course. Cast-iron streetlights and red maple trees line Main Street and there are park benches or big flowerpots on every block. It's the loveliest spot in Nebraska at Christmastime when the lights are up, especially on a clear, crisp night.

The stores on Main Street are cheek to jowl now and most of them have an Old West façade, even the Starbucks. On the inside, though, it could be any old coffeehouse, except that Olga Nordhagen, the franchise owner, put some booths in the back so folks could talk privately. Note to Howard: Every Starbucks should have a few of those.

Mr. Moore bought Laverne a small chocolate milk, me a grande latte, and himself a tall, no whip mocha. I like the whip myself; I don't see why a person wouldn't, but there you have it. Who would've ever thought that one store could invent so many drinks made out of coffee beans, milk, cocoa, and water?

We took a booth in the rear and I put Laverne in a high chair. By the time we were settled, I couldn't hold myself in any longer. I said, "If you knew about your daughter, why didn't you come back sooner? Lo would never admit it, but she needed you."

Mr. Moore looked down at the table before he answered, and then he looked into my eyes and said, "It wasn't my choice, Wilma."

"It wasn't your choice? I thought you were self-employed. Couldn't you at least . . . ."

"I was, Wilma, but I retired. That's all I can say for now, except that I hope you can trust me. God willing, things will work out in the long run."

Half the folks in Ebb have a theory about who—or what—Mr. Moore really was or is. The rest of us have three or four. "You're retired? But . . ."

All of a sudden, Mr. Moore's face became stern. Miss Giles, my six foot four, sixth-grade teacher used to look at me like that. It meant, "Close your mouth, Willy."

I started to reply anyway, but then I bit my tongue. I guess I didn't bite it hard enough. "Have you come to help us again?" I asked. "I have to know that much. Loretta's on death's doorstep, Matt could spend the rest of his natural life in jail, and half the storeowners in town are afraid they're next. I'm at my wit's end."

"I'll do my best, but I can only stay for a few days."

In the country, you learn to shut up and take what you can get. "A lot of people around here still think you walk on water," I said. "If a few days is all we can have, then a few days will have to be enough."

Mr. Moore changed the subject. "Tell me about you and Clem," he said.

"We're engaged," I answered flatly, "but you wouldn't know it."

"That's wonderful, I think. When's the big date?"

"That's why you wouldn't know it. We haven't set it yet."

"Whoa. That's a surprise. How long have you two been engaged?"

"For two years."

"Two years? What's the holdup?"

"Two words," I answered. "Pre-nup."

Mr. Moore sat back in the booth and Laverne giggled as if she knew what I was talking about. I shook my head and continued, "We tried to negotiate a marriage contract for months. When I say we, I don't mean Clem and me; I mean me and Clem's lawyers. Clem was preoccupied with a business deal."

"I take it you couldn't come to terms."

"It got to be a matter of principle, Mr. Moore: Clem wanted to keep all the principal. I'm not a greedy woman, not by a long shot, but a wife should have certain rights, and a fair inheritance is one of them."

"But you're still engaged?"

"It's odd but we are. Except for being unable to turn a matrimony into a business deal, we get along just fine." I didn't add that there would have been an uproar inside the Circle if Clem and I broke off.

"I take it you two live apart. Is that right? Do you see each other regularly?"

Normally, a woman of my age wouldn't admit to living in sin. On the other hand, a woman of my age wouldn't normally have the opportunity. I didn't know whether to be ashamed or proud, so I blushed. "Mona doesn't have to work weekends anymore. If we don't have any guests, I go down to the River House."

Mr. Moore smiled sweetly, as if he was forgiving my transgression. That's the way I felt anyway. "How is Clem?" he asked. "What's he been up to in the last two years?"

I replied, "The Big Buyback, plain and simple."

"The Big Buyback?"

"It was the most amazing thing anybody ever saw, Mr. Moore. Clem never said word one to me about it, but he decided to sell all the farmland owned by the family trust. A passel of it went to various Tuckers but most went to tenant farmers, nearly two hundred of them."

"Really? When did this happen?"

"Last year, which is when we gave up on the pre-nup. Clem was too busy to talk to his own lawyers about it. They were too busy with the legal particulars of the buyback."

Mr. Moore seemed a bit puzzled. "Just out of curiosity, how were the sales structured?"

"As I recall, everybody had three options: they could pay cash; they could borrow the money from HCB; or they could choose not to buy." HCB is Ebb's own Hayes County Bank, which Clem owns lock, stock, and barrel through the family trust.

"What happened if the farmers took the third option?"

"None of them did. They all knew that Clem could turn around and sell the land to somebody else . . ."

Mr. Moore finished my sentence, ". . . which would've put them out of a job . . ."

". . . and a home," I added. Farming is a hard life, and it's not just the backbreaking, fifteen-hour days, the capriciousness of the weather, and the dirt-cheap foreign competition. When a farmer loses his job, he loses his home at the same time. I live out here in the country, and even I don't know how they manage.

"Two hundred land sales and another two hundred loan transactions," Mr. Moore remarked. "No wonder Clem was so busy. I'm surprised he didn't sell out to one of the big agricultural conglomerates. It would've been easier and a lot less risky."

"He couldn't," I answered proudly. "There's a law against it. Farms have to be owned by families in Nebraska, which is the way it ought to be everywhere."

"Really?"

"It's a fact. The law was originally called Initiative 300, I think, or I-300. It became an amendment to the state constitution in 1982 or thereabouts."

Back then, we all believed that I-300 would stop rural flight, but all it did was slow the exodus down. Every year, a few more Nebraska towns evaporate into thin air. That makes the rest of us feel lucky and unlucky at the same time, like we're some sort of endangered species. I suppose we are in a way, but we aren't under federal protection.

Mr. Moore said, "I can see how that would be good for family farmers, but Clem's position is harder to understand. He seems to have concentrated his wealth in the local bank. Rural banks have always been a high-risk proposition, at least from an investment point of view."

"What are you saying, Mr. Moore?"

"It would appear that Clem is carrying too much risk in his investment portfolio. In normal circumstances, one would expect him to sell some portion of the bank so he could distribute his risk across a wider spectrum of investments."

"Sell the bank? Clem would never do that," I said confidently, as if Clem ever said boo to me about his business dealings.

"Not the whole thing, Wilma. Just a minority share."

That got me to thinking. "Maybe that's what Lulu was talking about. Everybody in the Circle is worried to death about what Clem will do next." I didn't add that Clem had been visited by a number of big banks in recent months. The Circle likes to keep tabs on things like that, but we don't talk about it much.

"If I may ask," Mr. Moore said, "why are you still worried about Clem? It sounds as if he did the farmers and the county a great service."

"Some folks have that opinion, but just as many believe that the farmers were forced to buy the land at an inflated price. Clem hasn't done much of anything since, either, except sit on his pile of money. It's like we're all waiting for the second shoe to drop."

"Really? Has he talked to you about this second shoe?"

"I asked once, in a nice way, but all he did was give me a bunch of mumbo-jumbo about continuously reevaluating the family's investment posture. I interpreted that as, 'Drop your question and back away from my business affairs.' "

"Hmmm. Is Calvin Millet still working for Clem?"

"He is. He did a lot of the spadework for the Big Buyback. Now he helps Clem manage the side of the family trust that's invested in stocks and bonds."

"He must be busy if Clem has that much money in play. Do you see him often?"

"Before the Big Buyback, I used to have Calvin over for dinner every week or so. Mona was so sweet on him when they were in high school. I hoped the spark would be rekindled."

"It wasn't, I take it."

"I don't know if there are very many sparks left in Calvin Millet's spark bucket," I answered. "Nowadays, people hardly see him at all. He flies all over the country on Tucker Trust business, but he keeps to himself when he's in town. I can't remember the last time I saw him in here or over at the Corn Palace."

Mr. Moore appeared to be distracted by Laverne. She had poured some of her chocolate milk onto her tray and was stirring it around, as if she was finger-painting. She stuck her index finger in the air so I could see it and said, "Juice?"

I pinched her cheek. "You should say hello to Calvin while you're here, Mr. Moore. Clem, too. They'll both expect to see you."

He checked his watch. "I'm having lunch with Clem at the River House in an hour."

"You're having lunch? Today?"

"I called earlier this morning," he said and pinched Laverne on the other cheek.

"How about Mona?" I asked. "Do you plan to visit her?"

"I stopped by the salon to say hello this morning during my walk. We're getting together this afternoon at three o'clock." Mr. Moore added, "There's one other person I'd like to see, but I can't seem to locate him."

"Maybe I can help. Who is it?"

"Silas the Second. I missed him the last time I was in town. I'd hate to miss him again."

"I'd help if I could, Mr. Moore, but I'm not doing any renovating at the moment, and that's when Silas usually shows up."

In case you're wondering, Silas the Second is Silas Tucker II, the man who built the Tucker mansion, which later became the Come Again. He's been dead for 125 years, but he still likes to drift in and check on the place every now and then.

"Is there something I can do that might attract his attention?" Mr. Moore asked.

"Well, you might try rearranging the furniture in your room, or you might invite somebody special to visit the Come Again. That'll bring him out sometimes, too."

Out of the blue, Mr. Moore asked, "Does he read?"

"Silas the Second?" I answered. "I suppose he does, or did."

"Then maybe I can leave him a note. Maybe that'll work."

Why didn't I think of that? If you want to visit a ghost, leave a note.

Chapter 5

The Opening Gambit

WITH THE EXCEPTION OF the Come Again, Clem's River House is the prettiest place in southeast Nebraska. It's built out of redwood logs, ranch-style, and sits high on a bluff overlooking the Missouri River. From the outside, it doesn't look much larger than any home you might see in an up-market subdivision in Lincoln or Omaha, but the appearance is deceiving. It has five bedrooms and eight bathrooms, most of which are in use. Clem doesn't live alone, our weekend trysts notwithstanding. His cook, Marie Delacroix, stays at the River House year round, and so does his new chauffeur and bodyguard, a man named John Smith.

I know what you're thinking: nobody is really named John Smith. But Dot Hrnicek checked him out. She says that there are fifty thousand John Smiths in the United States and he is the genuine article.

John is a former Army Ranger; a tall, muscular man with a burr haircut who is always wearing dark glasses. He's acquired a reputation for keeping to himself, but not around me. That's not to say he's chatty, but he's friendly and attentive: he never lets me open doors or carry packages. If he wasn't fifteen years my junior and employed by my fiancé, I might be suspicious of his motives.

He answered the door when my unusual lodger arrived at the River House for his luncheon appointment. I wasn't there, but I know what John was wearing: black. That's all he ever wears, head to toe. Mr. Moore was wearing a navy blue blazer, a pink shirt with a white collar, a maroon tie, and gray slacks. John introduced himself and escorted his guest to the dining hall, which is just what you would expect in any old hunting lodge, except it's bigger. There are twenty animal heads mounted on the walls, plus enough empty space for at least eight more, and that's without scrunching them together. Like I said, it's a large room.

While John went to fetch Clem, Mr. Moore admired the Waterford crystal and Wakely and Wheeler silver that had been laid out. In the meantime, Marie came in with the first course, a spinach, walnut, and tangerine salad with poppy-seed dressing. It was served on white Wedgwood. That's a whole lot of dinner service W's, but I have no explanation.

Clem tells me that I'm the best cook in the county, but anybody who has ever eaten at the River House knows better. Marie Delacroix could cook me under the table. She eats what she cooks, too, which might be the professional thing to do, but it has certain consequences. We've tried to enroll her in diet and exercise programs at the Circle, but Marie doesn't like to exercise and she says she's opposed to diets in principle. People have some funny principles around here.

Mr. Moore accepted her offer for iced tea—she remembered his preference—and Clem entered just as she was leaving. He was wearing jeans, cowboy boots, and a yellow cotton shirt. When the two men shook hands, Marie said they looked more like respectful adversaries than friends. I'm not sure that Clem has that many of the latter, me and Calvin excluded.

He said, "It was a pleasure to hear from you this morning, Vernon. I'm glad you got my email." Clem never told me he sent an email to Mr. Moore; I had to hear it from Marie.

"It was nice of you to send one," Mr. Moore replied, "but I'm afraid I missed it. As it turns out, I was in Cambodia for the last two weeks and I didn't take my laptop. I've never been able to get the hang of those Internet cafés."

"Did you say Cambodia? That's pretty far off the beaten track. I'm surprised they even have an Internet."

"They do, but the attractions are the ancient temples of the Khmer. What outstanding structures they are, and so similar to the Maya. I take it you've never been."

"I haven't, Vernon, and I doubt I'll ever go. The third world isn't my cup of java. When I can find time to get away, which is hardly ever, I prefer the first world. Usually, I go hunting or fishing in Canada."

Clem had mentioned his lack of enthusiasm for the third world a while back when I was reading a travel brochure about Costa Rica. I can pretty much figure out which countries are in the first world and which ones are in the third, but the second world is a mystery to me. I have no idea who they are, or if they qualify for special benefits like low-interest loans from the World Bank. I wonder if there is some place you can go in the U.N. to look up the criteria. If Costa Rica is in the second world, maybe I can get Clem to take me there.

The men sat down at opposite ends of the table, which meant that they were about fifteen feet apart. If you can picture it, that's about the length of a pickup truck. Clem tried to put me at the far end one time, but I couldn't hear a word he said, so I moved back up to his end. Mr. Moore stayed where he was put, which meant they had to holler at each other all through lunch. Marie, who has 20-20 hearing if there is such a thing, would've heard it all anyway.

Mr. Moore said, "You look fit, Clem."

"I am. I exercise, I watch my diet, and I get plenty of stress every day. How about you?"

"I've tried to eliminate the latter."

"Really? How did you do it?"

"The old-fashioned way: I retired."

Clem stuck a fork in a tangerine slice. "I'm envious. How are you finding the leisure life so far?"

"Misnamed. I'm no less busy than when I was self-employed."

"Is that a fact? Maybe it's the travel. Have you spent a lot of your retirement in far-off places with strange-sounding names?"

"I have recently, which makes it especially nice to be back in Ebb. But I'm so sorry to hear about Loretta and Matthew."

"That, Vernon, is why I asked you back. What a mess we're in! I don't expect you can do anything for Loretta, bless her soul, but Matt needs help."

"What would you like me to do, Clem?"

"That boy is looking down the barrel of a hundred and fifty years in the state pen, but all he has to do is name his partners and the sentence will be cut to ten. That's something any fool ought to do in a heartbeat, but Matt has refused, and none of us, including a six-hundred-dollar-an-hour lawyer I hired, have gotten through to that boy."

"Why?"

"Guilty conscience? Fear of reprisal? Whatever it is, he seems to have gotten it into his tiny head that he's doing the honorable thing, and he won't listen to anybody who has an opinion to the contrary. I want you to break through, to convince Matt to take the offer."

"What makes you think . . . ?"

"Forgive me for interrupting, Vernon, but you made yourself a reputation around here. You sold Calvin Millet some hope, and nobody believed that could be done. Hell, nobody even knew it was the right thing to do."

Mr. Moore paused for a few seconds before saying, "How is Calvin these days?"

"He works for me now. He doesn't exactly warm the room but he's made himself into a top-notch fund manager and he's the most trustworthy man I ever met. Have you ever had a right-hand man?"

"I can't say that I have."

"Well, next to a chesty woman on a cold winter night, it's damn near the best thing you can have. You should think about getting one."

And I thought Clement loved me for my mind.

Mr. Moore asked, "Is Calvin in town?"

"He's up in Omaha on business. He'll be back sometime tomorrow." Clem finished up his salad and yelled, "Marie, we're ready for the main course."

She came through the door moments later carrying her special mustard-seed pork chops with mushrooms and asparagus on the side.

After she left with the salad plates, Clem said, "How long do you plan to stay in town, Vernon? You're a retiree. You can't be in much of a hurry."

"Not as a rule, but I have to be in Phoenix by Sunday."

"That soon? Buford Pickett will be disappointed to hear that. I don't suppose you remember him."

Buford Pickett is the senior vice president in charge of loans at the Hayes County Bank and Clem's left-hand man. A few years ago, he married Lily Park, who was Calvin's administrative assistant at Millet's Department Store. Lily is a stay-at-home mom now, except that she is the treasurer of the Quilting Circle.

Clem continued, "Buford says you're the only survivor of a plane crash that nobody survived. He says you're a ghost, the only ghost who ever fathered a child."

"Is that so? People have odd beliefs, don't they?"

Clem smiled. "They do at that. Around here, you're in the middle of about half of them. Why do you suppose that is?"

Mr. Moore must have decided that that was a good time to move on. He said, "Wilma told me about your engagement. Congratulations. But two years is quite a long time, isn't it?"

"She's a fine woman, Vernon, and she's been patient as a monk while I've been getting some business affairs straightened out. When I'm done, we won't have any more problems with marital contracts."

"Do any of these business affairs have to do with the Big Buyback?"

"Wilma told you about that, too?"

"It wasn't the sort of thing I expected from you. Why did you decide to sell out?"

Clem went to college in England when he was a young man. More than anything else, it affected his eating habits. He's dined English-style ever since, which means he uses a dinner knife to shove food onto the backside of his fork. It's easy to see why the person who invented that system is not famous.

He replied, "I planted more than half a million acres a year ago last spring, Vernon. Do you have any idea how much I spent on seeds, fertilizers, pesticides, and herbicides?"

"None whatsoever."

"Well, that's more than you want to know. Tenant farmers are damn expensive these days, they're less manageable than a barn full of ferrets, and I had a hell of a time keeping up with the latest advancements in bioengineering. The big combines were starting to eat me up on yield. Either I had to get bigger or I had to get smaller, but getting bigger was nigh on impossible."

"Why?"

"An amendment to the state constitution called I-300. For more than twenty years, it's prevented Nebraska farmland from being bought by corporations."

"So the Big Buyback was the only way you could get out of the farming business."

"Not exactly, Vernon. I got out of the farm ownership business, but I nearly doubled my farm mortgage business. Hayes County Bank, which is owned by me and the trust, now holds the loans on more than two million acres of farmland in Rutherford B. Hayes and three adjacent counties. They're secured by the land."

"Did you divest your position in Millet's Department Store, too?"

Clem chewed on some pork before answering, "That's a private matter, Vernon. People around here get real emotional when I start discussing the department store. You'd think it was a goddamn shrine. Why do you ask?"

"I don't mean to pry. It's just that some of the townspeople seem to be concerned about what you're going to do next."

Clem dropped both of his utensils on his plate and exclaimed, "Concerned? Concerned? Isn't that just perfect? After Jesus cured the ten lepers, do you know how many thanked him?"

"As I recall, it was one."

"Well, I sold the farmland back to nineteen times as many tenants and I got exactly three. Makes you think there might be something to the Bible after all, doesn't it?" Clem shrugged and picked up his utensils again. "Who's worried now? Wilma? Lulu? Mary Wade?"

"I heard the rumor from Lulu Tiller."

"She's the Queen Bee of that infernal Quilting Circle, you know. Did she tell you they make quilts?"

"I've heard as much, yes."

"Well, I don't see how they have the time. As near as I can tell, they spend the fullness of their waking hours putting their noses into my business. What dastardly deed did the dreaded Ms. Tiller accuse me of this time?"

"If she knows anything of substance, she didn't divulge it to me. Her concerns seemed to be very general."

"There was nothing specific? If that's the case, you seem to be pressing a pretty lean point, Vernon. Do you have a theory of your own?"

"The obvious move would be to sell a minority interest in the bank."

"Why?"

"Otherwise, it would appear that too much of the Tucker Trust was tied up in one institution."

"Is that what you'd do?"

"Maybe, but I've never been fond of the obvious move."

Clem put his knife and fork on his plate and struck a thoughtful pose. "Do you remember the question you asked me at this same table two years ago?"

"Didn't I ask you several?"

"You asked me to name the three most memorable things I had ever done, in order. Number one was the birth of my daughter. You didn't seem to have a problem there, but I don't recall any huzzahs for memories two and three. Does any of that ring a bell?"

"It does. Yes."

"Well, stay tuned, Vernon. If things go according to plan, I'll have a new number two by the weekend."

When Marie heard that in the kitchen, she practically dropped a two-gallon bowl of marinara sauce. Mr. Moore kept his cool. "I'm glad to hear it, but I'm surprised that the Big Buyback didn't make your top three."

"Are you a chess player, Vernon?"

"Not a good one, but yes."

"Well, the Big Buyback was just the opening gambit." Without skipping a beat, Clem asked, "Can I interest you in some dessert? Marie made a blueberry pie from scratch this morning. Her pies are the best in the Midwest; even Wilma can't do better."

"I appreciate the offer, but I have to get back to town for another meeting."

"Do you mind if I ask who with?"

"Not a bit."

Clem said, "Okay. Who are you meeting with?"

"Mona Breck, Matt's mom."

"Now that's what I wanted to hear. Do you think you can help the boy?"

"I don't know. I don't even know if Mona will want me to try. That's why I'm going to see her."

"She'll want your help, Vernon, and not because you became some kind of overnight legend here. Mona is flat out of batters. Everybody else in the county has already struck out with Matt, me included. I don't want any grandson of mine, current or future, throwing away his life over some misguided notion of nobility."

The two men stood up and headed toward the front door. Just before he stepped outside, Mr. Moore said, "I'd appreciate it if you could do me a favor, Clem."

"If I can. What?"

"I'd appreciate it if you would call Mary Wade, the county prosecutor. I'd like to meet her at the courthouse at four o'clock this afternoon."

Clem grinned and replied, "I'll take care of it right away."

"And there is one more little thing. Do you mind if I walk around to the back of the house? As I recall, you have a lovely view."

"The river hasn't moved, Vernon. It's still the prettiest view in the state. Take all the time you like."

As soon as Mr. Moore was out of sight, Clem sprinted back to the dining room. Through a tiny gap in the kitchen door, Marie watched him pick up Mr. Moore's crystal-stemmed, iced-tea glass with a napkin, seal it in a plastic bag, and sneak it out of the room—as if he was stealing from himself.

Chapter 6

....

Shaky-head Dolls

MY ELDEST DAUGHTER MONA started to let her figure go toward the end of her marriage to that dentist up in Omaha, but she is back in the pink now. I don't know if I was ever that shapely. When she met Mr. Moore that day, she was wearing blue jeans, a blue cotton work shirt tied over a red tee shirt, and cowboy boots. She looked like two million dollars, country style.

They went into my den as soon as he got back from the River House. I should have asked if Mona wanted me to sit in, but I was afraid she would say no. Instead, I just followed them in as if I owned the place, which I do, after shoving an extra fistful of Kleenex into the pocket of my apron. A mother is always a mother, no matter how old her offspring get.

The main feature of my den is an antique, rolltop desk that used to belong to Clem Tucker. It has more drawers and cubbyholes than a roomful of Chinese boxes. I keep most of my business records and memories in it, but I better tell Mona where the important papers are before I pass on. Otherwise, she'll never be able to find it all.

I got to rooting around the desktop a few years after I bought it and found two hidden drawers in the back. One had a handwritten receipt from Harper's Feed Store that was dated April of 1932. Harper's went out of business that year, which was during the Great Depression. It was long before my time, but my mama used to tell me about it. I'd rather be living now; global warming, terrorism, reality TV, and all.

Mr. Moore took his blazer off and sat down in the chair at my roll-top desk. Mona and I sat on my settee, which is another antique of mine. It could use reupholstering but it's still as comfortable as can be. For a while, we talked about Mark and how well he was doing at school, plus his strange gin-rummy relationship with Clara, my third-floor recluse. Mona also filled us in on the rebuilding of Lo's salon, which was going fine except that they hadn't ordered enough paneling for the downstairs office.

After a while, I could see that Mona was starting to get fidgety. At exactly that moment, Mr. Moore asked, "How is Matt?"

She looked at me but didn't cry, for a change, then replied, "How much do you know, Mr. Moore?"

I answered, "He knows about everything, honey. He's completely up-to-date."

A single tear trailed down Mona's cheek so I handed her a Kleenex. She sniffled, "He's taking it like a real man: he admitted his guilt; he refused to be treated as a minor by the court; he won't name the other two boys; he won't accept any help. He won't talk to anybody, not even me. This afternoon, he wouldn't come to the visiting room at all, not even just to say hello."

Mr. Moore sat forward and said, just as softly as could be, "It's not your fault."

That was such a sweet thought, but Mona's hands came up to her face and the floodgates opened the instant he said it. I don't remember

her crying once during her divorce, but she has been a human Niag-
ara Falls ever since Loretta got hurt and Matt got put in jail.

I suppose I should have warned Mr. Moore, but he seemed to be
perfectly calm, so I rubbed Mona's neck and waited for her sorrow to
pass. It didn't. All of a sudden, she jumped up from the settee and ran
out of the room. I made my apologies and went after her. After a short
search, I found her curled up on the canopy bed in the white room on
the second floor.

I didn't say anything. I just went in and took a chair, a pearl white
item with a green brocade seat cushion that I picked up at auction in
Olathe. I couldn't have been with Mona for more than two minutes
when I heard Mark come through the front door.

Mark is thirteen years old and in the middle of a growing spurt. He
must be five foot eight, even though he just started the eighth grade.
He yelled, "Mama! Gramma! I'm home!"

Mona started to push herself up, but she had mascara running
from both her eyes down to her chin. There isn't a man in the world
who likes to see those thin black lines trailing down a woman's face,
not even a sapling of a man, because they're always there for the same
reason. I gave her a hug and told her to stay put and I went downstairs to field Mark.

He was nowhere in sight. It turned out that Mr. Moore had already
squired him into the kitchen, where they were sharing a soda pop and
discussing his new Chrysler. I guess it has a powerful engine. It's not
the sort of thing that most women care about, but nothing can grab
the attention of a teenage boy faster than an over-powered car—
other than a pretty teenage girl.

As soon as I walked into the kitchen, Mark said, "Hi Gramma! Is
Mom home?"

"She's upstairs," I replied. "She needs to be left alone for a while."

Mark looked at my unusual lodger, looked back at me, and said, "This is about my brother, isn't it? He's why Mr. Moore came back."

"Your mother is changing out of her work clothes," I said. "Changing clothes is something a woman generally does alone."

Mark wasn't fooled. He shook his head and said, "I have the stupidest brother in the known universe. Can you help him, Mr. Moore? Mom and Gramma have talked about it a zillion times. Gramma says you walk on water."

From the mouths of babes.

Mr. Moore said, "You know, I tried to walk on water once, but I sank like a stone. I'm not sure I can help your brother either. There's little time left."

Mark is the apple of his mama's eye, but that boy has a sharp tongue. That's one of the troubles with teenagers: their mouths are faster than their minds. You can only hope that they'll live long enough for their brains to catch up. He said, "You don't sound very confident."

"You have me, Mark. I'm not very confident, but maybe you can help. Do you have a few minutes?"

Mark checked his watch, just like he was a business executive or a retired salesman. I guess it was a watch-checking day. "I have a little time but I need to get my homework done by five o'clock. I'm supposed to play gin rummy with Aunt Clara, but she won't unless I've finished my homework."

"Your Aunt Clara is wise."

"Maybe, but she's not very good at cards. Uncle Clem says you're the best gin rummy player he ever saw. Did you know that? He says you cleaned his clock."

"No, I didn't know that. My clock-cleaning skills aren't remarkably better than my water-walking skills."

"I'm pretty good, too. Will you play me? Tonight? After dinner?"

"I'll take you on but not this evening. I have to drive up to the hospital to see Ms. Parsons after dinner. Why don't we try again tomorrow?"

"Okay." Mark checked his watch again. "You said you wanted my help with something. What is it?"

"I'd like you to tell me about your brother."

Without batting an eyelash, my grandson replied, "He's a dickhead."

I started to rebuke the boy but Mr. Moore asked, "Has he always been a dickhead?"

"Nope. Before we moved down here he was just a dork."

"What changed? Was it your parents' divorce?"

Mark shrugged, as if he was describing a mildly disappointing day at the office. "Maybe. Back in Omaha, before Mom and Dad split up, Matt hung around with dorks. After we moved down here, he started hanging with dickheads."

"Fair enough. What did he do in his dork days up north?"

"He and his dorky friends played video games. Matt thought he was hot stuff, but I had a friend named Donnie who could kill him at any game. It was embarrassing."

"Is there anything Matt did well? A subject in school, perhaps?"

"Matt used to like math. He got A's before . . ." Mark paused.

"What else is he good at?"

"Matt's a good baseball player. He was the starting second baseman for the Haymakers last year until he got thrown off the team." Mark meant the Rutherford B. Hayes High School Haymakers, the pride of the county.

"Why?"

"He skipped school. He flunked a couple of midterms. He got caught smoking in the school toilet. He got suspended for fighting. Like I said, he turned into a dickhead."

"He didn't do any of those things before your parents separated?"

"Dorks talk about skipping school and punching out other kids, Mr. Moore. Dickheads actually do it. That's the difference. Ever since Mom and Dad got divorced, Matt's been more of a dickhead than a dork."

Mr. Moore nodded and asked, "What did he usually do after school?"

"You mean before he set fire to the Bold Cut and beat up Laverne's mom? He hung around with his dickhead friends. What else?"

"Did he ever watch TV?"

"Yeah. Lots."

"What were his favorite shows?"

"Reality TV mostly."

"How about music. Did he ever listen to music?"

"Yeah, that too. My dad gave him an iPod last Christmas. He had it stuck in his ears all the time. Still does probably. I think they let him keep it at the jail."

"What kind of music does he like?"

"Vanilla rap, stuff like that."

"That's very helpful, Mark. Did your brother ever hang around with some boys from the Temple Ranch?"

"You mean Buddy and Richie, the Gault twins? Yeah. They were dorks, but they wanted to be dickheads like my brother. He used to give them cigarettes and let them listen to his iPod. They came over here and played video games a few times, too. They were pathetic."

"Perhaps they had few chances to practice. Is there anything else I should know? Did he have a girlfriend, for instance?"

"Nope. He's a dickhead, Mr. Moore. End of story." My grandson checked his watch again. "I have to do my homework."

"Thank you, Mark. Your observations have been very useful."

After he was out of earshot, I said, "I apologize for that boy's brashness. He must've gotten it from his father. How was your lunch at the River House?"

"The food was delicious and the conversation intriguing, as always."

"Was I right? Is Clem going to do something? Is there a second shoe?"

"It would seem so, Wilma."

Well, there it was. Anybody else might've softened me up; not Mr. Moore. "Do you know what it is?" I asked.

"I have an idea but I need to read I-300 first. I presume I can find a copy in the library."

"Of I-300? Why?"

"It has something to do with Clem's plan."

"It does? Oh, dear! That will make everyone so nervous. I have to tell Lulu Tiller. Do you mind?"

"I don't, Wilma. Follow your conscience, but be careful."

"Careful? Why?"

"Because your loyalties are in conflict: You're engaged to Clem but wedded to the Quilting Circle. This may be a test of your faith in Clem. It may be a test of everyone's."

As if I wasn't already confused enough. "What do you mean?" I asked.

"Clem is going to do something significant very soon, something unexpected and possibly controversial. If I'm right, he'll want you and the residents of Ebb to trust him, to have faith that he's doing the right thing. That's the test."

"To trust him? Are you sure?"

"Absolutely not."

Have you ever seen those bobble-head dolls that are so popular at sporting events? If they were like real life, they'd be shaky-head dolls. When it comes to men, that's what I do: I shake my head all the time. Men play the strangest, most foolish, most dangerous games. It makes life one crisis after another.

"What about Matt?" I asked.

"I have an appointment with Mary Wade in half an hour, but I'm not sure I should keep it. I don't have Mona's permission to visit Matt, much less help him. Should I see her for a few minutes before I go?"

"You don't need to. If she was here, Mona would plead with you to help Matt. She would get down on her knees and beg the devil himself."

"You're sure."

"I am. Absolutely. One hundred percent. If she had even the teensiest little misgiving, which she doesn't, I'd pull the hairs from her head a handful at a time until she got over it."

Mr. Moore remarked, "It won't be easy to help that boy. It may take some creativity."

"What do you mean?" I asked.

He stared off into space. "I'm not sure," he replied.

Mr. Moore has such a special way of building up my confidence.

Chapter 7

....

The Angles House

IF YOU'VE EVER SEEN a Jimmy Stewart movie from the 1930s, you know what the Hayes County courthouse looks like. It's a rectangular, three-story, Greek revival building with six columns in front, one short of a Jeep. It lapsed into a poor state of repair some years ago, so the Quilting Circle resolved to raise $200,000 to restore it to its original, pre-Depression dignity. We got two-thirds of the way there, but we got stuck in a financial rut until Clem Tucker stepped in. He offered to give us the rest of the money on two conditions: the county named the courthouse after his father, Silas the Fifth, and Buzz Busby did all the work. Now it's called the Silas C. Tucker Courthouse and Clem probably made money on the deal.

The inside of the building is dominated by a round, ground-to-ceiling foyer with yellow marble floors. It has the rare distinction of being acoustically perfect, meaning that you can whisper to the wall on one side and a person on the opposite side can hear you clear as day. The sheriff's office is to the left of the foyer entrance, directly across from motor vehicle registration, and the jail is in the basement.

The county attorney, Hail Mary Wade, is in the northeast corner of the third floor, right above the courtroom. Her office has a lovely view of Clem's "Angles House," which he built some years ago as a pied-à-terre because he got tired of commuting from the River House to his bank, which takes all of twenty minutes. The Angles House is the only place in Ebb that was designed by a frustrated geometry student. It has every angle you ever imagined, plus a few more that should've been left in the trunk. Calvin Millet lives there now. The other three bedrooms are empty, but Clem keeps one of his Porsches in the garage.

Mr. Moore was greeted outside of Mary's office by Dottie Hrnicek. Dot is squat and wide and strong as a man. I've never seen her out of uniform; she even shops in it. She keeps her hair short, too, and I swear her voice has dropped half an octave since she took the job, but she's a fine sheriff and a Quilting Circle board member. In some respects, I don't know how we managed when the sheriff was a man.

"Mr. Moore?" she said when he walked up. "My name is Dorothy Hrnicek. I'm the county sheriff. I know we haven't been introduced, but Ms. Wade has asked me to sit in on your meeting this afternoon. I hope you don't mind."

She stuck out her hand and Mr. Moore shook it. "Your reputation precedes you, Sheriff. I'd be delighted if you'd join us."

Dot held the door and Mr. Moore walked into the district attorney's office, which I've visited half a dozen times since Matt was indicted. Mary sits behind a large, dark mahogany desk in the middle of the room. There are four matching, straight-backed chairs in a row on the other side, facing her.

Did you ever notice that there are some chairs you sit in and others you sit on? All four of the straight-backed chairs were in the "on" category and equally, utterly uncomfortable; I've tried every one. She must want it that way.

Hail Mary Wade is a pretty brunette divorcée of thirty-odd years, and every inch of four foot ten. She can't weigh ninety pounds soaking wet. I get worried about her in a strong breeze. With the possible exception of Loretta, though, she is the smartest woman in the county; even Clem gives her a wide berth. Naturally, she's also a member of the Quilting Circle, but nobody knows where her nickname came from, not even us girls.

She was wearing a navy blue suit, a white blouse, and high, high heels. Hail Mary would wear high heels to a forced march. After Dot handled the introductions, Mary said, "Do you have a business card, Mr. Moore?"

"I don't," he replied. "I used to be a salesman but I'm retired now."

"Well, you certainly dress sharply. You must've retired well. I hear that you were a very good salesman."

The three of them sat down, Dot and Mr. Moore on the uncomfortable chairs. He replied, "I'm beginning to understand what people mean by 'larger than life.' I visited Ebb a few years ago and did what I could to help Calvin Millet. At that, I'm not sure I did a very good job."

"That's not the word I heard, Mr. Moore. Some of my constituents say you saved the town. Others say you stood toe-to-toe with Clem Tucker and beat him at his own game. I have no idea whether you're worth all that attention or not, but I've had four calls since you arrived in town this morning. One of them was from Lord Clem himself, asking for this meeting. It's a matter of county record that Clem Tucker never calls anybody himself. Isn't that right, Dot?"

"It is. If he wanted to curse himself, he'd call in a professional curser to handle the job, except he'd have his assistant call the curser."

"Did Clem explain why he wanted us to meet, Ms. Wade?"

"It would be more truthful to say that he called to set my expectations. He said he wanted me to give you free rein with Matthew Breck."

"To do what?"

"He implied that you could get Matt to accept the plea bargain I offered him four weeks ago. Was that wrong?"

"I don't know."

Mary sat forward. "You don't know? That's a confusing answer, Mr. Moore. What expectation do you have?"

"None at all. With your permission, I thought I might meet with Matt for a while this afternoon. I should have an impression after I ask him a question or two."

Dot and Mary exchanged glances. Dot said, "You can ask all the questions you want, hon, but the answers may be pretty sparse. Have you been briefed?" Dot calls every man "hon," even Clem. If the Pope came to Ebb, she would call him hon.

"Only the basics, Sheriff," Mr. Moore replied. "I'd appreciate your view. In particular, I'd like to understand why you were able to apprehend Matt but not the other two boys."

"I rode with Loretta in the ambulance. The poor girl was floating in and out of consciousness, but she managed to tell me that she was attacked by three men wearing black ski masks. One of them was wearing a sweater, a remarkable sweater for these parts."

"In what way?"

"Around here, you can get burned at the stake for concealing a Kansas State keychain in your backpack. Nothing against our neighbors, but it's not the sort of thing a patriotic Nebraskan would do. Fashion rebel that he was, Matt Breck owned the only K State sweater in the area. A wool fiber underneath Lo's fingernails matched it perfectly."

"I see. Was there any other evidence at the scene?"

"They used an accelerant to set the Bold Cut on fire: kerosene. That's evidence of premeditation and it gets them all a charge of first-degree arson and a second count of attempted murder. Unfortunately, it also did a fine job of covering their tracks. No fingerprints or other forensic evidence survived the fire and we've never found the ski masks or the baseball bat."

"If the fire was that severe, how did Loretta and her daughter survive it?"

"Loretta's salon was full of chemicals, but most of them were stored behind a fire door in her basement. If the fire had gotten down there, we would've lost half the block and the little girl for sure. Luckily, Laverne was asleep behind a closed door upstairs and suffered no injuries other than minor smoke inhalation. Loretta was dragged into Main Street by one of the perpetrators before they fled. The fire station is only a few blocks away. When the firefighters arrived, she was trying to crawl back into the fire to save her child."

"So Matt is the only hope you have of finding the other two young men."

"That's right, hon, and until we catch them, no woman in Ebb will get a good night's sleep. But that boy won't talk, and when I say he won't talk, I mean he won't say anything other than a cuss word or two—to anybody."

"I see. Then you have no idea who his accomplices were."

Hail Mary replied, "That's not exactly true, Mr. Moore. We do have an idea; a very good idea. Fortunately or unfortunately, a good idea is an insufficient basis for a charge of attempted murder in this state. We need hard evidence and we don't have any."

"Who do you suspect?"

"I can't say. Open felony investigations are confidential down here; that's the law. You're more than welcome to ask young Matt, though. You might also ask Clem Tucker's new bodyguard. He's been nosing around, too."

"I understand that Matt made friends with a few boys from some kind of religious group on the other side of the county. Are they on the suspect list?"

"The investigation is confidential, Mr. Moore. We've already said more than we should."

"Have any of them tried to visit Matt since his incarceration?"

"That's not information we can disclose either."

Mr. Moore began to speak, but Dottie stopped him. "You won't learn anything else about the investigation in here, hon. That's my final answer."

Hail Mary added, "What we can tell you is that Matt Breck has admitted his guilt to three class-two felonies. Since he was charged as an adult, that qualifies him for up to one hundred and fifty years in the state pen unless he names his accomplices, which he has fervently refused to do. Because of your reputation in this town, though, I'm inclined to give you a chance to change his mind."

"I appreciate your confidence, Ms. Wade, but everything about this situation tells me that I'll have little chance of succeeding unless I can be creative. That may require me to say or do things that may seem unusual. I'll need your support."

Mary replied, "Regardless of what Lord Clem says, I can't give you a blank check. Besides respecting the civil rights of our prisoners, you'll have to agree to three conditions."

"Three? What are they?"

"The first is that Matt's mother approves. I presume you already have her permission."

"Actually, I don't."

"You don't?"

"No. I was about to ask when she ran out of the room."

"Was she running for good cause?"

"She was weeping—for Matt."

"That poor woman. Were you hoping to see the boy today?"

"I was, yes."

"Then would you be kind enough to wait while I give Mona a ring?"

"Of course."

I answered when Hail Mary called. She's a real important woman in Ebb, but she can dial her own telephone. It took some convincing at my end, but I got Mona to talk to her. They had been chatting for about one minute when Mona started to sniffle again. I took the handset and said, "Did you get what you needed, Mary?"

"I did, Wilma. Thank you."

"Will you tell me how Mr. Moore is doing?"

"I suspect you'll hear before I do. You always do."

After we got off the phone, Mary said, "You're clear on condition one, Mr. Moore. The second is that you permit us to record your discussions with Matt. If you're successful, we don't want him to recant later. 'He-said, she-said' situations are real hard to resolve in a court of law."

"Has Matt been warned?"

"He has."

"I can't refuse?"

"You have no special privileges, Mr. Moore. You're not his lawyer, you're not his minister, and you're not his doctor. If you refuse, then I won't let you see him."

"Fair enough. What's the last condition?"

"Deputy Giant monitors your visits and handles the recording."

"Who?" Mr. Moore asked.

Dottie replied, "Deputy Giant. He's my chief of county corrections. You'll like him."

Chapter 8

Deputy Giant

DOT HRNICEK IS the only person in Ebb, man or woman, who can pronounce Luther Salevasaosamoa's last name, excluding himself. The rest of us call him Deputy Samoa when he's within earshot, Deputy Giant when he isn't. Luther was born and raised on the Samoan island of Upolu. After high school, he came to Nebraska to play defensive tackle for the Cornhuskers, but his right knee got blown out during the second game of his senior season by a vicious, crack-back block. The other team got a penalty; Luther got a permanently wonky knee that ended his football career.

Unlike a lot of scholarship athletes, Luther finished his degree, which was in law enforcement, and joined the Lincoln police force. He was assigned to cruiser duty, but some of his suspects got damaged en route to the police station, or so the story goes. Subsequently, Luther was transferred to Corrections, which he took to like a squirrel takes to cashew nuts.

Last year, one of the female deputies had trouble with an inmate in the Hayes County jail, so Dottie decided to recruit a man to run it. Luther read the ad and came down to Ebb for an interview. Dot hired him on the spot and put him on a diet. Luther, who is six foot seven in his stocking feet, is down to 315 pounds now and he says his knee is feeling better. On the occasional weekend, he makes extra money helping farmers with their heavy lifting. Rufus Bowe said he saw Luther pick up a four-hundred-pound tractor tire with his bare hands. I doubt that it weighed more than three-hundred myself. He still has the knee.

Luther is famous for one other thing: a deep, booming voice. Up in Lincoln, they say he once knocked down an angry inmate by yelling at him. Down here, I can tell you that there has been no trouble in the jail since Deputy Samoa joined Dot's team, not even a peep. We'd like to keep it that way so we've been trying to find him a match. The fly in the ointment is that he likes little women, but they're frightened to death of him. He would squash me like a bug and I'm not tiny by a long shot. Just the thought makes me gasp.

Deputy Samoa was waiting at the bottom of the basement steps when the sheriff and Mr. Moore arrived. Dot made the introductions. "Luther, this is Vernon Moore. He's come to visit with Matt Breck."

Luther stuck out his hand, which is the size of a plucked chicken, and said, "It's a pleasure, sir. We've been expecting you."

"Expecting me?"

"Everybody knows you're in town. The buzz is that you've come to get Matt Breck to plea down. It won't be easy, though. That boy won't even talk to himself."

Dot craned her neck so that she could look Luther in the eye. "Mr. Moore and I have made a deal, hon, which is that you'll monitor his visits with Matt Breck. Be warned: Mr. Moore says he may have to be creative. We don't have much time, so we want to give him as much latitude as we can, but he has to check with you before he does anything questionable. If you're uncomfortable for any reason, you come and see me beforehand. Okay?"

The deputy pulled a small recording device out of his upper pocket. "No problem, Sheriff. That's what I expect: no problems." Luther added, "Lockdown is at five thirty, Mr. Moore. If you want to spend some quality time with the boy today, we better get to it. He's around the corner and all the way down at the end of the corridor. We emptied out the cell next door so you could have some privacy."

"You cleared out the neighboring cell in advance?"

"Everybody said you were coming, Mr. Moore. Weeks ago."

Dottie excused herself, then Luther and my unusual lodger headed down the hallway. Gray, dimly lit cinder-block walls were to their left. The cells, which are eight feet wide by ten feet long, were to their right. Most were unoccupied, thank God.

There was no furniture in Matt's cell except for a bunk bed, a stainless steel sink, and a tiny, uncomfortable-looking steel toilet with a seat but no top. The floor was cement and the left and back walls were the same gray cinder block that lined the opposite side of the hall. Mona tried to bring Matt a rug and some posters, but they were against the rules so she had to take them home. Luther did allow her to leave an iPod and a few magazines behind, but Matt shoved the magazines under his bunk. I guess she forgot the *Victoria's Secret,* which was his favorite.

Matt Breck is a wisp of a boy. He has unkempt black hair, steely blue eyes, pale white skin, and poor posture. Like his fellow inmates, he was dressed in gray pants, a matching gray shirt, and work boots. Prisoners in most jails wear orange these days, which means that men are still in charge. Not many women like orange: it's too bright; it's hard to coordinate; and it stains easily. Gray may be harder to see in the dark, but it's better on all other counts.

When Luther and Mr. Moore got to the end of the hall, they found

Matt lying on the lower bunk with his eyes closed, earphones covering his ears. If he knew he had visitors, he didn't show it. He was in
the Land of iPod.

The deputy unlocked his cell door, walked in, and said in his deep
voice, "Sit up, junior. You have a distinguished visitor."

Matt opened one eye and peered at his guests, then closed it again.
That didn't make Luther happy. He said, "This is my last polite request, shithead. If you don't sit up and pay attention, you can kiss
your punk-ass iPod good-bye."

Matt opened his eyes and came up to his elbows, but he was still
in the supine position.

"Too slow," Luther said. He jerked the iPod away, headphones and
all, and then he grabbed Matt by the front of his shirt and pulled him
up to the sitting position. "Like I said, you have a distinguished guest.
I believe you two have met before. Is that right, Matt?"

Matt didn't answer.

"Your toothbrush goes next, junior. Have you two met or not?"
That was a threat to be taken seriously. For all his troubles, Matt is
the son of a dentist, meaning he is a fanatical flosser and brusher.

"We've met," Mr. Moore answered. He walked into the cell and
added, "Would you do me a favor, Luther? Would you bring me a
chair? An old man's back would be grateful."

"No problem. Are you okay on your own for a minute?"

"I don't know; he looks pretty tough. Is there a rear exit?"

"A few steps down the hall, past the weight room. Fire regulations.
An alarm sounds if the door is opened, and the staircase leads up to
the main floor of the police station."

Mr. Moore smiled. "I guess I'll be okay then."

Luther looked down at Matt. My grandson stared defiantly back.

"I could use that chair," Mr. Moore repeated.

"I'll be right back."

Luther quickly reappeared with a green-colored, metal folding chair, which he opened and placed a few feet away from Matt's bunk. Mr. Moore sat down and made himself comfortable while Luther stationed himself discreetly outside the cell. Then Mr. Moore said, "Nice place you have here. I can see why you went to all the effort."

Matt didn't answer.

"How's the food?"

Matt didn't answer again.

"Did I ask a controversial question?"

Again, there was no response.

"Have you been spending a lot of time with your Aunt Clara, Matt, or have you determined that keeping your mouth shut is a smart thing to do?"

No answer.

"I guess you know that our conversation is being recorded. Is that the problem?"

No answer again.

Mr. Moore waited a moment before saying, "Yeah, it might bother me, too. But what if I offered you your favorite meal in return for a one-word response to a simple question? Would that be enough of an enticement to speak? How about it, Deputy? If Matt answered my question, could you get the cook to make anything he asked for?"

"As long as it doesn't break the rule, Mr. Moore."

"What does that mean?"

"No lobster, no caviar, no fresh crab. That's the Last Supper rule. Anything else is no problem—if that's what you want to do."

"How about it, Matt? A one-word answer to a simple question will get you any meal you want."

Matt responded, "Is it about what I did at the whorehouse? If it is; no deal. I've said all I'm gonna say about that."

"Nope. That's water under the bridge."

"You don't care if I tell you who went with me?"

"I couldn't care less. My interest is in you."

"Why?"

"Because your grandmother asked."

My first grandson, the apple of my eye, replied, "That's a dumb-ass reason."

"She's your grandmother, not mine, but I came all the way here to help anyway. It seems to me that you could answer one little question in return. If you get the right answer, you can have whatever you want for dinner."

Matt chose not to reply.

"I'm not going to ask you to solve a quadratic equation. It's an easy little question. Are you afraid you'll make a mistake?"

"If the question's so easy, why do I have to answer it? Don't you know the answer?"

"I do, but a lot of people don't think you do. Prove them wrong and get any meal you want. What have you got to lose?"

"Will you get out if I say yes?"

"Hmmm. If you want me to leave right away, it'll cost you a second question, but you won't have to answer that one until tomorrow morning. How would that be?"

As fools go, Matt was no fool. "If I answer the second question now, will you leave me alone tomorrow?"

Mr. Moore said, "You're a canny negotiator, but I don't want the second answer today. I'll want it tomorrow."

"Okay. What do I get for answering the second question?"

"If you answer it honestly, you'll get your iPod back."

"Who'll decide if I'm being honest?"

"It's a straightforward question, Matt. For a guy who doesn't want to talk, you do a lot of talking. You could've answered my first question three minutes ago, I'd be gone, and Deputy Samoa would be in here taking your dinner order."

"What if I don't like the first question?"

"This is starting to get silly. It's one question."

"I don't trust you worth a shit, Mr. Moore; I don't care what Gramma says about you. What if I don't like your question? What if I refuse to answer?"

Mr. Moore kept his gaze on Matt and asked, "What's on the menu tonight, Luther?"

"Roast beef on white bread with the cook's special gravy, smashed potatoes, cling peaches from the can on chalky cottage cheese, and mixed green vegetables that were slow-frozen in pork fat after the harvest of ninety-four."

"What's for dessert?"

"That would be the peaches."

"Mmmm. I can see why Matt isn't interested in a special meal. Do you have any other prisoners who might take me up on my offer?"

Luther laughed. "If I could, I'd take you up on it myself, Mr. Moore. Have you ever smelled the cook's special gravy? Nobody knows what it's made from, but I hear she puts some kind of special shit in it to keep the inmates regular."

Mr. Moore stood up. "I'm out of patience, Matt. One answer; you get the meal of your choice. Another answer tomorrow; you get your iPod back. I'm done offering; it's time to make up your mind."

Matt remained silent, so Mr. Moore began to leave. When he reached the cell door, Matt asked, "What's the question?"

Mr. Moore turned. "Good call. The first question is: Is it better to be smart or stupid?"

"That's it? That's the question?"

"It's the sum total of your obligation. In return for a correct answer, you get the meal of your dreams, as long as it excludes lobster, caviar, and fresh crab."

"I want three waffles with butter and maple syrup, six strips of bacon, French fries, onion rings, and three Dr Peppers on ice. And I want a dozen Oreos and a bowl of vanilla ice cream for dessert. Did you get all that on your stupid tape recorder?"

Luther answered, "Yep. If you get the right answer, Cookie will make it. I'll make sure of it."

"Deal!" Matt said. "The answer is 'smart.'"

"Congratulations!" Mr. Moore replied. "It is better to be smart than stupid. Deputy Samoa will bring you your waffles tonight. While you're eating, I'd like you to think about the second question. It's a little more subjective, but not much."

"Okay. What is it?"

"The second question is: How are you doing so far?"

Matt retreated into the shadow of the upper bunk and didn't reply.

Mr. Moore said, "It's time for me to keep my end of the bargain and leave the premises. I'll see you tomorrow morning. Enjoy those waffles. I'm sure they'll be scrumptious."

You may be surprised to hear this, but Matt didn't jump up and thank Mr. Moore for getting him a meal so special that it had never been served in the history of American cuisine. Instead, he just sat there on his butt.

After Deputy Samoa locked the cell door, the two men walked back down the corridor together. When they reached the stairwell, Luther said, "Are you sure you didn't give away too much, Mr. Moore? All you got from that boy was a piddly-ass answer to a dead easy question."

"I see your point, but that's not exactly true, is it? We had to negotiate for five minutes before he would give it to me."

"I suppose you're right."

"I hope I am, Deputy, because I have a policy that we need to discuss."

"What's that?"

"I'm a full-service salesman. I deliver more than I promise."

Chapter 9

....

Patient Not Responsive

AFTER A LONG NAP, Mona put on a sweater and went out front to wait for Mr. Moore's return from the county jail. It had been drizzling all day so she sat on the bench under the porte-cochere. In the meantime, I got on the phone and invited Clem, Calvin Millet, Doc Wiley, Nurse Nelson, and Lulu Tiller to dinner. Clem declined and Calvin never returned my call, but everybody else jumped at the chance.

Mr. Moore got back shortly before sundown. Mona practically leapt upon the poor man when he walked up the driveway. "Did you see Matt? Did he talk to you?"

"We talked, but only for a few minutes. Rather than discuss it out here in the cold, I suggest we go inside."

He and Mona disappeared into my den without so much as a hello and how-are-you for the cook. From experience, I can tell you that a mother is always interested in the details about her children, which is why it can take longer to discuss a meeting than the meeting originally took. After Mr. Moore was done recounting, she asked, "What are you going to do? What can you do?"

He considered her question before answering, "I'm think I'm going to sell Matt some charity. I'm not sure it can be done but, with your indulgence, I'll give it a try."

"Charity? You're going to sell Matt some charity?"

"Yes. That's definitely it. I'm going to sell him some charity."

Sometimes, Mr. Moore could catch you flat-footed. I know he made me check my arches more than once. Flat feet must run in the Porter DNA; he had the same effect on my daughter. "Charity?" she asked. "What will that do for him?"

"If he learns to be charitable, he'll become a nice person. Everything else will take care of itself after that."

"Matt is an angry, introverted teenager. He's in jail. He believes his life is over. How can you teach him to be charitable?"

Mr. Moore sighed. "It's going to be a difficult sale for sure. The first step in the typical sales cycle is the establishment of rapport. That's an overcomplicated way of saying that the prospect has to trust the salesperson or there's no point in continuing, but Matt's trust is all used up. I'm going to have to open him up in a different way."

"How?"

"How. That, indeed, is the question." Mr. Moore added, "I think I'll use a banjo."

Mona probably checked her arches again. "A banjo? Do you even play the banjo?"

"I did. Once."

I guess the banjo road to charity wasn't obvious to my daughter, especially when she found out that she wasn't invited along for the trip. While she grilled Mr. Moore about his plan to help Matt, Doc Wiley, Nurse Nelson, and Lulu Tiller arrived, and young Mark came downstairs after his gin rummy game with Clara. He said he won, which was getting to be the norm. Clara had already told me in an email that he was getting to be too good. Clara only says yes and no out loud, but her fingers have a full vocabulary.

We ate under the chandelier in the main dining room. Laverne sat in her high chair between Mona and me and we traded off, which meant that one of us would eat while the other tried to minimize the quantity of food that was heaved onto my antique Persian carpet. My advice: If you're teaching a small child to eat, don't go walking around the kitchen or the dining room in your socks. Even with two women on duty, it's impossible to catch all the flying food. Laverne is such a cute little thing.

I served a pot roast with potatoes and carrots, plus broccoli, black-eyed peas, and my famous homemade biscuits. It was a complete success with everyone, especially Hank Wiley. After Luther Samoa, Doc Wiley is the largest man in Ebb, and he did it the hard way: He ate his way to the top. Nurse Nelson told me his cholesterol is through the roof, but he takes four medications a day to keep it under control. He says that's what they're for. Can you imagine? My ex-husband used to take some of those medicines and there were consequences. Every time he had gas, which was on the half hour, he would say, "It's a side effect."

Except for being a nurse in the same profession, Louise Nelson is the polar opposite of the doctor. She runs the Pilates course at the Circle and it shows. Her arms and legs are like rope. She's also the perkiest woman in the tri-state area. If the bank went down the toilet again, she'd find a silver lining in the bowl.

During dinner, Lulu Tiller and I got to talking on the side for a while, mostly about Clem Tucker. Ever since we got engaged, the girls at the Circle have expected me to keep them informed of every little thing he does, which isn't usually a problem. Mostly, that's all Clem tells me: the little things. He keeps the big things to himself. Then Mr. Moore comes along and learns in one lunch that the skies are going to darken and the ground is going to quake.

Sometimes, men get my goat.

Naturally, Doc Wiley and Nurse Nelson had to know what Mr. Moore had been up to since his last visit to Ebb. I was sitting right there at the table every minute but I don't remember much of his answer, except that he had retired and become a baseball-card collector. The latter seemed to interest the men greatly, but not the women. Note to the Circle: Never tell a man that baseball is just a game. Football either. It's risky.

After dinner, Mr. Moore and Hank Wiley agreed to drive over to the hospital in separate cars. In the meantime, Mona took Laverne upstairs to give her a bath before bedtime. Laverne is my goddaughter, but nobody wants to be her stand-in mother more than my Mona. For now, it's the closest she can get to fair compensation.

THAT SAME EVENING, Buford Pickett got a call at home. His wife, Lily, answered the phone. She may have been Calvin Millet's administrative assistant once upon a time, but she can get terse when people call her home after eight p.m.

"Picketts," she said.

The reply came back, "Lily, this is Clem Tucker. May I speak to Buford?"

Lily is not the most deferential woman either. She replied, "He's watching a *Fear Factor* rerun. The supermodels in the wet bikinis are eating bugs. It's one of his favorite parts, but I should be able to pry him loose for you."

A few moments later, Buford said, "Good evening, Mr. Tucker. Is something wrong?"

"Not a thing, Buford. Lily said you were watching *Fear Factor*. What channel is it on?"

"Channel six, sir."

"Thanks. I'm calling about the package John Smith delivered to you at the bank this afternoon."

"Oh, that. I was going to send you a note. It's a lovely piece of crystal. Can I ask why you sent it over?" Buford Pickett has his skills—he's the best money collector in the state, bar none—but he's not real good at reading his boss.

"You haven't heard? Vernon Moore is back in town."

"He's not! Is he really?"

"I'm surprised Lily didn't tell you. He's staying at the Come Again, which means the news is all over the county."

"Lily probably didn't hear, Mr. Tucker."

"Are you feeling okay, Buford? Your wife is one of the most powerful women in the Circle. Her position was cemented in stone the day she married you."

"Lily would've told me if she knew, Mr. Tucker. Vernon L. Moore is big news. Is there a reason he's back in town?"

"Hell yes, Buford. I invited him."

"You did what, sir?"

"I invited him."

"Uh, okay. Can I ask why?"

"No, but you can do me a favor. You've always been interested in Vernon's identity; me, too. That glass I sent you has his fingerprints all over it. I want you to take it up to the state police in Lincoln and have them run his prints for me."

Buford cleared his throat. "Uh, that probably won't be possible."

"The colonel owes me a favor; he'll do whatever I ask. Don't mail it; it'll get broken or end up in Nicaragua. Take it yourself."

"That's not what I meant."

"Okay. What did you mean?"

"There was no note. I didn't know what the glass was for, Mr. Tucker."

"So?"

"I brought it home. Lily washed it."

The phone went dead.

MR. MOORE AND Doc Wiley arrived at the hospital after visiting hours, as if that mattered to a physician. Hank walked the two of them straight up to the second floor.

Loretta was in a private room, which was good because she needed the space. She got bouquets every week from my family, from the Circle, and from a dozen other men in town, plus a daily delivery from an anonymous admirer. There were roses on the shelf along the wall behind her bed, daisies and lilies on the windowsill, and all kinds of flowers on three white tables that an orderly had brought into the room. Connie Kimball, who runs the floral section of the grocery store, stopped by three times a week to cull the wilting and rearrange the rest.

When I visited, which was every afternoon, Loretta would be lying straight in bed, legs down flat or slightly bent at the knee, arms to her side, with the blanket pulled up to her armpits. Her eyes were always closed and she looked calm, as if she didn't have a care. If it wasn't for the blinking monitors, the IV contraption, and the wire running down to the little thingamajig on her index finger, you'd have thought she was having a nap. Every day, I expected Lo to sit up, stretch like she does, and say, "Why Wilma, darlin', it's so nice to see you."

Mr. Moore stood at the foot of her bed while Hank checked the monitors and her IV. Doc is no spring chicken anymore. He's more of an autumn chicken, and his bedside manner has acquired a few annoying idiosyncrasies along the way. For one, he mutters to himself while he is puttering around your body. Nobody wants a doctor to be muttering while he is poking around, but it doesn't do any good to ask him what he's saying. He'll tell you that every little thing is fine, and then he'll go back to muttering.

After he was done, Doc said, "Every little thing is fine, Vernon, except for the coma, of course. Otherwise, I'd say she was the picture of womanly health."

"She certainly seems well cared for. Thank you. What are her prospects for recovery?"

"I wish I could say. The beating caused subcranial bleeding and swelling of both the left and right frontal lobes, ergo the coma. The good news is that her EEG appears to be normal and no lesions were visible on her MRI. The bad news is that she's been in this state for six weeks."

"So her chances are diminishing over time?"

"Yes, but no one can say how much with any certainty. I know it's a cliché, but she could wake up at any moment."

"Fair enough, Doc, but what I'm asking for is an approximation of her chances. Are they sixty-forty, fifty-fifty, twenty-eighty?"

"Touch her, Vernon."

Mr. Moore reached over and touched her arm lightly.

Hank said, "A sleeping person wouldn't notice that. Now pinch her. Don't be a sissy about it; pinch her hard."

Mr. Moore pinched her forearm. There was no reaction so he pinched harder, but there was still no response.

"That's called 'patient not responsive to pain.' It's not conclusive, but it's an indicator."

"So her odds are less than fifty-fifty. Is that what you're trying to tell me?"

"I am, but they're not zero either."

Mr. Moore inhaled deeply. "Can you leave us alone for a while, Doc. I thought I'd read to her." He took a paperback out of his jacket pocket.

"You're going to read to her?"

"I thought I would, yes?"

"That's a good idea. You also might massage her extremities from time to time; that's good, too. Can I ask what book you picked out?"

Mr. Moore showed the book to Hank. It was *Devil in a Blue Dress* by Walter Mosley, her favorite. "Do you think she knows I'm here, Doc?"

"It's a possibility. For all we know, she's been waiting for you."

Chapter 10

....

My Only Sunshine

THE NEXT MORNING, Mr. Moore left the Come Again empty-handed shortly after nine a.m. By the time he reached the courthouse, he was carrying a black, alligator-skin case with a rare, nineteenth-century Stewart Universal Favorite banjo inside it. I know because Ivy Henshaw called from Retreads, the local antique and secondhand store, about two seconds after he left. Like most of us women in Ebb, Ivy is a retread herself. We share an interest in refurbishing old furniture.

Before he went downstairs to see my grandson, Mr. Moore checked in with the duty deputy on the main floor. Most of the deputies in Hayes County are women. Not all, but most. The deputy behind the duty desk was a tall, lithe woman named Pokie Melhuse. Pokie was the most famous track star ever to graduate from Hayes High. She finished second in the one hundred meters at state her senior year and got a full ride to the University of Nebraska. Then she met a boy, got pregnant, got married, and subsequently dropped out of school to raise the child and help put her husband through law school. You know the rest of the story, including the part about the divorce a year or so after her husband passed the bar.

Like I said, most of us are retreads.

Pokie sat behind the duty desk, which is a big old, boxy thing that allows her to look down on all callers. The front of that desk is all scuffed up, like it's been kicked a thousand times. Of late, I've been inclined to give it the boot myself a time or two.

Pokie has heard of Mr. Moore, just like everybody else in these parts. She introduced herself and asked him to wait while she waved to Dottie Hrnicek, who was a few desks away.

Dottie came up and said, "Good morning, Vernon. What's in the case?"

"A banjo."

"A banjo?"

"Yes."

"Do you plan on taking it downstairs?"

"With your indulgence, yes."

Dot exchanged glances with Pokie and said, "You don't need any indulgences from me, hon. Luther will have to check it out." Dottie looked at the case a second time and added, "He's looking forward to your visit. He says you got the Breck boy to interact yesterday."

"It was a negotiation, Sheriff, and barely civil. We're a long way from a healthy, open dialogue."

"Well, you got further than anybody expected. Maybe the banjo will help. You don't plan to beat on him with it, do you?"

"Oh no, Sheriff. It's much too expensive for that."

"Good. Beating prisoners with costly musical instruments is against the rules. Do you plan to pop the big question after you play a tune or two?"

"You mean ask Matt to identify his accomplices?"

"Of course I do. What other question would I mean?"

"I don't plan to ask him that at all, Sheriff."

Dottie put her hands on her hips. She has substantial hips. "Excuse me. Did I hear you say you're not going to ask the big question?"

"I promised Matt I wouldn't, but I believe we'll get the answer in the end anyway."

"Is that so? How are you going to get the names if you don't ask?"

"Matt needs a code of conduct. I'm going to try to sell him one."

"You mean like the Ten Commandments?"

"Not exactly, Sheriff. That was a perfectly fine code in its day, but I'm not sure that 'thou shalt not covet' still resonates with America's youth. I thought I'd try to boil it down to something a bit simpler, like rules of thumb."

"Rules of thumb? How many of these rules will there be?"

Mr. Moore held up his hands as if he were cradling a hymnal and examined them, then he replied, "Two. Two rules of thumb. That should be enough."

"Did you say two rules? That's not very many. Will one of them be, 'Tell Aunt Dottie what she needs to know'?"

"In a manner of speaking, but I don't anticipate a lot of progress today. Today, I expect a bit of trouble."

Dottie looked up at Pokie again, who was pretending not to pay attention. "You're expecting trouble. Does it have anything to do with the banjo?" she asked.

Mr. Moore answered, "Matt's defenses will be up this morning, Sheriff. The banjo will help lower them, but probably not on the first try. It's more of an acquired taste. Did Deputy Samoa tell you about my special meal request?"

"He did. It's a good thing we put that boy around the bend by himself. If the other two inmates find out what Matt's getting, I'll have a jailbreak on my hands."

"Maybe, maybe not. Give it another day or two, then offer them the same deal."

Dot looked down at the banjo and sighed. "Is there anything else you need?" she asked.

"I appreciate the support, Sheriff. I may have another request or two, possibly as early as this afternoon."

"There's more? What do you plan to do—teach young Matt the mandolin? Maybe you two could do a duet."

"That's a lovely idea, but I can barely play the banjo."

"Is that so?" she replied. "Why don't I let Luther know you're waiting for him?"

Deputy Giant came up the stairs a minute or so later, but he didn't exactly bound. Stairs aren't his favorite thing. It's the knee. The two men shook hands and walked down to the basement where Luther opened the banjo case and inspected it for the presence of dangerous weapons. Besides the banjo itself, there were a few music books, a little cotton bag full of plastic picks, and a small, collapsible stand covered in chrome. He closed the case and remarked, "I'm not too fond of banjo music, Mr. Moore."

"No problem, Deputy. I'm not too good at playing it."

Luther did a double take. "Then why did you bring it? Do you plan on using it down here?"

"I do, if you'll indulge me."

"Why?"

"Back in the eighties, Army Rangers piped rock and roll music into Manuel Noriega's papal refuge around the clock until he agreed to surrender. I hope the banjo will have a similar if gentler effect on young Matt."

"You expect Matt to surrender to a banjo? That's pretty confusing, Mr. Moore."

"I agree. How did he react to breakfast this morning?"

"Ask him yourself."

The two men walked down the hall and around the corner to find Matt lying on his bunk. His breakfast tray lay on the floor, the food half-eaten.

Luther opened the door and took up his station outside the cell. Mr. Moore entered and said cheerily, "Good morning! Did you sleep well?"

Matt sat up. "Dinner was great last night," he exclaimed, "but they brought me the same thing this morning. Did you know that? It must've been a mistake." According to Luther, Matt's eyes were locked on the banjo case the whole time he was talking.

Mr. Moore asked, "Did you enjoy the meal the second time?" He put the case on the floor beside his chair and sat down, then he opened it and removed the metal stand, which he set up directly in front of him.

Matt's eyes remained fixed on the banjo, which was now visible. "Yeah. It was okay, sorta like leftovers. If I'd known I could have another special meal, I'd have asked for something else, a burger maybe. Is that a banjo?"

Mr. Moore took out a music book and placed it on the stand. He said, "It is, yes."

"You're not going to play it are you?"

"Only if I need to kill some time. I asked you a question last night before I left. Do you remember what it was?"

"Of course. A dickhead could remember that question. You asked me how I was doing so far."

"I did. That's exactly it. What did you come up with?"

Matt answered, "I know what you want me to say, Mr. Moore. You want me to say I'm stupid. I'm not going to do that. I'm not stupid."

"I know you're not, Matt. That's why I asked how you were doing so far. It's a different question, like a progress report."

"Why? Why do you want to know?"

"It's not me; I want you to grade yourself. Did you think about it overnight?"

Matt didn't answer. After a long time, Mr. Moore asked, "Was the question too hard? Can you tell the difference between smart and stupid?"

Matt replied this time. "Yeah. Of course I can."

"Good. A lot of folks can't. What is it?"

There was no answer.

"It's an important question, Matt. How do you tell the difference between smart and stupid?"

Once again, my grandson chose not to reply.

"Okay. I can see you've been stumped by the general case. Let's try a recent example. Yesterday, I asked you an easy question. You gave me the right answer and got your favorite meal for dinner. Was that smart or stupid?"

Matt remained unresponsive. Mr. Moore shifted his eyes toward Matt's leftover breakfast and said, "Deputy Samoa, would you remove the tray from Matt's cell? It's become a bit of a distraction."

Luther stepped into the doorway.

Matt said, "I'm not done with it. Who knows what we're having for lunch? The food here is usually shit."

"Do you want me to take it or not, Mr. Moore?"

"Leave the tray for a minute. Let's see if young Matt is willing to chat. As long as he is, I'm willing to let him keep it."

"I thought you said I'd get my iPod back."

"I did, but only if you answered this morning's question. You haven't."

"Where is it?" Matt demanded. "Where's my iPod? Do you have it with you?"

"It's in a drawer in the watch desk at the end of the hall," Luther replied.

"Someone could steal it. Go get it!"

A look of frustration crossed Mr. Moore's face. He turned to a particular page in the music book and said, "There's another excellent example of the difference between smart and stupid, Matt. Deputy Samoa is the jailer; you're the jailee. It's not smart for the jailee to tell the jailer what to do. It can make the jailer angry, which could be bad. Do you like your inmates to tell you what to do, Deputy Samoa? How does that make you feel?"

"It makes me mad."

"Is that a good thing or a bad thing?"

"Oh, it's never a good thing, Mr. Moore. It's bad."

"Do you ever do what they tell you to do?"

"Never."

Matt said, "I don't give a shit. If I don't get my iPod back right this minute, I won't answer your dumb-ass question."

Mr. Moore shrugged and picked up the banjo. "I can see we're not going to get anywhere this morning, Deputy Samoa. Would you remove his tray?"

"What about my iPod?"

Mr. Moore began to pick one string at a time, then adjust the appropriate knob on the neck of the banjo. "Nothing has changed, Matt. I said you'd get it back if you give me a good answer to last night's question. You haven't. Bottom line: no iPod. The offer's off the table until this afternoon." He finished twisting the knobs and strummed a few notes.

"Okay. Okay! I'll answer the question."

The strumming stopped. "Let's hear it. How are you doing so far?"

Matt grinned like a Cheshire cat. "I'm smarter than you, that's how smart I am. You wanna know why?"

"Sure. Why?"

"Because I know you can't make me talk, and you're too stupid to get the message. I don't give a shit if you throw my iPod in the sewer; I'm not talking. And you can take my favorite meal and shove it up your ass."

Luther took a step toward the boy but Mr. Moore held up his hand and said, "That, Matt, was example number three. Was it smart or was it stupid?"

Matt laid back down on his bunk and curled up facing the wall.

Mr. Moore smiled and asked, "Is there a particular song you'd like to hear?"

No request was forthcoming so Mr. Moore picked a bar of "You Are My Sunshine" and began to sing.

Luther told me later that Mr. Moore's banjo was passable but his vocalizing was pretty awful. Every sharp was flat and every flat was, well, still flat. Having no other defense, the deputy joined in. So did another prisoner down the hall who fancied himself a fan of blue-grass. Matt rolled up like a ball and stuck his fingers in his ears.

Sometime during an energetic rendition of "Camptown Races," my grandson covered his head with a pillow. This didn't escape Mr. Moore, who looked up at Luther after the song and asked, "Should I play one more?"

"That's a nice offer, but we're getting kinda close to meal time. I should probably confer with Cookie about Matt's luncheon menu."

My unusual lodger nodded and carefully placed his banjo back into the case. As the men headed down the corridor toward the exit, he said, "I was afraid of this. Matt has no appreciation of good, old-fashioned music."

Luther said his ears were ringing. I guess there's no place for banjo music to go in a cinder-block basement but back and forth. "What did you say?" he asked.

"Musical tastes notwithstanding, the real problem is that he's become emotionally entrenched. He could care less about pleading down; he believes he deserves the maximum sentence. It's his just deserts."

Luther grunted his agreement.

When they got to the foot of the stairs, Mr. Moore stopped and added, "Between now and Monday, all Matt wants to do is insulate himself from the rest of the world; to ride it out. We're going to have to raise the stakes."

"Higher than a banjo?"

"I'm afraid so. Do you have a suicide watch protocol?"

"There's a standard procedure for all county correction facilities, Mr. Moore. All of my officers are trained in it."

"What happens?"

"The inmate is separated from the jail population, which Matt already is. Anything he could use to harm himself is removed from his cell. The usual things are his belt, his razor, his shoestrings, plus toenail clippers and moustache trimmers; that sort of thing. Excursions from the cell are closely supervised or eliminated altogether. Visitation is suspended except for special cases."

"What about dental floss and his toothbrush?"

"Those are at the discretion of the chief of corrections." Luther hesitated and added, "You're not thinkin' of Matt Breck, are you? He's no suicide risk. If you gave that boy a gun, a knife, and a bottle of cyanide pills, he'd botch the job."

"That's not the point, Deputy. I'd appreciate it if you would clear it with the sheriff. Not for now, but soon."

"Are you sure?"

"No, but please get permission."

Luther shook his head. When it came to making people shake their heads, Mr. Moore was the champ. "If that's what you want."

"I'd also appreciate it if you'd throw his iPod in the sewer."

"The sewer? Why?"

"It's what he asked us to do."

Luther shook his head again. "You're the boss. What about his lunch? Is there someplace you want me to shove it?"

"No. I interpreted that part of his request as metaphorical. I'd like you to stay with the same drill."

"Okay, but do you want us to keep giving him so much food? He only ate half of it this morning."

"I'd like you to make the portions bigger, deputy. Add a waffle, more French fries, more Oreos. Increase everything. If he doesn't eat it all, leave his tray behind again. Leave it until the next meal."

"Give him more?"

"I'm a full-service salesman, Luther. I deliver more than I promise. It always works in the long run."

MR. MOORE LEFT the banjo behind the watch desk and walked upstairs. When he got to the top, Pokie said, "The district attorney would like to speak to you. She's in her office right now. Can I call to tell her you're on your way up?"

"You may, Deputy. Thank you."

We put a modern Otis elevator in the county courthouse during the reconstruction but Mr. Moore took the stairs. When he arrived at Mary's office, he found her reading a law book with her feet propped up on her desk. Now, this is no small feat for a woman of Mary's diminutive size, but she has the seat of her chair at the very highest setting. Her toes can't possibly reach the floor. A woman shouldn't put her feet on the desk, anyway. Thank God Mary was wearing pants. As soon as she saw Mr. Moore, she put her book down and her legs where they belonged: behind the desk. "Come on in, Mr. Moore," she said. "Take a load off."

He took a seat and replied, "Would you please call me Vernon, or just Vern? Mr. Moore makes me uncomfortable." He might have been referring to the chair.

"I will, and you can call me Mary. I'm not much for titles myself, or beating around the bush either. Do you mind if I ask you a personal question? You don't have to answer."

"Thanks for reminding me, Mary, but I know that questions are one thing and answers are another. What's on your mind?"

"It's about you and Loretta Parsons. Is that all right?"

"Ask anything you like."

"She said you fathered her child. Is that true?"

"It is, yes."

"But you left Ebb immediately afterward without so much as a word."

"That's also true."

"Yet Wilma Porter believes that you're the Second Coming and Clem Tucker says you can part the waters of the Nile. Why is that?"

"You'll have to ask them, Mary."

"I know for a fact that Loretta Parsons never looked at another man after you left Hayes County, even though you ran out on her and her baby girl. Did you know that?"

"No."

"Well, Loretta was a man's woman if there ever was one. It would be no different if Elizabeth Taylor gave up jewelry or Donald Trump gave up funny hair. Do you know why she gave men up?"

"I don't."

"Well, you're one hell of a mystery, Vernon; half the town agrees on that. I was on the fence myself until Dottie Hrnicek came into my office not fifteen minutes ago. She said you were taking a banjo downstairs to the jail, and then she told me that you don't plan to ask Matt Breck to name his accomplices. I don't care about the banjo; you can play any instrument you like if it will get Matt Breck to talk. But I don't see how you can get him to tell you who the other two boys are unless you ask him."

"Really? I think that would be a mistake."

"A mistake? May I ask why?"

"Of course."

Here's another piece of advice: If you ever have the pleasure of meeting Vernon Moore, don't pose a question that can be interpreted as asking for permission. He'll say yes or no and that will be it.

After an uncomfortable interval, Mary inquired, "Okay. Why won't you ask him? I thought that was our purpose."

"Is the question the goal, or is it the answer? How many times has Matt already been asked to name his accomplices?"

"I don't know."

"A precise answer isn't necessary; an approximation will do."

She shrugged. "I really don't know. Fifty? A hundred? A lot of people have asked him that question a lot of times, me included."

"Tell me if I'm wrong, but there seems to be a pattern there. How many times has he answered it so far?"

Hail Mary was well educated. She knew a rhetorical question when she heard one.

Mr. Moore continued, "From a statistical point of view, we can probably conclude that asking the question hasn't worked. Matt believes himself to be solely responsible for the crime. We won't get him to talk unless we stop focusing on his accomplices and start focusing on him."

"Do you mean he's trying to shoulder all the blame himself?"

"In my experience, human beings are not adept at sharing guilt, Mary. We're absolutists; we're very good at accepting all of it or none of it. To his credit, Matt has embraced the former, and with zeal. The consequence is that he won't name his collaborators."

"Okay. Do you have a strategy? Is that banjo part of some plan?"

"Matt used to get A's in math, which means he has the capacity to be logical. I hope to get him to use that same logic on himself, but I have to get his attention first. The banjo is a device, a gadget to help me get Matt's attention."

"That's it? You're going to teach him to be logical with a banjo?"

"Yes. If I succeed, the rest will fall in place."

You guessed it; Mary shook her head. "Clem Tucker called me

again this morning," she said. "That's two days in a row. He wanted to know how you did yesterday. I told him you made progress. Now I have to call back and tell him you're crazier than his sister Clara. Is there anything else you'd like me to do? Should we be planning to bus Matt and a few of his friends to the Grand Ole Opry?"

"It sounds like fun but I doubt that it would set a useful precedent. I did ask Deputy Samoa to check with Sheriff Hrnicek about another possibility, though."

"Oh dear. I'm not sure I have the courage to ask. What is it?"

"If the afternoon is anything like this morning, I'm going to ask that Matt be put on suicide watch."

"Now that," Mary replied, "is a darn good idea. You'll have my full support—on one condition: you come to my house for dinner tonight."

Later on, I asked Mary if Mr. Moore was surprised by her invitation, but she said he acted like he knew it was coming. "Thank you for the invitation," he said. "It's very kind, but I have another appointment this evening."

"An appointment? With whom?"

"With Loretta. By the time I drive to Beatrice and back, it'll be far past an old man's dinnertime."

I guess Mary was less used to being turned down than Mr. Moore was to being asked. After a while she said, "Do you plan to see her every night you're here?"

"Yes."

"And how long will that be?"

"Less than a week. I leave this Saturday."

"Do you think you'll be able to get Matt Breck to talk before then?"

"I hope so. With your help, there's a chance."

"A chance?"

"It's an uncertain world, Mary. Between here and history, chance is all there is."

Chapter 11

....

The Big Whopper

AFTER HIS MEETING with Hail Mary Wade, Mr. Moore dropped by the Bold Cut to see Mona. She had a lot of questions about the morning, of course. It worried her that Matt wouldn't talk, and it worried her more when Mr. Moore told her what he might have to do next. The term "suicide watch" may not bother a man much but it bothers the heck out of a woman. No woman likes any phrase with the word "suicide" in it.

Mr. Moore tried to calm my daughter but he wasn't immediately successful, so he took her to the Corn Palace for lunch. Afterward, Mona was composed enough to return to her work at the Bold Cut, which was a good sign.

In the meantime, Clem Tucker called me at the Come Again. Naturally, it was during Laverne's nap. Don't ask me why, but a man always calls during dinner or a child's nap time. It's like a sixth sense. Luckily, she didn't wake up.

After his usual pitter-patter, which was none, Clem said, "How many rooms do you have available tonight?"

"Two that are unspoken for. Why?"

"Some business associates of mine are driving down from Omaha this evening, but I don't have enough space for them all at the River House. Can you set aside your two empty rooms for the overflow? They should be arriving around six or six thirty."

"That's pretty short notice but we'll manage. How long will they be staying?"

"Just the one night."

"Do you have the names of these two gentlemen?"

"My AA will email the particulars over later. Is that okay?"

"How about supper?" I asked. "They won't be expecting me to cook, will they?"

"Marie will be serving dinner down here. It's a bit of a celebration; I'd be grateful if you could come along. John will pick you up in the limo."

"I suppose I can make it," I replied coyly, as if I wasn't suddenly curious about what was going on. "Will it be a dressy affair?"

"Business casual. Wear anything you like."

That wasn't what I wanted to hear. In the country, "business casual" means bib overalls and boots. I had no idea what it meant in the city, but I had a more pressing question. "Can you tell me what this is about, honeypot? It will help me decide what to wear."

"It's a surprise."

"A surprise? What kind of surprise?"

Clem answered, "A great big whopper of a surprise."

Well, that wasn't what I wanted to hear either because the surpriser of record was none other than Clement Tucker. The Quilting Circle had kept a tally of his whoppers over the years. About 80 percent of them were more like bad surprises than good ones, and he could sell the county and move to the coast any time he wanted to. "Can't you give me a hint?" I asked.

"That would spoil it, Wilma. You'll find out everything tonight."

I worked on him some more, I even used my feminine wiles, but that was all he would say. As soon as we got off the phone, I went straight into the den to check Mr. Moore's registration form. It was blank, meaning there was no cell phone number, but I had to talk to him right away so I geared up the network.

In the Quilting Circle, every woman is a Bee and every Bee has a hive. In an emergency, each woman calls her hive, which is six other Bees, then each of those Bees calls her hive, which is six more. No Bee is ever more than three degrees of separation away, so we can reach the entire membership in minutes.

I put out the call to my hive to find Vernon Moore. Five minutes later, I got a callback from the county librarian, a septuagenarian named Tulip Orbison who claims to be related to late, great Roy. Tulip said Mr. Moore was on the second floor reading the state constitution, so I asked her to bring him to the phone. It took a little while. Like a number of librarians I've known over the years, Tulip is more of a sitter than a go-gitter.

Presently, Mr. Moore said, "Good afternoon, Wilma. How are you?"

"I'm as nervous as a perfumed butterfly at a lizard convention," I answered. "Clem just invited me to dinner. Tonight."

"You've been engaged for what, two years? By now, I'd have thought that you two would be used to dining together."

"We are, but this is different." I recounted Clem's call, as close to word-for-word as I could remember. After I was done, I said, "What should I do?"

He replied, "You should enjoy dinner, Wilma. You have a number of lovely dresses, but my guess is that Clem prefers the low-cut ones. Forgive me for saying so, but I know I do."

A younger woman might take offense at a comment like that, but a mature woman will take a compliment and be happy with it, especially if it refers to a part of her figure that she's proud of.

I replied, "That's a nice thing for you to say, Mr. Moore, but it's not what I meant. I called because of what Clem said about a 'big whopper of a surprise.' At the Circle, we've been worried for upwards of a year that some kind of a second shoe was going to drop. Is this it? Do you have any idea what he might be doing?"

"I have an idea but it's hardly worth mentioning."

"It may be worth more than you think. Would you mention it anyway?"

Right out of the blue he asked, "Have you ever played chess, Wilma?"

Mr. Moore claimed to be a games salesman the last time he was in Ebb. For four hundred reasons, hardly anybody believed him. He did seem to know a lot about games, though. "I never have," I replied.

"In chess, there are three phases of the game: the opening; the middle game; and the end game. The Big Buyback was Clem's opening gambit; he said so himself. Apparently, he's been playing some sort of middle game ever since. You may see the results for the first time tonight."

"Do you know what that's going to be?"

"I only have a theory, Wilma. It's in I-300."

"The law banning corporate ownership of Nebraska farms?"

"I've been studying the exceptions. It's possible that Clem has found a way to use one of them to his advantage or, more accurately, to his double advantage."

"And that's what I'll find out tonight?"

"Perhaps, but there's also the end game. That has yet to come."

"An end game?"

"Look at it as a third shoe."

"A third shoe? Oh dear! What kind of shoe?"

"I don't know, Wilma."

"What am I supposed to do?"

"He's your fiancé. You're supposed to trust him."

Did you ever want to shake the nearest man until his eyeballs fell out? "Trust him! This is not a game! What Clem does affects the lives of everyone in Ebb."

Mr. Moore's tone didn't waver one iota. "That may be, Wilma, but it's a game to Clem. Trust him and you have your best chance of winning."

"Even if I can, the Circle never will."

I don't know what Mr. Moore said in reply because I lost the connection. It was just as well. Even though Clem was my Fiancé in Perpetuity, I had a responsibility to the community. I called Lulu Tiller and asked her to convene an emergency meeting of the Quilting Circle's governing board.

Chapter 12

....

The Abattoir

FROM TIME TO TIME, we still debate whose idea the Quilting Circle was, but we all agree that the first meeting was held in my dining room at the Come Again. Winnie Bowe, Rufus' wife, was elected our first Queen Bee. Quilting was never her forte, but she turned out to be an A-plus recruiter. There were more than twenty of us in the Circle after just a few months, so we had to find a clubhouse of our own.

The first place we rented was an abandoned old home with a pretty front porch three blocks over from the Come Again, but we had so many members two years later that we were splitting at the seams. Fortunately, we had accumulated enough money in the treasury by then to put a down payment on the Old Jenkins Abattoir on North Bean Street. It was a whitewashed, cinder-block building that had been vacant since the seventies, so it was dirt cheap. For the same reason, it took a lot of clean-up and remodeling, but it has served our purposes ever since.

For those of you who don't know, "abattoir" is a fancy-schmancy name for a slaughterhouse. When it was a going concern, the 4-H took a field trip there every spring. I went there five times myself, so I remember the process from top to bottom with disarming clarity.

Prudence forbids me from describing it though, except to say that I still can't eat hot dogs.

Lily Park Pickett once reckoned that more than five million cows of this variety or that had been butchered there over the years. It gave the place an eerie feeling, but we never changed the name. We still call it the Abattoir. In addition to our quilting bees, the day care center, exercise and diet groups, fund-raisers, and our political affairs, we have at least one luncheon every month for the full membership. We never serve beef, though. It would be disrespectful.

There are eleven rooms and meeting spaces in the Abattoir, not counting the kitchen and the two bathrooms, both of which are for women. Old man Jenkins' office is just down the hall and set up like a conference room. It has an elliptical, oak-veneer table and eight matching chairs in it that we bought at a going-out-of-business auction in Hastings.

I was the first to arrive for my own emergency meeting. That gave me time to reflect, but all I could see in my mind was dismembered beef. Thankfully, Lulu Tiller walked through the door a few minutes later, Dottie Hrnicek in tow. Bebe Palouse and Lily Park Pickett were right behind.

Everybody sat down and Lulu said, "Loretta Parsons is not present due to medical disability, bless her heart. The rest of the board of governors is in attendance. Let the record show that we have a quorum."

Bebe, who is the general manager of Millet's Department Store and the best-dressed woman in Ebb, got out her notebook and made a note in the minutes. She was elected secretary of the Circle last year, which is an important position. Sometimes, people forget what they agreed to, even women.

Lulu went on. "This is an emergency meeting; there are no carry-over items on the agenda. Unless anyone objects, I'm going to turn the floor over to Wilma."

Lily added, "It's your meeting, Wilma. What's going on?"

I don't know why, but I felt like I was testifying before a congressional subcommittee of some sort. "Ever since the Big Buyback," I said, "we've all been waiting for Clem Tucker's second shoe. It could drop this evening."

"Go on."

"Clem invited me to a business dinner tonight with no advance notice. He may be a lot of things, but he is not a spontaneous man. Five or six businesspeople are driving down from Omaha for the affair. Two are staying at the River House, the rest are staying at the Come Again. They're the guests of honor."

Dot Hrnicek is a natural investigator. She said, "It sounds like some sort of celebration. Did you ask him what the occasion is?"

"I did. He said it was a 'big whopper of a surprise.' Those were his exact words."

Everybody in the room shuddered. Dot said, "Did Clem tell you who these people work for?"

"No. I should've asked but it didn't come to mind."

"You can't think of every little thing, Wilma. Did he tell you anything else?"

"I tried my hardest but he wouldn't talk. He said it would ruin the surprise."

Lulu sat back with a pouty look on her face. "I knew it was no coincidence that Vernon Moore was back in town. Did you talk to him?"

"The moment I got off the phone with Clem."

"Does he know what Clem is going to do?"

"He has a theory, Lulu. He says it has to do with an exception in I-300."

"That doesn't make a lick of sense to me," Dottie said. "Clem sold off all of his farmland last year."

"I know," I replied.

"Yes, but does Mr. Moore know?"

"I told him about the Big Buyback yesterday morning, I-300 too. He was reading the state constitution when I called him after lunch."

Have you ever been in a meeting when everybody stops talking at once and starts looking at each other? That's what happened. After several seconds, Dottie said, "Wilma, does Clem have any other holdings in the county besides Millet's and the bank?"

"I don't know, Dot. He may have sold everything else off."

Dottie turned to Bebe. "Has the equity situation changed at Millet's?"

"Nope."

"Are you sure?"

"My employment contract requires Calvin to inform me of any material change in ownership."

"I'm not sure that that would stop Clem, Bebe."

"Maybe so, Dot, but it would stop Calvin Millet. If there was a change, he'd tell me."

There was a long silence again, but no one was looking around this time; everybody was looking at me. Lulu started to scratch her arm and said, "Lily, would you go into the accounting office and run an Internet search on Nebraska I-300? After you find it, would you print a copy for everyone?"

Lily is amazingly quick at that sort of thing. She nodded and left. The rest of us went into the kitchen where we proved, once again, that one woman can make a pot of coffee faster than four. By the time we got back to the conference room, each of us had a hard copy of I-300, which is officially called Article XII, Section 8 of the Constitution of Nebraska.

We drank our coffee and chatted amongst ourselves while we read the law. It didn't take long for Dottie to zero in on a single exclusion. Like I said, she's a natural investigator. "Have you all read paragraph L?" she asked. "It says that the restrictions shall not apply to 'a bona fide encumbrance taken for purposes of security.'"

I was a little bit behind but I skipped right down to it. Dot went on. "Don't I recall that almost all of the land Clem sold in the Big Buyback was mortgaged back through Hayes County Bank? Isn't that right?"

Lulu slapped the table and declared. "That's it. Clem is selling the bank."

Lily added, "Those mortgages carry adjustable rates. If the rates get so high that the farmers can't make their payments, the bank can seize the land."

"I don't believe it," I responded. "Clement would never do such a thing. He brought that bank out of bankruptcy and nurtured it into a going concern. It's like a child to him. He could never sell it."

Lulu doesn't like to back off a prognosis. "Wilma, honey, I'm afraid you're looking at this through rose-colored glasses. We've been fighting your fiancé from pillar to post for twenty years. He's selling out to an Omaha bank. That's the second shoe."

"I still don't believe it. Clem would never sell his baby; especially to some bank in Omaha. That might as well be Norway. Clem would never do that."

"What Lulu says makes a lot of sense," Dottie added. "We know that a bunch of banks have visited Ebb in the last several months. Big banks: First National of Lincoln; National Bank of the Plains; Omaha Industrial and Agricultural. That's off the top of my head. There may have been more."

Bebe said, "All those banks are huge, and they're all in-state. Any one of them could swallow up HCB like a pig eats peas."

Lulu slapped the table again and repeated, "Clem is selling the bank. We'll have to sue, of course. We'll get an injunction and sue. Meanwhile, we'll get Hail Mary to start some sort of investigation. If that peters out, we'll march on Lincoln."

For those of you who don't live out in the country, the local bank is like your liver. It may not be your favorite organ, but you can't survive without one. You don't want to sell your liver either, because you don't have a spare. All of a sudden, I was afraid that my Fiancé in Perpetuity was about to sell the town's one and only liver to a big-city bank.

Lily asked, "What's Mr. Moore going to do about this, Wilma?"

"I don't know. He didn't say that Clem was going to sell the bank, but he did suggest that whatever happens tonight is just a middle game. He says that there's going to be an end game, like a third shoe."

"Does he know what that is?"

"I don't believe so. He said it was just a theory."

Lulu switched to scratching the inside of her thigh. Bebe said, "I only know your Mr. Moore by reputation, but I think he's right. We may think we know what Clem's going to do, but we don't know for sure. He could be selling a minority stake in the bank. From a risk-management perspective, that would make a lot of sense."

"Mr. Moore mentioned the same thing yesterday," I added.

"Maybe so," Lulu interjected. "But would that be a great big whopper of a surprise, or would it be more like a medium-sized surprise?"

Bebe replied, "Clem could also be buying a castle in England, or an ocean-going yacht, or a hockey team. Rich old men like to buy sports teams. Maybe he's decided to spend a few hundred million dollars in a vain attempt to recapture his youth."

"That's a point," Dottie said. "Old men seem to like rubbing shoulders with young men in the locker room, which makes no sense to me at all. Have you ever watched beach volleyball on TV? If I was a rich old fart instead of an officer of the law, I'd buy a women's volleyball team."

Bebe rolled her eyes. "None of us knows what Clem Tucker is really up to, assuming he's up to anything. My proposal is that we hold our horses for now. We'll have a lot more information tomorrow morning. By then, maybe we'll know what Mr. Moore intends to do, too. His arrival can't be a coincidence."

"I second," Lily said. "Let's meet again when we know more."

Lulu was still scratching but she had moved up to her ribcage. I could tell she was itching for a fight. I said, "I'm in agreement too. Whatever it looks like, I can't really believe that Clem would sell our bank."

"What's your opinion, Dot?"

"I think we should hold off, too. I may be able to pick up a little extra information myself before the night is done."

"How?" I asked, even though I knew the answer.

The sheriff grinned broadly and replied, "In a way that only a law enforcement officer could truly love."

In the next four hours, every automobile with Omaha plates in

Rutherford B. Hayes County got stopped by one or more of Dot's patrol cars, whether the vehicle was moving or not. My new lodgers, two middle-aged men in three-piece suits who looked liked potbellied penguins, were stopped twice, and they were hopping mad about it when they checked in to the Come Again. I don't know if you have ever seen a hopping, red-faced penguin, but there is a certain element of humor to it.

By the time I arrived at the River House, I not only knew their names, I knew the names of Clem's other three dinner guests, I knew their job titles, and I knew their place of employment. In case you were wondering, they all worked for the National Bank of the Plains, commonly known as NBP, the biggest bank in Nebraska and the two Dakotas.

I didn't want to admit it but NBP was the worst-case scenario. Before I-300 was passed into law, they were the most aggressive institutional buyer of farmland in the state.

Chapter 13

Clementine

I was still at the Abattoir when Mr. Moore left the house with Laverne that afternoon. It was chilly outside, so Mona wrapped her in a Cornhusker-red parka and a pink jumpsuit. She looked like Little Red Riding Hood. Mr. Moore wore a blue blazer, gray slacks, a blue shirt with a white collar, and a red tie. He looked more like a Wall Street tycoon than the Big Bad Wolf.

Mona stood under the porte-cochere and waved as Mr. Moore pushed Laverne's stroller down my driveway. "Good luck," she called as they went. "Give my love to Matt." Then she went indoors and had another good cry.

It took Mr. Moore every bit of thirty minutes to get to the county courthouse. It ought to be a fifteen-minute walk for an old salt with a peg leg, but at least four of my friends stopped to say hello. To a woman, they were happy to see him with his daughter at long last but horrified to hear where he was headed. I know because each and every one of them was kind enough to phone me afterward and tell me so.

It is my experience that strollers are good for flat surfaces, but they don't do well on stairs. The county courthouse has a dozen steps leading up to the front entrance. When Mr. Moore arrived at the duty desk inside the police station, he had Laverne under one arm and the stroller in the other. I guess the sight caused another stir. As I said, most of the deputies in Hayes County are women, and they all know who Laverne Parsons is. Pokie called three of them over and they had a fine time passing Laverne around and cooing over how pretty she is.

Mr. Moore put up with it for a while, but then he took Laverne back and said, "Deputy Melhuse, I'd appreciate it if you could give Deputy Samoa a call. It's time for my session with Matt."

She replied, "You don't plan on taking Laverne down there, do you?"

"I do, yes."

The deputies stopped cooing. One of them might have touched her holster. Pokie asked, "Are you sure that's wise?"

"Not entirely, no."

"Couldn't Laverne get hurt?"

Mr. Moore took off Laverne's parka and stuffed it in the seat of her stroller. "No, Deputy Melhuse," he replied. "Deputy Samoa will be in the cell with us, so I don't believe there's any material risk. I'd appreciate it if you could keep an eye on her stroller though."

Pokie wasn't sold on the idea, but she knew who she was dealing with. She said, "Would you hang on for just one second? I'll go ahead and make the call." According to her, Deputy Giant appeared at the top of the stairs less than one millisecond later.

Laverne took one look at him and said, "Barney!"

Luther grinned and pinched her on the cheek. "Hello, Laverne, you sweetie-pie! Hello, Mr. Moore. Pokie tells me you want to take Loretta's little girl down to see Matt."

"I would, yes. Do you mind?"

"It's against the rules to take her into his cell," Luther said. "Minors aren't allowed in the incarceration area. I'll have to bring Matt to the visiting room. You can see him there."

"Can we head down to the jail, Deputy?"

"Sure. No problem."

On the way, Mr. Moore asked, "Did you throw Matt's iPod in the sewer?"

"No, sir. That didn't seem very environmental, so I pitched it in the kitchen trash. It's long gone now."

"Did you tell Matt?"

"No sir. He asked at breakfast but I told him he'd have to discuss it with you."

"That was the right thing to do, but I'd like Laverne to be in the cell when I talk to him. What if we brought an extra chair into the cell and you held Laverne while Matt and I talked? Then we'll all be safe. What do you say?"

Luther pondered a second or two before responding, "Minors aren't allowed in the incarceration area, Mr. Moore. I should call the sheriff. That's what I'm supposed to do if there's a question."

"I'm pretty sure she's in some sort of meeting right now. If I'm right, you'll have to make the decision yourself or escalate to Mary Wade."

Luther looked at little Laverne. "Can I ask why you're doing this?"

"Yes."

After the usual silence he said, "Okay. Why are you doing this?"

"Matt has been using his iPod to suspend himself in a State of Isolation. He has no chance of becoming the person he needs to become unless he can move to the State of Interaction. Under the circumstances, that will be a hard move for him to make. He needs help. Laverne may be able to help him."

"I don't understand, Mr. Moore. She's just a little girl. How is she going to help him?"

"I'm not entirely sure."

"You're not?"

"No."

"But you still want to do this."

"Definitely."

That prompted another long silence. Eventually, Luther said, "I don't know what you're doin', Mr. Moore, but you're supposed to have free rein. We're gonna break the rules, but just this time. I'll make sure that nothin' happens to Loretta's little girl."

"Thank you, Deputy. I owe you one."

"You do at that. Do you have to take the banjo, too?"

"I do. Maybe Laverne will like my playing more than Matt."

Luther held his tongue and went into the visiting room to get a folding chair while Mr. Moore retrieved the banjo from behind the watch desk, then the three of them toddled down the hall to see Matt. They found him curled up on his bunk, facing the wall. His meal tray was under his bed, the food piled high. Only the Oreos were gone.

Luther opened the cell and said, "Nap's over, junior. Your popularity is way up. You have two visitors."

Matt rolled over to see Luther and Mr. Moore seating themselves a few feet away from his bunk. The jailer turned on the recorder and put Laverne Parsons in his lap. She smiled and tugged at his badge, which he kept at a high sheen.

"What's she doin' here?" Matt asked.

Mr. Moore began to set up the music stand and answered, "I invited her along. She lives at the Come Again, you know. She's one of the family. She even has your old room."

Matt sat up, but with his back against the wall. "I don't want her here. Get her out."

"I thought you'd be happy to know that Laverne's okay. I can bring you up to date on her mother's condition, too."

"Get out of here, all of you!"

"Now Matt," Mr. Moore said, "we're not going to have another who's-the-boss contest, are we? The last time, two things happened: you lost and things got worse. Laverne is staying."

"Fine. I'm not talking."

Mr. Moore took a music book out of the case and put it on the stand. "You're not talking? What's new about that? How was lunch today?"

True to his word, Matt didn't answer.

Mr. Moore glanced at Matt's tray and continued, "Tell me if I'm wrong, but it looks like you didn't eat much. Does it look that way to you, Deputy Samoa?"

Without taking his eyes off Matt, Luther answered, "It sure does. I'm beginning to wonder if he told us what his favorite meal really was."

My grandson was never good at taking criticism. "I did so, but I didn't say I wanted to eat it for the rest of my life! I want something different."

Mr. Moore smiled. "Fair enough, but you're not there yet. Until you can tell me why you want something else, you'll be eating the same meal three times a day. Can you answer that question? Can you tell me why you want something else?"

"This is bullshit! You can't make me eat the same thing all the time. I have rights."

"You do have rights," Deputy Samoa said, "but they don't extend to menu selection. Mr. Moore is responsible for your meal planning right now. It stays that way as long as he says."

About then, Laverne managed to pull Luther's badge off the front of his uniform shirt, which left a small rip in the right flap of the pocket. She said, "Mine?"

He smiled down at her, frowned at Mr. Moore, and put the badge inside his breast pocket. Laverne turned her attention to his buttons.

Matt didn't seem to notice. "Are you going to play the banjo again?"

"Only if I need to kill some time. Will I?"

"I want to see my lawyer!"

Luther replied, "You fired your lawyers, junior. Mr. Moore is in charge of your visitation list now. No lawyers are on it. You'll have to ask him."

"I have the right to see a lawyer any time I want to."

"That used to be true," Mr. Moore said, "but you waived your right to counsel. Besides yourself, only Laverne, Deputy Samoa, and yours truly are on your visiting list, plus my trusty banjo, of course. No one else."

"Then I want to see my mama!"

"Only after we've made some progress. Until then, she's not on the list either."

Matt climbed out of his bunk and stood up. "Goddammit! I get sentenced on Monday and then I'm gone. I want to see my mama! Right now!"

Luther jumped to his feet and positioned his considerable frame between Matt and Laverne. In a deep voice, he said, "Sit down, junior, and shut up. Otherwise, things will get worse, and faster than you can say 'uncle'!"

Matt remained standing. "Worse? Worse? You stole my iPod. You're feeding me the same shit every meal. Some wacko from hell is playing a banjo in my cell. You won't let me see anybody. What else can you do? Are you gonna beat me? Are you gonna shove the banjo up my ass? There's nuthin' else you can do to me, you big, fat son of a bitch!"

Mr. Moore grimaced. "We probably need to clear up a bit of a little misunderstanding there. Deputy Samoa didn't steal your iPod."

"Really? That's terrific. It's mine and I want it back right now."

"I'm afraid it's gone, Matt."

"Gone? Where?"

"You told us to throw it in the sewer. Deputy Samoa was kind enough to oblige. Your iPod is sleeping with the roaches."

Matt sat down on the edge of his bed with a thud. Mr. Moore continued, "Yesterday I asked you whether it was better to be smart or stupid. You surprised everybody and picked the right answer. But when I asked you how you were doing so far, the conversation began to break down. Can you tell me why?"

There was no reply.

"The reason is that you can't face the answer. Until you do, things will get worse and for a very long time, possibly the rest of your life. This is your last chance to answer the question today. How are you doing so far?"

"How am I doing? Ever since you got here, my life has turned to shit. Now my iPod's gone. I don't give a shit what else you do."

Mr. Moore shook his head and replied, "Do you honestly believe your life went to hell yesterday? Do you have a clue where you're headed? Do you have any idea at all?"

Matt shouted, "Get out of my cell! Get out and take the whore's daughter with you!"

"I suppose I can interpret that as another refusal to enter into an open, trusting dialogue. I wonder: was it smart, or was it stupid?" Mr. Moore pulled the banjo out of its case. After some fiddling with the strings, my unusual lodger said, "Do you have a request, Deputy Samoa?"

Luther grinned. "I always liked 'Clementine.' Do you know that one?"

"I do. Feel free to sing along. You too, Matt." Mr. Moore played a few chords and then sang in his flat, nasal voice,

In a cavern, in a canyon, excavating for a mine,
Dwelt a miner, forty-niner, and his daughter, Clementine.
Oh my darling, oh my darling, oh my darling Clementine . . .

Luther joined in and Laverne laughed and clapped, as if she was watching an episode of *The Muppets Take Appalachia*. The bluegrass aficionado in the cell down the hall began to sing along, too, which was when my grandson snapped. He jumped up and grabbed the food tray underneath his bunk.

In the same instant, Luther stood and boomed, "NO!"

Matt ignored him and catapulted the contents of the tray toward his singing antagonists. It was impossible to miss at such close range. Deputy Samoa, Laverne Parsons, and Mr. Moore were struck by five waffles, a quarter pound of cold bacon, large quantities of cold French fries and onion rings, and splatter from a plastic bowl filled to the gunwales with melted ice cream.

Laverne put her index finger in some warm, vanilla cream on Luther's cheek and put it in her mouth. "Juice?" she asked.

Matt threw the tray down and retreated to the darkest corner of his bunk. Luther began to reach for him, but Mr. Moore pulled his sleeve and said, "There we go again, Matt. Was that smart, or was it stupid? I'll be back tomorrow to discuss it. You may want to review your position on the whole smart-stupid thing between now and then."

Matt said, "Kiss my ass," and rolled over to face the wall.

Once again, Mr. Moore had to restrain Deputy Giant, then he wiped off his banjo and packed it up.

As they walked down the hall, Luther grinned and said, "You used Laverne to provoke him, didn't you?"

"I suppose so. To be fair, the banjo played a role, too."

The giant snorted. "Whatever. It worked. What's next?"

"Put the boy on suicide watch."

"It'll be a pleasure."

"And one other thing. Increase the portions."

I WAS UPSTAIRS in my room when Mr. Moore returned to the Come Again from the county jail, but I could still hear Mona yelp when she saw Laverne. Apparently, the men hadn't been able to get much of the cream, butter, and grease off her pink and white jumpsuit. Mr. Moore was overdue for his game of gin rummy with Mark, but he tried to mollify Mona first. She's an understanding woman, but she was less than placated by his description of the day's play-by-play. As soon as she was done bathing and dressing Laverne, she came stomping into my room.

Women like to look at each other when they fume, but I was putting on my makeup, which meant my face was stuck in the mirror. I need to concentrate at my age. I let Mona rant a while—it's what a mother does—then I shook my head and said, "Mr. Moore may work in strange ways, but I think you have to trust him."

"Trust him, Mama? Forget Laverne. He's putting Matt on suicide watch."

"It's a ploy, honey. The boy will never kill himself. We Porters prefer to suffer; we stay with it. That's what you should do, too; you should stay with it. Mr. Moore has only been visiting Matt a short time, and he's your last hope. Give him another day or two to make some progress. I'm sure things will be better tomorrow."

Mona didn't answer me out loud so I looked at her reflection and said, "Do you have an alternative, honey? I don't believe you do, and nobody else does either. I bet Mr. Moore would say that all of the normal strategies have been used up and it's time to try something abnormal. From that point of view, he's just being logical."

"Do you hear what you're saying? How is it possible for him to be logical and abnormal at the same time?"

"He's a hard man to understand but he has a track record. Give him some more time."

Mona thought about it for a little while longer. "I'm concerned about Matt's diet, Mama. From what Mr. Moore said, he's living on Dr Pepper and Oreos."

"You're worried about that?" I said. "That's all he ate when he was living at home. He's a teenager. It's his job to accelerate the aging process by eating enormous quantities of the least nutritious food he can find. Mr. Moore is just helping him along. Now pick me out a lip gloss while I finish up my eyes. I'm leaning toward something of the ultra-red variety."

Mr. Moore won his game of gin rummy with Mark, across the board, but Mark wasn't disappointed at all. I guess he got a kick out of Mr. Moore's description of his brother's food dispersal skills. By the time I left for the River House, Mr. Moore had already gone to see Loretta, and Mona was getting Laverne ready for bed.

Even though I had my little black dress on, I felt like I was no better than dressed to the sixes. Maybe that's what business casual means: dressed to the sixes.

Chapter 14

The Second Shoe

THE GREAT ROOM in the River House may be the largest residential room in southeast Nebraska. For as long as I can remember, it's been arranged in four quadrants: one for watching TV; another for the library; one for playing cards; and a special area for the bar that has an old-fashioned, soda-fountain jukebox with original 45s, most from the doo wop era.

When I arrived, my potbellied penguins were looking over the songs on the jukebox along with a third man, probably in his sixties, who was slim and stylish-looking in a gray, double-breasted suit. Clem's other two guests were sleek, thirty-something blondes dressed in little black dresses and heels, like sisters from the same sorority. Thank God I had had the foresight to wear my own little black dress. It wasn't as small as theirs to be sure, but I still have my assets. The men kept their eyes on two of them for half the night.

The sorority sisters were in the library talking to Calvin Millet, who I hadn't seen for weeks. Calvin is a tall, wiry man, but he looked gaunt. That's what happens when a man cooks for himself or eats out too often. My Fiancé in Perpetuity and Mr. Smith were tending bar, both dressed in black from head to toe. Standing side by side, they looked like The Men in Black. It was black night.

Clem spied me in the foyer and came straight over, grinning like a Cheshire cat. That worried me some. Clem is not a natural grinner; he has to work at it. After helping me with my wrap and complimenting my appearance, two more things to worry about, he walked me around the room and introduced me to everybody. When we were done, I found myself at the bar with the classy, older man from Omaha. His name was Fabrizio Santoni, Fabi for short. He came to the United States when he was a young man, but he still had a lovely Italian accent. After college, he joined the National Bank of the Plains and eventually worked himself all the way up to Chief Operating Officer, which is just one rung short of CEO.

For a man so high up the ladder, he had a nice disposition. After telling me a bit about himself, he said, "I was stopped twice by the police on my way to the River House this evening. Both of the troopers were women. Is that common in this part of the state?"

"It can be," I answered coyly. "Why do you ask?"

"I am an old man, a widower. I'm looking for a place to retire. There's something to be said for a town where the police are women. The second officer was so attractive that I came very close to inviting her to dinner. Do you think she would have accepted?"

"She might at that. There's a surplus of eligible women in this neck of the woods. I have an idea that you'd get to know them all."

"I'm a foolish old flirt," he replied. "I admit it, but I can afford the consequences of success. Clem has spoken of you often, but I understand that you two have been engaged for a long time. Is this true?"

"It is."

"What's the reason for the delay? Do your parents disapprove?"

I laughed. "My parents passed on long ago, Mr. Santoni. But when they were alive, they were traditional, God-fearing folk: they disapproved of nearly everything."

"Ah, yes. I've been in this country for fifty years, but this is an attitude I still do not understand. Why are so many Americans so judgmental? Even the Bible says, 'Judge not.'"

"Nobody knows. I guess it's easier to judge not yourself and to judge the heck out of everybody else."

"Yes. That is always the easy way. How do you judge Clem? Is he worth such a wait?"

Mr. Moore would never say yes to a question like that, but I figured that Mr. Santoni was looking for a one-syllable answer. I looked him square in the eye and replied, "Yes. Clem's worth it. He's as fine as they come."

"Is he an honest man?"

"He is, but he doesn't get a lot of credit for it."

"Why is that?"

"When Clem says a deal is a deal, you can take it to the bank. But you better be thinking a step ahead, Mr. Santoni, because he is."

The old man rubbed his chin. "That is wise advice for all of us. Would you wait for him if he was a poor man?"

"If he was a poor man, my wait would be over," I answered. "Every problem we ever had was because of his money. Why do you ask? Do you plan on making him poor?"

"Oh no, Ms. Porter. To the contrary. I was only interested in your perception, but forgive my lack of manners. Would you care for something to drink?"

The dinner was just as congenial as could be. Clem sat at the head of the table between the sisters. I sat between Calvin and Mr. Santoni at the opposite end. Marie fixed steak au poivre and green-bean casserole for the main course. A casserole with mushroom soup in it is not the sort of thing a woman would choose for a formal dinner, but Clem asked for it. By now, you should appreciate the correlation between what he asks for and what he gets.

Because it was such an important evening, Clem asked Roberto Bocachica to help Marie serve. He and his wife, Consuela, are from Nicaragua. Neither one of them could speak a lick of English when they moved to Ebb, but they're more fluent than some of the locals now. She says they learned it from Oprah.

We tried to get Consuela to join the Quilting Circle a few years ago, but Roberto wouldn't have it. He said it was a violation of his arrangement with Clem. We may be the first woman's club ever excluded by an employment contract, express or implied. She attends meetings on the QT from time to time anyway, but we never ask her to pay dues or to bake.

For the longest time, Roberto swirled around the dinner table while everybody ate and talked about the one item that dominates the Nebraska male mind in the fall: football. It turned out that even Mr. Santoni was a dyed-in-the-wool Cornhusker fan. In between discussions about the latest recruiting violations, none of which were at our school, and the various merits of the West Coast offense, I managed to squeeze in a few words with Calvin Millet.

After we had speculated about the purpose of Mr. Moore's return for a while, I said, "Speaking of missing men, I haven't seen you lately. Where have you been?"

"Clem's had me running all over the country, Wilma. The Caribbean, too."

"The Caribbean?" I asked. "That must be nice. Which islands did you visit?"

"Just the Caymans, Grand Cayman to be precise. The local people tell me it's overdeveloped, but the beach there is incredible. They call it Seven Mile Beach but it's only five and half miles long. Did you know that?"

"I didn't," I replied, but you know what I was thinking: a man must've measured it and filed the usual report. "Is that a normal place to go on business?" I asked.

"It is, yes. Grand Cayman is the Switzerland of the Americas, without the mountains."

"So you keep money there?"

"We have an account or two. Everybody does."

"That's interesting," I answered, since I didn't know anybody else who had even been to a Cayman island, much less kept money there. "Is Clem going to keep you running all over Hell and Gone forever or are you going to have some time to catch your breath?"

"I don't know how much he's told you, Wilma, but we'll be making an important announcement tomorrow morning. I'll have some free time after that. I may even go back to the Caymans, but just to lollygag on the beach and swim with the tropical fish."

"Get a tan, too. You could use some color." I added, "Is Clem going to say anything about this announcement tonight?"

"He is."

"Can you give me a little hint in advance?"

"Clem asked me to keep everything confidential. He specifically instructed me not to talk to you about it."

In the time-honored tradition, I put my hand on my semi-bare bosom and asked ever so sweetly, "Me? Why?"

"You know why, Wilma: split allegiances."

"Split allegiances? You don't mean the Quilting Circle?"

"I do. You know you're going to have to choose some day."

"Choose? Between Clem and the Circle?"

"Yes."

Tell me if I'm wrong, but I didn't sense a smidge of hesitation in his answer. I turned from Calvin to cast my eyes toward Clem at the head of the table. The sorority sisters on his left and right were yammering away but he was stone silent and looking straight at me. I smiled. It wasn't my best, but he smiled right back. His was genuine, and a tad irritating.

When we were done with the main course, Marie and Roberto brought four delicious-looking chocolate soufflés into the dining room on matching silver trays. After the portions had been spooned onto our plates, Roberto came around the table and offered each of us some powdered sugar. Everyone accepted, but one of the sisters leaned down and smelled her soufflé afterward, like she was trying to inhale it. Naturally, the sugar went straight up her nose, which caused her to cough uncontrollably. That poor woman must have hacked and wheezed for three minutes. Marie and Roberto were visibly upset but, Lord forgive me, I was a bit tickled by it. A country girl is careful about where she puts her nose.

While we were eating our soufflés, Roberto brought a giant bottle of French champagne into the dining room and opened it up and Marie gave us each a special, crystal flute. Roberto filled them, then Clem stood up and tapped his water glass with a spoon.

"First of all," he said, "I'd like to thank our guests from the National Bank of the Plains for driving down to Ebb to dine with us tonight, especially Mr. Santoni. I know you're very busy people, but this is such an important occasion for me, the bank, and everyone in Rutherford B. Hayes County."

Clem held up his flute, "I'd like to propose a toast to you all, to NBP, and to our new relationship. May it endure to serve our grand-children and theirs."

Everyone held up their glasses and said, "Hear, hear." Everyone except me, that is. My mouth was open, but I sat there, stiff as a statue.

Clem was in fine form. "I'd also like to toast my fiancée, Wilma, for clearing out her busy schedule to be here tonight. She's the finest woman in the state. One of these days, I hope she'll do the honorable thing and make me her husband."

Everybody said, "Hear, hear" again and took another swallow.

I closed my mouth and blushed like a schoolgirl. Clem Tucker is a devious old coot; I swear he plans out everything in advance. I should have been paying attention to what he was saying about the bank but I was turning cherry red.

He barely stopped to catch his breath. "As you know, we're going to make the formal announcement tomorrow. The press release will go on the wires at ten a.m. and be in every newscast in the state by noon. I know it's the best thing for everyone, but the citizens of Ebb and some of the employees of Hayes County Bank may not see it that way at the start. We're going to have to do some selling. Before you all leave tonight, I'd like to remind everyone of tomorrow's schedule.

"Calvin, perhaps you'll be kind enough to do the honors."

Clem sat down. Calvin stood up and continued, "Bank manage-ment has been summoned to a meeting in the large conference on the top floor at eight a.m. Clem and I will brief them there and introduce them to you. Afterward, a continental breakfast will be served.

"Just before nine a.m., each of you will be paired with your corresponding HCB manager to make the announcement to bank personnel in small groups. Clem, Mr. Santoni, and I will circulate from meeting to meeting so that each group has an opportunity to ask questions. Buford Pickett will have the security guard close the bank until ten a.m. The bank has only thirty-seven personnel, so we expect the process to be completed well before then."

One of the penguins asked, "Will you have copies of the press release for your managers and employees?"

Calvin answered, "We will. We'll also put a stack of them in the bank foyer for our customers and a copy will be inserted in each bank statement through the end of the month. This is a great day for Ebb. We don't want to hide our light under a bushel."

The same banker said, "We anticipate considerable press activity by the afternoon. Will you and Clem be available for interviews?"

"I don't plan to go anywhere for the rest of the week. How about you, Clem?"

He answered, "Fabi and I have a few loose ends to tie down in Omaha, but we can be reached by phone at any time. Are there any other questions?"

I had about forty, but I didn't know whether I could ask them or whether I was supposed to keep my mouth shut. I chose the latter. So did everybody else.

Clem said, "Well then, why don't we all repair to the bar?"

Everybody stood except me. Calvin, who has always been the politest boy, stepped behind me and tried to help me with my chair. I didn't budge.

He said, "Wilma?"

The rest of the guests were filing out of the room. I whispered, "Can you please tell me what's going on here?"

He whispered back, "You didn't figure it out?"

"I'm ninety-nine percent sure I did, but I'd like to be completely sure. Did Clem sell the bank to NBP?"

"He did, Wilma, lock, stock, and barrel."

"He didn't keep even a little bit, for old time's sake?"

"No, Wilma. Not a share; not an option. It's all gone."

"Are the papers signed? Is it done?"

"Clem signed the final contracts three hours ago. The appropriate papers will be filed with the Federal Reserve and the state banking commission tomorrow morning."

"So it's over. There's no going back."

"That's right."

"The ink is dry?"

"It's a done deal."

My head was in a whirl. "You go and join the others. I need to be alone for a while."

"Are you sure?"

"All of a sudden, I'm not sure of anything except that I'd like to sit by myself for a minute. You go back to your guests."

Calvin put his hand on my shoulder and said, "Trust him. Wilma. That's all that I can say. That's all I'm allowed to say."

For a while, it was just me and the twenty dead heads on the dining hall walls, but Doc Wiley was looking down at me instead of the bear, Lily Pickett had become the elk head, and Lulu Tiller was the bighorn sheep. It was scary, so I wandered into the kitchen to commiserate with Marie. She was sitting at the butcher-block table, her apron stained with mushroom soup and dark chocolate, drinking sherry out of a purple plastic tumbler. The kitchen was a mess. Pots and pans were stacked on every counter and both sides of the sink were full of dirty dishes.

She looked up at me and asked, "Am I out of work, Wilma? This is the best job I ever had. I don't want to cook for an athlete again. I'll slit my wrists if I ever have to fry another chicken wing."

"Don't you worry," I replied. "Clem may have more time on his hands, but he can't boil an egg. You have the safest job in the county. It's everybody else I'm worried about."

"Didn't he tell you what he was going to do?"

"He didn't say a word. No, that's not fair. He told me I was going to get a big whopper of a surprise. How many words is that? Five? Six? Remind me to compliment him on his succinctness."

"Why wouldn't he tell you, Wilma? You could've warned us."

"That's exactly why he didn't," I answered.

Chapter 15

·······················

Revelations

AFTER I HAD FORTIFIED myself with a glass of Marie's sherry, I meandered back into the great room to find Clem, Mr. Santoni, and the two penguins playing gin rummy for money. Calvin was in the library having a drink with the sorority girls. John Smith was alone behind the bar.

I walked up to him and said, "I know the party's not over yet, but could you drive me back to the Come Again? If you get it over with, you can come back for the bankers later on and they won't have to drive themselves. I hear the sheriff has been paying special attention to vehicles with Omaha plates lately."

"That's a good idea, Ms. Porter," he said. "I'll check with the boss."

Clem came over a few seconds later. "Where have you been, Wilma? Fabi must have asked about you a dozen times."

"I just popped into the kitchen to see Marie. We had a dab of sherry together."

"That was sweet of you, but John says you want to head back to the Come Again. The night is still young. Can't you stay?"

"I'd love to, honeypot, but I have a houseful of guests to care for. I run a bed and breakfast, you know. Clara gets irritable if I'm late with her oatmeal."

"I should have asked. How is my elder sister? Is she well?"

"She could probably beat half the Haymaker track team in the metric mile, but she's going to be cranky tomorrow."

"Tomorrow? Why?"

"Because of the news, Clem. Because you sold the bank."

He smiled. "Oh, don't worry about that, Wilma. Clara is the second largest shareholder in the trust. She had to approve the deal in advance."

"Clara knew?"

"She did. She was very supportive."

To my knowledge, Clara and Clem Tucker hadn't agreed on anything since Johnny Carson quit TV. We were all so sorry to hear that he passed on.

Clem said, "You sat next to Fabi at dinner. Did you like him?"

"He's very friendly."

"He is that and he's a damn good banker, but he's looking right down the barrel of mandatory retirement. Isn't that a shame?"

"He mentioned something like that, but I thought he was pulling my leg. Can't a COO decide to stay on?"

"Not anymore, but seventy-two isn't what it used to be, you know. Armand Hammer was still running Occidental when he was eighty-eight."

"That is a crying shame," I said. In my mind, I thought eighty-eight was a fine number for piano keys, but it was probably pushing the age-discrimination envelope.

Clem went on. "Fabi has worked at NBP for forty-five years, but he never reached his goal. He wanted to be CEO, but he lost out to a youth movement."

I can be thicker than cold corn chowder but I was beginning to believe that Clem was trying to tell me something. As intelligently as I could, I said, "A what?"

"A youth movement. He's baby-sitting his third CEO now, and this one is the worst of the lot."

"My, my," I replied. "I guess he can't get a break."

"You were perfect tonight, Wilma. Thanks for taking such good care of Fabi. I know you impressed him." He bent over and kissed me on the cheek the same way you'd kiss an uncle's second wife. At the moment, it was about as much affection as I could handle anyway. I pecked him back and waited at the door while Clem returned to his card game.

Mr. Smith showed up with my wrap a few seconds afterward. Two opened doors and one "watch your head" later, and I was in the backseat of Clem's limo headed north. It's a big, black Cadillac with a black-leather interior that's been modified for the purpose of being driven by a chauffeur. A dark glass separating the front from the rear can be raised or lowered from either side, and there's extra legroom in back, plus two jump seats and a snazzy, polished-wood bar with crystal decanters and glasses.

Mr. Smith left the black glass divider down. We hadn't been on the road for a mile when he handed me a sheet of paper over the backseat.

"What's this?" I asked.

"It's a copy of tomorrow's press release," he replied to the rear-view mirror.

It gets real, real dark in the country at night; I couldn't read a word. Mr. Smith added, "There's a reading light on the C pillar behind your right ear. The switch is just below it."

I turned the light on and asked, "Did Clem ask you to give me this?"

"No."

I hate it when men don't embellish. A woman knows when to embellish. I asked, "Then why are you giving it to me?"

"It's big news, Ms. Porter. I thought you and Mona would want to know tonight."

I wasn't ready for any more revelations, but there it was. "Do you know my Mona?"

"She used to cut my hair every week—before the incident."

Well, that should have been plain obvious, shouldn't it? Mona had worked for Loretta ever since she had returned to Ebb. She had to know every man in the county; they all went to the Bold Cut.

"How is Ms. Parsons?" he asked. "Is she going to be all right?"

"I don't know. Nobody does."

"Have they made any progress on finding the other two boys?"

It's funny talking to a chauffeur. I couldn't decide whether to direct my attention to the rearview mirror or to the little bald spot in the back of his head. "I don't know that either," I replied to the mirror.

"How about your grandson, Matt? How is he?"

"It's a difficult time for him, Mr. Smith. It's difficult for all of us."

"I can imagine, but I don't understand how your daughter's son could do such a thing. Mona doesn't have a mean bone in her body."

"That's such a sweet thing for you to say, but I guess he did it. The question that has us all stumped is why. Do you have a theory?"

"I do," he answered.

"You do? What is it?"

"I can't say, Ms. Porter. Mr. Tucker asked me to back off for a while."

"Back off?"

"Yes. I was looking into the incident myself, but Mr. Tucker asked me to give it a wide berth until next Monday."

"Why did he do that?"

"I don't know. He also asked me to sneak up to Mr. Moore's room tonight and borrow a few things that he uses on a routine basis, like his toothbrush."

"He did what? Why in the world would he want to do that?"

"I had the same question. I doubt that Mr. Tucker cares about the brand of toothpaste Mr. Moore uses, and I'm just as sure that he hasn't hired a voodoo priest. That leaves one possibility: he wants Mr. Moore's fingerprints. Does that make any sense to you?"

I shook my head and shook my head and shook my head some more. I had no idea how Clem could have time for such shenanigans. In light of what I had just heard, though, I had to conclude that he had learned to delegate them. Clem Tucker had become a shenanigans delegator. That didn't sound like much of an epitaph to me.

I replied, "Some folks in Ebb have wasted weeks of their lives speculating about the true identity of Vernon Moore. Whoever he is or isn't, he may be the only man who can help Matt right now, and we're running short on time. We need him focused on my grandson, not on playing name games with my fiancé."

"I agree, Ms. Porter. What should I do?"

I had to mull that over for a while. The word "shenanigans" kept bouncing back and forth inside my head like a Ping-Pong ball. I answered, "You have to take something; that's for sure. Why don't I give you a few things that Mr. Moore hasn't touched? My lodgers have left oodles of toothpaste, hairbrushes, combs, and all kinds of toiletry items behind over the years. I keep a collection in a big blue Tupperware tub in the broom closet upstairs. How would that be?"

"It sounds like the perfect plan."

"Maybe, but won't you get in trouble when Clem finds out that those things never belonged to Mr. Moore?"

"Don't worry about me, Ms. Porter. I can take care of myself. Right now, I'm worried about Mona. If Mr. Moore can help her son, I'll do whatever's necessary to make sure he's not distracted."

There wasn't anything else to say on the matter, so I read the press release. I don't know why. I already knew what it said, just like I knew I would have to ask Lulu to call another emergency meeting of the governing board of the Quilting Circle.

SOMETIME LATER that night, Hail Mary called Mr. Moore on his cell at the hospital. When he responded, she said, "Vernon, this is Mary Wade. Are you with Loretta right now?"

"I'm at her bedside as we speak. How can I help you?"

"I apologize for the intrusion, but we have a bit of a problem. I just got a call from Dottie Hrnicek. Matt Breck has gone on hunger strike."

"I don't blame him."

"You don't blame him? Did you expect this?"

"No, but it isn't a surprising outcome."

"He threw food all over his cell tonight. Again. Some of it stuck to the wall this time. How's that for a surprising outcome? According to the night guard, it's a hell of a lot of food. Nobody wants to clean it up."

"Has Dottie taken any disciplinary action?"

"Not so far. The night guard called Luther; he called Dot; she called me; I decided to call you before I did anything. I suppose you have a recommendation."

"I do. Do nothing. Leave the food on the wall."

"How about his breakfast?"

"I'd appreciate it if you could increase the portions."

"Increase the portions? Sometimes, Vernon, your acts of generosity are a certifiable pain in the ass. Who's going to clean up Matt's cell?"

"I'll ask him to clean it up himself in the morning."

"Matt? Do you believe that there's one chance in hell that he'll do it?"

"I do, yes. About one."

"Goddammit, Vernon. Are you going to get this boy to talk to you? If you don't, Dottie and I will end up with egg all over our faces."

"One more day. Just one. Please. That's all I ask."

Hail Mary never expected to hear the word "please" from Vernon Moore. She said it stopped her cold. After a second, she replied, "Well, Wilma Porter believes in you, and she's a good friend. Her fiancé is also in your corner, and he's the richest man between Omaha and God. Even Luther has swung around in your favor. And I'm on your side, too, damn it—but not to the point that I risk my job."

"I understand, and I appreciate your patience."

"You have until noon, Vernon. I'll feed that boy the same meal one more time, but that's it. No more banjo-playing after that either."

"Thank you, Mary. Should I stop by after my morning visit?"

"I'd love to see you, but I'll be busier than a mongoose in a box of snakes. Have you talked to Wilma tonight?"

"I haven't, no."

"I thought she might have called. There's big news from the River House. Clem Tucker sold Hayes County Bank to the National Bank of the Plains, the whole kit and caboodle. Wilma said you wouldn't be surprised."

"I don't suppose I am. Is the formal announcement tomorrow?"

"So I'm told. I've been summoned to an emergency meeting of the Circle board, at sunrise no less. Whenever they call me, it's because they want legal advice. My guess is that they want to use the courts to stop Clem in some way. Is that how you read it?"

"Yes."

"What would be your advice?"

"Wait for the third shoe, Mary."

"That's exactly what Wilma predicted you'd say, word for word. Do you know what the third shoe is?"

"I have a theory."

"A theory?"

"Yes."

"Will you tell me what it is?"

"It's just a theory, Mary, but you might check the recent press coverage of the National Bank of the Plains."

"I don't need to; their problems are well publicized. The CEO is under criminal investigation and his bank is being scrutinized by half the regulatory agencies in Washington and Lincoln. If Lord Clem had to sell HCB, I'd have preferred that he sell it to the Chinese."

"On the surface, the choice of NBP does seem a tad counterintuitive, doesn't it?"

Mary said, "Yes it does. If that's the second shoe, it's a damned lousy fit. Do you have any idea how long we'll have to wait for this third shoe of yours, assuming there is one?"

"No, but I don't expect it to be long."

Mary sighed. "You're a confounding man, Vernon Moore. You ask people you barely know to put their lives in your hands, or worse, in Clem Tucker's."

"That's not true, Mary. I only ask that you be smart. That's all."

"But in your mind, being smart means waiting an indeterminate length of time for a indeterminate third shoe that nobody has heard about."

"Yes."

"How can you be sure, Vernon? Are you really that confident?"

"Not at all."

Chapter 16

....

Third Shoe Theory

I MAY BE A BED and breakfast girl, but sunrise meetings aren't my favorite. I'd rather not venture from the comfort of my home until the sun has warmed up the air. That's what it's for. Here's a hint: Be careful of voting a veterinarian to be the head of your club or committee. They're smart, caring people, but they go to bed early so they can get up at dawn to tend to the animals. If you like to sleep in, you'll be better off voting in a restaurant hostess or someone like that.

My alarm clock went off at five a.m., which was barely four hours after I had set it. I dragged myself out of bed, dressed in a running outfit, waved a comb through my ratty hair, and went downstairs to my kitchen to turn on the coffee machine. Mr. Einstein was right: time is relative. It takes longer to make coffee when a body needs it most. The first little drops were just beginning to squeeze through the filter when Vernon Moore ambled in. For once, he didn't look like a Brooks Brothers ad, meaning his tie was loose at the collar, his clothes were wrinkled, and white stubble dotted his cheeks and chin. Being the quick study I am, I judged that he had just gotten back from the hospital.

"If I didn't know better, I'd bet that you were up all night, Mr. Moore. Is Loretta okay?"

He replied, "I wouldn't say she's okay, but her condition hasn't changed."

"That's a relief. So many things have been going on lately; I haven't had time to worry for her like I should. Would you like some tea? It'll take me just a second to put the kettle on."

"That would hit the spot," he replied. "You're up at an early hour yourself. I take it that you're on your way to a Circle meeting this morning."

"I am. How did you know that?"

"Mary Wade called me at the hospital. She mentioned it."

"Did she tell you why? Did she tell you about Clem's announcement last night?"

"She did, yes."

"Were you surprised?"

"Not completely, no. I was expecting a controversial middle game. From that perspective, Clem appears to have done a masterful job."

I put some tap water into the teapot and plugged it in before I answered. "He has at that, Mr. Moore. If there was a Nobel Prize for Controversy, he would be an ironclad winner. He might as well have sold the county to Cuba."

"Mary's sentiments were remarkably similar. How do you expect your board to react this morning?"

"I talked to everybody last night. They were dazed, like a boxer who'd been knocked off his feet by a sucker punch. But the women of the Circle are fighters, Mr. Moore. They'll jump up and be ready to get at it this morning."

"Forgive me for pushing the metaphor, but would it be possible for you to convince them to dodge and weave for a few days?"

"Dodge and weave?" I shook my head. "I know those women. I doubt they'll be in much of a dodging mood. They'll be looking to mix it up, and right this minute."

I poured myself a cup of coffee while I waited for Mr. Moore to reply. He remained silent, so I got a Cornhusker china cup out of the cabinet and an English tea bag from the caddy. The tea bag was in tinfoil, which I removed—slowly—and put into his cup. After that, I took a sip of my coffee, and then I said, "You don't think we should fight, do you, Mr. Moore?"

"Given how little we know for sure, I believe that any sort of retaliatory reaction would be premature."

"I respect your beliefs, Mr. Moore, I really do, but the Circle has always had to fight Clem Tucker. If we hadn't, downtown Ebb would be deader than the woolly mammoth and half the farms in Hayes County would've gone to seed."

"Is that true? What about the Big Buyback? Did you have to fight Clem on that?"

Nobody in Hayes County believes that Clem Tucker sold all that land back to those farmers for any other reason than to enrich himself, but Mr. Moore had a point. The teapot began to whistle so I turned around to unplug it. While I poured the water into his cup, he said to my back, "It seems you've already made up your mind, Wilma."

I turned and handed him his tea. "I'm trying not to, but the situation looks dire. For all practical purposes, Ebb has been sold to a hostile foreign power. That can't be good news."

"I wonder. I wonder if that's true." Mr. Moore sipped his tea and added, "I have to be back at the jail in five hours. I should get some sleep."

"Oh dear. I was so caught up in the news that I forgot to ask. How are you doing with Matt?"

"Terribly, Wilma, but I'm hopeful."

That was it. That was my entire status report.

ON SUCH A COLD, dark day in Ebb, I half-expected the rain to be running horizontal, which can happen out here. As it turns out, the air was thick with fog and perfectly still. The great oak tree by my parking lot looked like an old-time, black-and-white photograph. It was so quiet that I could hear myself breathe, as if the town had been covered with a misty, gray army blanket.

A red orange sun began to peek through the haze as I walked toward the downtown, but it had disappeared into the fog by the time I reached the Abattoir. Lulu, Lily, and Bebe were already in the kitchen making coffee and microwaving a store-bought coffee cake that somebody had brought along. I worry about the preservatives in frozen foods, but some of those pre-prepared pastries are pretty tasty. I could never serve them to my guests but I buy one for the family every once in a while—which invariably makes me feel guilty because I didn't make it from scratch. I am a sucker unto myself.

I said hello to the girls in the kitchen and went straight into the office to make copies of the press release. Dot and Hail Mary were whispering about the topic of the day when I walked into the boardroom a few minutes later.

As soon as I sat down, Dottie looked across the table and asked, "How's Loretta?"

"There's no difference," I replied.

"Was Mr. Moore there last night?"

"He was. He didn't come home until sunup."

"Did you tell him about the Big Sellout?"

"I did, but he already knew. Mary had already told him all about it."

"What was his opinion?"

"I don't believe he has one, Dot. As near as I can tell, he plans to stay on the sidelines."

I was wondering how to explain a man I didn't understand when Lulu, Lily, and Bebe came walking through the door with breakfast. Lulu took her seat at the head of the table, Lily and Bebe served, and I handed out copies of the press release.

Lulu looked it over with a scowl on her face, and then she called the meeting to order. Lily had barely gotten her notepad out and started to record the minutes when Lulu asked, "Did Clem give you this last night, Wilma? I notice it's dated today."

"He didn't," I answered. "It was given to me by a confidante."

"A confidante? Marie?"

"I can't say, Lulu. I don't see why the source is so important anyway."

"I was just curious, dear. Did Clem announce the deal at the River House last night?"

"He did. The dinner was to celebrate it."

"Who was there?"

"Dottie has the guest list," I answered. "Besides Clem and Calvin, five bankers from NBP attended the affair. One of them was the COO, a classy, older man named Fabrizio Santoni. I sat next to him at dinner."

The questions stopped for a second while everybody looked at

everybody else except me. I can be pretty slow sometimes. I didn't figure out that I was on the hot seat until then.

Lulu asked, "Did you learn anything last night that might help us
put a stop to this thing; anything at all?"

"I didn't. It was a party, not a business meeting. There wasn't
much to learn."

"Did you talk to Marie?"

"We shared a glass of sherry after dinner and she was just as surprised as I was. The poor girl is a nervous wreck. She's afraid she's going to lose her job."

"That's interesting," Dot commented. "Why should she think
that?"

Bebe answered, "Because Clem has severed nearly every tie he has
to Rutherford B. Hayes County. With the exception of Millet's, he's
free as a bird."

"Which is why he'll stay," I said. "Everybody knows that Millet's
is the linchpin of the downtown area. Clem invested in it two years
ago because he was afraid . . ." I stopped myself.

Lulu said, "Go on, Wilma."

"Clem couldn't let Millet's go belly up because the values of all his
other holdings would have plummeted. That's why he wanted to invest in the store; to protect his other assets."

Lulu scowled. "Exactly, dear. Two years ago, Clem learned that his
entire Hayes County portfolio, literally millions and millions of dollars worth of investments, depended upon the continuing operation
of a small-town department store. Who would want that?"

Bebe commented, "Isn't he smart? Clem Tucker was held hostage
by my store, so he sold off everything that depended on it, and he did
it from the outside in, starting with the farmland and finishing with

the bank. Now he's shifted his risk out of the county. The implication is obvious. Once Millet's is out of the way, he can do anything he wants."

Lulu slapped the table. "That's it. Millet's is the third shoe. He's going to sell it, too."

Dottie has a gift for summing things up. "That's right, and we'll be up shit creek without a shoe. What can we do?"

Hail Mary had hardly said a word until that point, which is not what you'd expect from a woman who makes a living with her mouth. In response to Dot's question, she answered, "There are no obvious grounds for legal recourse here. Clem owned the bank; he had the right to sell it. I'm not aware of any state or federal statute that would prevent NBP from buying it."

"Even though they're being investigated?"

"As long as it's an investigation, the law requires us to presume innocence. It's not clear that any prospective remedy would deter their ability to acquire a small, rural bank anyway."

"Isn't there a limit on the number of branches a bank can have in this state?"

"There is, Dot, but there's no way that NBP would make such a silly error. If they did, the Nebraska Department of Banking would pick it up in a minute."

"They have to approve the deal?"

"They have to review it, so does the Federal Reserve. We'll have an opportunity to object in both cases, but it won't be for months."

Lulu asked, "What are the odds that we'll succeed?"

"Not good. Both are likely to take the view that NBP's greater financial resources will reduce the risk of bank failure in Hayes County. I can promise you that NBP management will say exactly that."

"What about some sort of class action?" Lulu asked. "We need to act now."

"In order to pursue some sort of civil action, we would have to prove criminal conspiracy and quantifiable damage to a specified set of plaintiffs. From where I sit, that looks like a muddy, uphill road to nowhere we want to go."

"What if we all pulled our banking relationships and moved them over to Beatrice or up to Nebraska City?" Dot asked.

Hail Mary replied, "That's an interesting idea, but it would take time and it would eventually undermine the local operation. Even though it's a branch, NBP will run Hayes County Bank as a business unit. If it doesn't perform, they'll replace it with an ATM overnight."

Dottie summed up again. "Isn't that it? Isn't that exactly what we're all afraid of? An ATM instead of a bank, then no Millet's, then no Bold Cut. Ebb will be another ghost town."

There was a long silence, then Hail Mary said, "I'll have my staff take a look at the state and federal reviews of the acquisition. It's a long shot, but we may have a case because of the criminal investigations at NBP."

"How about you, Wilma?" Lulu asked. "What do you recommend we do?"

"I've been thinking about it for some time. My suggestion is that we talk to Clem directly. Everybody has theories, but nobody . . ."

"That's not true, dear. We know that Clem sold the bank to NBP. That's not a theory. The theory is that Millet's is the third shoe."

"We don't know that for sure, Lulu, and we don't know why Clem sold the bank. We may think we do, but we don't have any facts. We might try asking."

"We, or you?"

"Clem has never discussed business with me. You should see him, but without me."

"We're Circle founders, Wilma. We've been on the board since day one. We both have to be there. If you aren't, Clem will interpret your absence as support for his position."

"Oh, I doubt that. Clem has always known about my role in the Circle. That's why he won't talk business with me. It's an unwritten rule we have."

"What's your view, Dottie?"

"Wilma should be there. She's the backbone of the Circle."

"Lily?"

"I have the same problem with Buford that Wilma has with Clem. It's like living on a tightrope. In my opinion, we should respect Wilma's position."

"Bebe?"

"For an age, life in Ebb has been a balancing act. Clem Tucker has been on one side and we've been on the other. This is a serious issue, maybe the biggest we've ever faced. I hate to say it, but I believe that Wilma has to pick one side or the other."

"How about you, Mary? What's your position?"

"I'm just an advisor, Lulu. I don't have a vote."

"Then advise us, dear. What do you suggest?"

"I suggest you look at the dilemma from another direction. What if Wilma simply refuses to choose? Are you going to haul her out of the Abattoir on a hook? She's a founder. You run the risk of splitting the Circle right down the middle when it most needs to be united."

No chairperson worth her salt likes to hear the divisiveness card played, and Lulu is worth her weight in salt. "You're absolutely right, Mary. You go ahead and research our legal options, including some form of litigation. We live in the United States of America. When the poor people get hurt by the rich people, it's our civil responsibility to litigate.

"We need to confront Clem Tucker, too. I'll handle that. The Circle controls a hefty portion of the bank's business. We ought to be able to force a meeting. Wilma, dear, your attendance will be optional. You decide whether to support us or not. Either way, I'd appreciate it if you could ask Clara where she stands on the sale of the bank."

"Clara approved the sale in advance," I stated.

"She did?"

"She's the second-largest shareholder in the trust. She had to agree."

"You talked to her?"

"No. Clem told me."

"I thought you and Clem didn't discuss business, dear."

"I asked Clem if Clara knew about the sale of the bank last night, Lulu. That was the answer I got." I would've pushed back more when I was younger, but I've since learned that somebody has to back off. Otherwise, the argument escalates until both parties reach mutually assured hard feelings. Hard feelings are the scars of discord. They're darn difficult to remove.

Lulu smiled and said, "There's one more thing: we need to call a general meeting of the Circle. They'll want to know what we plan to do."

"I agree," Dot seconded. "The rank and file will be just as worried as we are, if not more so. When people are worried, they do stupid things. As it is, I suspect I'll have to run a double shift and maybe even close the Corn Palace early tonight. There'll be plenty of drinking, and it won't be happy drinking."

"Is it your opinion that we should meet tomorrow morning, Dottie?"

"Yes."

Mary thought otherwise, bless her heart. "Do you really need to call a general session that quickly? That will give you one day to get in front of Clem. Even if you can, one day isn't nearly enough for my staff to sift through state and federal banking regulations, plus the criminal investigation at NBP. I won't have a thing to report tomorrow."

Bebe inquired, "How about the day after?"

Lulu began to protest but Lily chimed in, "Mary's right. We run the risk of having nothing but bullshit to feed the membership. They expect more from us."

I nodded my assent. I wanted more time because I wanted more time, plain and simple.

Lulu was in a box. "Okay. Friday it is, starting at ten a.m. I'll circulate an agenda and put in the call to Clem. I don't know what his availability will be like; you girls keep your cell phones handy. Mary, you'll need to have some sort of status report ready by Friday morning. I assume that'll be enough time."

"It'll have to be, won't it?"

"Now, what about the press release?" Lulu asked. "It's marked for publication at ten a.m. That's three hours from now."

"What do you mean?" I asked.

"We have an opportunity to seize the initiative. I propose that we go ahead and email it to the membership. I'll write a cover note telling everybody about Friday's meeting so they won't panic, and Lily can scan in the press release and attach it. We can scoop Clem by two hours if we get a move on."

"Is that fair?" I asked. "It was given to me in confidence."

"I don't see how an hour or two will make a pinch of difference to your fiancé," Lulu answered, "but it will show the membership of the Quilting Circle that we're on top of the situation. I vote we do it. Does anybody disagree?"

Nobody did, except me.

Lulu could be officious and headstrong but those things made her a good governor—most of the time. On that particular day, though, she was up my nose. The town was on the verge, Loretta was on the verge, Matt was on the verge, and Lulu had me worried that I would have to choose between Clem and the Circle. So did Calvin Millet and Bebe Palouse.

For the first time in my life, I had empathy for taffy.

Chapter 17

The Man in the Street

THE POTBELLIED PENGUINS came down for breakfast shortly after I got back to the Come Again. They were hung over and in a hurry; all they asked for was coffee and muffins. John Smith pulled up a few minutes later and they ran out to the limo, muffins in one hand, briefcases in the other. I had just a second to myself before Mona came down the back stairs into my kitchen, Laverne on her hip. She already had enough on her plate, but I felt like I had to tell her the news about the bank.

I gave Mona my copy of the press release, which she read while I got Laverne's breakfast ready. Her immediate reaction was less than unbridled enthusiasm. Even though she'd lived in Omaha with her ex for more than a dozen years, Mona had a natural, homegrown distrust for anonymous, big-city banks with no understanding of real life, rural or otherwise. From her comments, I could tell that Clem Tucker wasn't her favorite person on that particular day either. It would be fairer to say that he had never been her favorite person, but his stock dropped like a stone when I told her the news.

After Mona got Mark off to school, she came stomping back into the kitchen. "Does Vernon Moore know about the bank, Mama?"

"He does. We talked about it this morning, before I went to the Abattoir."

"What's he going to do about it?"

"I don't know that he's going to do anything, but I wouldn't wake him if I was you. He didn't get to bed until dawn."

Mona bit her lower lip, then said, "Let's go to the bank, Mama."

"What about Laverne?"

"I'll call Virgie. Let's go to the bank." Virginia Allen is a retired grade-school teacher who lives just down the street. My other daughter, Winona, had her in fourth grade. Poor Virgie misses her children so nowadays. She would rather baby-sit than eat bonbons.

"But why?" I asked, still surprised at the idea.

"Unlike you, Mama, most women aren't engaged to the scurrilous, dark-hearted owner of the local bank. My guess is that a lot of HCB's customers will be gathering there this morning to ask questions about their future prospects. I'm a customer and I have a few questions myself."

I wasn't in the mood, but I agreed because I knew Mona would go without me if I didn't. The fog hadn't burned off, so we bundled up, dropped Laverne off at Virgie's, and walked downtown to the bank. Along the way, half a dozen women stopped to offer me their commiserations or to ask me what the heck was going on, or both. I'm sure I wasn't at my best. I didn't know why I needed commiserations any more than the next person, and I had no idea what to tell them about the Big Sellout.

I've been in the information transfer business on an avocational basis for twenty years and I am still amazed at how fast bad news can travel. I wonder if Mr. Einstein ever measured its speed. He might have discovered that bad news is the only substance known to man that moves faster than the speed of light. In my experience, good news travels by barge.

I'm not good at estimating numbers, but a crowd of maybe fifty folks had gathered outside the main entrance of the bank by the time we arrived. That was large enough to restrict traffic to a single lane on Main, although that's not much of a problem in Ebb. We don't have a rush hour, even though we'd like one. It would be a growth indicator.

Mona and I stood across the street from the entrance to the bank so I wouldn't have to deal with any more commiseraters. The fog wasn't heavy; I could see that about half the crowd already had their Starbucks and more than a few were hung over, which I interpreted as good news. It is my belief that a dull-witted, latte-wielding throng is unlikely to cause a serious disturbance. A few of Dot's deputies were on hand anyway. Given the gravity of the situation, I suppose it was the prudent thing to do.

Just before nine a.m., none other than Mr. Fabrizio Santoni came out to the sidewalk to speak to the crowd, Buford Pickett in tow. A uniformed guard locked the door from the inside afterward, which looked a tad ominous to me. I suspect the crowd felt the same way, but they remained ruly while Buford introduced himself, which was a superfluous gesture if I ever saw one. Anybody who has borrowed a dime in Ebb since the Carter administration already knows who he is, and that's nearly everybody.

When he was done talking about himself, Buford gave a glowing introduction to Mr. Santoni, who didn't look a bit like a big-time banker. Instead, he was wearing gray slacks, a cabled, off-white sweater, and a black bomber jacket. He stepped forward, smiled warmly, and said, "I want to thank you all for coming. This is a great day for Hayes County and the National Bank of the Plains. I see that many of you already have a copy of the press release. Good. I'm glad that you got the news first and that you could spend some time with us this morning.

"Mr. Pickett and I are here to tell you that the bank will be closed for one extra hour today so that we can explain the benefits of the acquisition to our employees. I hope you will allow me to do the same for you."

An anonymous male voice from the crowd yelled out, "Forget the speech, bucky; we've read the release. When are you gonna close the bank?"

"Do you mean close the bank after normal business hours or shut it down permanently?"

"Shut it down, of course. Isn't that what always happens?"

Mr. Santoni smiled again. "It is not always what happens, but the contingency of closure is always considered before the acquisition. In this case, we plan to close down HCB when hell freezes over. Until then, we expect to operate it as a subsidiary of the National Bank of the Plains. If you come by later in the day, you may be surprised to see how many new services we will be able to offer the citizens of Hayes County in the coming months."

A man near the front of the crowd asked, "Our problems ain't nothing like city problems, Mr. Santorini. We don't need any complicated city services; we need simple country services. Will HCB be allowed to manage its business separate from NBP, or not?"

Buford began to answer but Fabrizio touched his arm and said, "Ah, the autonomous operations question. Someone always asks it and the buyer usually answers in the affirmative, but it is never true. Subsidiaries are never allowed to operate autonomously, but HCB is an important addition to the Bank of the Plains. It is positioned in a market we were unable to reach previously, but which we believe to have great potential. Our intention is to provide extra cash to HCB so it can increase its investment in Hayes County and the surrounding area."

I whispered to Mona, "That's Fabrizio Santoni. I met him at the River House last night."

"He's slick, Mama."

"Is that what you believe? I think he's a nice man."

"Do you believe he's telling the truth?"

"I do, honey. Don't you?"

Mona didn't answer me outright. Instead, she gave me an "are you kidding me?" kind of look. I recognized it because I taught that particular look to her when she was a little girl. Women hand down looks from generation to generation, like Hummel figurines. The best ones are pretty valuable.

While we were exchanging looks, Mr. Santoni was fielding a question from another man in the crowd. "How many bank employees are you going to lay off?"

"Ah, yes. That is a common result of acquisition, but it is not our intention in this case. We have carefully reviewed the employment level at HCB and believe it to be appropriate for the current business load. Naturally, that may change with the passing of time. If business goes up, which is our expectation, we will hire more. However, if business goes down, the consequences will be unfortunate but necessary."

A large man in overalls pointed toward the front door of the bank and replied, "Is Clem Tucker in there? I want to see him."

Fabrizio answered, "Do you have important business with Mr. Tucker, sir?"

"Yeah. I want to ask him why he sold my bank to a bunch of city slickers who don't know shit from shinola about farmin' or ranchin'."

"Mr. Tucker is a busy, busy man today. Please allow me to answer your question on his behalf. Would that be acceptable?"

The farmer mumbled something that sounded like, "I suppose so."

Fabrizio replied, "Even with the backing of a well-to-do and committed man like Clement Tucker, Hayes County Bank was small. It could not take advantage of monetary economies of scale in much the same way that a small factory cannot take advantage of production economies of scale. By selling HCB to the National Bank of the Plains, Mr. Tucker preserved the agricultural expertise of the bank, but he also acquired for it the economies of scale that are normally available only to a money center institution. As a result, your banking services will be more numerous and less costly in the long run."

"That sounds like a lot of bullshit to me."

Mr. Santoni nodded. "I know. Economics always sounds like bullshit, but the reality is that economics will make or break any bank, including NBP. What Mr. Tucker did was very smart and it will be very good for you, too."

Fabrizio stepped back and whispered something to Buford, who nodded and headed up the street at a brisk pace. Then he said, "I'm sorry, but we are out of time. The bank will reopen at ten a.m. this morning and keep normal business hours thereafter. For the rest of the day, the National Bank of the Plains will pay for all the coffee at the Starbucks down the street. Please enjoy yourselves and come back to visit us at ten."

With that, the guard opened the front door and Fabrizio disappeared inside the bank.

In an economically challenged town like Ebb, the loose use of the word "free" can cause a stampede, but not on the day the local bank is sold. The crowd began to meander over to Starbucks in small clusters. Mona had to go back to work at the Bold Cut and I didn't want to endure two more hours of commiserations while I waited for a free mocha, so I headed back to Virgie's house to retrieve Laverne. I got a call on my cell when I was about halfway there.

It was Clem. He said, "Thanks for taking such good care of my guests last night. Fabrizio was certainly taken with you." Before I could say "aw shucks" he continued, "My assistant said she saw you and Mona standing across the street just a minute or two ago. You should have come in to say hello."

"The armed guard in the foyer didn't look like he wanted to make new friends. Besides, we were interested in what Mr. Santoni had to say."

"How did he do?"

"He sent the angry mob to Starbucks for free lattes."

"I hear that he won them over. Was that your impression?"

"I'd say that he beat them to death with his wit. I'd say they weren't so much sold as subjugated."

"I'll tell him you said so. On another subject, Lulu Tiller called and requested that I meet with the Circle board today. Did you know that?"

"I did. It was my suggestion."

"Why?"

"They asked me why you sold the bank. I said they should get the answer straight from the horse's mouth."

Clem replied, "I have never been particularly fond of that phrase, Wilma."

Upon reflection, I had to admit that I wasn't either. All I'd ever gotten from a horse's mouth was stinky, steamy air. Who would want that?

While I was trying to think of something suitable to say, Clem asked, "What's your recommendation? Should I agree to the meeting?"

"I don't see how it could do any harm, honeypot. If you want to charm them, invite Mr. Santoni along. Mention that he's a widower. Lulu will eat him up."

"Fabi and I are heading up to Omaha this afternoon. I won't get back 'til Friday, which means I won't be able to sit down with you and your friends 'til next week."

"Well, I hope you can figure something out before then. The Circle believes you sold them out. They're in a fighting mood."

"You keep using the pronoun 'they,' Wilma. Don't you mean 'we'?"

I've never been a stickler for pronouns. Maybe that's a flaw. "I won't be at your meeting with Lulu and the Circle board, if that's your implication. It's a conflict of interest."

I guess Clem had already thought that over. Without a second of hesitation, he said, "I agree. Speaking of which, do you have any idea how the Circle got hold of my press release? A dozen of the bank's employees came to work with copies in their hands. My ability to manage the news to my own people was ruined, and I looked like a country bumpkin to Fabi."

I was walking at a good pace but that question brought me to full halt. "It was my fault, honeypot. I picked one up at the River House last night."

"Nice try, Wilma, but there weren't any to pick up. The few hard copies we had were in a locked briefcase. Who gave it to you?"

"I don't know. It was in my purse when I left and I didn't discover it until I got home."

"So you have no idea how you got it."

"Not a clue."

"You're sure?"

"I am."

The phone went quiet when I said that. Clem had hung up on me. A younger woman might have been concerned, but I've been hung up on so many times that I didn't give it a second thought. Well, maybe I gave it a second thought, but not a third.

Chapter 18
....

Circular Foods

THE SECOND MR. MOORE appeared in the county jail that morning, Deputy Samoa jumped up from the watch desk and said, "Did you hear? Clem Tucker sold the bank."

Mr. Moore answered, "Good morning, Deputy. The news is all over town."

"What's your take on it? Everybody down here is as nervous as a gay drake at a Southern Baptist duck shoot."

With characteristic clarity, my lodger replied, "Wait for the third shoe."

"Wait for the third shoe? Is that what you said?"

"The first shoe was the Big Buyback. My belief is that the Big Sellout is the second shoe. There should be a third—a Big Something Else."

"Do you know what it is?"

"No, but I doubt that we'll have to wait long. How's Matt?"

Luther paused for a second or two before he answered. "He's got a new career, Mr. Moore. He's become a food decorator. Last night, he covered the back wall of his cell with waffles, Oreos, and various carbohydrates."

"That's interesting. How did he react to his breakfast this morning?"

"He stuck more circular foods to the wall."

"Did he eat anything?"

"No. He's gone on a hunger strike. I wanted to call you myself, but the sheriff said I had to follow the chain of command."

"Your chain of command works. The county prosecutor called me last night with the news."

"That's good, Mr. Moore, because we have a problem. If Matt doesn't eat lunch, I'm going to have to call Doc Wiley, and that will be the end of Matt's famous meal."

"You know that, and I know it. The important thing is that Matt doesn't. Let's make sure that it stays that way this morning. Shall we go see him?"

Luther grinned. "I'm sure he's looking forward to seeing you, Mr. Moore. You're his favorite visitor." He added, "Don't forget your banjo."

Luther handed the instrument to Mr. Moore and they set off down the hall. Along the way, Luther stopped in the visitor's room to pick up the folding chair that had been removed from Matt's cell when he was put on suicide watch. Once upon a time, some creative but depressed criminal must've beaten himself to death with a cheap metal chair.

The smell of Dr Pepper, maple syrup, bacon, and onion rings reached the men as they rounded the corridor corner. Matt was curled up on the lower bunk in his fetal, wall-facing position. French fries and bacon strips were strewn haphazardly around the floor and the back wall was speckled with waffles, onion rings, and Oreos that had been sliced in half. One of the deputies told me later that Matt had used the syrup to glue the circular foods to his wall.

Luther unlocked the door, put the chair down, and assumed his position outside the cell. Mr. Moore went inside, carefully avoiding the food on the floor, and said, "Good morning, Matt. I see you've become an artist of the trompe l'oeil, but everything is so round. Is there something symbolic in it?"

My grandson rolled over and sat up, which required him to pull at his beltless pants. He was in his socks—his shoes were at the side of the bunk with the shoelaces removed—and his cheeks and eyes were red, as if he'd been crying. "Maybe it's a hint that I'm sick and tired of the same thing every meal," he said. "What are you going to do to me this morning?"

Mr. Moore sat down and opened the banjo case. "What would you like me to do?" he replied. "Would you like some more round, flat foods with little or no nutritional value? How about pancakes? They'd fit your décor perfectly."

"All I want is for you to get out of my cell. Get out and never come back."

"I can't quit, Matt; not until this weekend. What about English muffins?"

Matt lay down and rolled over to face the wall again. "Get out!" he demanded.

Mr. Moore set up the stand and placed one of the music books on it. "Are you sure that's what you want me to do? Let's consider the consequences. If I go now, you'll get the same meal for lunch, except the portions will be larger. Judging from the condition of your cell, I'm not sure that's what you want."

"Stick it up your ass."

"The second thing you might want to consider is who I might bring along this afternoon."

Matt replied to the wall, "Like I give a shit." Then he paused and added, "Who?"

"There are so many possibilities. At the moment, though, I'd have to put your brother Mark on top of the visitor's list. I'm sure he'd like to see you, your food art, and your beltless, shoeless outfit. He might like my banjo playing. What do you think?"

Clem once told me that there is one moment in every contest when victory is decided. That was it.

Matt didn't answer immediately, but eventually he rolled over and sat up. According to Luther, he was fighting back the tears. "You can't bring my brother here," he said. "Not Mark."

Mr. Moore took the banjo out of its case and laid it across his knees, then said, "Yes I can, Matt. I have free rein. Of course, there is an alternative."

Matt sniffled and used a sleeve to wipe his eyes. "What? That stupid question?"

"Yes. You have to answer it."

"I don't even remember what it was."

"I'll remind you. If you don't want your brother to see you like this, though, you're going to have to do a few more things."

"Like what?"

"For openers, you'll have to clean up your cell. I'll arrange with Deputy Samoa to have the proper cleaning materials delivered to you."

"What else?"

"You're going to have to enter into an honest dialogue with me. You're going to have to talk freely about you and about life in general."

"I thought you said I had to answer one question."

"That question was the beginning of a dialogue."

After some time, Matt asked, "All I have to do is talk? Is that it?"

"Except for cleaning up the mess in here, that's the sum total of your obligation."

"For how long?"

"Half an hour or so, maybe less, once or twice a day 'til Saturday. That's not much time. You have some free time, don't you?"

Matt thought it over. "What about food? I can't take any more of that shit. It's making me gag."

"I'd be thrilled to put you back on the standard jail regimen, but we'll have to discuss it first. Having the same meal three times a day should have taught you an important lesson. I'll have to make sure you learned it."

Matt shook his head. "What lesson: that the same food every day makes me want to puke? Is that a lesson?"

"It is, but there's more to it. You'll pick it up quickly if we talk about it."

"What about this suicide shit?"

"I'll have the suicide watch removed this afternoon, but only if we're making progress."

"And the banjo?"

"I won't play as long as we're making headway. How's that?"

"Okay. Give me a hamburger and a glass of milk and I'll talk."

Mr. Moore's brow furrowed. "A hamburger? More circular food?"

"I don't care. All I want is a hamburger and a glass of milk."

"Why?"

"Because I'm sick to death of waffles and fries. I can't even look at them."

"Why, Matt? Why are you sick to death of waffles and fries?"

"Because you forced me to eat them every freakin' meal. Why else?"

"You said it was your favorite. You ordered it yourself. It's only the third day and you can't stand it. Why?"

"I . . . I don't understand. I don't get it. Do we have to play these stupid games? I just want something else to eat."

"It's not a game, Matt. Use your brain. If you had all the hamburgers you could eat for the next forty days and forty nights, would you be sick of waffles?"

"Waffles? No. I'd be sick of burgers."

"Good answer. What's the lesson?"

There was a long silence. Eventually, Matt replied, "It's easy. If you eat the same thing three times a day every day, you get sick of it."

"What if you had to watch the same movie three times every day for a month? How would you like that?"

"I'd get sick of it, too."

"If you had to listen to the same song forty times a day, even if it was your favorite, would you get tired of it?"

"I get it, Mr. Moore. That would suck."

"Good. You seem to have a decent grasp of the basics; let's try the next plateau. Why haven't you been sick to death and bored to tears for your entire life?"

Matt looked at Luther, who shrugged his shoulders. "I don't understand," he said. "Why?"

"Isn't it because your life has been an endless bounty of diversity? Isn't it because you've always had choices? Isn't it because things constantly change? Isn't it because you often don't know what to expect? Based on what you've learned in the last two days, would you rather have the same meal every time or a different meal every time, even if you didn't know what it was going to be?"

Matt rubbed his forehead.

Mr. Moore said, "It's a simple question, Matt. Would you like everything to be the same all the time, or would you prefer a steady diet of choice, change, and surprise? It's a no-brainer, but I want to hear you answer it."

"Okay. I'd take the different stuff."

"Why?"

"Because I'd be bored out of my mind otherwise."

"That's right. So answer this question: Is diversity important?"

"Uh, yeah. Obviously."

"Is it barely important, important, or extremely important?"

"It's really important, okay. I get it."

"Fine. If it's so important, then why did you try to get rid of the only black woman in Ebb six weeks ago?"

Matt sat back and pulled his knees up in front of his face. "I don't want to talk about that, Mr. Moore. You said I wouldn't have to."

"Fair enough, but tell me one thing. Would you do it again if you had the chance?"

Matt sniffled and said, "It was a bad thing to do. I knew that before you ever came down here to torture me."

"Why was it bad, Matt? Why was it a bad thing to do?"

There was no answer.

Mr. Moore gripped the banjo by the neck and stood up, then he yelled, "Which is it, Matt? Is diversity a fabulous gift that you should value and nurture, or is it a needless burden that you can exterminate at whim? It's a simple question! Answer it!"

Matt pushed himself against the wall. "I get it. I'm sorry! I'm really sorry! I understand why it was wrong."

Mr. Moore sat down and replied calmly, "I'm glad to hear it. We've made some progress today."

Matt peered over the top of his knees and asked weakly, "Does that mean I can have something else for lunch?"

"Deputy Samoa will bring you the things you need to scrub out your cell. After it's been cleaned to his satisfaction, he can put you back on the normal jail menu. If you work quickly, you could have a new, surprising meal for lunch."

"Can I have my belt and my shoelaces back?"

"I'm not that easy. You can have them back if we have a good talk this afternoon."

"What about Mark? Are you going to bring him here?"

"Not as long as we're making progress. If you start to slide backward, he'll be here in a heartbeat."

"What about my iPod?"

"Don't push me, Matt. For now, let's focus on cell cleanliness, food variety, and open dialogue. I'll be back this afternoon. Between now and then, I'd like you to think about the answer to an important question."

"Jeez. Another one? What?"

"It's not another one; it's the same question I asked you our first day. After you said that it was better to be smart than stupid, I asked you how you were doing so far. I'd like you to answer that question this afternoon."

Matt looked down and then replied, "I know the answer, Mr. Moore. I don't have to wait until this afternoon."

"Fair enough. What is it?"

"I'm doing shitty, okay? Anybody can see that."

"Do you mean you haven't been very smart?"

"Yeah. That's what I mean."

"How do you know?"

"Isn't it obvious? I'm seventeen years old and I'm going to be in jail for the rest of my freakin' life! I have to eat the same meal three times a day. I can't even wear a belt. That's how stupid I am."

"You're right. In the past, you have been stupid, appallingly stupid. Should you continue to be stupid, or should you be smart from now on?"

"I don't see why it makes any difference. I'm going to jail and I'll be there 'til I croak. Even if I get paroled, I'll be older than you when I get out. My life will be over."

"So you believe you should be stupid while you're in jail? Tell me, Matt, how has stupid been working lately, as in the last two days?"

Matt shrugged his shoulders and answered, "Okay, okay! I get it."

"Are you sure? You don't look like you get it."

"Jesus! I said I get it, Mr. Moore!"

"Is it better to be smart or stupid, Matt? Answer the question."

Matt said softly, "It's better to be smart."

"Good answer. When should you start being stupid again?"

Matt thought for a second, then said, "Never. Never, okay?"

"Excellent. You can start by cleaning up your cell. Do you think you can do that?"

"Yeah. I know how to clean."

"Good. It's an underrated skill. While you're at it, I'd like you to think about a different question for this afternoon, a new question."

"Another question? How many of these stupid questions are there?"

"Do you want a new lunch or not?"

With resignation, Matt asked, "What is it?"

"Since you're going to be smart from now on, let's test your grasp of the English language. The new question is: What's the difference between fact and belief?"

"Fact and belief?" Matt asked.

"They're short, everyday words, Matt. Think about the difference." Mr. Moore stood again. "What's on the luncheon menu today, Deputy Samoa?"

"The cook's special lamb stew, biscuits, and fruit cocktail in Jell-O."

"Biscuits: another circular food, I believe. Would the dessert be the Jell-O?"

"It would, Mr. Moore, and that's a fact."

Mr. Moore packed his instrument away and the two men walked back down the corridor. As they approached the watch desk, Luther said, "You got him to talk today. That was major. Did it go the way you wanted?"

"More or less."

"Well, it looked good to me, and I'm an expert on jailer-jailee relations."

Mr. Moore handed the banjo case to Luther. "I wouldn't call it a victory yet, Deputy. We've got just three, action-packed days left."

Deputy Giant stopped in his tracks. "Action-packed?"

ON HIS WAY OUT of the county courthouse, Mr. Moore took out his cell phone and called Doc Wiley. Nurse Nelson answered, "Vernon, is that you? Hank told me you were in town. Why haven't you stopped in for a game of cribbage?"

"It's a pleasure to hear your voice, Louise. I would've been by but Wilma's got me running all over town. I called for Hank. Is he in?"

"He's making house calls. Would you like me to take a message?"

"Yes, please. I'd like to ask a favor. Would you ask Doc Wiley to meet me at the hospital at ten tonight."

"Can I tell him why? You're not worried about Loretta, are you?"

"Of course I am, but that's not the reason. I have a few questions to ask about Loretta's care for the long term. I know it's an imposition, but I'd appreciate it if he could meet me there."

"Oh, you're no imposition, Vernon. He's got an open slot here at the clinic later today. Could you drop by then? We could squeeze in a game of cribbage."

"I'd love to, but my schedule is full for the afternoon."

"Is it Matt Breck, or are you working on the Big Sellout?"

"A little of both. It seems to be a busy day."

"How about tomorrow then?"

"I'm afraid that tomorrow will be just as hectic. I'd really appreciate it if Doc Wiley could meet me at the hospital this evening."

"Okay, Vernon. I'll ask, but I can't promise he'll say yes."

"Thanks, Louise. Will you call me back when you get an answer?"

"I will, but on one condition."

"Of course."

"You stop by before you go."

"Before I go?"

"Everybody knows you're going to leave again, Vernon. The only question is when."

Chapter 19
....

The Left Behind

EVEN THOUGH HAYES COUNTY BANK had been acquired by a financial institution with more money than the gross domestic product of seventy-four sovereign nations, some of the staff felt like they'd been demoted. Buford Pickett was a case-in-point. On Tuesday, he was HCB's Senior Vice President of Loan Services and Clem's left-hand man. On Wednesday, he was a vice president who reported to a senior vice president, who reported to an executive vice president, who reported to a business unit president, et cetera—but he was also the highest-ranking NBP manager in Hayes County.

After the employee meetings were over, Buford took the elevator up to the fourth floor to discuss the matter with his former boss. Nobody liked to go to Clem's office, even when he wasn't there. It wasn't a whole lot bigger than Matt's cell, and it wasn't much more comfortable either. Clem's desk was bought secondhand from the high school—I kid you not—and he sat in a cheap, black-vinyl chair he must've ordered on the Internet from thehouseofuglychairs.com. A battered metal filing cabinet, a red wool couch that had seen better days, and a squarish, chrome-and-glass coffee table were squeezed into the remaining space, which wasn't much.

I asked Clem one time why he couldn't get himself a bigger office and some decent, hardwood furniture. He pointed out to the hallway and mumbled, "Multiplier effect. Every dollar I spend in here costs me ten out there."

That, in a nutshell, is my Fiancé in Perpetuity. Everything he does has some kind of multiplier effect on everybody else in Hayes County.

Buford waited at the door until Clem waved him in. Two glasses and a crystal pitcher with ice water were already sitting on the coffee table. The pattern looked vaguely familiar, but Buford elected to sit down and keep the observation to himself.

Clem rocked back in his chair and said, "Well? What do you think?"

"I don't know, Mr. Tucker. I had no idea this was coming."

"C'mon. You can talk to me. Are you happy? Are you sad? What?"

"Honestly, I haven't thought it through."

"Fabi took a long, hard look at your loan portfolio, Buford. It was the key to the acquisition. He said it's the finest ex-urban portfolio he's ever seen."

"That's nice."

"You're in charge of the sub now; the head banking honcho in Hayes County; the big cheese. Won't that be nice, too?"

"Yessir. I guess it will."

Clem sat forward quickly. "Uh oh. I know that tone. Are you gonna tell me what's eating you or not?"

Reluctantly, Buford answered, "I don't know what to expect, Mr. Tucker. The only thing I know for sure is things won't be the same."

"That's right. Things won't be the same. We all have new challenges. Didn't anybody ever tell you that uncertainty is the spice of life?"

"Uh, no."

"I'm surprised; I hear it all the time from Wilma. Anyway, the bottom line is that our lives will be spicier. That's good, isn't it?"

"I don't know, sir."

Clem opined, "Well, I do. I was stuck in a rut. I spent half my days fighting that damn Quilting Circle and the other half trying to squeeze a few more basis points out of the family trust for a bunch of small-minded, shortsighted, second-guessing relatives. Except for courting Wilma and shooting at the odd endangered species, I wasn't having any fun at all, so I decided to shuffle the deck. Now we've all got a brand new hand to play."

"Maybe, but I liked the old hand, sir."

"Why? You're running the show now, and Fabi will be keeping a friendly eye on you all down here. If you have any trouble with those MBA geniuses up in Omaha, give him a call."

"I will, Mr. Tucker. He seems like a nice man. If I may ask, what are you going to do?"

"To tell the truth, I'm not entirely sure. Things are in motion; things I can influence but I can't control. They'll determine what I end up doing, and where."

"Where?"

"Don't look so surprised. I'm out of the banking business as of today. My trust management responsibilities have been delegated to Calvin Millet. I can go anywhere I want."

"Don't you still own a big chunk of Millet's Department Store?"

"I do, but I'm a minority owner, which is a polite way of saying that I can't say squat about the paper clips they buy. Millet's is Calvin's store to own and Bebe's to run, which puts me out of work. Does that make me retired or unemployed?"

"I don't know, Mr. Tucker."

"Me either, and I have another little piece of news that's just for you."

Buford perked up for the first time in a long morning. "You do? What?"

"Even as we speak, John Smith is driving up to state patrol head-quarters in Lincoln with some repatriated items from Vernon Moore's shaving kit."

"He's doing what?"

"The colonel's got two of his best fingerprint people standing by. They'll work through the night if they have to. By this time tomorrow, we may know who Vernon Moore really is."

Buford became contemplative. Clem said, "Is something bothering you?"

"I don't know. I guess so."

"You guess so? What?"

"I don't know about fingerprinting Mr. Moore. I kind of like the theory we have now."

"You don't mean that cock-and-bull, World War II story about the *Lady Be Good*? If Vernon was the sole survivor of that crash, which was in the middle of the goddamn Sahara Desert, he'd be ninety years old. You can't believe that."

"Yes I can, sir, and I want to. It gives Mr. Moore an aura of mystery; Ebb, too. It makes us all special. You said it yourself: uncertainty is the spice of life."

Clem rocked back in his chair. "Do you want me to call John back? I still can, you know."

"No, Mr. Tucker. If my theory is right, Mr. Moore's fingerprints won't show up anywhere. We'll still have the mystery, but it'll be better."

"You're a good man, Buford. Let's roll the dice."

WHEN I'M UNDER PRESSURE, I like to bake. It's a fine form of therapy, especially for the proprietress of a bed and breakfast. On that particular Wednesday, I decided to start with my cinnamon rolls, which are surpassed in local renown only by my biscuits. After I put Laverne down for her morning nap, I went into my kitchen and got out the flour, the butter, the sugar, the cinnamon, and the pecans, and then I went to work. It used to be that the hard part of making cinnamon rolls was kneading the dough, but I have a Japanese machine that does it for me now. I had no idea they liked cinnamon rolls, but there you have it. There's no difference in the taste and it saves my hands from a lot of wear and tear.

I was finishing up the layering of the pecans in the pan, which has to be just so, when Vernon Moore strolled into my kitchen looking like the cock of the walk.

"Good morning," I said. "Or is it good afternoon? I never know what to say at this time of the day."

He replied, "Have you eaten lunch yet?"

"No."

"According to the British Army, it's morning until you've eaten lunch. What's that smell? Is it cinnamon? Are you making cinnamon rolls?"

"I am, but they won't be ready for another hour. Sit yourself down and I'll make you a sandwich."

"It won't be too much trouble?"

"You'll earn it," I said. "I could use a little help. But before I tell you my sad tale of woe, how did things go at the jail this morning?"

Mr. Moore sat down in his usual spot. I remained standing; I had work to do.

He said, "Matt and I had a civil conversation for the first time. I even saw a trace of introspection. If I was an optimist, I'd be optimistic."

"Matt talked to you? Of his own free will?"

"More or less, yes."

"That's wonderful! Do you see him again this afternoon?"

"I do."

"If things go well, will you still be an optimist tonight?"

"Maybe, Wilma, but it's not Nature's way. In the normal course of events, more things go wrong than right."

I turned back to my pan and replied, "Isn't that a fact?"

As a general practice, I don't eat lunch. If I did, I'd be bigger than Rufus Bowe's barn. I fixed Mr. Moore a glass of iced tea and a roast beef sandwich with some potato chips on the side. While he ate, we talked about Matt, Mark, Mona, Loretta, and the Big Sellout, especially the latter. He must've said "third shoe" nine times; I don't remember precisely. I'd have a better recollection if we had been discussing the topic I really wanted to discuss, which was my own predicament, but personal problems are not my best category as a rule. I'm usually better at talking about other folks' predicaments than my own.

Finally, I said to Mr. Moore, "You keep telling me to trust my fiancé, but I have it on good authority that he asked John Smith to take some of your toiletry items up to Lincoln for fingerprint analysis."

He chuckled and replied, "Is Clem still trying to figure out who I am?"

"Apparently, and he has the Nebraska State Patrol ready to throw in with him."

"How intriguing. I feel like a *Marvel Comics* superhero with a secret identity, but I don't remember anything missing from my shaving kit. Are you sure John got some of my things?"

"He didn't," I replied proudly. "We put our heads together and decided he could get a few things from the 'left behind' stock in my broom closet. As I remember, he took a can of shaving cream, a razor, and some old, rusty fingernail clippers."

"That was sweet, Wilma. I'll have to call John and thank him."

"You're not worried?"

"Not in the least. Now, tell me what's bothering you."

That was it. No lead-in; no introduction; no prologue; no warning. I don't know about you, but I have difficulty answering a question like that without some sort of preamble. After I collected my thoughts, I answered, "Last night, Calvin Millet told me I would have to choose between Clem and the Quilting Circle. Lulu Tiller said the same thing in front of the Circle board of governors this morning. I don't know what to do."

"Why do they say you have to choose?"

"The Big Buyback notwithstanding, Clem and the Circle have always been on opposite sides of the fence. Now that Clem has sold the bank, the sparks are really going to fly."

"Really? From where I sit, it looks like Clem has sold off everything he owns in Ebb with the possible exception of a minority position in Millet's Department Store. Why is he still the Circle's adversary?"

"I don't understand. Clem just sold the bank."

"Isn't that exactly what the Circle wanted him to do? In your fondest dreams, didn't you want him to sell out and quit?"

"What are you trying to say, Mr. Moore?"

"The game of cat and mouse between Clem Tucker and the Quilting Circle is over, Wilma. You won. Declare victory and move on. For the same reason, there has never been a time when it was less necessary for you to choose between Clem and the Circle."

"But the Circle doesn't believe the game is over. They believe they've been sold out. Lulu Tiller thinks Millet's will be the third shoe."

"Would that be bad? If she's right, Clem is selling the last piece of his local portfolio. You should be dancing in the streets."

I had to think that over. Even when we weren't involved, I never felt like Clem was the Circle's enemy. He was just the Champion Bull, the one, untamable critter we had to keep fenced in.

Mr. Moore asked, "Is the board convinced that Millet's is the third shoe?"

"They seem to be," I replied. "It makes some sense."

"Are you certain? Clem is attempting to do something memorable, possibly extraordinary. Selling the local bank wouldn't make the grade, nor would the sale of a store. As a rule, selling isn't nearly as memorable as buying. If you think about it, buying isn't as memorable as dozens of other verbs either."

"Then what's he really doing?"

"I only have a theory, Wilma; a belief. All I can say is that Millet's may be a red herring. You may be better served if you focus your attention on the National Bank of the Plains."

"But we have. The board is very focused on NBP."

"Are you, or are you in a rush to get into a fight? Fights have winners and losers, and the outcome is never certain. You might consider slowing down. Give Clem's strategy time to unfold; allow yourselves time to gather information."

"What about me? What about choosing between Clem and the Circle?"

"What will the Circle do if you refuse to choose, Wilma? Will they break your sword, strip off your buttons and epaulets, take your horse, and send you into the wilderness on foot?"

I guess Mr. Moore had seen *Branded* with Chuck Connors. The thought made me shiver. "What are you telling me?"

"I know it's not the American way, but put it off. Delay, dither, dilly-dally. Dawdle in the depths of indecision."

"What if Clem says I have to choose?"

"He won't."

"He won't? Why not?"

"Because the game is one shoe short of done. He didn't care that you were a member of the Circle when the game was afoot; he certainly won't care after it's over. You shouldn't either." Mr. Moore stood up and added, "Thank you for lunch, Wilma. I don't know how anyone could make a simple roast beef sandwich into such a delight, but you managed. I look forward to a cinnamon roll."

I had one more question to get off my chest. "We women talk a lot in this town, Mr. Moore. In particular, we like to keep up with the local news."

He smiled and replied, "I hadn't noticed."

"Well, we compare notes a lot, and sometimes we come across something that appears to be a bit inconsistent."

"Is there a particular inconsistency you have in mind?"

"A little one, yes. When Mona asked you how you were going to help Matt, you said you were going to sell him some charity. When Dottie asked, you said you were going to give Matt a code of conduct. And when Mary Wade asked, you said you were going to teach Matt to be logical. We're a teense confused."

"Don't be," he replied. "They're all the same." Full stop. End of story. That's all he said on the matter, as if the answer should have been intuitively obvious.

I stood silently at the kitchen sink while my lodger called John Smith on my kitchen phone. When he left the Come Again a few minutes later, he was whistling and carrying a small, brown paper bag. I had never heard Mr. Moore whistle before. He wasn't good at it.

As for myself, I had intended to make a cake after the cinnamon rolls but I decided to put it off. Instead, I went through all the rooms upstairs, checking for dirty laundry and dishes. In Mr. Moore's room, I found an open, handwritten note on his bedside table. It read:

Dear Silas,

    I'd very much appreciate the opportunity to meet you before Saturday morning.

Kindest regards,
Vernon L. Moore

Chapter 20

Another Word for Guess

OVER THE YEARS, I've known men who fought in World War II, Korea, Vietnam, and the Middle East. The quietest, most introspective ones had killed men in battle. John Smith won't talk about what he did in the army, but Mona asked him why he wouldn't eat chicken at the house one afternoon. He replied, "Tastes like snake." Tell me if I'm wrong, but I don't think he was a bookkeeper.

John was sitting on the courthouse steps by himself when Mr. Moore walked up with his little brown bag. John jumped to his feet and said, "I didn't expect a call from you, Mr. Moore. How can I help?"

"I understand you've done some research into the Bold Cut incident. Is that true?"

"Yes, sir. Matt didn't act alone, but the sheriff never charged anybody but him. Mr. Tucker asked me to find out who else was involved."

"Can you tell me what you've learned?"

"Sure. The sheriff wouldn't help so I had to start at ground zero: with Matt's friends and associates at the high school. Some time around the end of the last school year, he started to spend a lot of time with two boys, identical twins named Buddy and Richie Gault. Earl, their father, is the leader of the Divine Temple of the Everlasting God Almighty. On half a dozen occasions, Matt visited them at the Temple Ranch out on the county line."

"Did Matt actually join their church?"

"I had the same question but I never got an answer. They escorted me off the lot, so to speak. Naturally, that increased my curiosity, so I looked into the history of the temple in general and Earl Gault in particular. He was a second-string, All-American linebacker at a small Baptist college in Texas . . ."

"Did he graduate?"

"Yes, sir."

"With what degree?"

"Business administration. He got pretty good grades, too, but he tried to make it as a pro ballplayer after school. That didn't work out, so he went into show business and eventually landed a gig with a TV ministry out of Atlanta. Sometime in the nineties, he split off and created the Divine Temple. He moved his people up here two years ago after a tax dispute with the state of Georgia. That's as much as I know."

"Are you still working on the investigation?"

"No, sir. Mr. Tucker asked me to give it a rest while you were in town."

"I see. How's your schedule for the next twenty-four hours?"

"Before I answer," he inquired, "can I ask why you want to know?"

"Of course."

After the usual awkward silence, John said, "Okay. Why?"

"I'd appreciate it if you could drive me out to the Temple Ranch. I'd like to have a chat with Mr. Gault."

"He won't see you, Mr. Moore. I got a friendlier reception in Mogadishu."

"Why don't you let me worry about that? I have a small talent for getting people to talk to me. Can you go tomorrow?"

"Okay, but I'll need to get permission."

"Clem has a vested interest in our mission; I expect his answer to be in the affirmative. When can we go?"

John pulled a little black book out of his pocket, then replied, "I have to take Mr. Tucker and Mr. Santoni up to Omaha later, but I might be able to drive back tomorrow morning."

"Then let's meet here at eleven hundred hours."

"I'll be right here on the dot, sir, assuming the boss gives me an affirmative."

"Thank you for indulging me, John. It's not the sort of adventure I'd want to undertake alone. If I may, I have one other small request."

"Yes, sir."

Mr. Moore handed him the small brown paper bag. "I'd like you to drop these things off at state police headquarters in Lincoln as soon as possible."

John opened the bag carefully, as if the contents might be dangerous. Inside was a tube of toothpaste, a toothbrush, a few old-fashioned plastic collar stays, and an empty container of men's cologne. "Wilma told you?" he asked.

"Yes."

"But I've already taken some of your stuff up there."

"So I understand, but it wasn't really mine, was it? These things are, and my best fingerprints are all over them."

John peered inside the bag again. Mr. Moore said, "Just give forensics a call and tell them you were given items from the wrong shaving kit. I'm sure they'll understand."

For a fact, John didn't. As soon as he was on his own, he called me to inquire into Mr. Moore's sanity. I did my best to convince him that my unusual lodger was of sound mind but I'm not sure I succeeded— probably because I've had my own doubts from time to time.

MATT WAS READING an old magazine when Deputy Samoa and Mr. Moore arrived at his cell. Except for the unmistakable odor of household cleaner, there was no evidence that the walls had once been decorated with circular foods, but Matt's laceless shoes were at the foot of the bed and he was still missing his belt.

Mr. Moore stood the banjo case in the corner and remarked, "Short of an army barracks, this may be the cleanest billet I've ever seen. You did a terrific job."

Matt wasn't used to getting compliments and suspicious of the few he got. He replied, "Uh huh. Like, are you going to play the banjo again?"

Mr. Moore sat down on his metal folding chair. "Think of it as a backup plan. Were you just reading the *Sporting News*?"

"Yeah. I like baseball."

"Is that so? Me, too. Do you read the box scores?"

"Uh huh."

"When I was your age, I could fiddle with the box scores for hours. I didn't know it, but it helped me with math in school. Now I collect baseball cards. Do you?"

"Naw. I did when I was kid, but not now."

"That's when I started. I have cards that stretch all the way back to the nineteen thirties but my favorite players are relief pitchers. I have all the greats: Hoyt Wilhelm; Dennis Eckersley; Mariano Rivera; many more. Did you have a favorite position?"

"Yeah. I was a second baseman."

"Who was your favorite player?"

"You mean like now, or all time?"

"All time."

"Nelson Fox. He played for the Chicago White Sox, my favorite team. He was a twelve-time All-Star. Did you know that?"

"No, but I remember him well. Do you have his baseball card?"

"Nah. I used to, but not anymore. That kind of stuff is for kids." Mr. Moore couldn't have known, but Matt's entire collection was in a big box in his closet at the Come Again.

"You're probably right; kids and old men. Speaking of old, what's the date on that copy of the *Sporting News*?"

Matt checked the front page and replied, "September."

"September? Ugh! It's a month out-of-date and the play-offs are in full swing. Would you like me to bring you the latest issue tomorrow?"

"That would be cool, but I'd rather have my . . ."

Before Matt could finish, Mr. Moore said, "Earlier today, I asked you to think about the difference between fact and belief. Did you?"

With hesitation, my grandson answered, "Yeah. Some."

"Good. What did you come up with? What's the difference?"

Matt glanced at Deputy Samoa. "Facts are things you can be sure of, like baseball statistics. Beliefs are things you think are true, but you can't be sure of."

"That's an excellent answer. Can you give me an example of a belief?"

Matt looked at Luther again. "Sure. A belief is like when you think your team is gonna win a game. You know when it's over, so it's a fact afterward."

"That's another good answer. Belief is a synonym for guess. In comparison, facts are better because no guesswork is involved. Still, people seem to have a lot of beliefs, don't they?"

"Uh, I don't know, Mr. Moore."

"Belief in God, belief in democracy, belief in vampires, belief in Santa Claus. We all have beliefs, Matt, and we don't have a choice. Do you know why?"

"No."

"Because there aren't enough facts to go around. If a man with a baseball bat approaches you in an alley, do you know if he's going to attack you?"

"No."

"That's right, but your life may hang in the balance so you have to guess, even though there aren't enough facts. Does that make sense?"

"Yeah. If the guy with the bat looks pissed off, I'm getting my butt out of that alley."

"Me, too, so facts and beliefs are both important. However, it turns out that understanding the difference between fact and belief has a great deal to do with being smart or stupid."

"I don't get it, Mr. Moore."

"Let's try an example, but it's a little close to home. If the going gets too rough, you let me know and we'll talk about something else, okay?"

"Okay."

"Why did you and your friends attack the Bold Cut?"

Matt pulled his knees up and sat back on his bunk.

Mr. Moore said, "All we're talking about is the difference between fact and belief. I'm not going to ask you who was there with you."

Matt caught sight of the banjo and replied bravely, "I can do this. We took down the Bold Cut because it was a whorehouse."

"A whorehouse. Fair enough. Was that a fact or a belief?"

Matt didn't answer.

Mr. Moore repeated, "You said it was a whorehouse. Was that a fact or a belief?"

"It was a fact."

"Really? How did you know? Were you a client? Did you go to the Bold Cut and pay for sexual services yourself?"

Matt pushed himself closer to the wall.

"I doubt it, especially since your mother worked there. Who said it was a whorehouse?"

"Everybody. Everybody said so."

"Everybody? Did your grandmother? How about your mother? She actually worked there. Did she ever tell you that she or her associates traded sexual favors for money?"

Matt didn't answer again.

"Okay. Did you peep in the window and witness any of Ms. Parson's girls providing sex to their clientele?"

"No, man. That would've been sick."

"Then how did you know that the Bold Cut was a whorehouse?"

Matt hesitated before replying, "My friends told me. They said they'd been there."

"Did they tell you they paid money for sex?"

"They saw it. They said they saw men go into the back room and come out thirty minutes later. They said they heard giggling and groaning, a lot of it."

"Did you ever go in the back office yourself?"

"Yeah, with my mom."

"What did you see?"

After a moment, Matt said, "A desk, a sofa, a massage table."

"Did you ever get a massage from any of Loretta's girls?"

"Duh, no. My mom would've freaked."

"I got one—from Loretta herself. She was good at it, too. As I remember, I did a little groaning myself. Did that make Loretta a whore?"

Again, Matt didn't answer.

"Did your mother give massages? Did you ask her?"

"Are you shittin' me? I could never ask that. The thought makes me want to puke."

"I understand, but I still haven't heard any hard evidence that the Bold Cut was a whorehouse. Do you have anything else?"

Matt hesitated before answering, "Maybe not. I guess not."

"You guess not? What's a guess, Matt? Is it another word for fact, or is it another word for belief?"

There was no reply.

Mr. Moore folded his arms and said, "Do you know what a delusion is, Matt?"

"Yeah. Sorta."

"A delusion is an irrational belief. Have you ever heard of the Heaven's Gate cult?"

"The who?"

"They were a group of well-educated men and women who lived and worked together in San Diego. Unfortunately, they were also a cult whose leader claimed to talk directly to God. Does that sound familiar? He said that the Hale-Bopp comet would carry them all to God, but only if they were disembodied. As the comet passed Earth, do you know what they did?"

"What?"

"They committed suicide. Even though they were highly intelligent people, they killed themselves because of the blatantly irrational claims of a delusional man. That's what stupid people do, no matter how well-educated they are: they act on delusion. Does that ring a bell?

"You acted on a delusion that the Bold Cut was a whorehouse when, in fact, it wasn't. You also acted on the delusion that it was your job to penalize the owner of the establishment, and you acted on the delusion that beating the proprietress into a coma was a suitable punishment for such a crime, even though there was no proof of any crime."

"I didn't hit Loretta, Mr. Moore. I would never hit her. We were just supposed to trash the place and get out. That's all."

"Okay, but then you acted on the belief that your accomplices would confine themselves to the unfair, emptyhearted, and mean-spirited demolition of her business. Was that smart?"

"No."

"That's right. Smart people act on fact, Matt. They avoid acting on belief except as a last resort because they know that beliefs are guesses. Do you know what stupid people do?"

"They act on delusion?"

"Yes. They also have a confounding ability to confuse fact and belief. When an advertisement implies that you'll have sex with beautiful women if you chew a certain kind of gum, are they selling you a fact, a belief, or a delusion?"

"That's easy. A delusion."

"When Galileo was incarcerated for demonstrating that the sun is the center of our solar system rather than the Earth, were his judges acting on fact, belief, or delusion?"

"Duh. That was delusion, too."

"Not at the time, Matt. At the time, it was belief. That's the problem with beliefs: some of them are subsequently proven to be delusions. When a religious terrorist murders a hundred innocent women and children, is he acting on fact or belief or delusion?"

Matt thought for a long time. "Belief or delusion," he answered. "I don't know which."

"Me, either. One of the great ironies of humankind is that we rarely become emotional about facts but we are often passionate about our beliefs. Beliefs may be necessary, but it's not clear that our passions have served us well. Over the course of history, millions of people have been murdered and tortured by religious zealots who acted on belief or, worse, on delusion.

"Beliefs are the Gray Area between fact and delusion. Until we can prove which one they are, they're guesses, even belief in God."

According to Luther, Matt practically jumped out of his skin when he heard that. "Belief in God, Mr. Moore?" he asked. "Don't you believe in God? Gramma said you did."

"She's right, Matt. More precisely, I believe in a benevolent and loving God, and very strongly. Do you?"

"Yeah."

"Do you believe in Him, or are you absolutely certain that He exists?"

"I'm sure. I'm a hundred percent sure."

"Really? How can you be? Have you met Him? Have you seen Him interviewed on the evening news? Have you solved a mathematical equation that proves His existence? What hard, verifiable evidence do you have?"

Matt thought, then replied, "How about the Bible? Isn't that proof?"

"The Bible is an extraordinary collection of observations and ideas, but it was written thousands of years ago. Since then, it has been translated and edited and retranslated and reedited over and over again. Now it exists in countless versions. Scholars can spend a lifetime trying to understand how much of any one version is fact and how much is fiction."

"Nobody knows?"

"Nobody knows for sure, so it's all down to you. In your heart, do you believe that Noah and his family built a single ship—out of gopher wood no less—that was big enough to hold two examples of every species on the planet? How did the animals from the Americas, Australia, and Antarctica get to the loading dock? And where did they put enough food for one hundred and ninety days? Next to the swimming pool for the hippos and the crocodiles?"

"Are you saying the Bible is bogus, Mr. Moore?"

"No. Does the story about Noah have to be completely true or completely false, or can it be something in between?"

My grandson squirmed. "Something in between?"

"Probably, maybe. The Bible in all its forms is part fact, part metaphor, and part myth, but there is little consensus about which is which. Therefore, you may believe what you wish, but you must never confuse your beliefs with cold, hard facts. Do you understand?"

"I-I think so."

"And I hope so; I truly hope so. There is nothing more stupid than the use of violence to advance a belief, and there is nothing more hypocritical if that belief is in a loving God. Promise me you'll never do it again."

"I won't," Matt said. "Not ever."

Mr. Moore stood slowly and moved his chair to the side of the cell. Luther grinned and gave Matt a thumbs-up.

Matt said tentatively, "Are we done for today?"

"We are. You did a good job of hanging in there. Your belt and shoelaces will be returned after I leave. I take it that the food has already improved."

"Naw. It's still crap, but at least it's different."

Mr. Moore picked up the banjo case. "I'll bring you the latest edition of the *Sporting News* tomorrow. In the meantime, there's another question that I'd like you to think about."

"Like, what?"

"Is it wrong to make a mistake?"

"I don't understand, Mr. Moore."

"It's another simple question, Matt. Is it wrong to make a mistake?"

"Duh, it's wrong. Mostly."

"Mostly? How do you tell when it's okay and when it's not?"

Matt looked through the bars at Deputy Giant, who nodded.

My grandson said, "Okay. I'll think about it."

"Good. I'll see you tomorrow morning at ten a.m."

On their way back down the corridor, Mr. Moore said, "Thanks for being so patient, Deputy Samoa. You've been very helpful."

"I'm just doing the job, Mr. Moore."

"Maybe, but you've gone the extra mile and I appreciate it. Forgive me, but I have to ask you to do it again. I'd like you to get permission to take Matt on a walk. Friday morning, weather permitting."

"To do what?"

"To look at houses."

"Houses?"

"What else?"

Chapter 21

Men Frying Fish

A BANK OF BILLOWING, purple-black clouds had appeared in the north by the time Mr. Moore left the courthouse. Everybody who has ever lived in Nebraska knows what that means: it's going to get wet and it's going to get cold. It was more than an hour before dusk, but the sun was already obscured and a chill wind had begun to ripple through the fields around town. There are no mountains in Nebraska and darn few hills, trees, and big buildings. When the wind blows, there's nothing much to slow it down.

On the way back to the Come Again, Mr. Moore got a call from my fiancé, who said, "Vernon, I'm glad I caught you. Have you heard the news?"

"It was smart, Clem, very smart."

"Really? I'm flattered, but why do you think so?"

"Because you sold the Tucker Trust farmland twice. First you sold it back to the farmers, then you sold the bank, therefore the loans on the farmland, to the National Bank of the Plains."

"That's exactly right. From what I hear, the Quilting Circle doesn't share our enthusiasm for the deal. They've demanded a meeting . . ."

Clem's voice trailed off. Like I said, cell reception isn't real good in the countryside. Nasty weather doesn't improve it.

Mr. Moore yelled, "What was that, Clem? I couldn't hear you."

"Sorry. I must've faded out. Is it raining down there yet?"

"No."

"Well, we're halfway to Omaha and it's raining cats and dogs up here. The temperature must've dropped twenty degrees, too. If you've got somewhere to go, I suggest you get there pronto."

Mr. Moore turned his collar up and increased his pace. "You were asking about the Circle?"

"Yeah. They've demanded a meeting, but I won't be back in Ebb until the weekend. What do you recommend I do?"

"Calvin's still in town, isn't he? Why don't you delegate the meeting to him?"

"Calvin's calendar is wall-to-wall . . ." Clem's voice faded again.

"Are you there, Clem?"

"Yeah. We're still here. That's a hell of an idea, Vernon. I'll do it. My read is that the Circle is out for blood; Tucker blood. Do you see it that way?"

"That's the indication, but it's too soon to tell for sure."

"Well, Wilma says they're spoiling for a fight, and she's on the inside. I'll get my dander up if they try to throw a monkey wrench into this deal. I'm a hell of a lot easier to get along with when my dander is down."

Vernon turned right on Pea and said, "I understand, Clem, but you're just guessing. I wouldn't worry about it now. You have bigger fish to fry."

"Bigger fish? How could you know that?"

"I don't, but logic suggests that you haven't reached your end game. The sale of the bank is significant, but it looks more like a rook sacrifice than a checkmate to me. And the deal is closed, but you're on your way up to Omaha. The inference is that there's more to do."

There was a long silence before Clem said, "How are you doing with Matt? The grapevine says you're playing the banjo down there. Is that right?"

"Not anymore. We're talking now."

"I was never one to care for the banjo myself. Is Matt paying attention to what you say, or is he just bullshitting you?"

"It could be either. It's too soon to tell."

"You don't have a lot of time left, Vernon. When do you see him again?"

"Tomorrow morning."

"Good. John tells me you want to borrow him and the limo. He says you plan on visiting that Gault character. Is that right?"

"I'd like to see what the reverend is made of. It'll help me down the road."

"What the hell does that mean?"

"You have your end game, Clem. I have mine."

WHEN MR. MOORE got back to the Come Again, I was sitting in the kitchen splitting a warm cinnamon bun with Laverne. She got a big grin on her face when he walked in, but she didn't hold out her arms like she does for Mona. Maybe it was his hair, which had been blown in every direction of the compass and then some.

"You look like you just walked in from a tornado," I said. "Sit yourself down and talk to your daughter. I'll fix you some tea and a cinnamon roll."

"Thank you."

Mr. Moore kissed Laverne on the top of the head and sat at the table next to her high chair. She picked up a chunk of cinnamon roll from her tray, lobbed it over the side, and said, "Ball?" Mr. Moore caught it before it hit the floor and popped it into his mouth. He could've been a mom.

"How was your second appointment with Matt, today?" I inquired. "Did you make more progress?"

"I hope so."

"The underground says that Matt has improved a bushel and a peck in the last twenty-four hours. Everybody knows it's you. I hear Dottie's thinking of changing the way she feeds uncooperative prisoners."

Laverne heaved another chunk of cinnamon bun over the side, but it was on the opposite side of her chair and Mr. Moore wasn't fast enough. He started to lean down but I said, "Never mind; I'll sweep up afterward. Will you be staying for dinner tonight? I'm fixing pork chops and mashed potatoes."

"I'd love to, Wilma, but I feel guilty. You should change the name of this place to a Bed, Breakfast, Lunch, and Dinner."

"Oh, I don't think so, Mr. Moore. There's no way I would want to advertise that. I wouldn't fix a cold bowl of grits for some of my guests if it wasn't a trade obligation. Will you be going out to see Loretta tonight?"

"Yes."

"I heard that you've asked Doc Wiley to meet you there. Is she all right?"

"She's in a coma, Wilma."

"Yes, but she seems to be stable. Is that going to change?"

"There's no way I could know that. I'd like to talk to Hank about her long-term care."

"Is that all? Do you promise?"

"Yes."

"Well, that's a relief. We don't need another disaster today, for heaven's sake. It would be just like Loretta to upstage Clem somehow."

Mr. Moore's forehead furrowed up. "Another disaster?" he asked.

"The Big Sellout," I replied. "They've started a pool down at the Corn Palace. You pay one dollar and pick the month that the bank gets replaced by ATMs."

"That's a bit fatalistic, don't you think?"

"I don't know, Mr. Moore. I'm feeling fairly fatalistic myself. Lulu Tiller has called a general meeting on Friday morning. They're going to vote on whether the Circle should oppose the sale of the bank. Hail Mary Wade is working on the strategy as we speak."

Mr. Moore asked, "Can I ask what the back-up proposal is?"

"The back-up proposal?"

"Didn't you say that Mary's preparing a strategy to prevent the sale of the bank? What's the alternative? What's Plan B?"

"An alternative? I don't know. Should there be one?"

Mr. Moore pulled at his earlobe and said, "People are predictable, Wilma. If you put two hundred of them in a room, whip them into a frenzy, and then tell them that they can fight or do nothing, which option do you think they'll pick?"

I didn't have to, but I thought about it for a few seconds. "I don't have another proposal, Mr. Moore. Do you?"

"Nature isn't fond of black-and-white situations, Wilma. Nature prefers a broad spectrum of outcomes. When only two alternatives are proposed, it's usually a rhetorical contrivance, a fallacy. You should distrust it. To sue and not to sue are only two alternatives, and starkly opposing ones at that. Distrust them. Ask yourself what else the Circle might do."

"I don't know, Mr. Moore. Clem has sold the bank. Lulu believes that Millet's is the third shoe. If she's right, the town is done for."

"I don't agree. Instead, I suspect you'll need to revise your shoe forecast."

"What on earth does that mean, Mr. Moore?"

"If Millet's is the third shoe, it's likely to be a distraction. The end game will be the fourth shoe."

"A fourth shoe?"

"Yes."

"Oh dear! What do you want me to do?"

"Find an alternative to litigation, something colorful. For instance, you might consider offering Clem a membership in the Circle."

All of a sudden, I felt faint. "A what?" I asked.

"You said so yourself: Clem and the Circle have always been on opposite sides of the fence. Why not invite him to join the Circle instead? What have you got to lose?"

As I live and breathe.

JUST BEFORE DINNER, Mr. Moore came down the back stairs with little Laverne riding high on his shoulders, grinning and gripping his hair with both fists like she had a wild stallion by the mane.

The stallion said, "I forgot to ask you earlier, Wilma. Could you get me Bebe Palouse's home phone number? I'd like to give her a call."

I started to ask why but I wasn't sure I wanted to know the answer, so I went to my den and got her number. While I was rooting around the desk drawer for my Circle directory, I happened to glance outside.

By the light through the window, I could see wet, quarter-sized snow-flakes drifting slowly to the ground.

It was a lovely scene to be sure, but Hank Wiley is no snow person. Minutes later, he called to ask if he still had to go to Beatrice to see Loretta, but Mr. Moore volunteered to drive them in his new Chrysler. It had all-wheel drive.

After dinner, Mr. Moore went off to pick up Doc Wiley, Mona took Laverne upstairs to give her a bath, and Mark went into the parlor to watch TV. I had a rare spell alone, but I didn't feel like doing the dishes because I was going to have to dump the dishwasher first, which is a pain in the back. I'd been thinking about buying a new car myself, possibly with all-wheel drive because it's supposed to have good traction on slick surfaces, so I dug the Sunday want ads out of the recycling bin and took them into the dining room to read.

That's where I went wrong. To begin with, I'd like to know who is inventing all these new kinds of money. What are lease cash, loyalty cash, bonus cash, mobility cash, and customer cash, and how are they different from cash cash? And what in God's creation are all these rebates? I saw one car—one car, mind you—that offered a manufacturer's rebate, loyalty cash, customer cash, mobility cash, some kind of realty association rebate, a college grad rebate, and a military rebate. I'm not kidding. The fine print was smaller than my ex-husband's working IQ, but I eventually determined that I could get the advertised price if I had just graduated from college, if I was a disabled real-estate agent on active military duty, if I already owned the same brand of car they were selling, and if I had good credit—all at once!

What are they thinking?

Chapter 22

....

Mr. Moore Makes a Mistake

IT WAS STILL SNOWING when Mr. Moore and Doc Wiley drove over to the hospital, and the temperature had dropped below thirty-two degrees so it had started to stick on the road. Apparently, Hank didn't have a high degree of confidence in all-wheel drive. He said he asked Mr. Moore to slow down fourteen times on their way. I don't know if Mr. Moore ever did, but they got there safely.

A single night-light illuminated the head of Loretta's bed. An IV ran into her left arm, another wire went down to the thingamajig on her right finger, and the monitors behind her bed beeped and blinked off and on. Being sick these days is like being a DVD player; you're hooked up to every device in sight. When I was by myself in Loretta's room, I sometimes found myself wondering if God's finger was on Lo's clicker.

Mr. Moore took a seat in a visitor's chair and Doc Wiley went about checking her vitals. After a while, Mr. Moore said, "Well? Has there been any change?"

Hank stared at a monitor and stroked his chin. "Every little thing looks fine, but her pulse and breathing rate are both slightly elevated and I don't know why. Can you wait here while I go back to the nurse's station to check her medication?"

"Sure."

Mr. Moore touched Loretta's arm with his fingertips, then he picked up the paperback he had left on the shelf behind her bed. Before he could turn the first page, the beeping began to increase in frequency and the lights on the monitors began to flash. He jumped out of his chair and put his ear to Loretta's chest. Seconds later, Doc Wiley came rushing back into the room with the night nurse right on his heels.

"What's going on, Hank?" Mr. Moore asked.

Before the doctor could answer, they heard a slow, slight moan, followed by a weak, barely audible whisper, "Vern, darlin', is that you?"

Both men looked at Loretta as if they didn't believe their ears. Her eyes had opened and she had turned her head slightly to the left, toward Mr. Moore. "Where the hell am I?" she squeaked. "In a florist shop?"

"You're in the hospital, Lo," he answered. "The flowers are for you."

Loretta's voice was weak and raspy. "Where's Laverne? Have you got her?"

"Wilma and Mona have been taking care of her since your accident. She's a beautiful little girl."

"Accident?" Loretta tried to push herself up to her elbows but had no success.

Doc Wiley read the monitors while he felt her pulse. "You've been asleep for quite a while, Lo," he said. "Take it easy. You'll find that you are very, very weak. Your strength will come back, but it'll take time."

"Forget my muscles, my mouth is drier than a box of salt. How long have I been out?"

"Six weeks, give or take."

"Six weeks? When did the salesman show up?"

Hank began to answer, but Mr. Moore replied, "I got here a few days ago."

"That was the best you could do?" She added, "I feel queasy, Doc. My throat hurts and I'm very, very thirsty. Is that normal?"

"Considering how long you've been asleep, I'd say that it was better than normal. We'll get you some ice chips as soon as we give you a once-over. You may have a little trouble swallowing at first, but it'll come back in time. Vernon, I'd appreciate it if you'd leave the room until we're done."

"Vernon Moore, don't you go without giving me a kiss. I could fall asleep again . . ." Loretta's voice trailed off.

Mr. Moore smiled and gave her a lingering kiss on the lips. Doc Wiley joined him in the hall about ten minutes later.

"What's the prognosis, Doc?"

"She seems to be doing remarkably well, considering. Her respiration rate is still slightly elevated, but otherwise her vitals are strong. I can't find any evidence of neural impairment. That's the best news. Don't push her voice, though. Like the rest of her, it's very weak."

Doc Wiley paused and then continued, "Loretta's recovery will come in steps, Vernon, and it will require a team effort. By tomorrow, she'll have half a dozen doctors and nurses working to restore her strength, her range of motion, and her emotional well-being. The process will take weeks, possibly months."

"Thanks for the warning, Doc, but I've had some experience with long-term rehabilitation. That's not my worry. In Loretta's case, we'll also need to keep a lid on her recovery."

"On her recovery? Why?"

"Matt's accomplices are still out there and Loretta is the only eyewitness."

Hank shrugged his shoulders. "I understand, but the women in Ebb have a network that would bring the CIA to tears. I'd be surprised if the news hasn't already reached the Abattoir. As we speak, they're probably planning a Chippendale Night to celebrate Loretta's return."

"You're right. Sheriff Hrnicek will have to post guards around-the-clock."

"Beatrice is in Gage County, Vernon, not Hayes."

"Fine. She'll need to contact the Gage county sheriff." Mr. Moore peered inside the room and added, "I can't tell you how grateful I am that you came tonight, Doc."

"You're more than welcome, Vernon."

"Can I go back in now?"

"In a minute or two, when the nurse is finished. I need to talk to the resident physician, then I'll hang around the nurse's station for another hour or so. If Loretta's vitals are still good, the local staff can take over and we can go back home in that fancy car of yours."

"No problem, Doc. It'll be my pleasure."

Instead of heading down the hall, Hank stared at his shoes.

After a second or two, Mr. Moore asked, "Is something bothering you?"

Hank replied to his feet, "It seems like an incredible coincidence that we were here at the exact moment when Loretta woke up, especially on such a God-forsaken night."

"What are you trying to say, Doc?"

He answered haltingly, "Did you know this was going to happen, Vernon?"

"No."

"You didn't?"

"To the contrary. For no rational reason whatsoever, I was afraid that Loretta would stop breathing and you wouldn't be here to bring her back."

"Really? Are you saying you made a mistake?"

"I did, and I've never been happier about it."

The nurse emerged from Loretta's room with a small container of tubes, vials, syringes, and damp cloths in her hands. Mr. Moore said, "Can I go in now?"

"Yes, but don't talk her to death. It may sound odd, but she needs her rest."

"I understand, Doc. Thanks."

The top half of Loretta's bed had been angled upward and she was propped up on her pillows. Mr. Moore kissed her on the forehead and ran his fingers lightly down her cheek. He said, "How are you?"

Loretta whispered in reply, "I don't have any strength. I can hardly swallow."

"Your muscles have been inactive for a long time, Lo, even your throat muscles. You'll need to exercise them back. It'll take a while."

"What kind of while? I don't even know what day it is."

"It's late Wednesday night."

"Wednesday? When are you leaving?"

"Saturday morning."

"Saturday? I should have known. Why didn't you wake me up earlier, darlin'?"

The nurse came into the room with a small plastic glass half-filled with ice chips. For the next ten minutes, Loretta struggled to swallow the small amount of water they produced.

After the nurse left, Loretta asked, "Were you reading to me, Vern, or did I dream that?"

"Yes. *Devil in a Blue Dress*. Would you like me to read some more? We have half the book to go."

"In a minute. Have you spent any quality time with Laverne?"

"Every chance I get."

"Did you tell her who you are?"

"I did."

Loretta tried to clear her throat. "Has she been a good girl?"

"The best. She not only talks, she speaks with her eyes and expressions, just like you."

"She's my baby, isn't she? I need to see her. Will you bring her up tomorrow morning?"

Mr. Moore didn't answer immediately. Loretta said, "You're meddling in other folk's affairs, aren't you? Are you going to get the boys who beat me up?"

"You remember?"

"Flashes, like photographs I can see for a split second. One of them was wearing a K State sweater. Was it Matt Breck? Was he there?"

"I'm sorry to say so, but yes."

"I'm sorry, too. Where is he now?"

"In jail. He admitted everything."

Loretta frowned. "Poor Mona must be going crazy. Is she okay?"

"She'll feel better when she hears that you've woken up."

"Weren't there two others? What about the other two boys?"

"They haven't been caught."

"But you're going to get them before you leave. Isn't that right?"

"I am. You can bank on it."

Lo smiled and said, "That's my Vern." After a few more seconds, she added, "You're not angry with me are you?"

"Angry with you. What for?"

"For seducing you into fathering my child."

"Heaven's no. She's a wonderful little girl."

Loretta smiled again. "Can you stay tonight?" she asked.

"I'd love to, but I have to drive Doc Wiley back to Ebb in an hour or so."

The mother of my goddaughter started to object, but I don't think she had the strength. "Will you ask Wilma and Mona to bring Laverne as soon as they can? I need to see my girl."

"I won't be able to hold them back."

"And one last thing, darlin'. Would you bring me a latte next time, a double shot? These ice chips aren't going to cut the mustard. I need some zip."

"It'll be my pleasure."

"Good. You can read to me now, but kiss me good-bye before you go."

"I will."

"Promise?"

"Cross my heart." He didn't add, ". . . and hope to die."

I DREAMT ABOUT my high school days for the jillionth time that night. The bell had rung and everybody else had left my algebra class, but I stayed behind because I'd forgotten to wear a skirt. My subconscious was probably trying to tell me that I had forgotten something, but I have no idea what it was. Frankly, I don't see why the mind has to be so obscure. If I've forgotten something, why can't somebody in my dream just hold up a sign that says, "Your sunglasses are in the green bowl in the den"? That would be more informative.

I was still trapped in algebra class when I felt someone grab my arm and say, "Wilma, wake up."

I opened my eyes to see Vernon Moore standing by my bed, in my bedroom no less. That was something else I had dreamed of, involuntarily of course. Before I could clear the cobwebs and get my bearings, he said, "Loretta woke up tonight."

I sat straight up in bed, like I was spring-loaded. It's a good thing I was wearing a nightie. "Loretta! She's awake?"

"I just left her at the hospital."

"Have you told Mona?"

"No. I thought you might want to do that."

"I have to get up! Mona has to get up! We have to get Laverne and go!"

"Go ahead and wake Mona, but wait until the morning to drive to the hospital. The roads are awful and Loretta needs rest. Doctor's orders."

"Is she okay?"

"She looks fine. Doc Wiley says her numbers are very good."

That stopped me dead in my tracks. "You made Hank go up there, Mr. Moore. You almost had to drag him by the collar. You knew she was going to wake up, didn't you?"

Chapter 23

······················

Cruel Ironies

IT HAD STOPPED SNOWING but six inches of white, wet snow remained on the ground in the morning. When it snows like that in the city, the plows come out and clear off the roads. In the country, the plow, singular, comes out of the firehouse and clears off the main road, and then the plow-driver, a squat, bullet-shaped man named Flathead Williams, goes to the Corn Palace to warm himself up. Flathead hasn't been the same since he fell off the back of his daddy's pickup forty years ago. His mama, a nice woman named Beryl, takes care of him to this very day.

Because the roads were so slick, Mr. Moore insisted that Mona and I take his new, all-wheel drive car to the hospital. That would have made me feel safer except that I was worried sick that I would wreck it. Thankfully, Mona volunteered to drive, which absolved me from responsibility. As soon as breakfast was over, she bundled up Laverne while I transferred the baby seat from Mona's minivan to Mr. Moore's Chrysler. I don't know if you have ever had the pleasure, but moving a child safety seat from one vehicle to another is harder than rebuilding a tractor transmission in the dark, and it takes longer when your fingers are numb from the cold.

While I was learning to be a safety seat engineer, Bebe Palouse was getting an unexpected call from Calvin Millet. Bebe was not quite dressed and made up for work, but she has a phone on the wall next to her toilet, just like in Hollywood. After Calvin identified himself, she said, "Good morning to you, too. It's early. To what do I owe the pleasure?"

"You'll have to forgive me, Bebe. I had hoped to walk over to the store today to see you privately, but Clem called last night and insisted that I meet with you and the other governors of the Circle. That was the last open spot on my calendar for the rest of the week. Would it be okay if we talked personally on the phone?"

Bebe steeled herself for the third shoe. "We've known each other nearly two years, Calvin. What's on your mind?"

"Clem and I have decided to restructure the ownership of Millet's Department Store. I thought you should be the first to know."

She gulped and replied, "Is Clem selling out?"

"I can't answer that one way or the other, but I can say that forty-nine percent of the equity in the store is being put up for sale. The ownership of the other fifty-one percent will remain confidential to everyone but the new investor or investors."

"Okay, I guess. Do you have a buyer in hand?"

"We hope so. We'd like to offer the forty-nine percent to you."

Bebe plopped down on her toilet seat. That's why a woman always leaves it covered, because you never know when you'll need to plop. "To me?" she asked. "Forty-nine percent?"

"Yes."

"But I can't afford . . . How much will it cost?"

"We retained two independent consultants to appraise the store. The average values your forty-nine percent at 3.35 million dollars. We think it's a fair price."

"I agree, but I'm afraid it doesn't matter. I don't have that kind of money."

"Hardly anybody does, Bebe. That's why banks were invented. I'd be happy to set you up with Buford Pickett early next week. I'm sure he'll be amenable to making you a loan."

When you sit on Bebe's toilet, as I have on the odd occasion, you can talk on the phone and see yourself in the mirror at the same time. I never wanted to observe myself in that particular location, but there you have it. When Calvin called her that morning, Bebe said she looked like a deer caught in the headlights of an oncoming train. "Thank you," she replied. "It's a very nice offer, but totally unexpected. If you don't mind, I'd like to think about it before you set anything up with Buford. Will you be around in case I have a question or two?"

"I'm in meetings for the rest of the week, but leave a message on my cell phone. I'll get back to you as soon as I can."

After saying good-bye, Bebe hung up and stared at herself in the mirror for a while longer. When she felt like she had come to grips with Calvin's proposition, she picked up the phone again and called the store to say she would be late. Bebe never, ever missed work, but Thursday was a horse of a different hue—for a lot of folks.

FOR THE SECOND DAY in a row, Vernon Moore left the Come Again for the county courthouse with bag in hand. In this instance, it contained a copy of the *Sporting News*, baseball cards, a notepad, and a ballpoint pen. When he reached the downstairs watch desk, Luther Samoa said, "I'll have to check that sack, Mr. Moore. I can't have you sneaking a cordless jackhammer in to young Matt, or worse, another musical instrument."

"I give, Deputy. You have me. I brought some things that appear perfectly harmless to the untrained eye, but they're more dangerous than a banjo."

Luther peered inside the bag and asked, "Is that a ballpoint pen?"

"I picked it up last week in the British Secret Service surplus store down in Kansas City. Besides being a fine writing instrument, it contains a battery-powered laser with enough energy to cut through a foot-thick, cinder-block wall like whipped butter."

"You're a hoot, Mr. Moore. What about the rest of these things?"

"They're equally dangerous. You'd be wise to confiscate them."

"So there's nothing in here that you could make music with? No harmonica? No comb and paper or anything like that, right?"

"Not this time."

"I had to check," he said. "It's the rule. Can we leave the banjo at the watch desk today? Matt said he dreamed about it last night. It woke him up in a cold sweat."

According to Luther, Mr. Moore stuck out his lower lip. "Sure," he replied. "No problem. It can stay behind."

"Great. Let's go see how junior's doing."

On their way down the hall, Mr. Moore asked, "Did Matt eat his breakfast this morning?"

"Yeah. There was a lot of leftover batter so the other two inmates had waffles, but I had Cookie fix Matt a bowl of Frosted Flakes."

"That was charitable of you, Deputy Samoa. Thank you."

"You're welcome."

They found Matt brushing his teeth. He finished rinsing and remarked, "I have an electric toothbrush at home, but they won't let me have an electrical outlet in here."

"Perhaps you can have one at your next destination," Mr. Moore answered. "How are you doing?"

"Okay, I guess. I'm just bored." Matt looked for the banjo and appeared to be pleasantly relieved by its absence. "What's in the sack?" he asked.

Luther took up his customary position outside the cell. Mr. Moore handed the bag to Matt. "It's the latest issue of the *Sporting News*, as promised, with all the stats right up to the league championships."

"Cool. What's the rest of this stuff? Are these baseball cards?" Matt reached inside the bag and pulled out an inch-high stack of cards in a rubber band.

"I know they're for kids and old men, but I thought you might enjoy them."

"I can keep them?"

"You may. I have thousands more."

"Jeez. Thanks, Mr. Moore." My grandson flipped quickly through the cards. Puzzled, he commented, "Like, all these guys are white."

"Is that a good thing or a bad thing?"

"It's a bad thing. A lot of the best players are Latino and . . ."

Mr. Moore finished the sentence, ". . . Afro-American and Asian." He reached inside his coat pocket and pulled out a second, rubber-banded stack. "You got the right answer. Here's the rest of the cards. In total, they're the best players in the game today."

Matt nodded as he looked through the second set, one by one.

"As soon as you've had a quick riff, we need to get back to business. You'll have the rest of the morning after I'm gone."

Mr. Moore waited until Matt had put the baseball cards aside, then he said, "Do you remember the question I asked you yesterday afternoon?"

"Yeah. You asked me if it was okay to make a mistake."

"Right. Is it?"

Matt lowered his eyes and glanced at Luther before replying, "It seems to me that the answer is both yes and no."

Before he could say anything else, Mr. Moore replied, "That's exactly correct."

"It is?"

"Yes. The answer is both yes and no. The trick is knowing when it's okay to make a mistake and when it isn't. Did you think about that?"

Tentatively, Matt replied, "Y-yeah, but it's kinda hard, Mr. Moore. How can you know when it's okay to make a mistake?"

"Let's try an example. Suppose you're on a famous TV game show and you've just won a shot at the grand prize, a Chevrolet Corvette. You can pick from three doors, but the Corvette is behind only one of them. What are your odds of picking the right door?"

"That's easy. It's one in three."

"Right. So is it okay to make a mistake and pick the wrong door?"

"Duh, yeah. Like, the odds are against you."

"Right again, but is that why? What if there are six doors and a brand new Corvette is behind five of them? Is it still okay to make a mistake?"

"Yeah. It's luck, man. There's no way you can know ahead of time."

"Correct. Real life is a lot like *Let's Make a Deal*. You often have to make a decision even though you don't have perfect information. For instance, you can afford to buy one of three TVs. Which one will last the longest? You have three similar job offers. Which one will be the best over the long run? Two politicians are running for Congress, but they spend their campaigns attacking each other. Which one will be least inept in office?

"In real life, there are never enough facts. You have to supplement them with guesses. But when decisions are based on guesswork, mistakes are inevitable. Let's change the scenario slightly. A Corvette is behind one of three doors as before. You're unlucky; you guess door number two, which is empty. The producer takes pity on you and decides to let your brother Mark have a chance, but he picks door number two again. Is that okay?"

"No, man. That was bone dumb."

"Why?"

"Because he made the same mistake I made. It was way stupid."

"That's right. Smart people avoid repeating mistakes, not only their own but mistakes that others have made before them. Doesn't that make sense?"

"Yeah, but . . ."

"Yeah, but what?"

"Like, parents don't tell kids about a lot of the mistakes they made."

"That's true, but do you know why?"

"No."

"When you were born, how much experience did your parents have in child-rearing?"

"I'm the oldest. They had like none."

"It's an irony; isn't it? The majority of children are born to parents with very little experience or worse, none at all, so mistakes are inevitable. Then, when parents are finally savvy enough to raise children well, they're too old to have them. That's a cruel irony, isn't it?"

"I guess."

"By the time you were a teenager, weren't your parents smart enough to tell you not to smoke?"

"Yeah, but that's sorta what I mean. My dad smokes."

"Okay. You had conflicting input. It happens all the time. How did you resolve the conflict? Did you research the consequences?"

"What? Nobody does that."

"A smoking habit can cost more than a quarter million dollars, Matt, and knock four or more years off your life. Along the way, it makes you more vulnerable to a host of nasty diseases. Would a smart person spend two hundred and fifty thousand dollars to be sicker, die sooner, and have stinky breath? Is that a sensible purchase?"

"No-o. I guess not."

"It's not a guess. Smart people consider the consequences before they make important decisions. They avoid a lot of mistakes that way."

"Okay, so smoking was a dumb move."

"True, but don't be too hard on yourself. You were victimized by another cruel irony of Nature."

My grandson looked at Luther and said, "Another what?"

"Your teenage years are a unique time in your life, Matt. It's when you're permitted to make life-threatening decisions long before you're smart enough to make them. At the ripe old age of sixteen, for instance, you're allowed to operate a motorized, four-thousand-pound projectile that can travel at triple-digit speeds. Thousands of teenagers die every year because they do exactly that."

"Didn't you drive fast when you were a kid?"

"Yes, which meant what?"

"I dunno."

"It meant that I was repeating the mistakes of others. Was that smart?"

Matt didn't answer. Mr. Moore continued, "As a teenager, you're also allowed to torpedo the remaining eighty percent of your life by the simple expedient of screwing up in school for a few short years. Millions of teenagers seize that opportunity, too, even though millions before them have already made the same dull mistake. Do you know what a lot of those past teenagers are called today?"

"Underemployed?"

"Excellent answer. For the record, they're also called parents, which leads us to a third, cruel irony of Nature."

"What?"

"Teenagers are programmed to rebel against their parents. It's in our DNA, our hormones, or perhaps in an undiscovered location in the vast wasteland of the human brain. Ten thousand years ago, the instinct to rebel pushed our forbears to go forth from the caves and multiply, but there are billions of us now. We should be done multiplying, but the innate drive to rebel against our parents remains, and it has a certain logical consequence."

"Which is what?" a deep, booming voice asked.

Both Matt and Mr. Moore turned to look at Luther. He replied sheepishly, "I rebelled against my pa. I feel bad about it now. He wasn't such a bad guy."

Mr. Moore asked, "How, Deputy Samoa? What did you do?"

"I stayed out late. I stole the pickup and went joyriding a few times after he and Mom went to bed. I wouldn't do my chores. That kind of stuff."

"Were any of those things smart?"

"Nope."

"That's the irony. Most parents have gotten reasonably smart by the time their children are teenagers. Unfortunately, the easiest way to rebel against smart people is to do the opposite, which is what?"

Luther answered, "To be stupid."

Matt began to protest but Mr. Moore said, "Did your mother speak to you about the consequences of getting lousy grades in high school?"

My grandson the inmate sat back on his bunk, legs crossed. He answered, "Like a zillion times, yeah."

"Did you ever listen?"

"No."

"You were a classically stupid rebel. Congratulations. Did you talk to your mother about the probable consequences before you and your pals attacked the Bold Cut?"

"What? Like, no. Of course not."

"Did you research the consequences elsewhere? For instance, did you seek the advice of an expert arsonist?"

"No."

"Really? Why not?"

"Jeez. I don't know, Mr. Moore."

"Okay. Let's think about it. Where's the best place to find experienced arsonists?"

"On the Internet?"

"Not bad. Convicted felons are known to adore Internet chat rooms. But how could you be certain that the one you hooked up with was the genuine article? What if you happened instead on a bald, sixty-year-old tax accountant with an acne condition whose real purpose was to get a date with a cute, teenaged boy?"

In unison, Matt and Luther said, "Blecchh!"

"My sentiments exactly. Luckily, there's a much more reliable source."

"What? Where?"

"Any state or federal penitentiary. Do you suppose that's a clue? Do you suppose it tells us anything about a career in arson?"

Matt shook his head slowly as he answered, "I didn't think it out. I was the dumbest idiot on the face of the Earth."

"True. You stood with the titans of stupidity, but you're going to be smart from now on." Then Mr. Moore picked up the pace of the conversation. "Do smart people consider the consequences of their actions in advance?"

"Yeah."

"Do they repeat mistakes?"

"Like, no."

"Do they confuse fact and belief?"

"No."

"Did you think about any of that before you attacked the Bold Cut?"

"No."

"Was it even your idea?"

Matt began to speak but stopped himself.

Mr. Moore stood up abruptly. "I thought as much. That's enough for this morning."

"We're done?"

"Until the afternoon, yes we are."

Apparently, Matt had learned one lesson. "Cool. Like, what's the next question?"

"It's multiple choice. Are you ready?"

"I asked, didn't I?"

"Here it is: Is life a team sport, an individual sport, or both?"

Matt took the tablet and ballpoint pen out of the bag and wrote the question down. Then he said, "You don't want to talk about this now, do you?"

"That's right; I don't."

"Me, either. Thanks for the baseball stuff, Mr. Moore."

"You're more than welcome."

Matt didn't get up from his bunk. I guess it would have been too much to expect. Luther locked up and the two men walked quietly down the hall. As they passed one of the cells, the inmate said, "No more banjo?"

Mr. Moore answered, "No. Probably not."

"Gee. That's too bad. I don't suppose you've got a cigarette on you."

Luther stopped and turned to face his charge. Nothing more was said.

Chapter 24

Ten W. Forty

BECAUSE THE WEATHER was so awful, Mona and I dropped Mark off at school on our way to the hospital. If I wasn't sold on all-wheel drive by then, I was by the time we got to Beatrice. The roads were slicker than a Teflon skating rink, but Mr. Moore's Chrysler drove like it was on rails. It would have been nice if I had had all-wheel drive on my shoes, too. I slipped in the parking lot while I was getting Laverne out of her harness and ended up on my rump on the cold, wet ice. Just as I was getting ready to feel sorry for myself, Laverne stuck out her lower lip and said, "Owie?" Leave it to a child to turn the knob on your perspective.

Loretta beamed when Mona and Laverne flew into her room, me limping along behind. I don't want to dwell on it, but there was a lot of hugging and kissing and crying all around, especially the latter. That's an area where men could learn a thing or two from women. Crying is whole lot better than "what's up, dude?" in the same way that hugging is better than a handshake. It reveals the heart. That's why a woman can laugh and cry at the same time, and why I carry facial tissues most everywhere I go.

After we had wiped the tears from our eyes, Mona put Laverne on

Loretta's lap and we stepped back. Laverne beamed at her mother and said, "Mee-maw?" Under the circumstances, I thought it was a darned good deduction, and so did Loretta, who started crying all over again. After they had hugged and talked a bit, Mona chased Laverne around the room while I brought Loretta up to date on the local news. Naturally, Lo had lots of questions. It took me half an hour to cover Matt and Mr. Moore and the same again to tell her about the sale of the bank to NBP.

After an "uh oh," Mona took Laverne to the restroom to change her drawers and put some cornstarch on her tush. There's nothing better for little bottoms than plain old cornstarch right out of the box. As soon as they were gone, Loretta asked, "What's the board going to do about the bank, Wilma?"

"I don't know," I answered. "Lulu Tiller is on the warpath and Hail Mary Wade is looking into legal remedies. I expect that's next."

"But didn't Vern say that there's a third shoe? Didn't you just tell me that?"

"He said it was a theory, Loretta. He said there might even be a fourth shoe, but the board isn't in much of a mood for any more shoes."

"Forget them, honey. What do you think?"

"I don't know for sure. Mr. Moore had another proposal. I thought it was silly at first, but it's starting to grow on me."

I explained his proposition to Loretta. She shut her eyes for a few moments, then said, "That's an odd idea, but it would shake things up, wouldn't it? I'm usually in favor of shaking things up. Do you have a plan?"

"I may at that," I said. "I got it from vegetarians."

Loretta liked my idea but she tired quickly, so our visit was brief. Still, it did my heart so much good to see my best friend back among the living. Mona's, too. We were downright giddy on the way home. Even the weather was looking up. The snow and ice had turned to slush by the time we left the hospital, and a warming breeze was beginning to blow in from the southwest.

As soon as Mr. Moore's morning session with Matt was done, he walked upstairs to the duty desk and asked, "Would it be possible for me to stop in and see the county attorney, Deputy Melhuse?"

Pokie put in a call to Hail Mary's AA and then replied, "She's in a closed-door session with some lawyers from Lincoln for the rest of the day, but she said she could step out for a few minutes. Everybody seems real tense up there. Does it have to do with Matthew Breck, or is it about the bank?"

"I don't know. Should I go straight up?"

"You go ahead. I'll let the county prosecutor know you're coming."

As was his custom, Mr. Moore took the stairs to the third floor, where he was met by Mary's AA and ushered into her office. He was looking at the melting snow on the many roofs of the Angles House when she came in moments later.

Hail Mary can be brisk when she's in a hurry. "Hello, Vernon," she said. "How's Project Breck coming along?"

"We continue to make progress."

"Are you going to get him to name those other two boys?"

"I'm hopeful."

"You're hopeful? If I was that poor boy, I'd be digging the molars out of my gums with a fruit-baller. How can I help you today?"

"I understand that you're advising the Circle on their legal options with respect to the sale of Hayes County Bank."

"Forgive my bluntness, Vernon, but that's none of your business. My impression was that you were on the sidelines. Was that wrong?"

"Not exactly. I'd rather describe myself as an avid bystander. It's been my experience that civil litigation can be used to postpone almost anything in this country for an indefinite time. Is that your experience, too?"

"No, Vernon, it's not. If there's no case, the court will throw it out."

"Does that happen to you very often?"

"It hasn't happened to me since my second year out of law school. When I take a case to court, it sticks."

"Do you always win?"

"I win a lot more than I lose, but I always get heard, win, lose, or draw. My opponent always knows he's been in a fight."

"I don't doubt it for a minute, Mary. Have you taken the time to consider what might happen if you take Clem Tucker to court, win, lose, or draw?"

"What do you mean, Vernon?"

"Clem is in a bind. Virtually all of the family's wealth is tied up in the local bank. If the sale is held up by litigation, what do you think he'll do? What would you do?"

"I don't get what you mean. If I'm Clem Tucker, I fight."

"I'd fight too, but I'd also explore alternatives. The bank's value is in its loan portfolio. Instead of fighting in the courts indefinitely, I might package the loans into bundles and put them up for sale. It's a common, everyday business strategy. A thousand banks and investment institutions could be interested—in Nebraska, elsewhere in the United States, even in Europe and Asia."

"Maybe, but then the bank would be worth much less than it is now."

"Exactly. Once the loans had been sold off, I'd probably have to close the bank and hope that a neighboring institution would put a few ATMs in Ebb. For sure, no large, metropolitan bank would be interested anymore."

"What about the bank's deposits?"

"The depositors would have to shift their accounts to an out-of-town bank."

Mary became pensive, then said, "I think I get the picture, Vernon. Are there any other options you might consider?"

"I don't know. I'm not a banker. As a businessman, though, there is one option I wouldn't consider, under any circumstances."

"Which would be . . . ?"

"The current situation; the status quo. As the sole owner of Hayes County Bank, the Tucker Trust has too many eggs in one basket. Too much of its wealth is tied up in the local bank. No matter what you and the Circle do, Clem can't allow the existing situation to continue."

Hail Mary pursed her lips and said, "There are two very expensive lawyers in my conference room. I have to get back to them, but will you do me a favor? Will you call me if you have any more ideas?"

"I will. Thank you for your time."

"You're more than welcome. I hear that Loretta came out of her coma last night. We're all very happy for her. For you, too."

"Thank you. The odds were against her. She's very lucky."

"That's not what I heard. I heard that you were there. I heard that you took Doc Wiley with you, in the middle of the night, smack in the middle of the snowstorm."

"It was a lucky coincidence, Mary. That's all."

"After all this time, that's one heck of a coincidence, Vernon. When you see Loretta, please give her my very best. I'm thrilled that she's back. We all are."

MR. MOORE PLACED a call to Bebe Palouse when he got down to the main floor of the courthouse. She was still at home, half dressed and half not, trying to figure out if fortune or calamity had landed on her doorstep.

Mr. Moore said, "I don't believe we've been introduced, Ms. Palouse, but I thought I should give you a call while I'm in town."

"It's nice to hear from you, Mr. Moore. I know you by reputation; everyone does. And I heard that Loretta came out of her coma last night. You must be very happy."

"I am. She seems to be doing well."

"If you see her today, would you say hello for me? She's a good customer, a wonderful friend, and the heart of the Circle."

"I hope to see her this afternoon, Ms. Palouse. I'll do just that."

"Thank you. Now, how can I help you?"

"I was calling to ask if you had heard from Calvin Millet?"

Bebe froze. "Calvin? Why?"

"It was just a long shot, really. I thought he might call to offer you an equity position in the store, but I can see that I was wrong. I apologize for interrupting your busy day."

"Calvin hasn't called, Mr. Moore, but the day is still young. If I may ask, what did you expect him to offer me?"

"A minority position in Millet's, perhaps as much as forty-nine percent."

"That much? Why would he do that?"

"Clem appears to be divesting his local holdings, and in a precisely planned order. Millet's should be the last to go."

"So you believe that Calvin might offer me Clem's share?"

"I thought he might. I also thought the offer might put you in a bit of a bind."

"Really? How come?"

"I have some experience in the retail business, Ms. Palouse, and it looks to me like you've done an excellent job. Millet's is healthy now, which means that a large equity stake will be expensive. Not many people have that kind of cash lying around. There's the bank, of course, but that's a lot of debt to load on a pair of young, single shoulders. On the other hand, you might have a unique opportunity."

"What, Mr. Moore?"

"It doesn't really matter, does it? Calvin didn't call."

Bebe replied, "It's not even eleven a.m. Most of the day is still ahead of us. You said I might have a unique opportunity. I'd appreciate it if you would tell me what it might be."

"It's an outlandish idea. I'm almost embarrassed to tell you about it. If I do, you have to promise you won't tell anyone else."

"It's a deal. I swear on a stack of Bibles."

"Fair enough. If Calvin does call with an equity proposal, I thought you might turn around and offer some of it to the Circle. It would take some negotiation, but the Circle could end up owning a significant defensive position in Millet's. That's a lot of ifs, though. It might not be worth the trouble, even if you're given the opportunity."

Bebe didn't answer. Mr. Moore said, "I'm sorry to waste your time, Ms. Palouse. If Calvin calls, I hope you won't take my idea too seriously."

She replied, "Now I know why Wilma Porter calls you her unusual lodger, Mr. Moore. It is an outlandish idea, but I appreciate it anyway. And do give my best to Loretta."

As soon as she got off the phone with Mr. Moore, Bebe put a call in to Lulu Tiller. "Where are you?" Bebe asked.

Lulu whispered, "Lily, Dottie, and I are sitting in the lobby on the top floor of the bank waiting for Calvin Millet. I thought you weren't feeling well. Are you on your way over?"

"No. We need to talk right away, but not there."

"Our meeting is set to start in a few minutes, Bebe. Can I call you back?"

"That wouldn't be wise. I need you to cancel your visit with Calvin immediately and convene an emergency meeting of the board of governors."

"Another emergency meeting? We have a general session tomorrow morning."

"You'll need to cancel that, too, Lulu. We're not ready."

"Can you hold on for a minute? I have a another call coming in."

Bebe paced around her kitchen while she waited for Lulu to get back on the line. After a small eternity, Lulu said, "That was Hail Mary. She asked me to call an emergency meeting of the board of governors, too. This afternoon. Are you two in cahoots?"

"No. Did she say what it was about?"

"Not in so many words, but it may have to do with legal issues. Why?"

"I was just curious. Did she say anything else?"

"Yes. She said that I should postpone the meeting with Calvin."

"Things seem to be happening quickly, Lulu. It could be a very bad time to confront either Calvin Millet or Clem Tucker. You need to get out of the bank, and then we need to get over to the Abattoir and compare notes."

Lulu replied, "I'll discuss the matter with Lily and Dottie and let you know what we decide."

"Don't discuss it, Lulu. You're the Queen Bee. Make the decision now, while I'm on the phone."

LATER THAT MORNING, Calvin called Clem from a speakerphone in the bank conference room. Buford Pickett, the new general manager of the Hayes County subsidiary of the National Bank of the Plains, was also there. The three men rattled on about the weather for a bit, then Calvin said, "Before we get into business, you should know that Loretta Parsons woke up last night."

"She did?" Clem replied. "That's terrific! She's one hell of a woman, and I haven't had a decent haircut in months. When did she come to?"

"Late last night."

Buford added, "Vernon Moore and Hank Wiley were there at the time."

"Is that so? Did they revive her?"

"Maybe, Mr. Tucker. Lots of people think it was Mr. Moore. It's pretty spooky."

"You worry me sometimes, Buford. Let's just be thankful she's back and stay away from the spooky shit, okay? How did your meeting with the Circle board of busybodies go?"

Buford added, "There's something else you need to know, Mr. Tucker, and it's pretty spooky, too."

"Can it wait for just a minute? I apologize for playing the prick of the day, but I'm up to my armpits in alligators right now. How did the goddamn meeting go, Calvin?"

"They canceled. Lulu, Dottie, and Lily were sitting in the waiting area right outside my office, but they asked for a rain check just minutes before we were supposed to meet."

"Is that a fact? Did Lulu say why?"

"She said that Bebe was under the weather and Wilma was up at the hospital, so she didn't have a quorum."

"She didn't have a quorum? For a business meeting?"

"Yep."

"Well, you have to give her a bonus point for creativity. Did you say that Bebe wasn't there?"

"Yes."

"That could be interesting. I take it you got through to her this morning?"

"I did, yes."

"Was she thrilled?"

"She seemed more shocked than anything."

"What did she say? Does she want the deal or not?"

"I think she does, Clem. She's worried about the cost, though."

"Did you tell her that Buford will loan her the money?"

"Yessir, but . . ."

"But what? If necessary, I'll cosign the loan."

"She was blindsided, Clem. She didn't see it coming. My guess is that she needs some time to deal with the shock."

"When are you planning to call her back?"

"If I'm right, it won't do us any good until next week."

"Next week? That long? Why?"

"The offer's on the table, but it's a lot of money. We're not going to get the result we want if we push Bebe too hard. How are things up there?"

Clem grumbled and replied, "Burt Nettles is a slippery, goddamned piece of work. If truth in labeling laws applied to people, his name would be Ten W. Forty."

"I take it he's resisting your proposal."

"You could say that, but Fabi and I have him cornered. I have to get back in there. You had something urgent you wanted to tell me, Buford. What is it?"

"The state patrol called, Mr. Tucker. They have some preliminary results on Mr. Moore's fingerprint identification."

"Did you clue Calvin in on this?"

"Yessir."

"Okay. Go ahead."

"They've run Mr. Moore's prints against a number of federal, state, and municipal data bases. So far, they've found four matches."

"Would you repeat that, Buford? They found what?"

"They've found four matches, Mr. Tucker."

"I'm sorry. It sounded like you said four matches. That can't be right, can it?"

"That's what they said, sir."

"Does that mean they've found four different people with identical fingerprints? How the hell can that be?"

"They wouldn't say, sir. They seem pretty confused, too."

"Are they still looking?"

"Yessir. The analyst said they were about halfway done."

"Halfway? How many goddamned matches do they need?"

"I have no idea, sir, but I thought you'd want to know."

"Calvin, what's your opinion of all this?"

"I think you should be careful what you ask for, Clem."

Clem replied, "Is that a fact? I haven't had this much fun since I stole my father's pink Lincoln when I was fourteen years old."

Chapter 25

The Temple Ranch

WHEN MR. MOORE EXITED the county courthouse that afternoon, he found Clem's black Cadillac limousine waiting in the handicapped spot at the foot of the steps. John Smith was leaning against the front, passenger-side quarter panel reading a book, but he jumped to when Mr. Moore approached.

Mr. Moore surveyed the location of the car and frowned.

John opened the rear door and offered, "Mr. Tucker always has me park here. If a handicapped person ever comes, I'm supposed to move it."

"Doesn't the sheriff ticket you?"

"Never has, sir."

"Why don't we ride together up front?" Mr. Moore said. "It'll be easier to talk." Before John could respond, my unusual lodger was settling himself into the front passenger seat.

John came around to the driver side, got in, fiddled with the electric side mirrors for a moment, and turned the ignition. As he pulled away, he said, "Last night it snowed flakes the size of poker chips. Now the snow has practically disappeared and there's a warm front blowing in from the southwest. Some guys in my old outfit warned me about the weather in this part of the country. I should have listened. When that much warm air hits this much cold air, sparks will fly. Large sparks."

"Have you heard today's weather report?"

"Yes, sir. They're predicting thunderstorms: heavy rain; high winds; lightning; maybe hail. It's nearly November. Is hail even legal this time of year?"

"Apparently, weather in Nebraska is like pharmaceuticals in the Netherlands: everything is legal whether it's dangerous or not. Did they mention when the storm would hit?"

John turned onto State Highway 4 and answered, "All they said was sometime this afternoon. Judging from the size of that front, I'd say it's going to be sooner rather than later."

The clouds to the west were as tall, dark, and bulbous as they had been the day before, but they were brown instead of purple. In Nebraska, the clouds are color-coded for the convenience of the farming community: white is nice; gray is usually good but sometimes so-so; brown and purple can be bad. If the big brown clouds, which are warm fronts from the southwest, ever run into the big purple ones, which are cold fronts out of the north, it can be very, very bad.

Mr. Moore inquired, "Do you think we can get to the Divine Temple and back before the front hits town?"

"I don't know. How long do you intend to spend with Earl Gault?"

"An hour, maybe less."

"That'll give us a chance. It's not my place, but how did you get him to see you?"

My unusual lodger smiled and replied, "I just asked. It's something

I learned as a salesman. If you ask, it's remarkable how often people will say yes."

Before John could comment, his riding companion got a call on his cell phone. He said, "Vernon Moore speaking."

"Vernon, this is Clem Tucker. How the hell are you?"

"I'm fine. How are you? How is Omaha?"

"We're fighting tooth and nail up here. I haven't had so much fun since I snuck into the girls' locker room when I was in eighth grade. Hoo whee! That was too much for a country boy to see; I can tell you that. Are you en route to the Divine Temple?"

"As we speak. I have an appointment with Reverend Gault in about twenty minutes."

"Well, be careful. I wouldn't trust that son of a bitch any further than I could throw his ox. If you don't mind, I've taken a precautionary step. I asked Dottie to have one of her deputies meet you at the Temple Ranch gate. I know you don't need the help, but John can have a hard time backing down. It's that military training of his. He still believes he's invincible, even though he's getting a little long in the tooth for all that martial arts crap."

"I appreciate the thought, Clem. Is that why you called?"

"Partly. I also heard that Loretta woke up last night. My source says it was an abetted miracle, meaning a mysterious character brought her out of it."

Mr. Moore started to object but Clem went on. "Don't give it another thought, Vernon. Coincidences happen every day. Have you heard the latest about Millet's?"

"No, I haven't."

"Well, Calvin and I just offered Bebe Palouse damn near half the store. You'd think she'd be doing cartwheels, but Calvin says she's in shock. Why would she do that?"

"Who knows? Maybe it's the amount of money involved."

"The bank will loan her the money. What's the problem?"

"That would be a lot of debt for a young, independent woman to take on. And it would handcuff her to the store indefinitely."

"I might have thought about the handcuff part myself, but wouldn't you take the deal? The annual dividend distribution will more than cover the burden. We're offering her equity, a board seat, and the chance to make a boatload of money."

"Well, a boatload of money will turn most heads, even a boatload of nickels. I'm sure she'll give the deal careful consideration."

"That's why I called, Vernon. Would you do me a small favor? Would you talk to her?"

"I don't know her. We've never been introduced."

"Did you know Earl Gault? Did you know me when you first came to town? Hell, when did not knowing anybody ever stop you from stirring the pot?"

"Why me? Can't Calvin talk to her?"

"It's a small favor. It wouldn't take more than thirty minutes of your time. Buy her a burger at the Corn Palace. I'll pick up the tab."

Mr. Moore sighed and replied, "The last time I got involved in one of your business deals, it didn't work out exactly the way you'd planned. Do you want to run that risk again?"

"Hell, Vernon, I'm counting on it. I don't give a shit how Bebe does it. I don't care if she uses food stamps. I just want her to take a significant minority position in the store. Will you at least give it some consideration?"

"I'll think about, yes."

"Let me know what she says. How's Matt coming along?"

"We seem to be headed in the right direction."

"That's good to hear but the clock is ticking. Is he going to plea down?"

"It's too soon to tell."

"Well, don't let Loretta distract you too much. She can be a helluva distracting woman, but your top priority is to get that boy to cop a plea so he has a particle of a future left. I can count on you, can't I?"

"Clem, I've never heard you so wound up. You're not on a new kind of medication, are you?"

"Hell no. I'm jazzed on adrenaline; I'm in the hunt. I have the target in my sights and my finger is itchy on the trigger. If everything goes according to plan, I'll have a brand-new trophy for my dining-hall wall tomorrow afternoon. In the meantime, I need you to sort out Matt Breck and Bebe Palouse. Remember what I said about that Gault character, too."

"I will, Clem. Thanks for calling."

After they had hung up, John inquired, "Was that the boss?"

"Yes."

"With news?"

"No. He was calling to say he cared."

John looked in the rearview mirror. "He's not the only one. We have a county mounty coming up on our six."

"Don't worry. She's backup. She'll park at the gate and wait for us."

"For us. Did you do that?"

"No. Your boss did. Like I said: He cares."

JUST BEFORE THEY REACHED the county line, John turned left onto the kind of hard, flat gravel road that connects so many of the farms to the highways in our state. A half mile later, the men came up on a wide, ironwork gate that opened at the middle. The words "Temple Ranch" ran across the top of it. There was a small, white placard to the right of the entrance, the sort you might see on the sidewalk in front of a small city restaurant. In large, red, handwritten letters, it read, "Welcome, Mr. Moore."

John said, "Isn't that special? They didn't put out a sign for me."

"I'm touched," Mr. Moore replied.

The sheriff's deputy stopped outside the gate. John turned and proceeded through, where they were met by two men in cowboy hats who had been waiting inside a muddy white pickup truck. The driver waved and pulled onto the dirt road in front of them. A rifle rack was visible through the rear window. It must've been for spiritual guns.

John followed, but he stayed back so the pickup didn't throw mud on the limousine. A few minutes later, he pulled into a parking space perpendicular to a large, circular, asphalt driveway. A faded, frayed American flag flew high over the center of the circle, its wire cable clanging in a slow, semi-rhythm against the metal pole. According to John, the only other sound was a brisk southwesterly breeze.

Directly in front of John and Mr. Moore was the Divine Temple of the Everlasting God Almighty. It was a rectangular, redbrick building covered by a steeply angled white roof with six leaded glass clerestory windows on each side. Near the edge of the roof, directly above the main entrance, was a twelve-foot cross plated in chrome that blazed in the sunlight.

The pickup parked on the opposite side of the driveway. Its occupants, both of whom were dressed like old-time cowboys down to the red bandanas around their necks, walked over to where John had parked the limousine. Before he could exit the car, the taller one spit some tobacco juice on the tarmac and said, "That's a real nice set of wheels, Mr. Smith, but I wouldn't park it here if I was you. On a day like today, the afternoon sun will hit the reverend's cross just right and the reflection will cook a dashboard crispy brown in no time at all. If you park on the other side of the circle like we did, you won't have any problems."

The shorter cowboy opened the passenger-side door and said, "Welcome to the Temple Ranch, Mr. Moore. Reverend Gault is on his way out to meet you. You can wait here while Mr. Tucker's man parks the limousine over there."

Mr. Moore exited the car and used the moment to soak in the local color, of which there was very nearly none. There wasn't a tree or a bush in sight. The fields were muddy brown and peppered with the broken, dried stalks of alfalfa and corn that the harvesting machines leave behind. Save the church, every building in sight was painted white: several houses, what seemed to be a school or meeting place nearby, long fence lines, and a horse barn on a distant ridge.

After John had moved the limousine, Earl and Evelyn Gault emerged from the Divine Temple. The reverend was a barrel-chested man in his late forties, balding, with black curly hair on the sides and a full moustache. He was wearing a long white robe over a white, buttoned-down shirt, blue jeans, and white, silver-toed cowboy boots. His wife, a tall, ample woman in her thirties, was wearing a gray, ankle-length dress with a white cotton bib and a lace-trimmed bonnet covered her hair. Both were smiling.

The Reverend Gault stuck out his hand and said, "Welcome to God's little acre, Mr. Moore. I'm so pleased you could visit with us, today. You already met Mike and Gabe, there. They're the O'Rourke boys from Arkansas. This here is my wife, Evelyn. Like me, she hails from Texas."

Mr. Moore shook hands and replied, "The pleasure is mine. Thank you for meeting with me today."

"No sir, the privilege is ours. I take it from your manner of speech that you're not from around these parts, but there's a hint of somethin' southern in your tone. Are you a country boy by birth?"

"Yes and no."

"Well, a little country is better than none. We don't have much occasion to drive over to Ebb these days, but I hear that you're some kind of local legend over there. Some say you're close to God. Is that true?"

"To tell the truth, Reverend, I don't know if we're close to God, if He's close to us, or neither of the above. He's a mystery to me."

"Isn't that a fact? He's a mystery to us all. I know you've come to chat a bit, but would you like to accompany Evelyn and me on a little tour of the ranch first? It won't take but a minute or two. Afterward, we'll come back to the Temple for a sit-down."

"What about John, my driver? May he come with us?"

"It depends, Mr. Moore. Does he have an ax to grind, or he is just here to cover your back?"

"He's company, Reverend. He has no agenda of his own."

"Then bring him along, but I'd appreciate it if you'd have a chat with him first. He got a little confrontational with a few of my boys the last time he was here, so I had to have him escorted off the ranch. That's not the sort of thing a man of God likes to do, but I insist on a sociable temperament. I hope you understand."

"I do and I agree," Mr. Moore replied. He excused himself and went across the circle to have a brief conversation with John, then they returned together and followed the reverend and his wife down the sidewalk toward one of the outbuildings behind the church. As they walked along, the reverend turned his head sideways and said, "I hear that you were followed by a deputy sheriff. Do you usually get a police escort?'

Mr. Moore replied, "Not as a rule, no."

"Was it something you asked for?"

"No. I'm as surprised as you are."

"Oh, I wouldn't say I was surprised. That particular deputy cruises by the ranch all the time. I just wondered if she was more interested in you or me this time."

Mr. Moore shook his head. "It's another mystery," he replied.

Mrs. Gault repeated, "Isn't that a fact?"

The reverend stopped at a small, white-washed fence next to a one-level building that looked like a school. He rested his forearms on the top of the fence and said, "Do you now what this is, Mr. Moore?"

"It looks like some sort of corral."

"That's exactly what it is. We teach our children to ride as soon as they can walk. That across the way is the schoolhouse. Besides traditional schooling and education in the scriptures, every child on the Temple Ranch learns how to ride a horse, drive a tractor, milk a cow, and hoe a row by the age of ten. Like the Good Book says, "It is good for a man that he bear the yoke in his youth."

"Where are the children now?"

"They're home having lunch. That's an advantage of having a school so close by. But if the weather holds, they'll all be out here or over at the milk barn come this afternoon."

"Do your children go to school year-round?"

"Somebody told me you were good at asking questions, Mr. Moore, but I'd say you were just this side of psychic. Our children attend school eleven months out of the year, and we think that's the way it should be. Unfortunately, our opinion isn't shared by the U.S. government. Millions of children who are at the peak of their intellectual curiosity have to waste upwards of three months out of twelve on video games, television, troublemaking, and who knows what else? No wonder we have so many problems with our youth. Isn't that right, Eve?"

Mrs. Gault answered, "It is, honeybunch. That's why we've decided to launch the Temple Ranch Summer Camp for God's Children. For up to eight weeks at a time, we're going to allow right-minded parents to send their children here for a summer school of scripture and good, old-fashioned farm work."

"That's interesting. Will the coming summer be your first session?"

The reverend answered, "We ran a two-week prototype this last August for ten boys and girls. It went real well. This summer, we plan to lengthen the program to four weeks and expand to twenty children, maybe more."

Eve added, "We've listed our program on our new Web site. The Internet is such a revelation. Thirteen children have already signed up. We may have to turn some away come springtime, and that would be too sad for words."

The reverend and his wife began to walk again. Mr. Moore asked as they went along, "Do all of the temple's children attend school here at the ranch? I thought you sent your teenagers to high school in Ebb."

"As the Book of Psalms says, Mr. Moore, they're a 'stubborn and rebellious generation.' No matter what we want, we have to expose our children to the outside world sooner or later. At least there are rules in high school. There's a start time and an end time, and plenty to learn in between."

"So you allow your children to associate with outsiders."

"No, Mr. Moore. We invite our older children to mix with other boys and girls, and we open our hearts to them if they want to visit us here. It's God's way. Don't you agree?"

"I do, Mrs. Gault. How many families reside at Temple Ranch now?"

She opened her mouth to respond but Earl Gault said instead, "It's nice you're interested, but that's not a question we like to answer. Some of the families who've joined our ministry came from sad, unwholesome situations. All they want is to be left alone in the service of the Lord, but the sheriff is poking around here all the time. There isn't a religious leader in the country who doesn't remember Waco or Ruby Ridge."

"Waco? Ruby Ridge? Why are they significant to you?"

"Because they were calamitous examples of unlawful government intervention. All those people wanted was to be left alone. That's all we want, too, but we won't repeat their mistake. Whenever John Law calls, I remind my people of Proverbs 25, verse 21: 'If thine enemy be hungry, give him food to eat; and if he be thirsty, give him water to drink.'"

"That's touching. I'll have to read up on my Proverbs. Is your community growing?"

"God-fearing people don't have many places to go anymore, Mr. Moore. We have a waiting list."

"A waiting list?"

"That's right. Families and individual adults of majority age can apply to join the Divine Temple of the Everlasting God Almighty on the Internet. Regrettably, we can only take a few each year so we have a waiting list."

"Do you check out the applicants before you let them in?"

"It's the Age of Instant Gratification, Mr. Moore, the Quick Fix. The world is chock full of freeloaders and half-believers looking for a no-sweat road to the Promised Land. This here is a ranch. We sweat every day in the service of the Almighty, so we don't have a choice; we check everybody out."

"Forgive my indelicacy, but is wealth ever a factor in your decision?"

The Reverend Gault opened his arms and spun around in a circle, as if he was doing a pirouette in slow motion. "Look around you, Mr. Moore. What we have created is a highly productive farming and ranching operation covering just this side of eight thousand acres. Next year, I'll open the doors of the church to families in the surrounding area. The year after that, we'll open a retail arts and crafts operation on the Internet. In three or four years, we'll be at ten thousand acres or more and running one of the largest summer camps west of the Mississippi River.

"The book of Genesis says, 'The Lord made all that he did to prosper at His hand.' We believe that prospering is the natural result of hard work, as long as it's done in the service of the Lord. Isn't that right, Eve?"

"It is, Earl."

He gave her a squeeze around the waist. "Thou art all fair, my love, and there is no spot on thee. Thy neck is like a tower of ivory."

"I am fearfully and wonderfully made," she replied.

The reverend said to Mr. Moore, "We need to head back to church now. Mr. Tucker's man can come along, but it'll just be the three of us. Evelyn teaches reading and the culinary arts to the children in the elementary school. She'll be needed there real soon."

Chapter 26

Chapters and Verses

JOHN HELD THE DOOR while Mr. Moore and the Reverend Earl Gault entered the side entrance of the Divine Temple of the Everlasting God Almighty. It opened to a crimson-carpeted walkway between the stage and the front row of pews, which were cushioned, also in crimson. An elevated pulpit was on the far side, beyond an ornate organ and a stone, waist-high, baptizing bowl. Gray, faux stone tablets with the hymns of the day were hung high on each wall.

The reverend waved his hand toward the front pew and said, "Why don't we all sit down and rest our weary souls?"

John chose to remain standing near the side exit. Mr. Moore sat in the second row. An array of Bibles and hymnals were shelved in the back of the front pew. He picked up a Bible, the King James version, and leafed through it as he said, "These pews are actually comfortable. That doesn't coincide with my memories as a young man."

"The service of the Lord is discomfort enough, Mr. Moore. The pain should be in the heart, not in the sacroiliac."

"Especially when there are cows to be milked and rows to be hoed?"

"Amen, brother. The youths shall bear the yoke so that old men can drive the tractors and pay the bills. You know, I find the book you have in your hands to be a constant well of inspiration. It tells me everything I need to know about the spiritual life. Have you studied it?"

Mr. Moore closed the Bible and put it back on the shelf. "No. I've read it but it would be unfair to say I've studied it."

"Then you're informed if not a scholar. The book of Psalms says, 'The fear of the Lord is the beginning of wisdom.' I believe that. Do you?"

"No. I can't believe that an infinitely powerful God would either need or want to be feared. I believe that curiosity and courage are the forebears of wisdom."

"Okay then. If we can't talk as one God-fearing man to another, maybe we can talk as one curious man to another. You had a purpose for coming out here; I had a purpose for seeing you. Do you want to start, or should I?"

"Why don't you?"

The reverend glanced briefly at John and then asked, "I hear you were in the room when Loretta Parsons woke up last night. Is that true?"

"Yes."

"How is she? Is she well?"

"She seems to be in remarkably good shape."

"As long as we're speaking man-to-man, her shape was never in question, but I'm glad to hear it's been preserved. How is her mind?"

"Her considerable faculties seem to be intact with one exception: she has no memory of the attack on her salon. I suppose it was the trauma. According to the doctor, any recollection she might have had has probably been blotted out for good."

"I wouldn't be surprised. The subconscious mind can be a blessing sometimes. I hear you're staying at Wilma Porter's bed and breakfast and you've been spending a lot of time with her grandson, Matt Breck. May I ask why?"

Mr. Moore frowned. "You seem to have heard a lot about little old me, Reverend."

"Until the Big Buyback, you were the main topic of conversation at the Bold Cut. After that, it was Clem Tucker. He stole your thunder."

"Well, good for him."

"Like Mr. Tucker, you have a reputation for getting into other people's business, which is why I was asking about Matthew Breck. He's to be sentenced on Monday. I don't see what you could be doing down there. I hear you've even been takin' a banjo along."

"My musical arrangements with Matt are a family matter, Reverend Gault, therefore confidential." After a brief lull, Mr. Moore continued, "If I may ask, did you know Loretta Parsons personally?"

The reverend changed positions on the front pew. "She cut my hair on a few occasions. Did a fine job, too."

"Why did you stop going?"

"Cash money, Mr. Moore. The Bold Cut was a small luxury for a few of my men, but it became a financial burden when all my parishioners started goin' there for manicures and pedicures and such as that. Last year, I sent two of my own to a school in Wichita so they could learn the art of cutting hair. They're pretty good at it now. If the Bold Cut doesn't reopen, I might start up a salon right here on the ranch."

"Do you have a theory about what happened that night?"

"Not much of one. It was Homecoming at the high school and the

Bold Cut had a certain, salacious reputation. Some disappointed schoolboys with alcohol in their bellies probably had sexual mischief on their minds. It was hot blood boiled over by bad spirits, plain and simple. Isn't that what you believe?"

"No. My theory is more sinister than yours. I believe that Matt Breck fell victim to a malevolent and very adult controller with some sort of perverted justice on his mind. Skillful controllers can be extraordinarily dangerous and Matt was an exceptionally soft target: young; unsure of himself; angry at his mother for breaking up his family; desperate to be a part of something, possibly even a cult; blind to consequences, as most teenagers are."

"Woo-wee! It sounds to me like you're a fan of conspiracy theory. I bet you believe that Lee Harvey Oswald didn't act alone."

"He didn't. He was the patsy, too."

"Is that so? Then I suppose you think I'm this godless controller you're talking about. Is that why you came out here?"

"Matthew Breck spent a lot of time with your sons, Reverend Gault. I just wanted to see what he found at the Temple Ranch."

"We're simple, God-fearing people, Mr. Moore. If that's what Matthew Breck was looking for, then that's what he found on my ranch, and that's all."

"I have just one last question, Reverend."

"Fire away."

"Do you speak to God personally?"

"Of course I do. I'm a man of the cloth."

"Does he talk back to you?"

"He does. He chose my path; he guides me down it."

"Really? Over the course of my lifetime, I've known a dozen men who made the same claim, but not one of them ever put Him on the speakerphone."

"On the speakerphone? What does that mean?"

"For the benefit of your parishioners. When God speaks to you, do you ever put Him on the speakerphone so they can hear, too?"

The reverend stood up and said, "I know what I wanted to know, Mr. Moore. You may have a scripture or two, but you're no man of God."

"I never said I was. I don't have the courage to make an assertion like that."

"Well, I do, and I am not a man to be trifled with. I have resources beyond your imagination. When you get home, you may want to read the Gospel of Saint Matthew. Verse ten of chapter three says, 'Now also the axe is laid unto the root of trees: therefore every tree which bringeth not forth good fruit is hewn down, and cast into fire.'"

"That sounds like a warning. Is it?"

"It's a forewarning, Mr. Moore. Leave me and mine alone and I'll leave you and yours alone. Make sure Mr. Tucker's man does the same thing. That's all I ask."

The reverend turned and began to walk down the aisle. Mr. Moore stood up, smiled at John, and looked around slowly. After a second or two, the two men followed their host through the thick, double doors that opened to the circular drive. The breeze had stiffened into a southwesterly wind and the sun had disappeared behind tall, darkening clouds. As they walked toward the limousine, the hat flew off the head of one of the O'Rourke boys of Arkansas, sending him off in pursuit, and the reverend's white robe flapped in the speeding air like a single, spasmodic wing.

When they reached the limousine, Reverend Gault said, "I want to thank you for coming, Mr. Moore. It was a very informative visit."

John Smith opened the passenger-side door. Mr. Moore put one foot inside the car, then he paused and replied, "You were also helpful, and kind enough to leave me with a departing quotation. I'd be a poor guest if I didn't have one for you, too."

"That's fair. You go right ahead."

"Proverbs, 22:7. Do you recall it?"

"I can't say as I do. What does it say?"

" 'The rich ruleth over the poor, and the borrower is servant to the lender.' "

"The borrower is what? Are you under the impression that I owe you something?"

"Not at all. Enjoy the day." Mr. Moore got in the car and closed the door. John drove away without another word.

Later on, I asked John what the reverend and his wife were like. He said they were night and day. Evelyn smelled of expensive perfume, but he had never met another man, inside the military or out, who smelled as much of raw testosterone as the Reverend Earl Gault.

That was his answer. It was all about smells.

Chapter 27

....

Slaughterhouse Three

MONA DROPPED ME OFF at the Abattoir on the way back from the hospital, which meant that I was early for our daily emergency meeting. I had nothing else to do so I fixed the coffee and sat myself down at the elliptical table in Old Jenkins' office to watch the storm roll in from the southwest.

I don't know why, but the phrase "under the weather" popped into my mind. I've heard it a hundred times, but it confuses me to this day. People say they're under the weather when they feel ill, but they never say they're over the weather when they feel good. Of course, the only people who ever get to be over the weather in a physical sense are astronauts. The rest of us are under it all the time, whether we feel good or not. The saying makes no sense at all.

Lily Park Pickett came into the room about ten minutes after I did. You can always tell she's coming because she turns on every light in sight. She's not alone. A lot of women who had restraining orders against former boyfriends or ex-husbands have lost their fondness of the dark.

Lily and I were chatting about Loretta's miraculous recovery when Bebe, Dottie, and Hail Mary came into the room talking about the

weather. I looked out the window and saw that it had started to sprin-
kle, which meant that Lulu would be late. Her backyard is surrounded by a tall chain-link fence so she can let the socially amenable
animals outside, but she has to reel them all back in when it starts to
rain or snow, except for the alpacas. Buzz Busby built a tin-roofed
shed for them in the rear corner of the yard. It's sort of like a flow-
through mini-barn with hay on the floor. The alpacas wander in
whenever they feel like it, rain or shine. They have interesting faces;
like camels, but without the stress.

Lulu came running into the conference room a few minutes late
wearing a raincoat and carrying a furled umbrella. Everybody else already had coffee and we had beaten the weather to death, so we were
chomping at the bit. Lulu got herself settled as quickly as she could
and said, still out of breath, "I don't know how I ever thought I could
be a veterinarian and Queen Bee at the same time. If I say I'm going
to run for reelection, Wilma, I want you to have me forcibly re-
strained. Will you do that for me?"

"You said that last year, Lulu," I replied.

"I know, but I'm serious this time. The dogs are real put out with
me today. We were supposed to have a seminar on owner care this afternoon, but I had to cancel it because of the meeting here at the
Abattoir. Now they're sulking in the mini-barn and the alpacas are
standing out in the rain. I think we're having too many emergency
meetings, don't you?"

"I couldn't agree more. I should be at the hospital with Loretta
right now. I bet that everybody here would rather be somewhere else."

The other girls nodded and Lulu asked, "How is Loretta, dear?"

Dottie added, "Yes. How is she? Will she be up for a chat later
on?"

"Mona, Laverne, and I were at the hospital almost all morning," I answered. "Her voice is weak and squeaky, but her appetite has improved and her color is a whole lot better. She sent her love to everybody at the Circle and said she'd be back on her feet in no time at all."

Lily Park Pickett touched the back of her hair, which was in need of a cut, and asked, "What does Doc Wiley say?"

"This morning he said her blood pressure was back down to where it belonged and everything else checked out A-okay. He said it's a miracle."

"Did he mean a miracle miracle, or a Vernon Moore miracle?"

"I don't know, Lily," I answered. "I was afraid to ask."

Lulu has a perfect last name; she likes to keep her hand on the tiller. She said, "I'm tickled pink that Loretta is on the road to recovery, but we have work to do. Both Hail Mary and Bebe asked for an emergency meeting today. Which one of you two would like to start off?"

Bebe spoke up first. "Calvin Millet called me this morning."

Lulu said, "And . . . ?"

She could hardly hold herself back. "He offered to sell me forty-nine percent of the store. Can you believe it?"

I practically jumped out of my various undergarments. "He what? He offered you that much?"

"He did at that," she said. "I had no idea it was coming."

Bebe recounted her five-minute call with Calvin Millet three times, then Lily Park Pickett said, "We're all so pleased. What do you plan to do? Have you decided?"

"I thought about it a lot this morning and there's no way that I can afford to purchase the entire forty-nine percent unless I borrow myself to the hilt," Bebe replied. "No disrespect, Lily, but the thought of borrowing that kind of money from your husband gives me the willies."

"Don't worry yourself for a minute. Anybody who borrowed that much from Buford would have to be a salted nut-ball. But what else can you do?"

"Well, I could get back to Calvin and say I'm interested, but in a somewhat smaller stake. There are two problems with that though: the first is that Calvin might say no and my big chance would be gone; the second is that he might say yes and then sell the rest to an assault weapons manufacturer in New Jersey."

"That would scare me, too," I said.

"But what if I bought some part of the forty-nine percent, say half, and the Circle bought the rest? It would take some negotiating, but the Circle would have a say in the running of the store. I might even be able get two board seats: one for me and one for the reigning Queen Bee."

"Would that be a paying position?" Lulu asked.

"It would have to be negotiated but it often is."

"Who else would be on the board?"

"I don't know, Lulu. I would expect that Calvin Millet would be the chairman and there would be three or four others."

"Would one of them be Clem Tucker?"

"Maybe, but my guess is that Clem is getting out, just like you said."

Lulu turned to Hail Mary. "What's your take on this? Would we have to reincorporate as a for-profit outfit?"

"I doubt it. Lots of not-for-profit institutions have investment port-folios, universities for example, but I'm no expert in corporate law. I'd have to have the matter researched."

"Are you worried about having to pay taxes, Lulu?" Lily asked. "Is that why you asked?"

"Yes," Lulu answered. "I'm against it in principle."

Lily never got a college degree, but she was Calvin Millet's right-hand man for years. Even though she's a full-time mom now, she still has one of the best financial minds in the Circle. She said, "Don't worry. If we convert the Circle to a for-profit corporation, we would have to pay taxes only if we made a profit. That shouldn't be much of a problem."

"Whoa, Lily," Dottie interjected. "Haven't we made money almost every year?"

"To be precise, we've generated a surplus almost every year. It's perfectly okay for a legitimate not-for-profit to make a surplus almost all the time because there's no tax liability, but that's not what a for-profit company wants to do. If we change our status, we would want to avoid making a profit. Either that, or we'd have to pay both federal and state income taxes."

"I'm a simple public servant," Dottie said. "Let me see if I heard you right. As long as we're a not-for-profit company, it's okay for us to make money hand over fist. But the moment we become a for-profit company, we need to start losing money. Is that what you just said?"

"There are a lot of nuances but that's basically it, Dot."

Dottie shook her head. "No wonder this country is so screwed up. That's the stupidest, backwardest thing I've ever heard."

Lulu ran her own business. She said, "Well, it makes perfect sense to me. When do you have to get back to Calvin with a decision, Bebe?"

"I can't call him back until the Circle decides whether it wants to become an investor in Millet's or not. Until then, I won't know what to say."

Lulu turned to Lily. "Can we afford that kind of money?"

Lily asked, "How much are we looking at, Bebe?"

"Two million dollars, give or take."

"That would put a lot of pressure on the treasury, Lulu, but we could swing it. We'd probably borrow some of the money ourselves."

"From Buford?"

"Who else?"

Lulu said, "Mary, how long will it take you and your team to research the legalities?"

"A week, two, worst-case."

"That long?"

"It's a complicated issue, Lulu, and the cost of error could be high. We need to be on sound legal footing before we go forward with this."

Lulu sighed. "That's a fair point. But before we start looking down the barrel of a two-million-dollar investment, I better ask if we're even interested in Bebe's proposition. The floor is open."

Dottie said, "We don't need any discussion, Lulu. We all want to do it. Just ask for a show of hands. I propose that the Circle become a minority owner in Millet's Department Store, contingent on all the stuff that Lily and Mary are talking about. Is there a second?"

Lily's hand shot up. "I second the motion," she said.

Lulu asked, "All in favor?"

It was a slam dunk; five to zero. Then we agreed that we wouldn't disclose the opportunity to the general membership until our ducks were in a row. Otherwise, we would just get everybody's hopes up.

After Lily had recorded all of the to-do's, Lulu said, "You asked for an emergency meeting, too, Mary. What's your topic?"

"As you all know, my team has been looking for a way to stop the Big Sellout. The first thing I'm going to tell you is that Clem Tucker is on firm ground. As far as we've been able to determine, the sale of a rural Nebraska bank to a national bank domiciled in-state has never been overturned by either the state banking department or the Federal Reserve. It doesn't happen."

"Are you saying that we should throw in the towel?"

"No I'm not, Lulu. What I'm saying is that the deck is stacked against us. I'm also saying that I would have a very hard time spending public money on this case. If there were any obvious grounds to suspect fraud, that would be another matter, but there aren't any."

Dottie asked "What about all the trouble that NBP is in? That looks pretty fraudulent."

"I agree, but the focus of the investigation is on the CEO, not the bank itself. Have you checked NBP's stock price lately?"

"No. Checking on stocks isn't part of my regular routine. Why?"

"It's been going up. That wouldn't be a normal indicator that the bank is in trouble."

"What are you trying to tell us, Mary?"

"We need to rethink the whole proposition."

"What? Yesterday, we were all ready to draw and quarter Clem Tucker in the town square. Now you're saying we should back off? Why in the Sam Hell should we do that?"

"Suppose the sale falls through, Dottie. It doesn't matter why; just suppose it does. What do you think Clem would do next?"

"I don't know. I suppose he'd go off and shoot some poor, endangered critter."

"And what would he do after that? Do you think he'd sit in his chair and rotate, or do you suppose he'd go out and find himself another buyer, or worse?"

"Or worse? What could be worse?" Lulu asked.

"Let your imagination run wild. He could sell the bank to a foreign investor who can't speak English and hates corn. Or he could bundle up all the real-estate loans the bank has and sell them to outside investors. If he did, the bank would be gutted. There would be very little reason to keep it open."

Dottie summed up with her usual eloquence. "Shit!"

Lulu jumped right in. "He couldn't do that, could he? It sounds illegal."

"It's garden-variety business behavior. Loans are bundled up and sold on the open market every day. If HCB's loans were sold, the bank would be an empty shell with a marginal retail operation. Do you seriously believe that Clem Tucker would keep it open after that?"

Lulu scratched her elbow and said, "Can we take a break? I need to pee."

We all took a few minutes to powder our noses, clear our heads, and refill our coffee cups. Nobody wanted to talk about the bank, so we talked about the weather some more. It was getting worse.

When we reconvened, Lulu turned to Mary and asked, "Will you net this out for us, dear?"

"Yes. Unless the investigation of the NBP's CEO turns up something juicy, any legal objection to the acquisition of HCB looks like a fool's errand. But we should be more worried about what happens if the deal falls through. From where I sit, Clem's alternatives are pretty ugly."

"So we're the ones who should sit and rotate. Is that what you're saying?"

"No. My recommendation is that we keep one eye on the investigation at NBP and the other on Clem Tucker. If the deal gets in trouble, though, I may end up recommending that we support it at the state banking department's hearing in six months."

"Support it? Is that what you just said?"

"It's a bird in the hand, Lulu. If Clem loses the deal, we'll have no way to influence what he'll do next; no way at all. He could turn the bank into a car wash and we'd be left holding the hose."

Lulu began to scratch some body part below the table. Judging from the altitude of her chin, which was level with the table, I'd say it was her ankle. Nobody said anything until I stuck up my hand and offered, "Excuse me. I may have a little idea of my own."

Lulu stopped scratching and said, "What, Wilma?"

"Well, it's not really my idea," I replied. "It came up in a conversation I had with Mr. Moore. He said that Clem Tucker is no longer our enemy, but in the next breath he implied that Clem could be more dangerous now than ever."

"Why?" Dottie asked.

"He has all his money in stocks and bonds now. He doesn't have anything to manage anymore but the Trust, except that Calvin does that, so Clem has nothing to do."

Lulu said, "That's the scariest thing I've heard since the invasion of those African bees. What did Mr. Moore say?"

I didn't see any reason to beat around the bush. "He suggested that we invite Clem Tucker to join the Circle."

"He said what?"

"That's just how I reacted, Lulu, but then the idea is growing on me."

Dottie sat forward and said slowly, "We have never allowed one man to set foot in the Abattoir, Wilma, except to fix something that broke. The Circle is still as virginal as Mary herself. Now you want to open it up to men? I don't believe it."

"Not men, Dottie. I think we should make a one-time chicken exception."

"A one-time what?" Lulu inquired.

"How many of our members are practicing vegetarians? Fifteen? Twenty?"

"I don't know, Wilma. Does it matter?"

"Not really. What matters is that some of our vegetarians make one exception: they eat chicken. That's what the Circle should do: we should make an exception. We should allow one of our members to be a man: Clem Tucker."

Dottie Hrnicek said, "I wish to correct myself. I thought all that for-profit, not-for-profit bullshit was the stupidest thing I ever heard, but inviting Clem Tucker to join the Circle takes the cake. No disrespect, Wilma, but it's the brand-new stupidest thing I ever heard."

Bless Lily Park Pickett's heart. She sat back in her chair and commented, "It could be a mistake to dismiss Wilma's idea out of hand. We'd have to exclude Clem from certain events, Chippendale Night for instance, but otherwise we'd have him on the inside, surrounded by women. There's a certain irony to that. What's the worse thing that could happen?"

We talked about Mr. Moore's proposition long enough for three clear positions to develop: I was on the pro side with Lily; Bebe and Hail Mary were on the fence; Lulu and Dottie were dead set against it.

The stress of three unexpected propositions began to get to Lulu. She was scratching a thigh with one hand and a knee with the other. "Let me see if I have this right," she said. "As a result of this meeting, we're going to consider investing in Millet's Department Store, we're going to consider supporting Clement Tucker if the HCB deal gets in trouble, and we're going to consider making a one-time 'chicken exception' so that he can join the Circle. Did I leave anything out?"

I smiled and answered, "That's it. Won't it be fun?"

Dottie said, "Is it too late to tape record this meeting? I'd like to listen to it in my dotage."

Lulu wasn't amused. "What do we tell the membership? We can't drag them in here tomorrow just to say we're researching three issues that will change the Circle forever, but we can't put any of them to a vote yet because they're all so unbelievably bizarre."

"Postpone the meeting," Dottie said. "Send everybody an email saying that there's been some exciting new developments, but we have to do more research before we can go to the general membership with any recommendations."

"I don't know," Lulu countered. "That sounds like ten gallons of horseshit in a five-gallon bucket to me."

Lily stuck up her hand. "Me, too. I second Dot's motion."

It was raining sheets when we left the building, so Dottie gave me and Hail Mary a lift in her patrol car. I sat by myself in the back, behind the thick, Plexiglas divider. I'd like to say it was fun, but all I could think about was my grandson. He had ridden to jail in the very same car, and I bet it wasn't fun for one minute.

Chapter 28

A Team Event

DEPUTY SALEVASAOSAMOA WAS WAITING at the watch desk when a drenched Mr. Moore descended the stairs, leaving wet, fully-formed footprints on every step. "Did you take a shower in your clothes," Luther asked, "or is it raining like the devil outside?"

Mr. Moore shook his head like a dog shakes his body after a bath. "I sprinted from a parked car up the courthouse steps. What's that? Ten yards? I'm soaked."

"Yeah. Welcome to Nebraska, where Lucifer himself is the weatherman. Come back next spring and you can two-step with a tornado. Can I get you a towel or something?"

"Thanks. I'll be fine." Mr. Moore took off his dripping jacket and asked, "Is there someplace I can hang this?"

"I'll take care of it," Luther answered. "What's on the agenda for young Matt this afternoon?"

"If you don't mind, I'd like to change the scene. Would it be okay if we moved the conversation to the visiting room?"

"I don't see why not. Nobody's visiting my other two guests, but if somebody comes, we'll have to go back to his cell. Okay?"

"Yes, of course."

Deputy Giant hung Mr. Moore's wet blazer on a coat hook and led him into the visiting room, which is to the left of the corridor about ten feet down from the watch desk. It's a square, windowless room with lime green walls, as in Three Mile Island green. They may glow in the dark. There are three card tables in the room, each with two or three unpadded, metal folding chairs: some rusty brown, some dark green, some rusty chrome, all creaky. The doors to the women's and men's restrooms are to the right of the entrance. The pop machine, which is red and white and the closest thing to an art form in the whole jail, is to the left.

Mr. Moore made himself comfortable at the table furthest from the entrance. Luther brought my grandson in a few minutes later. "You want a soda, junior?" Luther asked. "It's on the house."

Matt said, "I'll take anything but a Dr Pepper. Okay?" Then he looked at Mr. Moore. "What happened to you? The wet look is way over, man."

"It's raining outside. Floods haven't been ruled out."

"Floods? Cool. They'll have to move me to higher ground."

"They have at least one other option, Matt. Think it through before you wish for a flood. How was lunch today?"

"Chipped beef on biscuits. The gravy was white and runny, like snot. It was yummy."

"Would you rather have . . ."

"Naw, Mr. Moore. I don't want any more waffles."

Deputy Samoa gave my grandson a 7-Up and sat down at the table closest to the exit. Matt sat opposite Mr. Moore, who then said, "I left you with a question this morning. Do you remember it?"

"Yeah. You asked me if life was an individual event, a team event, or both. That's it, just like you asked."

"What's your answer?"

Matt took a long swig from his soda and replied confidently, "It's both of the above.'"

Mr. Moore settled back. "Both of the above? Okay. Tell me what you do alone."

"Jeez, Mr. Moore. I sleep alone; I brush my teeth alone. I do everything alone now. When I was in school, I studied by myself and took tests on my own. Sometimes, I went outside and had a cigarette by myself, too."

"So having a cigarette was an example of an individual event?"

"Yeah. Sometimes I just wanted to be alone and have a smoke."

"Did you grow the tobacco?"

"What? No. Why?"

"I'm curious. Did you cure it?"

"The tobacco? Like no."

"Did you manufacture the cigarette?"

"No.

"How about the lighter?"

"I didn't make that either. So what?"

"Indulge me for a few moments, Matt. Did you earn the money for your cigarettes, or did you get it somewhere else?"

"I got an allowance, Mr. Moore. I never took money from anybody."

"I didn't assume you did. Tell me, were you naked when you smoked?"

Matt pushed back from the table but he glanced at Deputy Giant, who was listening intently. He kept his seat and answered, "Was I what?"

"It's a simple question. Were you naked when you smoked?"

"No. No way. That would be nuts."

"So you were dressed. Good call. Did you make the clothes yourself?"

"No. Of course not."

"Did you make the money to pay for them?"

"This is starting to get pretty stupid, Mr. Moore. I was a kid. My mom paid for my clothes."

"Okay. Let's summarize: other people grew and cured the tobacco; other people manufactured the cigarette; others made the lighter; others provided you with the clothes you were wearing; and others gave you the money to buy everything. Is that about it?"

Matt squirmed in his chair.

Mr. Moore said, "Exactly. You may smoke a cigarette by yourself, but it's only the last, small act in a long series of team events. But smart people don't generalize from the particular; that's for politicians. We need a second example. Pick another of your individual events."

"Like what?"

"It doesn't matter. Didn't you say that you took tests alone?"

"Yeah. Like, who doesn't? It's cheating otherwise."

"Okay, but who wrote the textbook and who published it? Who built the school and made the desk? Who made the pencil and paper? Who created the test and graded it? How did you get to school? If a vehicle was involved, who made it and who sold it? Who washed and ironed your clothes? Who made your breakfast that morning? Who made the soap you used to shower with? Who manufactured the showerhead? How did the water get to your house and why was it hot? Who built the house? Who . . . ?"

"I get it, okay."

"If you get it, then what's the right answer to the question?"

"Life is a team event."

"Is it partially a team event, or is it completely a team event?"

Matt grinned and answered, "I pick my nose alone."

"Do you? You're a teenager. You've survived because of years and years of grueling, thankless team effort by your parents, grandparents, teachers, coaches, and doctors, just to name a few. Otherwise, you wouldn't have a nose to pick or a finger to pick it with. Do we need more examples, or have you grasped the basic concept now?"

"Okay, Mr. Moore. I get it."

"Fair enough. If you really do get it, then you're ready for a little inferential thinking."

Matt looked at Luther before replying, "I don't even know what it is."

"It's something else smart people do. You're a smart kid; you'll get the hang of it. Are you ready?"

"No."

"Let's take a stab at it anyway. If everything we do is a team event, we're on teams all the time. Isn't that right?"

"Yeah. I guess so."

"No guessing, Matt. When you were having a smoke, you were on the tobacco team, the cigarette team, the lighter team, the clothing team, the family team, and a hundred other teams, all at once. Human life is nothing more than a continuing chain of team events. True or not?"

"I said I get it. True."

"Good. As you go through life, do you want to be on good teams or bad teams?"

Matt rolled his eyes and answered, "Duh. I want to be on good teams."

"Incisive answer, but here's the hard part: How do you tell the good teammates from the bad teammates?"

My grandson looked at Luther again, who shrugged.

Mr. Moore said, "If you were the captain of a baseball team, would you pick the best players you could?"

"Duh, yeah."

"Why?"

"So I could win. What else?"

"Are you sure? What if the best players were more interested in playing Frisbee than coming to practice? Would you win?"

"No. I'd get really pissed off."

"Another superb answer. The first requirement of picking good teammates is not how capable they are, it's whether you can trust them to work with you toward a common goal. Of all the people you've known in your many years of sentience, who can you trust the most?"

Matt had no answer. Mr. Moore asked, "How about a pro basketball player in a shoe commercial on TV? Can you trust him?"

"Jeez. I don't know. How can I know?"

"That's exactly right. You can't possibly know whether he's trustworthy or not. However, you can determine something of nearly equal importance. Does that basketball player have the same goal you have?"

"I don't get it, Mr. Moore. What do you want me to say?"

"I'm not trying to get you to say anything, Matt. I'm trying to get you to use your head. Do the professional athletes you see in TV commercials want you to have great shoes, or do they want something else?"

"Like what?"

"Like millions of dollars in endorsement fees. Do you even know if they wear the shoes they're promoting?"

"No."

"That's right. They get paid millions of dollars for one reason: to induce you and your peers to spend one hundred and eighty dollars for a forty-dollar pair of shoes. Is their goal the same as yours?"

"No."

"Then are they on your team?"

"I get it, okay. They're not on my team, but who cares? It's just a pair of shoes."

"Good point. We need a more pertinent example. How about your friends? Can you trust them?"

"Duh, yeah. They're my friends."

"Are you sure? What if they want you to torch the hair salon where your mother works? Do they have the same goal you have? Are they on your team?"

Matt sat back and crossed his arms. Mr. Moore said, "It's a simple question, Matt. You were part of a team that ransacked and burned the Bold Cut. Was that a shared goal, or did your teammates induce you to do something you desperately didn't want to do?"

Matt stood up and turned toward Deputy Samoa. "I'm done," he said. "Take me back to my cell."

Luther looked at Mr. Moore, who remained seated. In a slow, booming voice, he said, "Sit down, junior. You're done when Mr. Moore says you're done."

My grandson sat down reluctantly. "You keep bringing that night up, Mr. Moore. I don't want to go there. It's behind me. I need to move on."

"Fair enough. Let's fast forward to today. You're in jail because you were a classic teenage sucker. In an act of rebellion that traces back thousands of years, you rejected the two teams you could truly trust, your parents and your teachers. In their stead, you chose vicious, superficial friends and a malicious, manipulative, authority figure who cared nothing about you."

Matt didn't say anything. Mr. Moore continued, "Good teammates don't want you to do something destructive with them; they want to do something constructive with you. Good teammates don't hurt others; they help."

"I get the team thing, okay? I picked a lousy team."

"Are you sure? It's an uncertain world. Everything is constantly changing. Do you always know who your teammates are going to be?"

"What does that mean?"

"You're driving home from school one day when a dog runs into the road, causing you to swerve and smash into an oak tree at forty-five miles an hour. Your head lurches forward from the impact just as the airbag deploys, breaking every bone in your face. Do you want the first person on the scene to be the geeky kid you beat up during lunch hour?"

Matt didn't answer.

"What if you had picked the geeky kid to be on your volleyball team in PE that day? Would that singular gesture of kindness have cost you anything that mattered?"

Again there was no reply.

"You and a friend sit behind an old couple at the movies and taunt them until they leave in disgust. The next day you find out that they own the apartment complex where you live. Was that smart or stupid?"

Matt answered, "Stupid."

"Why?"

"Because you never know who's going to be on your team."

"So when is it smart to be callous and mean?"

"Never?"

"That's right, but why?"

"I don't know. Because I may need their help some day?"

"That's precisely it. From one minute to the next, you never know who you may need to be on your team." Mr. Moore paused, then added, "We're done for the day."

My grandson brightened up. "We're done?"

"For today, yes. Since you're smart now, you won't be surprised to learn that there's another question for tomorrow."

"Yeah. Okay. So what is it?"

"Is it better to be strong or weak?"

"Jeez. That's way simple. What's the second question?"

"How do you tell the difference?"

Matt was about to answer but Pokie Melhuse came running into the room and shouted, "Mr. Moore, you have to come to the phone! Right now!"

The color drained from his face. "Now?"

"I just got a call from Wilma Porter. She's at the hospital. Loretta Parsons stopped breathing. They're trying to bring her back but it's not working."

"What did you say?"

"Loretta stopped breathing. You have to come up to the duty phone!"

Chapter 29

We Are Struck Dumb

AT THE SAME EXACT time that Pokie was chasing down Mr. Moore, I was standing just outside Loretta's door while a doctor and three nurses tried to pump the life back into her. The doctor was stressed as could be—you could see the veins protruding from his neck—and the nurses were running all over hither and yon, trying to do this or that. It was such a horrid scene and I felt like such a helpless fool. My best friend was lying lifeless in her hospital bed, alarms were going off everywhere, and I was standing in the hall with a cell phone stuck in my ear, hoping against hope that I could talk to a biennial lodger.

Now, I know that I embellish from time to time, but I'm not at all comfortable with what happened next, and I'm not exaggerating one iota either. Pokie Melhuse was on the other end of the line at the very same time and she saw it all.

As soon as Mr. Moore heard the news about Loretta, he stood up without a word and walked deliberately out of the visiting room, Pokie in tow. In the same steady gait, he went up the steps and past the duty desk, where she grabbed his arm and said, "Mr. Moore, Wilma Porter is on the phone. Line two. She has to talk to you, right this minute."

Mr. Moore shook her off and continued through the door, across the marble foyer, and straight out of the courthouse into one of the heaviest October rainstorms in the history of southeast Nebraska. Pokie followed him but stopped under the eave just outside the door. The water drops were large and hard, like liquid ball bearings, and so dense that the wind was blowing them down the street in a succession of cold, gray waves, one after the other.

John Smith had parked the limousine in the handicapped spot at the base of the courthouse steps because he knew that Mr. Moore would need a ride home. When he saw Mr. Moore walking down the courthouse steps, he jumped out and opened the passenger-side door, but my lodger marched right past him and straight into the middle of the street, where he stopped, he looked up, and he shook his fist at the deluge. Then, in an angry, deep-throated voice, he screamed, "NO-O-O-O-O-O-O-O!!!!"

At the same, identical moment, a giant-sized lightning bolt struck Beatrice General Hospital, followed by an eardrum-piercing clap of thunder. A split second later, a wall of wind slammed into the side of the building with a WHUMP! so hard that you could feel the floor shift. And then the lights went out all at once, like they'd been doused by God.

In the dark, the doctor yelled, "Goddammit! What happened to the back-up system? I'm trying to save a woman's life!"

As if they were in casual conversation, Loretta answered, "Well, give yourself an A-plus, darlin', and get your cold, clammy hands off my chest."

The lights came back on a tick or two later. I guess the back-up system was working after all. My best friend was sitting up by then, humming and buttoning up the front of her PJs, and her hair was standing straight on end. The rest of us were as motionless as chess pieces, struck dumb by thunder, lightning, and Vernon L. Moore.

I kid you not.

Chapter 30

Tempo

MY LIFE WENT INTO some kind of holding pattern when Loretta was revived before my eyes. I could see her smiling sweetly, like the cat who had just swallowed a bird. I could see the doctor and nurses darting around the room like little fish in a bowl. I could hear Pokie Melhuse giving me the play-by-play description of Mr. Moore's rage against the rain, but I had stopped participating in the play myself. I had moved out-of-body; I had become a pure observer. For those few moments, I didn't even want a life of my own. I wanted to watch the drama unfold until the credits ran. I was especially interested in the credits.

Pokie snapped me out of my reverie when she said over the phone, "I have to go, Wilma. The rain hasn't let up, but Mr. Moore is still standing in the middle of the street in his shirtsleeves. If he doesn't get run over, he'll get killed by pneumonia."

"Loretta is breathing again," I replied.

"Loretta is what?"

I began to cry. "Loretta's fine, Pokie. Tell Mr. Moore. Tell him his work is done."

Pokie ran down the steps to help John Smith bundle Mr. Moore into the limousine. She told me later that he was soggier than a saturated sea otter but docile, like a small, sleepy child, even when he heard that Loretta was okay. John said he fell asleep on the way back to the Come Again, which is a three-minute ride by car. After they arrived, John helped Mr. Moore upstairs and waited while my unusual lodger showered and changed.

Meanwhile, I got my composure back and called nearly everybody, starting with my daughter Mona, then Lily Park Pickett and Lulu Tiller. I called Dottie and Hail Mary Wade too, but Pokie had beaten me to the punch, so I called my Hive next. By the time John Smith and Mr. Moore were back in the black limousine and headed to the hospital to see Loretta, I suspect that everybody in a hundred-mile radius of Ebb knew what had happened. The only exception was Buford Pickett, who was on the line with Clem Tucker when Lily tried to call.

"Buford?" my Fiancé in Perpetuity said. "What an unexpected surprise! Have you heard from Bebe Palouse? She should be calling to set up a meeting with you."

"No sir, Mr. Tucker. I phoned for a different reason altogether."

"Well, I don't have a lot of time. Whenever I get a minute to myself, some lawyer comes in here with the stupidest question you could imagine. Shoot. What have you got?"

"I just got another phone call from the state patrol, Mr. Tucker. They're extremely interested in talking to Vernon Moore."

"Well that shouldn't surprise you, Buford. How many people do you know with four fingerprint matches?"

"Seven."

"What did you say?"

"The number is up to seven, sir, and counting. They're expanding the search overseas. They're also sending a car down to pick up Mr. Moore. What do I tell them?"

There was no answer at the other end.

Buford said, "Sir? Are you still there?"

"Yes, goddammit! Is the car on its way?"

"Yessir. Do you want me to tell them something?"

"Did you give them his description?"

"Yessir."

"That's terrific. Did you tell them where he was staying?"

"Yessir. I did that, too."

"You're an upstanding citizen. I suppose you told them what kind of car he's driving."

"I did, Mr. Tucker. Everybody in town has seen that big white Hemi of his."

"Swell. That's just perfect. Do you have a pen and a piece of paper handy?"

"Yessir."

"Good. I'm going to tell you precisely what to do. There are to be no deviations. Do you understand?"

"Yessir, but . . ."

"There are to be no goddamned buts either. First, I want you to telephone the colonel at state police headquarters and have him call me on my cell phone immediately, and I mean right now. As soon as that's done, I want you to get on the line to John Smith and have him call me in thirty minutes. Not twenty-seven minutes, not thirty-two minutes; thirty minutes. Last, I want you to purge this tawdry little tale from your memory banks forever."

"I'm sorry, sir, I didn't mean to . . ."

"It's not your fault, Buford. I blame myself. I shouldn't have started a game I couldn't control at both ends of the board. Now the tempo is all wrong."

"The tempo, sir?"

"Make the calls, Buford. Leave me a voice mail when you're done."

BY THE TIME Mr. Moore and John Smith got to the hospital, there were fifty people either inside Loretta's room or milling around in the hallway. If we'd had a bar and a band, it would've been a cocktail party. Everybody was talking about the same topic: Loretta's shocking recovery.

Have you ever watched the conductor of an orchestra? He can be waving his wand all over the place and every instrument in the symphony can be making all kinds of music, but all of the musicians stop playing the instant the conductor drops the baton to his side. In the blink of an eye, you can hear a pin drop. That's how it was when Mr. Moore appeared. Everybody was talking and laughing and crying one second and the entire floor of the hospital was utterly silent the next. If we had been drinking champagne, wineglasses would've been falling to the floor like losing tickets at a racetrack. As it was, jaws dropped right and left.

The crowd parted like the Red Sea as Mr. Moore walked down the hall. When he got to me, he said, "How is she?"

"She's perfectly fine," I answered. "Her hair is a little frizzed and her tongue is black, but she says she feels a lot better than she did yesterday."

"Her tongue is black?"

"What did you expect? She got struck by lightning, but you need to talk to her yourself. She's been asking for you every two seconds since she woke up."

"I'd like to see her alone. I don't suppose you could help me."

Loretta's room was like an elevator full of strangers: jam-packed but silent as could be, and everybody was facing the door, meaning Mr. Moore and me. I said, "You won't need my help. Just go on in."

When Loretta saw Mr. Moore she said as loud as she could, "Everybody out!" He held the door while they all filed out of the room, including Lulu Tiller, Lily Park Pickett, Dottie Hrnicek, Hail Mary Wade, and my daughter Mona. On the way, Dot stopped and said, "If you don't mind, Vernon, I'd like a quick chat before I head back to town. Would that be all right?"

"Of course, Sheriff. Just give me fifteen minutes."

"Thanks. I'll be waiting in the hall."

After they were alone, Mr. Moore bent over and kissed Loretta gently. She said, "Look at my hair, Vern. I haven't had a natural since I was thirteen, and that was for a school play. And look at this." Loretta stuck out her tongue. It was pink on the bottom but black as anthracite on top. "It's sore and I can hardly taste a thing."

Mr. Moore sat on the edge of the bed and held her hand. "You're alive."

"I am. According to half the county, I have you to thank for it. Is that true or not?"

He rubbed his forehead and replied, "I don't have that kind of sway, Loretta."

"Then what were you doing in the rain in front of the courthouse?"

"You heard about that?"

"From Wilma, Mona, Dottie Hrnicek, and a dozen other women. What were you doing?"

"I was angry. I was complaining."

"Complaining? Why?"

"Because you, the mother of my child, were suddenly dead. In my mind, that merited a strongly worded complaint."

"That was so sweet, Vern." Loretta held out her arms. When Mr. Moore bent down, she hugged him and asked, "Was I really dead? I don't remember."

"I wasn't here at the time, but the report of your demise was unequivocal. Where's Doc Wiley?"

"He's around here somewhere. He went off to see the other doctors."

"How did he explain your revival?"

"He said you did it."

"No, he didn't. He couldn't have."

"He did, Vern. He was talking to me when he said it."

"That can't be right. There has to be a medical explanation. What did the attending doctor say?"

"He said it was the lightning bolt."

"Good. There you have it. You were struck by lightning."

"Everybody says you caused it, Vern."

"But I wasn't here, Lo. I was at the courthouse."

"That's not what I hear. Wilma said you were standing in the middle of the street in front of the courthouse, in the driving rain, yelling at God."

"At the same time the lightning struck? I didn't know that? How could you know that?"

"Pokie Melhuse was on the courthouse steps talking to Wilma, who was standing outside the door to my room. They were on the phone to each other at the time."

Mr. Moore didn't respond. Loretta said, "You didn't know, did you? You didn't know you brought me back."

Chapter 31

Mr. Moore Sets a Record

AFTER MR. MOORE HAD VISITED with Loretta for a while, Dottie hauled him off to the hospital café on the first floor. It's a postage stamp of a place run delicatessen-style by a Vietnamese American named Bobby Ho Gallagher. His father was an Air Force man with some kind of secret job and his mother was a Vietnamese translator. Wouldn't you know it? Bobby Ho makes the best corned beef sandwich in southeast Nebraska.

Dot and Mr. Moore got themselves some tea and sat off in a corner so they could be alone, relatively speaking. Like I said, it's a small place. Right off the bat, Dottie said, "Thanks for bringing her back, Mr. Moore. Ebb hasn't been Ebb since Loretta went down."

"I didn't . . ."

"Don't say another word. I'm a police officer. I know the evidence is circumstantial, but I have two eyewitness reports."

Mr. Moore began to speak, but Dottie said, "That's not why I wanted to talk, hon. I was hoping you could tell me about your visit at the Temple Ranch. My deputy says you were there for upwards of an hour. I take it you had a chance to interview the Reverend Gault."

"I also spoke with his wife, Evelyn. They gave me the cook's tour."

"Hmmm. That's better treatment than I ever got. We don't have much of a file on the missus. How did you read her?"

"Disingenuous: too sweet; too fond; too supportive."

"I'm a country girl, Vernon. I'd appreciate it if you would share your observations in simple, straightforward language."

"Fair enough. She plays the doting wife, but my guess is that she plays a significant role in the sect."

"Like the power behind the throne?"

"Maybe. The Reverend Gault can quote from the Bible at will, but he's more businessman than religious zealot. The question is, 'Who's the zealot?' It could be his wife."

"Evelyn? Are you sure?"

"Not at all."

"Do you believe that the Gaults were involved in the attack on the Bold Cut?"

"I don't have any evidence, Sheriff; just a belief, a theory."

Dottie shot forward in her seat. "Well, I have a theory, too, Vernon. It was Matt's friends, the Gault twins. Is your theory the same as mine?"

"I can't say."

"Why not?"

"Because the finger has to be pointed by Matt Breck. When the accusation comes from him, it will carry the weight of fact."

Dottie sat back. "If it comes from him. We're almost out of time."

"One way or another, Sheriff, you'll know by Saturday. In the meantime, I'd appreciate it if you could keep a close eye on Earl Gault. He said something near the end of our visit that was troubling."

"What was that?"

"When I asked him how he would react to a visit from your office, he said he would never repeat the mistakes that were made at Waco and Ruby Ridge. He quoted Proverbs: 'If thine enemy be hungry, give him bread to eat; and if he be thirsty, give him water to drink.' "

"You said he's a pragmatist, hon. That sounds pretty pragmatic to me."

"The Reverend Gault is an expert on the scriptures, Dottie, but he omitted the next verse."

"Which is what?"

" 'For thou shall heap coals of fire upon his head.' "

"Uh oh."

"Yeah. Uh oh."

MR. MOORE GOT A call on his cell phone as he and Dottie were leaving the café. It was from Clem, who said, "You'll have to forgive me for bypassing the usual niceties, Vernon, but I'm up to my eyeballs in lawyers and I'm running out of hours in the day. Have you got a second?"

"Two calls in one day, Clem? What can I do to help you?"

"The shoe's on the other foot this time. I need to know where your car is. I believe it's a Chrysler, a white Hemi sedan. Is that right?"

"It is, and it's somewhere in the Beatrice General parking lot. I loaned it to Wilma and Mona so I don't know where it's parked. Why do you ask?"

"I just got off the phone with John Smith. He figures you're going to be at the hospital for another hour or two. Is that right?"

"Yes."

"Good. I don't have time to explain, but a couple of my people are on the way to the hospital right now to steal your car. I'd appreciate it if you could give them at least an hour to get it done."

Mr. Moore excused himself and stepped into a men's restroom. "Steal my car?"

"Yep. It has to be done right away, and you won't be able to report it missing either."

"Why not?"

"Let's just say I'm doing you a favor."

"A favor? By stealing my car? Does this have anything to do with that fingerprint analysis you requested?"

"You know about that? How in the hell . . . ?"

"It was an interesting idea. What have they found?"

"I'd rather not answer that, Vernon."

"I'd rather not have my car stolen, either. What did they find, Clem?"

Clem hesitated before answering, "So far, they've found nine matches going back to 1954. At least that's what they say."

"Nine? Wow! Where did they find them all?"

"Federal, state, and local databases all over the country. Apparently it's something of a state record—by a margin of eight."

"I'm surprised myself."

"Apparently, so are they. The state patrol wanted to talk to you tonight but I told them you left for Denver earlier in the day. Now they have an APB out for you across Interstate 80 to the Colorado border. My people will take your car south to the Kansas line and they'll stay off the state highways."

"Will I get it back?"

"I'm afraid not, Vernon. Cars don't come back from where yours is going, but I'll buy you a new one. Or would you rather trade up to a Cadillac? I've got an in with a dealer down in Kansas City."

"That's a fair offer, Clem. I'd like to think about it."

"Well, you're about to be sans wheels so don't think about it for too long. Before I let you go, did you have a chance to talk to Bebe Palouse?"

"No. I've been a little busy."

"So I hear. John Smith tells me that you brought Loretta Parsons back from the dead this afternoon. Is that true?"

"I doubt it."

"Did I hear you right? Did you just say you doubted it?"

"I did, yes."

"Jesus Christ, Vernon. What the hell is going on down there?"

DOC WILEY THREW EVERYBODY out of Loretta's room at eight p.m. that night so that she could get her rest. I can't remember being so happy and so tuckered out all at once, except for the birthing of my girls, of course. To everybody's surprise, John Smith was waiting for us in the parking lot. He told us that Mr. Moore's car had been struck by an inebriated, fifteen-year-old driving a stolen pickup truck, so he had had it towed off to Lincoln to be repaired. Mr. Moore didn't seem upset, even though his car was brand-new. To be fair, though, he never seemed to get too upset about anything much—except for the temporary demise of the mother of his child.

John drove us all home in Clem's black Cadillac limousine. Mr. Moore sat in the back with me; Mona sat up front. John put up the black glass divider so I have no idea what they talked about. Mr. Moore fell asleep.

After we got home, I quick-thawed some of my spaghetti reserve for everybody while Mona went to Virgie's to pick up Laverne. It was the wrong side of midnight by the time John left for Omaha and the rest of us crawled into bed. Before I drifted off, I prayed to God that no one would come to visit the next day because my kitchen was a disaster.

I guess He wasn't listening.

At around three a.m., the smell of burning wood woke me up. By the time I got my robe and slippers on, Mona was headed down the stairs with Laverne, Mr. Moore was calling 911, and little Mark had gone up to the third floor to fetch Clara. When we got outside, we saw my grand oak tree, the one that's more than 150 years old, burning up in huge, red-orange flames and millions of tiny sparks that disappeared into the night sky.

That old tree was forty yards from the front edge of my porte-cochere, but the fire was so hot that Mona, Laverne, and I had to move around to the side of the house. Mr. Moore, Mark, and Clara joined us just a minute or two before the two county fire trucks arrived. Clara was wearing an orange-colored, fire-retardant suit, just like a real fireman. When you're a rich recluse, I guess you have time to consider the contingencies.

Fire fighting is one of the few professions in Ebb that is still dominated by the male of the species. It's not that women wouldn't like to play cards all day and run through walls into raging infernos at night, but men have a better physique for the latter. Once the firemen got themselves hooked up to the hydrant by the road, it took only a few minutes to put out the fire. But my oak tree had already burned down to a leafless, charred remnant of its former self, which broke my heart. When I said as much to Mr. Moore, he replied, "It was my fault, Wilma. I thought the reverend was speaking metaphorically, but he was being very specific."

Mr. Moore had made another mistake.

Chapter 32

The Axe Is Laid unto the Root

LITTLE LAVERNE WAS WIDE awake and ready to boogie at six thirty the next morning. I felt like something the cat dragged in myself, as did Mona, so we determined who had to get up with the baby in the usual way: by rock, scissors, paper. Naturally, I lost, so I threw on an old blue terry cloth robe and struggled down the stairs to my dirty kitchen with a giggling Laverne under one arm and a basketful of laundry under the other.

Mr. Moore came down the back stairs into my kitchen just a smidge before eight a.m. I figured he'd be just as haggard as I was, but he was showered, shaved, and dressed in a navy sweater, pressed blue jeans, and tan walking boots that looked brand new. I was more depressed than the market for Russian rubles myself, but Mr. Moore never said a word about my poor tree or my distressing appearance. He just kissed me on my cheek, and then he pulled Laverne out of her high chair and gave her a huge hug.

After he was done squeezing, Mr. Moore put Laverne back in her chair and took over the feeding chores while I plugged the kettle in. The next thing we knew, there was a "wham, wham" from the front door knocker, followed by, "Wilma? Are you up and about? It's Dottie Hrnicek."

Dot is not one to wait for folks to open the door, friendly or otherwise. She just lets herself in, like she has a warrant to search the place.

"We're in the back," I yelled.

A few seconds later, the Hayes County sheriff moseyed into my kitchen, where she stopped and looked me over. "Oh my! I'm so sorry, Wilma," she said. "I didn't know you were caught in the fire last night. Did you file a ten twenty-three?"

I'm so dumb. "What's a ten twenty-three?" I asked.

"An incinerated hairdo report. If you don't file one, the insurance company won't cover the damage."

That came from a woman who has her hair cut like a man, who has bigger biceps than most men, and who acts more male than half the men in town. Before I could reply, she said, "Hello, Vernon. Hello, Laverne; you're such a cutie-pie. You don't look like somebody set your hair on fire. Where's your other momma?"

"Mona's still in bed," I answered.

"Rock, scissors, paper?" Dottie asked.

"I went with scissors," I answered flatly. "Sit down and I'll make you a nice cup of chamomile tea."

"Thanks a lot, Wilma, but I'd rather drink dandelion wine out of a cardboard box."

"I know, dear. I've seen you."

Dottie seated herself at the opposite end of the table from Mr. Moore and inhaled deeply. "Is that coffee I smell?" she asked.

"It is, but it's only for the nice people. Are you going to be nice for the rest of the morning?"

Dottie ran her index finger down the butt of her pistol. "Don't force me to resort to harsh measures, Wilma. I'm an officer of the law. All I want is a cup of black coffee and a few minutes with you and Vernon."

"What's up?" I asked while I poured.

"What's up? Loretta died and came back to life last night, and then somebody murdered your oak."

Before I could say anything in response, Mr. Moore asked, "Did you find any evidence at the scene, Sheriff?"

"Which scene, hon: the hospital or Wilma's tree?"

"The tree."

"That's what I came to talk about. We have enough to know it was an act of vandalism. An accelerant was used, probably kerosene, and the tree was spiked before the fire was set. Even if it had survived the fire, the poor thing would've starved to death."

"Mr. Moore knows who did it," I offered.

"No, I don't," he replied. "I have a suspicion, but that's all."

"Do you think it was the Gault boys?" Dottie asked.

"I can't say that, but Earl Gault warned me yesterday. If I hadn't been so thickheaded, I might have prevented it."

"Warned you? How? Was it his intention to heap coals on your head instead of mine?"

I had no idea what she meant at the time, but Mr. Moore was perfectly tuned in. He answered, "No. Shortly before I left the ranch yesterday, the Reverend Gault quoted a verse from Saint Matthew. It went, 'Now also the axe is laid unto the root of trees: therefore every tree which bringeth not forth good fruit is hewn down, and cast into fire.'"

"Wow! That's pretty explicit in the rearview mirror, isn't it?"

"Yes, and larger than it originally appeared."

"Was anybody else around when he said it?"

"John Smith. You can verify it with him."

"I will. Did anybody else have a reason to kill your tree, Wilma?"

"Not that I know of, Dottie."

"No disgruntled lodger who disliked those four-pound blueberry muffins you make?"

"Heavens no. Everybody loves my muffins."

"Me, too. I don't suppose you have one lying around."

"I'm sorry, Dot. They're all gone. The cinnamon rolls, too. I suppose I need to bake today."

"Don't worry about it for a second. I need to get off my bottom and get out to the Temple Ranch. I'd like to hear what the reverend has to say; maybe leave behind a quotation or two of my own." Dottie took a long swig of blistering-hot coffee and added, "Would you be kind enough to escort me to the door, Vernon? I have one more question for you. Wilma, you say hello for me if you see Loretta before I do. And give me a call when the muffins are done. Okay?"

I said I would. Who can refuse an officer of the law? After that, Dot and Mr. Moore walked out to my front porch, where they were in clear sight of what was left of my poor old oak.

Dottie said, "A funny thing came across my desk first thing this morning."

"What was that, Sheriff?"

"The state police have issued an all-points bulletin for you. Did you know that?"

"Yes."

"You did? Do you know why?"

"I do, yes."

"Would you care to share it with your Aunt Dottie, hon?"

"Uh, I'd rather not."

"I thought you might say that and I can't compel you to incriminate yourself, so I called state police headquarters in Lincoln. You know what? They wouldn't tell me what they want you for either. In the past, they've been more than willing to explain to me how they're saving my county from vicious evildoers. I find their obstinacy odd, don't you?"

"Actually, Sheriff, it's extremely odd."

"The APB said you were headed west on I-80. Given your continuing presence in my town, that would seem to be a tad inaccurate. Who told them that?"

"I don't know."

"Well, a little bird told me that John Smith gave you a ride back to town from the hospital last night. Where's that big Hemi of yours? It's not parked out back; I checked."

"I don't know where it is either."

"Did somebody steal it?"

"I was told that it was struck by a pickup in the hospital parking lot. It had to be towed away."

"Is that so? I didn't see an accident report."

"Would you expect to see one, Sheriff? Beatrice isn't in Hayes County, is it?"

"It isn't, but it's darn intriguing that your car was damaged so bad that it had to be towed away at the very same time that you were supposed to be driving it to Colorado. Did you file an accident report in Gage County?"

"No."

"Why not?"

"I'd rather not say."

"That's unusual, Vernon. Most people file accident reports after they're in an accident. Otherwise, the insurance companies won't pay up. It's also the law, but I'd need a scrunched-up vehicle to prove you violated it. Do you know where your car is now, hon, or would you rather not tell me that either?"

"I have no idea where it is."

"You don't?"

"No."

"Are you ever going to get it back?"

"Apparently not."

"But I don't suppose you're going to file a stolen vehicle report either."

"No. I'm not."

"So your brand-new Chrysler has just evaporated, like it was a soap bubble and somebody stuck a finger in it. Is that right?"

"Apparently, yes."

Dottie put her hands on her substantial hips. "Half the people in this town think you're the most straightforward man on the planet, Vernon Moore, and the other half can't understand a goddamned word you say. My vote is starting to swing to column B. Can you give me one single reason why I shouldn't run you in this minute?"

"That's easy, Sheriff. I'm small potatoes. Matt's accomplices are the big potatoes, and I'm your last chance to get them."

"That's right, and you get extra credit for Loretta's revival too, so you have a forty-eight-hour hall pass, meaning it expires Sunday night. If you're still here at suppertime, I'll slap on the leg irons, Clem Tucker or no Clem Tucker."

"Clem called you?"

"He wanted me to make sure that the state police didn't send another car down here for you today. Isn't that a corker? He knew about the APB before I did. Now, how in the Sam Hell did that happen?"

Chapter 33
....

The Kangaroo's Tale

WHEN MR. MOORE ARRIVED at the county jail later that morning, he found Pokie waiting for him in the downstairs visiting room, along with Deputy Samoa and Matt Breck. All three were wearing green nylon police jackets, which was a nice touch, and they hadn't put any handcuffs on Matt.

Before Mr. Moore could ask, Luther said, "Deputy Melhuse is walking the walk with us this morning. It was the sheriff's call. Pokie's the fastest man in Hayes County, bar none. If Matt tries to take off, she'll run him down in two seconds flat. If he's faster than we think, I'll shoot him. Isn't that right, Pokie?"

Pokie turned beet red but didn't respond. After Loretta's revival, she had promised herself that she wouldn't speak in Mr. Moore's presence unless spoken to. She said later that it had something to do with unworthiness.

My grandson had no such affliction. He said, "Where are we going, Mr. Moore?"

"I thought we'd walk downtown; maybe stop at Starbucks at the end. How's that?"

"Like, cool," he answered, and off they went.

The rivers in seven counties were still swollen from the previous day's rain, but the front had left behind a warm breeze and bright, clear skies. Matt had to stop and cover his eyes when he stepped into the light of day. It was the first time he had seen the sun or breathed unfiltered air in weeks. For a full minute, he squinted skyward and held out his arms to soak it all in.

While they waited for Matt to acclimate himself to the outdoors, Luther pulled Mr. Moore aside and whispered, "The Reverend Gault tried to visit Matt this morning. I thought you'd want to know."

"Did you let him in?"

"Hell no, Mr. Moore, and he wasn't too happy about it. He was insistent; he said he was the boy's minister."

"What did you do?"

"I did my sworn job as a civil servant: I made him wait and then I sent him away mad. That man sure knows a lot of quotes from the Bible."

"So I've heard. A lot of them seem to include the 'f' word."

"The 'f' word?"

"Fire."

Mr. Moore started down the courthouse steps, Matt at his side, Pokie and Deputy Giant behind. Luther said, "The buzz around the jailhouse is that you brought Loretta Parsons back to life last night, Mr. Moore. Is that true?"

"It's a silly rumor, nothing more. I was miles away when Loretta returned to consciousness."

"Pokie here says she saw you do it."

She turned red again but kept to her oath.

Mr. Moore replied, "Deputy Melhuse saw me complaining; that's all."

Luther looked at Pokie but no words were spoken.

Matt asked, "Is Ms. Parsons okay now, Mr. Moore?"

"That seems to be the case. On the other hand, we thought she'd recovered the night before. The doctors are optimistic, but cautious."

The foursome turned the corner at Sorghum Street and headed south toward Main. Mr. Moore said, "Do you remember the question I asked you yesterday afternoon, Matt?"

"Yeah. First, you asked if it was better to be strong or weak, which is a seriously dumb question, and then . . ."

"A dumb question? Had you ever asked it—of yourself?"

Matt hesitated. "Uh, not 'til last night."

"Better late than never. Now that you've thought about it, what's the difference?"

"Between strong and weak?"

"Yes. That's the topic for the day."

"It seems to me that it's hard to say one way or the other. You have to go case by case."

"Fair enough. Why don't we start with an example?"

"Okay."

The group reached Main Street but continued southward. Luther said, "We should've turned left to go to Starbucks, Mr. Moore. It's just a couple of blocks over."

"I know, Deputy. We'll circle back. I wanted to walk down to the residential area on the south side of town. Is that all right?"

"Anything's all right as long as we keep junior here on a short leash."

They stopped a block later, where Mr. Moore pointed toward a cute little Arts and Crafts cottage painted in white with forest green trim. By coincidence, it belongs to Constance Kimball, the town florist and an absolute genius at arrangements. She does the center-pieces for all the Circle events, and she was responsible for most of the flora in Loretta's hospital room.

Mr. Moore said, "How many hours do you suppose it took to build that house, Matt?"

"Gee. I don't know. I never worked construction."

"Me either but I'm not looking for precision; an approximation will do. Do you suppose it took hundreds of hours, thousands of hours?"

"I don't know. Hundreds for sure."

"I agree. For discussion purposes, let's say the house took five hundred hours to build. How long would it take to tear it down?"

Matt thought for a second and replied, "That depends, doesn't it? If you used a bulldozer, it might take like half an hour. If you blew it up, it would take a few seconds. If you burned it down . . ."

"Right again. So what's harder, Matt: building a house or destroying it?"

"Duh. It's harder to build."

"A little bit harder, harder, or a lot harder?"

"A lot harder."

Mr. Moore turned parallel to Main and headed east. As the group followed, he pointed to a car parked along the street and said, "Let's try automobiles. How long does it take to make one of those?"

"A Camry? Gee, I don't know."

"Me either, but it takes a dealer a day to change a set of brake pads. Even in the assembly-line era, I think it would take a lot of hours to build an entire car, wouldn't you?"

Matt answered slowly, "Yeah. I guess so."

"In comparison, how long does it take to steal one?"

"Like, seconds. Right?"

"Like, yes. Let's try one more. How long do you suppose it takes to make a person?"

"Nine months?"

"You can get a baby for that, but how much more time does it take to turn a baby into an adult?"

"Sixteen years?"

"Assuming a single parent and a girl: maybe. Assuming two parents and a boy: twice that and more. That's thirty to forty years of work to raise one child, excluding the help of teachers, doctors, dentists, and others. You have some recent experience in this area. Wouldn't you agree?"

Matt didn't say one way or the other. Mr. Moore went on. "In comparison, how long does it take to kill someone?"

"One second."

"Okay, which is more: one soulless second of hostility or many, many years of hard work, patience, and frustration."

"I get it, Mr. Moore."

"Do you? Are you sure? What's the message?"

"It's harder to make things."

"Correct. More precisely, it's vastly more difficult to build things of value than it is to destroy them, isn't it?"

"Yeah."

"So, which is strong and which is weak?"

"It's obvious. Making stuff is a lot harder."

"True, but the difference between strength and weakness can't always be measured in effort. Let's say, for instance, that you see an old woman in the street carrying two big grocery bags. You have three choices: you can ignore her, which takes no effort whatsoever; you can help her, which takes some effort; or you can steal her groceries, which may take even more effort than helping her. Which of the three choices is the strongest?"

"Like, to help her?"

"Yes, but why?"

Matt thought for a second. "Because I don't get anything for it?"

"That's precisely it. In some cases, acts of strength require great effort, but in all cases, acts of strength require an element of selflessness. At some level, they're always acts of charity. In comparison, what can we say about weakness?"

"Gee, I don't know."

"Acts of weakness create victims, Matt. In fact, there are only two ways to create victims: by acts of Nature such as earthquakes and disease, and by acts of weakness such as substance abuse, deceit, or assault. When an act of weakness is man-made, do you know who one of the victims invariably is?"

"No. Who?"

"The weak person himself. For instance, you and two others assaulted a defenseless woman with a baseball bat and burned down her store. Were she and her child the only victims? Or were you one, too?"

Matt slowed briefly and said, "Can we go back to the jail, Mr. Moore? I don't want to go to Starbucks. People will just stare at me."

"Sure. Is there someplace else you'd rather go?"

"Yeah. I'd like to keep walking to the Missouri state line. It's a long way, so I'd have to be strong, right?"

Mr. Moore laughed, "In a physical sense, perhaps. We'll keep going but we can skip the coffee. Where were we before you requested an itinerary change?"

There was another long silence before my grandson answered, "You said I was the victim of my own weakness. If that's so obvious, why did I do it?"

"That, Matt, is a question with many answers. One of them is that you were stupid because you didn't stop to think about the consequences in advance, not even for a minute. Another is that you ignored the baby kangaroo in you."

"I did what?"

"You ignored the baby kangaroo in you. Do you know how big baby kangaroos are at birth?"

"Like, who would know that?"

"I do, as a matter of fact. They're pink, blind, and about the size of your thumb. But from the moment of birth, each one of them is strong enough, and smart enough, to crawl all the way up its mother's belly and into her pouch, where it attaches itself to a nipple. The mother doesn't help. Isn't that remarkable?"

"Yeah. I suppose."

"Here's the question, Matt: How does a baby kangaroo know where to go and what to do? It's just been born. Did it go to prenatal kangaroo school? Did it listen to Baby Kangaroo Einstein tapes in the womb? Did it get directions from mapquest.com? How did it know?"

Deputy Samoa interjected, "All of this talk about kangaroos is making me thirsty, Mr. Moore, and I already had my face fixed for a peppermint soy mocha. We're two blocks due south of Starbucks right now. Why don't we turn left here? You all can wait on the other side of Main while I get everybody a coffee. It's on me."

The travelers huddled at the corner, then Luther hurried up the block while Matt, Mr. Moore, and Pokie followed at a more leisurely pace. Two ladies from the Circle came out the side entrance to Starbucks as Luther entered and headed down the street. When they saw Matt and his escorts, they crossed to the other side and began to whisper to each other.

Mr. Moore frowned. "Let's get back to our discussion of postnatal marsupial behavior. How does a baby kangaroo know what to do, Matt?"

"I don't know."

"There's only one explanation, isn't there? Blind, thumb-sized, baby kangaroos are born with enough knowledge to know that they have to undertake a long, furry trip. It makes you wonder how much knowledge a seven-pound human baby could be born with, doesn't it?"

"Yeah, maybe. But so what?"

"What I'm about to tell you is a personal belief. It stems from years of observation, but it's never been proven, so it's not fact. You have to decide whether it makes sense to you or not. Okay?"

"Yeah. Okay."

"I believe that human beings are born with the knowledge that it's far better to do something of value than something of no value or, even worse, something destructive. Do you know why?"

"No."

"Because we feel good after we study for a test; or after we help an old lady; or after we help to build a house. Isn't that true? Don't you feel proud after you've done the right thing? Isn't it a good feeling?"

Matt didn't answer.

"In comparison, how did you feel after you cut class, or after you burned the Bold Cut?"

Matt didn't answer again.

Mr. Moore said, "Smart people are honest with themselves, Matt.

They see through to the truth even when it hurts. How did you feel after you attacked the Bold Cut?"

Pokie, Mr. Moore, and Matt continued north until they reached Main. As they crossed, Mat answered, "I felt shitty, okay? I said so a hundred times."

"Three of you went to the salon. One of you had a baseball bat. Loretta Parsons was alone and defenseless. Was the attack an act of strength or an act of weakness?"

Matt began to walk faster.

Mr. Moore kept pace. "You hid behind ski masks. Was that an act of strength or an act of weakness? Do strong people need to hide?"

Matt sped up again, but Mr. Moore remained in step. "When you burn down a place of business that took years to build, is it an act of strength or an act of weakness?"

Matt lurched forward as if he was going to run, but Pokie grabbed him by the collar from behind and said, "Whoa there, horsey. We're supposed to be taking it easy."

Matt came to a stop and backed against the brown, brick wall of Whipple and Sons, the local office of the "good hands people."

Mr. Moore got right in his face. "Is working forty years in a boring job to support a family an act of strength or weakness? Is being truthful when it's easy to lie an act of strength or weakness? Is facing up to your mistakes an act of strength or weakness?"

Matt spat back, "I faced my mistake! I admitted what I did and I'll pay the price."

"That's right, but what about your accomplices? They haven't admitted anything. Are they strong or are they weak?"

"I don't know, Mr. Moore, but you better be careful. Those guys can be pretty tough."

"Pretty tough? How did you come to that conclusion? Because they beat a defenseless woman with a baseball bat?"

"No. I heard about Gramma's tree last night. Everybody knows. Do you think it was a freakin' accident?"

"No, Matt. It was the senseless, shameless slaughter of a grand old oak, done in the dead of night by a person or persons unknown. Was it an act of strength or an act of weakness?"

"It doesn't make any difference, Mr. Moore. He was warning me and he was warning you. If you don't leave him alone, they'll burn down Gramma's house next. They'll do it in the middle of the night when my mom and my brother are there and it'll be your fault."

"My fault? Those two vermin are on the street for one reason: because you won't name them. The moment you do, the threat is over."

"No. No, it's not. There's more of them. They'll get my mom just like they got Loretta Parsons. Mark and Gramma, too."

"So you believe you're being strong by keeping silent?"

"Yeah, I do. If I keep my mouth shut, he'll leave me and mine alone."

"That's interesting, Matt. Someone else I know used a nearly identical phrase yesterday. A mutual acquaintance. Do you know who?"

"No. Who."

Mr. Moore looked Matt right in the eye and replied, "Earl Gault."

Luther Samoa crossed the street and half-jogged up the sidewalk, limping slightly. He was carrying a gray cardboard tray with four coffee drinks on it, one of which was extremely large. When he reached his traveling companions, he took a deep breath and exclaimed, "What a line! Half the town was in there talking about Loretta's recovery. It's a good thing you didn't go in with me, Mr. Moore."

"Really? Why?"

"Everybody was talking about you. They say you brought Loretta back. Some folks are saying you'll save the bank, too. If I were you, I'd keep a low profile from now on. People are starting to get an unnatural impression of your capabilities."

Mr. Moore took a sip of his mocha. "Remember the story of the Heaven's Gate cult, Matt? Too many people, even intelligent people, are so desperate to believe in something that they'll grasp at anything. Is that smart?"

"Uh uh."

"That's right. Intelligence is a gift of Nature, like the ability to wiggle your ears. Being smart is a choice; being strong is an even harder choice. In the future, I hope you'll be strong enough to be smart and smart enough to be strong."

There was no response for a second or two, then Mr. Moore added, "I'm done for the morning. If you don't mind, Deputy Samoa, I'll head back to the Come Again from here."

Out of nowhere, Pokie broke her oath and asked, "Are you going to the hospital, Mr. Moore? Won't you need a ride?"

"Does everyone know about my car, too?"

Luther answered, "It's a small town, Mr. Moore. Word spreads fast. We don't get to post a grand theft auto on the Big Board very often."

"I didn't file a stolen vehicle report. How did that happen?"

"Sheriff Hrnicek filed one for you this morning."

"That was considerate. I guess it means I'm on this Big Board of yours?"

"Three times, Mr. Moore. The sheriff is treating last night's fire as arson and you're listed as a material witness. She already had you down as a person of interest in the Bold Cut case, and the rumor mill says you're involved in the sale of the bank. If the county attorney decides to investigate, you'll probably get a fourth entry."

"Four entries? Should I be flattered?"

"No, sir. Most folks don't like being on the Big Board. It usually means trouble."

"Well, like you said, I probably need to lower my profile."

Pokie repeated, "Do you need that ride, Mr. Moore? If the sheriff doesn't mind, I'd be happy to drive you over myself."

"I suspect I do, Deputy, thank you."

"Where should I pick you up?"

"At the Come Again. I'll be ready in thirty minutes."

Matt asked, "What about this afternoon? Will you be back?"

"At four on the dot."

"Okay. Like, what's the question?"

"There isn't one, Matt; not this time. You get to do a little role-playing instead. Won't that be fun?"

"Role-playing? You mean you want me to pretend to be somebody else?"

"That's it on the button."

"I'm not very good at acting, Mr. Moore. Do I have to?"

"Trust me. It'll be a cakewalk."

Matt asked plaintively, "Can you at least tell me who I'm supposed to be?"

Mr. Moore smiled and replied, "Sure. You get to be God."

Chapter 34

....

The Last Shoe

WHEN MR. MOORE ARRIVED at the hospital, Mona, Laverne, and I were already visiting with Loretta, along with Lily Park Pickett, Louise Nelson, two of Loretta's girls from the Bold Cut, and half a dozen other women from the Circle. We were drinking coffee from Bobby Ho's delicatessen, passing Laverne around from lap to lap like a new toy, and gossiping while Loretta's girls gave their boss a manicure and a cut.

As fate would have it, Loretta was the first to see Mr. Moore. He was standing in the doorway with a latte from Bobby Ho's in his hand. Loretta said, "You remembered, Vern. That's so sweet."

The chitchat stopped dead in its tracks. We started to get our things together because we figured it was our cue to leave, but Loretta wouldn't have it. "You all stay put," she said. "He'll be back tonight. Isn't that right, darlin'?"

"Yes," he replied without moving, as if he would get cooties if he entered the room. After a second or two, Nurse Nelson jumped up from her chair and took the latte. "Loretta can't have coffee, Vernon," she said in a stern, nurse-like voice. "All she can have is thickened water."

I know what you're thinking, but I have no idea what thickened water is either.

Mr. Moore is not exceptionally tall for a man, but Louise is just a sylph of a girl. She stood on her tippy-toes and added in a whisper, "You owe me a game of cribbage."

He whispered back, "I called your office. The receptionist said you were here."

"If you try to wiggle out of it, I'll tell everybody who taught me to cheat."

"I didn't teach you to cheat, Louise. I taught you to alter the odds in favor of a very special opponent. Sadly, my time in Ebb is growing short. Even though I don't want to, I may have to take a rain check."

Loretta said what the rest of us were thinking, "Would you two stop whispering? I'm starting to get suspicious."

Louise replied in a normal voice, "Loretta says you're leaving tomorrow morning. Is that true?"

"I'm afraid it is."

"Does that mean you're coming back?"

"I hope so."

Loretta interrupted again. "That's good enough, Vern. Don't add the part about not being sure. Just come over here and sit on the edge of my bed while Nurse Nelson finds a straw for my latte." She added with a pout, "Please, Louise."

Nurse Nelson frowned and disappeared.

"Were your ears burning, darlin'?" Loretta asked. "Everyone in the room was talking about you. According to my friends, you've saved me once or twice; there's a controversy about the actual number. Now I hear that you confronted that bullshitter of a reverend at the Temple Ranch. You didn't tell me you were going over there."

"I wanted to meet the man; that's all. Apparently, Matt spent quite a bit of time with his sons."

"Well, I'm glad you got back in one piece. That man used to come to my store, and he brought a posse in with him. They were always friendly, but in a slick, superficial way, like used-car salesmen. After a few visits, the reverend demanded a massage—from me—in front of them. I refused, of course, and he lost his temper. That man sure knows a lot of quotes from the scriptures, but none of them are nice. He must've missed Sunday school the day they read, 'Blessed are the meek.' "

"Did he threaten you?"

"Between all the 'thines' and 'haths,' I don't honestly know. For sure, he and his men never came back to my store. It's an un-American thing to say, but I was happy to lose his business. They made my girls nervous every time they came in; the other customers, too. Isn't that true, girls?"

The two young women who had been working on Loretta's nails nodded together, chin up and down in unison. The younger one, a dropout and single mother who had gotten her GED after going to work for Loretta, said, "That reverend is a certifiable whack-job. I'd rather kiss an exhaust pipe than trim that man's greasy hair ever again."

Mr. Moore nodded and asked, "Do you believe that Reverend Gault was involved in the attack on you and the Bold Cut?"

"I don't know," Lo answered, "but I'm starting to get worried. I heard that Wilma's tree was burned down, and now I've got a guard outside my door. Are you going to get the other two boys or not?"

We were all sitting on the edges of our chairs. He answered matter-of-factly, "I am."

One second later, everybody started talking at once, and then Lily went downstairs and ordered three vegetarian pizzas. Loretta couldn't have any, poor girl, but Louise let her sip some of her latte through the straw.

After lunch, Mr. Moore rode back to town with Mona, the baby, and yours truly. He sat in the back with Laverne, but she was so tuckered out from all the excitement that she fell asleep in her child safety seat as soon as Mona turned the ignition. I know it wasn't kosher, but Mr. Moore took her out and held her in his arms the rest of the way home. By the time we arrived, he had fallen asleep, too.

NOT EVERYBODY WAS having an afternoon snooze. Sometime before the end of the business day, Clem Tucker got on the phone to Calvin Millet.

"Where are you?" Calvin asked.

"I'm at NBP headquarters, in the executive conference room on the top floor."

"Are you alone? Can you speak?"

"Of course. Why the hell would I call if I couldn't talk?"

"Good point? Is the deal done?"

"Yep. That Nettles is an elusive son of a bitch, but Fabi kicked his ass when the chips were down. He'll be a hell of a CEO."

"What was the problem?"

"Nettles wanted an eight-digit exit package; I wanted to hang him from the yardarm by his private parts, the prick. Except for Fabi, the rest of the board cowered in the corner like a bunch of wet puppies. What in the hell happens when these tough-guy executives take a board seat? Do they get their balls hacked off on the way in the door?"

"I don't know, Clem."

"Well, a few of them will have to be put down, but that can come later. Burt got out with seven digits. He hasn't seen the last of me, though."

"How did we come out?"

"Right where I said we would. Where else?"

"That's absolutely amazing, Clem. I could never have done it."

"I know. That's why I'm in the left-hand seat and you're in the right-hand seat, for now anyway. I have to say I'm pretty pleased myself."

"When will the official announcement be made?"

"The release will be put on the wires just before the markets open Monday morning. The lawyers sent a notice to the exchange asking that off-hours trading be suspended until then."

"Then should I go ahead and make the offer to the Circle?"

"That's the question, isn't it? Have you seen any indication that they're going to try to interfere?"

"None. They haven't tried to reschedule the meeting, and I haven't heard any saber rattling either. It's been surprisingly quiet."

"Okay. Let's roll the dice, but not 'til tomorrow afternoon. I'd like to keep it under wraps 'til then for my own purposes."

"No problem. I thought I'd make the offer through Lily. Is that okay with you?"

"I don't care if you make it through a Siamese translator as long as we have a deal memo next week. Hold on a minute . . ." There was a pause on the line, then Clem asked, "Do you think she'll tell Buford?"

"Unless I ask otherwise, I expect she will."

"Good. If Lily tells him, then I won't have to. Make the call."

"Consider it done. Is there anything else I need to know for now?"

"One last thing. I want to meet with Vernon before he goes, but I won't get back to the River House until ten tomorrow morning. Could you call him and arrange something after that, say lunch around noon? If he's got some kind of conflict, call me back. Otherwise, I'll assume we're set."

"Thy will be done."

"Save that kind of shit for Vernon Moore. Okay? That reminds me. His car was stolen last night."

"It was?"

"Yes. At the hospital. Dreadful luck, but that's the risk you take when you drive a high-profile car. Tell him John Smith will pick him up at the Come Again and bring him down."

"If you don't mind, Clem, I'd like to ask Vernon a question or two myself. Would it be all right if I drive him to the River House?"

"Join us for lunch, Calvin, by all means. But I want John to drive Vernon down."

"No problem. I'll see you at the River House around noon."

As soon as Clem hung up, Calvin auto-dialed Lily Park Pickett. She was driving back to Ebb from the hospital but she picked up the call. Mothers always pick up now, especially on school days.

Minutes later, I got a call from Lulu Tiller. "I just got off the phone with Lily," she said. "She's requested an emergency meeting of the board. She wants to do it tomorrow."

"Tomorrow? That's Mr. Moore's last day. Can't it wait until Monday?"

"I asked the same question, Wilma. She said she would bust a gut before then."

"But she wouldn't tell you what it was about?"

"Not over the phone, except to say that your fiancé is involved."

"Clem? Uh oh. Is it the fourth shoe?"

"I don't have a clue, Wilma. I lost count of all the shoes yesterday. Maybe it's just the last shoe."

"Wouldn't that be a breath of fresh air?" I replied.

Chapter 35

Empathy for God

POKIE MELHUSE WAS AT her usual duty station when Mr. Moore arrived on Friday afternoon. As soon as he walked in the door, she said, "The county attorney would like to see you before you go downstairs, Mr. Moore. Would you mind?"

"Not a bit. Shall I walk up now?"

"I'll go with you," she said. "Let me give her AA a call so they know we're coming."

Pokie was probably the only person in Ebb besides Mr. Moore who preferred two flights of stairs to an elevator. On their way up, he remarked, "Thanks for driving me to the hospital, and for coming along on our walk yesterday. I hope it wasn't too much of an imposition."

"Oh, no, Mr. Moore. It was a nice break from the duty desk. Is that how you've been talking to Matt all along?"

"More or less, yes. Did he say anything on the way back to the jail?"

"Not too much. He and Luther talked about you mostly."

"Me? Why?"

"Luther told Matt he had to be worth saving because you brought Loretta Parsons back from the dead in a lot less time than you've spent with him . . ."

"You know that's untrue, don't you? I didn't bring Loretta back to life."

Pokie answered, "If you say so, Mr. Moore." There are a dozen ways to end an argument with a man, but the most deadly is, "If you say so, dear." It works every time.

When they reached the third floor, Pokie handed Mr. Moore over to an administrative assistant who ushered him into the county attorney's office. Hail Mary was dressed in a gray, pinstriped pants suit with a red silk blouse that day, along with her usual seventy-three-inch high heels. They shook hands and she pointed him at the four extraordinarily uncomfortable seats in front of her desk. Mr. Moore chose one while she sat in her reclining leather chair.

After making herself more comfortable than he could ever be, she said, "I heard all the stories about your first visit to Ebb, Vernon, but I didn't believe a one of them. Now you've been back for one week— one week—and my town is in chaos: the bank has been sold; Loretta Parsons has died once and come back twice under inexplicable circumstances; Wilma's oak tree has been burned to a nub in a flagrant act of arson; the state police have issued an APB for you and refused to tell us why; and your car has mysteriously disappeared from the surface of the planet. The Circle is even thinking of offering a man a membership, if you can believe that, and I'm getting paranoid. I believe you're involved in all of it. Are you?"

"I doubt it."

"You doubt it?"

"Yes. I'm not sure."

"You're not sure?"

"To be honest, I'm rarely sure of anything."

"Okay, Vernon. I got a call from Lulu Tiller thirty minutes ago.

She's convening an emergency meeting of the Quilting Circle board tomorrow morning. Do you know how many that makes this week?"

"Three?"

"Four, which is twice as many as we've had in the last two years, total. Naturally, it has something to do with Clem Tucker. Do you have any idea what it's about?"

"Just that: an idea."

"Do you want to share it with me?"

"No. That should be up to Clem."

Mary sat forward and clasped her hands on her desk. "Is it my hair, Vernon? Do I need to change my perfume? For some reason, I don't sense that you're being entirely forthcoming."

"You hair is perfectly lovely and so is your perfume. Is it Chanel?"

Mary touched the back of her coiffure. For some reason, a woman has to touch her hair whenever she gets a compliment about it. I do it myself. Don't ask me why.

Mr. Moore continued, "Is there some other reason you asked to see me, Mary? I'm late for my meeting with Matt."

"Yes. I wanted to know how you're doing. Is he going to name his accomplices?"

"I believe so."

"You believe so? When? He goes before the bench Monday morning."

"Tomorrow morning."

Mary said she was so excited that she nearly jumped out of her knickers. "Tomorrow? Are you sure?"

Mr. Moore replied, "No."

I could have told her he would say that.

• • •

DEPUTY GIANT WAS PACING back and forth in front of the watch desk when Mr. Moore arrived. "You're late," he said. "You've never been late before. It's not about that APB, is it?"

"You heard about that, too?"

"At the sheriff's briefing after lunch. You made the Big Board for the fourth time."

"What did she say?"

"Other than a word or two about your ability to insinuate yourself into police matters, she reported that eyewitnesses had seen you leaving the county yesterday afternoon for parts unknown. We were required to memorize that part in case we get any more inquiries."

"That was sweet of her."

"Yeah. That's what everybody says. She's a real sweet person. Are you ready to see Matt? I thought you'd be putting the squeeze on today so I left him in his cell."

"We're almost there, Deputy Samoa, but I can't close the sale until tomorrow. Would you bring him to the visiting room?"

"No sweat. You go ahead and take a seat. I'll have the boy on deck in two shakes."

A few minutes later, Matt and Luther entered the visiting room. As before, my grandson sat directly opposite Mr. Moore while the deputy took a chair at the table closest to the door.

Matt said, "I heard your car got stolen. Do you think it was another warning? His boys will do anything he tells them. Anything."

Mr. Moore replied, "I doubt it. If I've judged the reverend correctly, auto theft is not his transgression of choice."

"Don't be too sure. That man can be mean, real mean."

"I appreciate the insight, Matt. Are you ready to take on your new role?"

Matt fidgeted. All Porters are fidgeters. It's genetic. "Pretend to be God?" he asked. "I don't think so, Mr. Moore. I don't know if I can do it."

"Why? Do you believe you'll be damned for trying to understand Him?"

"I-I don't know. It just doesn't seem right."

Luther said, "You won't be struck by lightning, junior. The man at your table is in charge of lightning. Banjos, too. If I were you, I'd worry about him."

Mr. Moore let the jailer's comment pass. "Let's try something a little less lofty for openers," he said. "You've played a lot of baseball. Do you suppose you could coach a Little League team?"

"Sure. It would be a piece of cake."

"Okay. Let's start there. You're the coach of a Little League baseball team. You're older, bigger, and stronger than your players, aren't you?"

"Duh, yeah. Like, Little Leaguers can only be twelve years old, max. They're just kids."

"Fair enough. You're the coach. What do want your team to do?"

"Win?"

"Yes, Matt, but how?"

"B-by doing their best, right?"

"Okay. But how about playing together? How about playing as a team?"

"Yeah. We'd have to do that to win."

"I think so, too, but suppose your team was losing. Would you put yourself in to pitch?"

"What? That would be whacked, man. I could never do that."

"Really? Why not?"

"Because it would be cheating. I'd get thrown off the field; I'd get suspended."

"You're thinking about the consequences in advance, Matt. Excellent. It sounds to me like you'd make a fine baseball coach, which means you're ready to be promoted to God. Trust me; it won't be much different than coaching little kids. Do you think you can handle it?"

Matt answered haltingly, "N-no."

"Indulge me. Give it a try. If you get uncomfortable, we can always send you back to Little League. For now, though, you're God. You're the Maker. In your infinite wisdom, you've given life to billions of tiny creatures called human beings. In your infinite generosity, you've also given them free will. Do they have to do what you tell them to do?"

"I, uh, I don't know, Mr. Moore. I don't get it."

"It's easy, Matt. You've created billions of little human beings. They aren't as strong or as smart as you are, but you've given them free will anyway. Do they have to do what you tell them to do?"

"Like, no. They don't have to."

"That's right, but you're a benevolent God, aren't you? You care for your people. Don't you want them to prosper?"

"Yeah."

"I agree, but how? What do they need to do?"

Matt thought about the question for a bit. "Help each other? Play as a team?"

"Very good. That's precisely what they should do, but let's not stop there. You're infinitely strong and infinitely wise, but you're all alone at the top. Do you have any special needs? Is there anything else you might want your people to do?"

"Like, like what, Mr. Moore?"

"Like fear you? Would you want your people to fear you?"

"Naw. That would be dumb."

"Why?"

"If I was God, I'd be super strong. I'd never hurt my people; I'd help them. They wouldn't have to be afraid of me."

"Hold it right there, Matt. If you helped them, wouldn't that be like putting yourself in to pitch for your Little League team? Could you do that without ruining the game?"

My grandson hesitated and then replied. "Maybe, but I'm God, right? I'm super smart. Maybe I could figure something else out."

"That's an interesting idea. After all, you are the Creator of the universe. As far as we know, it's an unprecedented achievement. Do you want your billions of people to worship you for it, to pay you homage?"

After another pause, Matt replied, "Yeah. I created the universe. I ought to get some props for it."

Mr. Moore rubbed his chin. "Are you sure? You're infinitely powerful. Do you need a bunch of little human creatures to puff up your ego? Why would you need that? What would you get out of it?"

There was no answer this time. Mr. Moore continued, "But you did give your people free will. They can worship you if they want. True?"

"Yeah, I guess so."

"Then tell me this: do you care if one group worships you one way and another worships you in some other way?"

"Duh, no. Like, why would I care about that? They have free will."

"Good answer, but what if one group of your worshipers claims to have exclusive rights to heaven?"

"Excuse me?"

"You're God. Do you care if one group of worshipers claims that only they can enter the kingdom of heaven and everybody else is doomed to hell? Would you care about that?"

Matt was silent for several seconds before answering, "That's what the reverend said."

"It's what a lot of religious people say, Matt, but they're only people. You're an all-knowing God. Would you allow mere men to determine who could enter heaven and who could not, or would you make that decision yourself?"

"I'd want to do it myself."

"Why?"

"Because men make mistakes. I'm God; I wouldn't."

"Bravo. That's exactly right. Now tell me this: Would it be fair of you to condemn a man to hell forever because of one mistake, or even two or three? Eternity seems like a pretty long time to pay for a few mistakes."

My grandson didn't answer.

"You're a benevolent God, Matt. Would you send misbehavers to hell forever, which is an infinitely long, infinitely horrible punishment, just for an error or two? Or might you find some sort of alternative?"

"Like what, Mr. Moore?"

"How about a shorter sentence—say a thousand years of shoveling out the stables in a mile-long barn full of Clydesdales, then back to real life for a second try? How would that be?"

"Have you ever cleaned out a stable, man? I'd never punish my people that way. I'd give them another chance."

"Okay, but suppose one of your humans screwed up so badly that a thousand years of shoveling horse manure fit the crime. Would you be more lenient if he or she gave you money?"

"What? I'm God; I don't need money. I can have anything I want."

"How about a sacrifice? A goat? A virgin? Would that cool your jets?"

"No, man. That's like still a bribe, but way, way worse. It would really piss me off."

"Okay. What if the misbehaver said he was sorry? What if he repented?"

Matt paused. "I'd listen to that, I guess."

"Good. Would you want your misbehavers to repent to other men, to certain special men, or could they apologize directly to you?"

"What? They should apologize to the person they hurt, not to me or anybody else. I don't need it and nobody else matters."

"You're right, Matt. It was a stupid question. I take it back. Are there any other things you might want your people to do?"

Matt scratched the side of his head. "I'm God. I don't need anything from my people. I'd just want them to live good lives. End of story."

"By being smart and strong? By helping each other?"

"Yeah. Definitely."

"That's exactly what I would want if I were God. I'd want people to be charitable, to help each other. In an uncertain world, charity is where being smart and being strong intersect. But life isn't always that simple, is it?"

"What do you mean?"

"It's rare, but being smart and being strong can be in conflict. In fact, they can be directly opposed, can't they?"

"Excuse me? I don't get it, Mr. Moore."

"You underestimate yourself, Matt. Of all the people I know, you get it best. You face one hundred and fifty years in prison. If you're smart, you'll give up your accomplices and cut your sentence to ten years. But if you're strong, you'll never give them up because you fear for the lives of your mother and brother."

There was no answer.

Mr. Moore went on. "It's a difficult dilemma, isn't it?"

My grandson hung his head and said softly, "Yeah."

"There's a solution. We'll discuss it tomorrow."

"A solution? You have a solution? Jeez, Mr. Moore. Can't we talk about it now?"

"I'm not ready. I'll be ready tomorrow."

"But . . ."

"Tomorrow, Matt."

My grandson opened his mouth to protest again but Deputy Giant said, "We're done for today, junior. The man has called the game."

When Luther returned from escorting Matt back to his cell, he was surprised to find Mr. Moore still sitting in the visitor's room. "Is there something else?" the deputy asked.

"Do you play cards, Deputy Samoa?"

"Yes, sir."

"Cribbage?"

"Is that the game with the little board? I don't know that one."

"Would you like to learn?"

"Why, Mr. Moore? Is there a reason?"

"I'll just come straight out with it. I was supposed to play cribbage with Louise Nelson sometime this week but I won't have the time.

I was hoping you could pinch-hit for me. You know Louise, don't you?"

"Nurse Nelson? Sure. I've been to Doc Wiley's office a dozen times to see about an old football injury. She's nice, and petite. Do you think she'd teach me to play cribbage?"

"She might. You'd be doing me a huge favor if you'd give her a call."

Chapter 36

Conduct Unbecoming

THAT EVENING, CALVIN MILLET got a call from Bebe Palouse. At the time, he was sitting in his fourth-floor office at the Ebb branch of the National Bank of the Plains, recently known as Hayes County Bank. For the record, Calvin's office was even smaller than Clem's. If a wood dowel had been run from one wall to the other, it would've been two hangers short of a closet.

Bebe said, "I know it's getting toward closing time, Calvin, but do you have a minute?"

"Of course. How was business at the store this week?"

"Considering the distractions, very good. I thought folks might be a little cautious after the sale of the bank, but they've been buying like there's no tomorrow. Receipts are up versus last October. If Christmas comes in on forecast, we'll beat our targets for the quarter and the year."

"That's great, Bebe. Have you had time to think about our offer?"

"I have, Calvin. The price is fair, but I can't afford the whole forty-nine percent, and I don't want to borrow that kind of money either. I can't imagine owing Buford Pickett three million dollars."

"I understand, Bebe. Believe me, I understand. But we'll sell you less than forty-nine percent, you know. We're more than willing to find another buyer for the balance."

"I do and I know it sounds strange, but I'd like to make you a counteroffer. My idea is a little on the unusual side, so hear me out. There are some real upsides for the store and the shareholders."

"There's nothing wrong with an unusual proposal," Calvin replied. "If we don't like it, we can always suggest an alternative. What do you want to do?"

"What if I took twenty percent and the Quilting Circle bought the other twenty-nine percent?"

Five minutes later, Calvin called Clem Tucker, who was in an Omaha hotel room getting dressed for dinner at the Santoni residence. After Calvin described Bebe's offer, Clem asked, "Where in the hell did that come from?"

"I don't know."

"Did you ask her?"

"Yes. She said it was her idea."

Clem remarked, "Well, it smacks of Vernon L. Moore to me. Doesn't it smell like Vernon to you?"

"I don't know. I've never paid much attention to his aroma."

"Either way, it's a hell of a coincidence, isn't it?

"There's no question about that. Do you want me to pull the plug?"

"Pull the plug? Shit no. Doubly redouble your efforts. That reminds me: Is lunch set for the River House tomorrow?"

"It's all settled. John will pick Vernon up at eleven thirty at the Come Again."

"Good. And you'll be there, too. Right?"

"Yes."

"Excellent. Remind me to thank the guest of honor tomorrow."

"Thank Vernon? For what?"

"For Bebe's proposal. What else?"

THAT AFTERNOON, MONA, yours truly, and a few of our friends removed most of the flowerpots from Loretta's room. That created enough space for a second bed, which an orderly brought in and we pushed next to hers. Just before we left for the night, we helped her change into a lovely, white silk nightgown.

The poor woman could hardly move, but she could still set a scene. When Mr. Moore arrived, Lo was sitting up against a bank of pillows with the blanket at her waist, as if she had been posed by David O. Selznick. He came over to the bed and kissed her lightly on the forehead, then the cheeks and lips, lingering at his final destination. To the best of her ability, she kissed him back.

"You look ravishing," he said. "How's your tongue? Is it back to normal?"

Loretta stuck it out. It was more gray than black on top.

"How do you feel?"

She replied, "I feel like a dishrag, but without the energy. If I could lift my arm, I'd check my watch, if I had my watch. Where have you been all day?"

"Here and there. I'm not quite finished with Matt Breck." Mr. Moore sat on the edge of the bed and took Loretta's hand, but he seemed distracted by the addition of the second bed.

"Don't worry about that," Loretta said. "It's just for company.

According to Doc Wiley, it's going to take four to six weeks of therapy to get me back in the saddle, so to speak. Do you know how
many people I had to see today?"

"No. How many?"

"I have a speech therapist, even though I seem to be doing just fine
in that category. I also have a physical therapist, an occupational therapist, a dietician, two doctors not counting Hank, and six nurses,
counting Louise. Every time I get comfy, somebody new comes in here
with something exhausting for me to do. This morning, they propped
me up on some parallel bars to see if I could drag my pitiful, half-dead
legs across a mat."

"How did you do?"

"I dragged my legs across the mat, as requested. The therapist, I
can't remember if she was the physical or the occupational, said it was
a remarkable achievement for a woman in my condition. Wasn't that
nice of her?"

"Well, you look terrific to me."

"You're so sweet, darlin'. Have you been taking positive rein-
forcement lessons from Louise? That's the kind of thing she always
says. Speaking of Louise, she said Luther told her that you've been
playing the banjo for Matt Breck. That's the strangest thing I've ever
heard. You never told me you played the banjo."

"It would've been an exaggeration."

"I heard that, too. Is Matt going to name the other two boys or not?"

"Either he will or I will."

"You? You know who they are?"

"I'm ninety-eight percent there, Lo. You could push me across the
finish line."

"Me? How?"

"I know it'll be hard, but it would help me greatly if you could recount what happened that night at the Bold Cut. I hate to ask, but I need the details."

"I don't have any details, Vern. All I have are flashes, and I have darn few of those."

"What if I helped you?"

"Helped me? How? Are you going to mesmerize me with your charms? That's supposed to be my department."

"Nothing so dramatic. I thought you might remember if you were relaxed."

"Relaxed? Look at me. I can hardly be anything else. Besides, I don't want to go back to that place. I don't want to get beaten up again."

"You won't relive it, Loretta. You'll merely observe it."

"Do you promise?"

"No."

"That figures. Are you sure this is necessary?"

"Not completely, no."

"Then I have to go back, don't I, darlin'? What do you want me to do?"

Mr. Moore got up and turned down the lights in Loretta's room. "Close your eyes," he said. "Inhale deeply. Relax."

After a few seconds, he inquired, "Are you comfortable? Are you warm enough?"

"Uh huh."

Mr. Moore stroked her hair gently and said softly, "You have no cares, Lo. You're warm and comfortable and perfectly safe. There's never been a better time to reminisce. Do you remember the first time you came to Ebb?"

"Yes."

"Was it a nice visit?"

"Uh huh. That's when I met Wilma."

"Would you tell me about it? Don't relive it. Describe it as if you were watching an episode of your life. How did you meet her?"

"I had seen a TV special about Ebb, so I made a reservation at the Come Again. Wilma and I were friends five minutes after I arrived. It was the strangest thing: we had so little in common, but we were like two peas in a pod."

"Can you see her as she was then?"

"Like it was yesterday."

"How did she look?"

"She was so much younger. Her girls were still at home, but she walked me all around town after they left for school. That was so nice."

"What kind of day was it?"

"It was a crispy, sunny day in the fall."

"Were the leaves turning?"

"They were red and brown and yellow, and blowing everywhere in the wind."

"Did you stop at Starbucks?"

"There was no Starbucks back then. We had fried clams at the Corn Palace."

"When did you make up your mind to move to Ebb?"

"Before we got to the Corn Palace. Everywhere we walked, people stopped to say hello. It was as if Wilma was the queen of Hayes County and I was her royal cousin from the Duchy of Africa. Every woman we met was white, but nobody made me feel like I was a second-class citizen. I'd never felt that way before."

"Do you remember the day that Laverne was born?"

"Laverne? Of course I do, in living color."

"Tell me about it. Don't relive it; just observe it."

"I was in labor in Doc Wiley's little clinic for nine hours. He came in and out, but Wilma and Louise were there every minute. I cursed you a thousand times and they both joined in. Louise may be a perky thing, but she's good at cursing. After my water finally broke, little Laverne came busting out and it was the best day of my life."

"What did she look like at birth?"

"Her face was puffy, her nose was squished, and she was covered in goo. You've never seen a more beautiful baby. Somebody should've been there."

"Somebody wanted to be. Did she cry at birth?"

"Uh uh. Laverne has never cried. Not once, not even when she hit her head on the foot of the fireplace in Wilma's parlor."

"If Laverne didn't cry, then what woke you up the night of the break-in? Did you smell smoke?"

"No. It was noisy downstairs, like an old war movie was playing on the TV. But I won't allow a TV in the salon because it would ruin the conversation, so I went down to investigate."

"What did you see?"

"Three boys in ski masks. One of them was smashing the armrests off my most expensive barber chair, the one with the built-in vibrator. Another was throwing red paint on the mirrors and the third was trying to break into my cash register."

"What did they do when they saw you?"

"The boy in the purple sweater grabbed me and held me while the tall one with the baseball bat hit me across the arm. I tried to get loose, but he was holding me from behind."

"What were the other two boys wearing?"

"They were dressed like cowboys: jeans, jean jackets, and boots."

"No hats?"

"No. Black ski masks."

"Did any of them say anything when they saw you?"

"The short one at the cash register said, 'Hot damn! It's the whore!'"

Mr. Moore stroked Loretta's hair. "Don't forget; you're just observing. What happened then?"

"The boy behind the cash register started to come toward me, and then everything went black. That's the last thing I remember."

"You said you were held from behind. Did he hold you so that the other boy could hit you, or did he try to turn you away?"

"I'm not sure."

"It's just a rerun, Lo. Look at the scene again; take your time."

After a bit, she said, "I think he was trying to turn me away. That's how I got hit in the arm. We were spinning away."

"Thank you. There's no reason for you to go back to that night ever again. You can forget it completely." Mr. Moore kissed Loretta and added, "I wanted to be with you at Laverne's birth. I'm so sorry I wasn't."

She opened her eyes. "You knew?"

"Yes."

"That was conduct unbecoming, Vern. I expected more. Why weren't you here?"

"Forgive me, Loretta, but there are some things I can't explain, even to you."

"You can't? That's what Wilma told me you'd say." Loretta paused for a moment. "Can I ask you another question?"

"Of course."

"Was it your decision?"

Lo waited for an answer, but Mr. Moore didn't reply. Eventually, she asked, "Is it always somebody else's decision?"

Mr. Moore didn't answer again. Loretta frowned and said, "Okay, but you have to make it up to me anyway, darlin'. How are you going to do that?"

"I'll do whatever I can for as long as I'm here. What do you want?"

"Three things, Vern. First, you have to stay the night. It's all arranged with the hospital staff. I told them you'd be a gentleman— this time."

"It would be my pleasure. I don't suppose they can find me some pajamas."

"Probably not, but I bet they can get you a little blue gown with a great big gap in the butt. They have lots of those. I can have a good cackle every time you walk across the room."

"That would be fine. What's the second condition?"

"You get those other two boys."

"I'm already on record, Lo. Number three?"

"You have to come back. I know you're leaving tomorrow for God knows where, but you have to come back. Whatever happens, you have to come back to see your daughter."

"You have my word, but in return I have one small request for you."

"A request for me? Is it something I can do lying down?"

Mr. Moore smiled. Loretta said later that it was more like a melancholy smile than a cheery one. "When you're well," he replied, "I'd like you to take Laverne over to the Angles House."

"To see Calvin?"

"Yes. You have to promise."

THE NEXT MORNING, the hospital staff brought Mr. Moore breakfast and the newspaper in bed, and they brought Loretta a small bowl of applesauce. It was her first real food since her second recovery. She ate slowly while Mr. Moore read the paper out loud, and they laughed and cried about what passes for news these days. Then their morning together was interrupted by the inevitable nurse, who informed Loretta that her physical therapy session was near. Mr. Moore got dressed, but unhurriedly, as if he was a matador preparing for a bullfight.

When he was done, he sat on the edge of Lo's bed for the last time. She said, "I won't see you again, will I?"

"Not this trip. No."

"Will you be all right? I feel like something's in the air, but I can't put my finger on it."

"It's just another day at the office, Lo. I'll be fine. Everyone will be fine." Mr. Moore was fibbing, but there was no way she could know.

"Will you say good-bye to Laverne before you go?"

"Yes."

Loretta paused for a moment before asking, "When will you come back to me?"

There was no immediate answer. She continued, "Don't overcommit, Vern. It'll take me six weeks to get back to full speed. Anytime after that will be okay."

Mr. Moore bent over and kissed Loretta softly on the lips, he touched her hair, and he replied, "I'll be back as soon as I can."

Chapter 37

A Gray Stray

THE LORD MAY STRIKE me dead where I sit, but I am not a cat person. My mother couldn't turn them away, so we had two or three of the little critters in the house all the time when I was growing up. On my eighth birthday, it became my job to feed them and clean out the litter box. Wasn't that nice? Even at that age, I couldn't understand why a normal person would spend actual money to cover every piece of clothing and furniture in the house with cat hair, cause the kitchen to smell like dead fish, and make the garage reek of cat litter and you-know-what.

Naturally, the one day I could beat Mona at rock, scissors, paper, a gray stray came to our back door. For reasons just explained, Mona was deprived of an intimate association with felines during her childhood so, being among the uninitiated, she brought it in the house and fed it half a can of tuna. By the time I got downstairs, it was sleeping on one of the chairs in my dining room, meaning we had been officially adopted. For all I knew, the official papers were in the mail.

My personal aspersions aside, proprietors of bed and breakfasts should not harbor cats, so I mustered up my resolve and went into the kitchen to confront my eldest. Before I could open my mouth, Mona said, "Did you see the cat, Mama? Isn't he the cutest little thing? I always wanted one, and he just loves Laverne."

"That's so sweet," I answered bravely.

Laverne was eating oatmeal in her high chair. She scooped some up with her spoon and held it over the side of her tray so that it would slide slowly to the floor. After it landed with an audible plop, she looked up with pride and said, "Yogie?"

That's when Mr. Moore walked in, looking more than a bit rumpled, the stray cat at his heels. He said, "Good morning, all. I noticed that you have a new lodger, but he has a certain, permanent air. Have you checked his credit?"

"No," I answered coldly. "He won't be staying long." Before Mona could protest, I added, "Cats are bad for the bed and breakfast business. It's in the manual. Thirty-one percent of lodgers have an allergy." I made that number up. I have no idea how many people are allergic to cats.

"But Laverne loves him so," Mona said. "As soon as she saw him, she said, 'kitty.'"

I was unmoved. "Laverne calls every critter 'kitty.' If she saw a manatee in the Missouri River, she'd call it a kitty." I needed to change the subject, so I turned to Mr. Moore and asked, "Are you leaving today?"

"This morning," he replied.

I knew it in my head but my heart was unprepared for the news. "When?" I sniffed.

"John Smith is picking me up at eleven thirty. I have to see Matt between now and then."

"When are you going over to the courthouse?"

"As soon as I shower and change."

"Will you be coming back to the Come Again before you leave?" Mona asked.

"Yes. John will be picking me up here."

"Mama has to go to a meeting at the Abattoir. Would you like Laverne and me to stay until you get back?"

"If you don't mind, Mona. That would be very nice."

It hit me then. I couldn't be sure that I would get back from the fourth emergency Circle board meeting of the week before Mr. Moore left for good. I said, "We have to say good-bye before you go. Don't we, Mr. Moore?"

He smiled sweetly and replied, "I suspect so, Wilma. Why don't we wrap things up after I shower and pack?"

Mr. Moore came down the back stairs into the kitchen about thirty minutes later, clean as a whistle and dressed in a black blazer, a black turtleneck, light gray slacks, spit-polished shoes, and a warm, engaging smile. It was just the two of us: Mona was upstairs dressing Laverne.

I could tell by his ease that Mr. Moore had experience at leaving people behind. I didn't, not people I cared about anyway. I was standing over the sink with my old red sweater rolled up to the elbows so I wouldn't get it in the dishwater, and I was in no mood to say good-bye to anybody, not even the cat.

"Do you have time for some tea?" I inquired without looking up.

Rather than sitting at the kitchen table where he belonged, Mr. Moore leaned against the counter only a foot or two away. "I don't, Wilma. I can only stay a few more minutes."

I turned to face him. He was so close that I could smell his aftershave. "How was Loretta this morning? Is she going to be all right?"

"Loretta is indomitable," he replied. "She's doing much better than anyone could have expected. Hank predicts that she'll recover fully and in record time. A thousand times last night, she told me how much she appreciated what you and Mona have done for her and Laverne."

"It was never enough. I doubt that Mona will ever get over it. A mother never does, you know."

"You need to help her, Wilma. Mona will need to move on, as will you."

"I know. It'll be easier for us all when Loretta comes home and the Bold Cut reopens. Then the only person missing will be Matt."

Mr. Moore smiled again. "Matt will return to Ebb one day when he's older and wiser, just like wayward grandsons are supposed to do."

"Will you be back when you're older and wiser, Mr. Moore?" I asked.

"I hope so. In the meantime, I left something for Matt in the roll-top desk. Please keep it in confidence until he's released from prison. I also left a package for the Reverend Earl Gault on the settee. I'd appreciate it if you could mail it for me later today."

"Can you tell me what it is?"

"It's a gift, Wilma. Please mail it anytime this afternoon. Is that okay?"

"I promise I will." I could tell Mr. Moore was getting ready to leave. "Did you ever meet Silas the Second?"

"I'm sorry to say I didn't. Maybe next time."

"Maybe next time . . ." My voice trailed off. I couldn't think of anything else to say.

Mr. Moore put his arms around me. It wasn't a hug; it was a hold. He held me for a long time before he said, "I have to go now."

He kissed me on the forehead and then poof, he was gone, like a ghost. My kitchen was empty of sound and fury and I was all alone. A single tear rolled down my cheek. There should have been more, there would have been more, but I was distracted by the thought of that package Mr. Moore had left behind for the Reverend Gault.

After arguing with myself for all of three seconds, I went into the den and opened it up. That is something every grown woman can do, and without detection, because we wrap all the packages in the first place. Inside was a small, gray-colored, sort of Y-shaped appliance with a bunch of buttons on the top. The side of the box said it was a speakerphone. There was a note inside that had been addressed to the Reverend Gault. All it said was, "The Epistle of Paul the Apostle to the Galatians, chapter 6, verse 7."

I rummaged around the bookshelves until I found my Bible. Galatians 6:7 reads:

> Be not deceived; God is not mocked:
> For whatsoever a man soweth, that shall he also reap.

I don't know what Mr. Moore was trying to tell the reverend—at least I didn't at the time—but that saying never made a whit of sense to me. The men I know don't reap what they sow. The richest and the meanest men reap, the poorest and the nicest ones sow. The law of the jungle trumps the word of God—but maybe it doesn't when Mr. Moore is in town. Maybe he changes the rules. Maybe he can make paper beat scissors.

Is that what angels do?

Chapter 38

Matt's Dilemma

REVEREND GAULT WAS SITTING on a bench in the marble-floored foyer of the courthouse that morning, dressed in a black, preacherlike robe and reading the bible. Pokie Melhuse was keeping an eye on him through the open double door to the sheriff's offices. By coincidence, that meant she could hear anything said in our acoustically perfect foyer.

As soon as Mr. Moore walked through the front door, the reverend jumped to his feet and called out, "Can I have a moment of your time, Vernon?"

Mr. Moore stopped and the two men met in the center of the foyer, but about six feet apart. "Certainly. What can I do for you?"

"I take it you're seeing young Matt Breck again today."

"I am, yes."

"I tried to see the boy myself this morning, but the jailer wouldn't let me. Why are they letting you visit the boy?"

"I'm a friend of the family. Why do you ask?"

"I fear for his soul. The boy needs to see his minister."

"Take it from me, Reverend, Matt's soul is not the one you need to worry about. Right now, we need Matt to focus on preserving his future, which means naming his accomplices. Don't you agree?"

"Uh, yes. Of course I do. Yes indeed."

"I'll tell him that you said so. I'm sure it'll have a big impact."

Mr. Moore began to turn toward the sheriff's offices, but the Reverend Gault remained rooted to the floor and said, "I heard that Loretta Parsons died and came back to life. Is that true?"

"That's the abridged version, but yes, she did. Isn't it a miracle?"

"Two nights in a row? It's some kind of miracle; that's for sure. My sources believe you did it. They say you brought her back."

Mr. Moore lowered his voice. "My public stance is clear: her recovery was a massive stroke of luck. Between us, though, I want you to know the truth: I did it. I summoned a lightning strike from the heavens."

"That's one hell of a claim, Vernon Moore. It's a blasphemy. 'Beware of false prophets, for they are as ravening wolves.'"

Mr. Moore grinned and replied, "I'm just kidding, Reverend. I know less about her recovery than her doctors, and believe me, they're baffled." Mr. Moore went on, "Is there anything else? I'm about to be late for my appointment with Matt."

"I heard about Ms. Porter's tree the other night, too."

"Did you? What a magnificent old oak! What a tragedy! Did you hear it was arson? Why would someone want to harm an ancient, defenseless tree?"

"I don't know, Mr. Moore. Maybe it was a message."

"I can see you've given the matter some thought. What kind of message do you suppose it was?"

"I can't say for sure. A warning maybe."

"You're probably right, but I wonder. Communications go two ways. Do you suppose the warners are expecting a return message?"

"A return message? What does that mean?"

Mr. Moore answered, "I don't have a clue. Have a nice day." Then he pivoted and headed through the double doors into the sheriff's office. When he reached the duty desk, he said, "Good morning, Deputy Melhuse. Is Sheriff Hrnicek in?"

Pokie watched the reverend uproot himself and head toward the courthouse doors before she answered, "No, sir. She called in to say that she'll be stopping at the Abattoir for a meeting before she comes to work. I don't expect her 'til lunchtime."

"That'll be too late. Who's the ranking deputy on duty?"

"I am. What's on your mind?"

"How many exits are there from the Temple Ranch?"

"Three maybe. I'm not sure. How come?"

"Give the reverend time to get back to the ranch, but once he's there you'll need to station cars at all three exits so that no one can leave."

"Why?"

"They may try to run for it."

Without a hint of hesitation, Pokie said, "I should call Dottie, shouldn't I?"

"That may be a very wise move. If she needs to speak with me, I'll be downstairs with Matt and Deputy Samoa."

"You should wait here, Mr. Moore. She'll want to talk to you right away."

A minute later, Mr. Moore was on the phone with Dottie Hrnicek. Two shakes after that, Dottie was on her way to the courthouse and the meeting at the Abattoir had been canceled. I had just finished getting dressed when I got the news at home, so I got in my old station wagon and headed to the hospital. Two of Dottie's cars passed me on the way. Their lights weren't flashing, but they had to be going three hundred miles an hour.

AFTER MR. MOORE HAD sorted everything out with Dottie and Hail Mary, he walked downstairs for his last meeting with my grandson. Deputy Giant met him at the watch desk and said, "I heard the news, Mr. Moore. Pokie says you know who attacked the Bold Cut."

"I do, Deputy Samoa."

"Did you tell Sheriff Hrnicek?"

"No. That will be Matt's job."

"You didn't tell her? Didn't that piss her off?"

"Only in passing. I told her where to go instead. That seemed to help."

"You told her where to go?"

"Yes."

Luther shook his head. "You're a strange man, Mr. Moore."

"Let's go see Matt."

When Mr. Moore and Deputy Giant reached to my grandson's cell, they found him sitting on his bunk with piles of baseball cards stacked all around him. They waited patiently while he put them into a shoebox and stowed it under his bunk.

After everyone was situated, Mr. Moore said, "How are you, Matt?"

"I'm okay."

"Okay? Is that all? This is our last meeting. You should be thrilled."

"Yeah. Like, when do I get to see my mom?"

"She'll be here after lunch."

"By herself?"

"I'll make sure she is, and Deputy Samoa will resume responsibility for your visitor list. Does that meet with your satisfaction?"

"I suppose. Yeah."

"Good. Are you ready to discuss your dilemma?"

My grandson paused, then replied, "Uh, no. Not really."

"Why not?"

"It's like you said, Mr. Moore. The smart thing would be to rat the other guys out, but they threatened to hurt my mom and my little brother if I did. What would be good for me would be bad for them, so that would be weak, right?"

"That's right, Matt. You have a serious dilemma. How do you resolve it?"

"I'm a man. I'm strong. I keep my promise; I don't tell."

Mr. Moore said, "That's very noble of you. When being smart and being strong are in conflict, it's usually better to be strong than smart. That's what nobility is; helping others even when it hurts you."

"It is?"

"Yes. You were given a choice and you chose the noble path. Good for you. Unfortunately, though, the game has changed. Nobility is no longer an option."

"What do you mean?"

"Your accomplices are going to get caught, Matt. In less than an hour, no matter what you do."

"What? How do you know?"

"Because I have their names. I know who attacked the Bold Cut beyond a shadow of a doubt, and I'm obligated to turn them in."

My grandson sat forward and snapped, "You're lying."

"Am I? If your two accomplices were major-league baseball players, they'd be on a team in the western division of the American League, wouldn't they? More specifically, they'd play in Anaheim. Isn't that right?"

Luther began to pace back and forth. My grandson sat back against the wall and said softly, "What do you want me to do, Mr. Moore? If you tell the sheriff, I'll spend a hundred and fifty years in jail for nothing. That's bone stupid. But if I tell, they'll hurt Mom and Mark."

"No they won't, Matt. The cat will be out of the bag. Your partners-in-crime will be in jail. Reprisals will be pointless."

"How do you know? I don't see how you can possibly know that."

"I just do, Matt, but it doesn't matter. If you won't name your accomplices, I will. It's that simple."

"Even if my mom and brother could get hurt?"

"Remember our discussion about fact and belief? There are no relevant facts between us now, only beliefs. You believe your mother and brother may be hurt, but I believe the risk is small and justice must be served. More to the point, I'm willing to act upon it. No one who hurt Loretta Parsons and my daughter will go unpunished. This game is over!"

Matt considered his options, as if he had any, and concluded, "I have to rat them out. That's it, isn't it."

"Yes, but don't forget our lesson on charity. If you use your head, you can still be charitable."

"Charitable? I'm sending them to prison. How is that charitable?"

"Charity is a gift, Matt, any kind of gift, as long as it's selfless. What can you give them?"

"I don't know. What?"

"Use your brain. If you were in their shoes, what would you want?"

My grandson pulled his knees to his chest and answered, "Like, to escape."

"Perhaps, but that option is off the table. As we speak, the ranch is being surrounded by deputies from the sheriff's office."

"You told already?"

"No, Matt. I told Sheriff Hrnicek where to go, not who to arrest. That's your job. You still have a chance to give your partners something, even if it's less than outright freedom."

My grandson shook his head. "I don't know," he said. "What?"

"How about this?" Mr. Moore replied. "What if you call them? What if you offer them the chance to turn themselves in? Maybe they can strike a deal of their own."

"A plea bargain?"

"The county attorney will want to know who ordered the attack on the Bold Cut. That might give your accomplices an opportunity to negotiate a deal."

"They'll never do it; they'll never say. He won't let them. He'll tell them to go to jail forever or he'll make them run."

"Possibly, but you can at least give them a chance. It's the charitable thing to do."

Matt didn't respond. Deputy Giant stopped pacing and grabbed a bar with each hand as if he was going to pull them apart.

Mr. Moore checked his watch. "It's ten forty-seven," he said. "If your two friends don't turn themselves in by eleven o'clock on the dot, I'll tell Sheriff Hrnicek who they are myself. I suggest you go with Deputy Samoa right now. Tell me if I'm wrong, but it looks to me like he's raring to go. If you don't get moving, he may throw you over his shoulder like a cheap rug and carry you upstairs."

Mr. Moore stood up. Luther released his grip, opened the cell door and said in a deep voice, "Get your butt up, junior. The clock is ticking."

My grandson remained seated. "And you're sure my mom will be okay?"

"You have my word, and you'll be okay if you remember two rules of thumb: It's better to be smart than stupid, and it's better to be strong than weak. Everything else will follow."

Matt stood up and said, "I'm really sorry. I didn't mean for Ms. Parsons to get hurt."

"I know. When you get the chance, you'll need to tell her that. Laverne, too. It's the strong thing to do." Mr. Moore held out his hand. "Good luck," he said.

Without looking up, Matt shook Mr. Moore's hand, then Deputy Giant ushered him down the hall. Mr. Moore followed at a distance but stopped at the watch desk to leave a short note. It asked Luther to give the banjo to the inmate who liked bluegrass.

Chapter 39

The Understatement of the Year

CLEM'S LIMOUSINE WAS PARKED near my poor old oak when Mr. Moore returned to the Come Again. The tree and the car were both black in color, but they stood in sharp contrast against a gray, cloudy sky: one sleek, sharp, and shiny; the other gnarled, charred, and recently deceased. Mr. Moore stopped to touch the trunk of the oak before he went inside, where he found John Smith and Mona having tea in the parlor.

John immediately stood, teacup in hand.

Straightaway, Mona asked, "Did my son name his accomplices today?"

"He did, yes. As I left, he was calling them from Sheriff Hrnicek's office."

"So he'll get the reduced sentence?"

"I have every expectation that he will."

Mona began to tear up but she managed to keep her composure. "Will he see me now? Will he talk to me?"

"He's expecting you this afternoon but you should go alone, and you should wait until three o'clock at least. The sheriff's office will be very busy 'til then. Matt, too."

I wasn't there with a tissue and Mona never carries any. She had to dab the corners of her eyes with the sleeve of her sweater. Then she gave Mr. Moore a hug and said, "Thank you." From a grateful grandma's point of view, that was the understatement of the year.

Mr. Moore was gracious in victory. "You're welcome," he replied. "Matt was a victim, too, but he was courageous in the end. You can be proud of him for that."

Mona began to tear up again. Mr. Moore asked, "Is Wilma back from her meeting?"

"It got canceled so Mom went on to the hospital. I don't think she could've endured another good-bye. I'll call her with the news."

"That would be nice, thank you. How about Laverne? Is she having her morning nap?"

"Uh huh. Would you like me to bring her down?"

"Oh no. I'd rather go to her, if that's okay. Why don't you stay here and keep John entertained?"

According to Mona, Mr. Moore's eyes were glistening more than usual when he brought Laverne down the stairs a while later. Laverne was all bright-eyed and bushy-tailed herself. He had dressed her in a little blue-checked frock with white sockies and pink, sequined tennis shoes.

While John went upstairs for his luggage, Mr. Moore hugged Laverne and said, "After I'm gone, I want you to take your mommy to see an old friend of mine named Calvin. He may be grumpy and a bit standoffish at first, but you'll know what to do. In no time, you'll have him eating out of your hand."

They walked outside and waited while John put the bags in the trunk of the limousine. When he was done, Mr. Moore kissed Laverne on the forehead and handed her back to Mona. "Can you say good-bye to me now?" he asked, the sparkling in his eyes growing ever more apparent.

Laverne held out her arms and said, "Mee-maw?"

Mr. Moore kissed her one last time and got into the car. As they drove away, Mona could see him waving from the front seat.

His glistening had runneth over. Tears were streaming down his cheeks.

Chapter 40

. . . .

Roostitution

FOR LUNCH THAT AFTERNOON, Clem asked Marie to fix club sand-wiches, "hold the turkey," which is his barely clever way of asking for double-decker BLTs. He orders them the same way in restaurants, which can be a tad embarrassing. Marie also prepared homemade French fries, which she slices paper-thin from Idaho potatoes and flash fries in canola oil. They're more like warm potato chips than conventional fries and cholesterol free, which can hardly be said for Clem's diminished club sandwiches.

John escorted Mr. Moore to the dining room and then disappeared into the kitchen, leaving the three men to their own devices. After they had seated themselves and been served, Clem said, "Calvin tells me you've been busy this week, Vernon. Hell, everybody tells me you've been busy. I don't see how a man can have so much energy. You have to be my age. If Buford's theory is right, you're twice my age. How do you do it?"

Mr. Moore swallowed and replied, "I wonder myself, Clem. The last few days have been more demanding than any in recent memory."

"I'm more than sympathetic, except that I have no idea how much energy it takes to call in a lightning strike. Do you?"

"I haven't the faintest idea, but I can tell you that weather complaints should be filed indoors. I don't recall ever being that wet, even when I was taking SCUBA lessons in Belize."

"So you deny you brought Loretta back to life," Calvin said.

Mr. Moore sat back in his chair. "Is it a denial if it's a fact, or is it just a fact? You tell me."

Before Calvin could answer, Clem asked, "How is Lo? Is she on the comeback trail? Buzz tells me that the restoration of the Bold Cut will be complete within the month. If Loretta's in shape to reopen, I'm going to start letting my hair grow now."

"Doc Wiley says it will take her six to eight weeks to recover fully, but I'm sure she would appreciate the gesture. A hairy Clem Tucker would be a lovely welcome-back gift."

Clem took a big bite out of his sandwich, which Marie cut into little triangular quarters. "Consider it done," he said. "Now, tell me about Wilma's grandson. Did he take the plea?"

"He did. I got a call from Sheriff Hrnicek en route. His co-conspirators surrendered just minutes ago."

"They did?" Calvin asked. "That's terrific. Who were they, the reverend's sons?"

"No. He's much too smart for that. The leaders of the attack were Michael and Gabriel O'Rourke. Matt was their accomplice, not the other way around."

"Who the hell are the O'Rourkes?" Clem asked.

"Brothers; hard-core members of the Divine Temple of the Everlasting God Almighty; the rod and staff of the Reverend Earl Gault."

"Well, well. So it was that bunch after all. A lot of people around here had their suspicions, John and me included. How did you get to the bottom of it?"

"I asked a few questions and listened to the answers; that's all. The last piece of the puzzle didn't fall into place until last night."

Calvin interjected, "If you don't mind, Vernon, what was that?"

"One of the unidentified assailants was noticeably shorter than the other. That eliminated the Gault twins."

"That was it?"

"That was the last part of it, yes."

Clem held up his glass, which was crystal and filled with Perrier and ice. "So the case is closed. Bravo!"

Before Calvin could raise his, Mr. Moore replied, "Not quite. Those boys didn't attack the Bold Cut on their own. They were under orders."

"Orders? From whom?" Clem asked,

"Earl Gault, more likely an intermediary. Even Matt doesn't know. No one ever will unless one of the O'Rourke boys negotiates a deal with Mary Wade."

"Do you think that will happen?"

"No. It'll be offered but I seriously doubt that either will accept."

"Why not? You'd think they would've learned something from Matt."

"That's the problem, Clem: religious zealots don't learn. They believe they have all the answers, and it is that one, divine delusion that makes them so dangerous—and so vulnerable. Without question, the O'Rourkes were programmed to believe that their crimes were God's will and heaven will be their reward. With equal certainty, they were told that they will rot in hell if they give up their vicar. In another time or place, they would die first."

"So the book isn't closed," Clem said.

"It's not, but it needs to be. For that, I'll need your help."

"Mine? What can I do?"

"What can you do?" Mr. Moore asked. "You can do anything you want. Aren't you the new chairman of the board of the National Bank of the Plains?"

Calvin dropped his sandwich. My Fiancé in Perpetuity wiped his mouth and answered, "You, Vernon Moore, are a piece of work. What was the tip-off?"

"There were several. In the first place, you set my expectations for a new number-two memory, this week. On its own, I doubt that the sale of HCB would make your top forty. But then you went to Omaha. That was the tell."

"Couldn't I have been going to a board meeting?"

"A three-day board meeting is too long for business-as-usual, but it's about right for a coup. And even though the CEO was under investigation, the stock had been trending up. My guess: Calvin had been accumulating it quietly for months. How am I doing so far?"

Clem inhaled deeply. "You're right on point."

Mr. Moore went on. "The hard part had to be deposing the CEO. Most corporate boards are chock full of feeble-minded old men these days. Even if you had acquired a lot of stock, you would have needed inside help. Is that right?"

"It is. Would you like to know how the deal went down?"

"I would."

"My main contact at NBP was Fabrizio Santoni, the COO. From our first meeting, I could tell that he was one hell of an executive: supercompetent; as honest as they come; a lifelong employee of the bank. But the board passed him over and recruited a CEO from the outside, then another after that. The third, Burt Nettles, turned out to be a bare-assed thief. As is the fashion these days, he brought a crooked CFO with him and Fabi was cut out of the loop."

"Until you came along."

"That's right. I'd already made the decision to divest. The flap over Millet's two years ago taught me that. So I was looking to unload my bank, and Fabi was looking for a way to save his. We had dinner after our second meeting. By our third, we were in league."

Mr. Moore asked, "How did the mechanics work?"

"With Calvin's help, I managed to acquire five percent of the bank through a series of funds and off-shore accounts. The sale of HCB netted another 3.4 percent."

"I take it that there wasn't a lot of cash involved in the actual sale."

"Right again. The press release said the deal was for cash and stock, but the amount of cash involved was one Yankee dollar. That was a diversion. I didn't want anybody catching on before we closed the trap."

"So you went into the game with 8.4 percent of the bank's common stock. How much did Fabrizio bring to the table?"

"Remember, he's been a top executive at the bank for years. By the time we walked into Burt Nettles' office on Wednesday afternoon, we had just shy of twelve percent in our pockets, plus proxies from the bank's two largest institutional investors. That put us at twenty-six percent and change. Nettles was a goner, but the slippery bastard had to flop around on the deck like a hooked fish for another day and a half anyway. I finally gutted him yesterday morning."

"I take it that Fabrizio is the new CEO."

"That's right. He's earned it and he'll do a fantastic job. To be frank, it was the last thing I wanted for myself. I've never had a full-time job. From where I sit, it looks like work."

"So what's your next move?"

Clem grinned across the table. "Hell, Vernon, I should be asking you that question. What would you do if you were in my shoes?"

"If I was in your shoes, I'd buy a chunk of Campania and write my memoirs. My suspicion, though, is that you're not quite done. My suspicion is that you have something in mind for the Quilting Circle, a parting gift if you will."

Clem and Calvin exchanged glances. Calvin said, "Would you care to be more specific?"

"I can't. Like I said, it's just a notion."

Clem offered, "Do you want to know what it is? Confidentially, of course."

"I would, yes. If you don't mind."

"We're going to structure Hayes County Bank as a subsidiary. We've offered nineteen percent of it to the Quilting Circle, plus a board seat. How about that?"

"I'd say it was unprecedented, but why?"

"Why? For two decades, those women have been sitting in the bleachers and throwing monkey wrenches into my business deals. Calvin and I were sure we'd see some wrenches after the sale of HCB, but we haven't, so far anyway. That's a surprise, isn't it, Calvin?"

"Definitely, and completely out of character."

"I think so, too. What's your view, Vernon?"

The eyes of the two men met and locked. Mr. Moore shrugged but didn't reply.

Clem went on. "Well, I'm putting those armchair wrench-chuckers into the game. I'm making them at least partially responsible for the economic viability of the town. Somewhere in between their quilting bees and bake sales, they're going to have to make some actual business decisions."

"Do you think they'll buy it, Clem? I'm not sure I would. To me, it sounds more like retribution than a business proposition."

Clem sat back in his chair and crossed his legs. "I see it more as roostitution, Vernon, as the chickens coming home to roost. I made the price real sweet; they'll buy it. That reminds me: did you ever have a chance to chat with Bebe Palouse?"

"I tried but I could never reach her."

"Is that so? She came back to Calvin and me with a real innovative proposal for the store. I wanted to thank you. I figured you were behind it."

"Your gratitude is kind but misplaced, Clem. I have no idea what she proposed." Mr. Moore touched the edges of his mouth with his napkin and checked his watch. I guess it was a watch-checking week. "Oh dear," he added. "It's getting late. Lunch has been a joy but I'd like to get down to Kansas City before nightfall."

"That's a good idea. You never know what the weather will be like en route. Are you going to take me up on my offer for a new Cadillac? It's a fine car; I can tell you that."

"Thanks, but I've decided to stay with the Hemi for the time being. There's another way I could use your help, though. It has to do with minimizing risk. Sending the O'Rourkes to jail is a fine start, but the real threat remains at the ranch."

"I agree, but I still don't see what I can do about it."

"Isn't the Temple Ranch a customer of Hayes County Bank?"

"You mean the Hayes County subsidiary of National Bank of the Plains, but yes, they are. We hold a number of their loans, and their deposits."

"Do their deposits cover their debts?"

"Hell no. That Gault character is up to his eyeballs in debt, just like every other clod-buster in this county. It's a damned shame."

Mr. Moore pushed back from the table and began to reflect.

Clem said, "I have a suggestion, Vernon: Don't try to be a banker. Just tell me what you want."

My unusual lodger looked up slowly and replied, "I want you to call his loans, all of them, and freeze his deposits until they're covered."

"Woo-wee! Do you know what you're asking me to do?"

"Yes."

"Are you sure? Are you double damn sure? I don't give a shit about the reverend. You're asking my bank to take a half-million-dollar write-off."

Mr. Moore looked Clem square in the eye and said, "Bill me." That's exactly what he said, full stop. I have it from three independent sources.

Calvin asked, "What did you say?"

"Bill me. Send me a bill."

"Bill you? Do you have that kind of money?"

"Not on me. Will you take a check?"

Calvin started to say something, but my fiancé held up his hand like an Indian chief and sat back in his chair, where he began to twist the corner of his napkin, a wine-colored, cotton item. After some amount of twisting, he rolled it up slowly and placed it on the table, then replied, "Keep your checkbook in your pants, Vernon. Considering your performance this week, I might prefer that you owed me a favor down the road. Besides, this little deal might end up working to our advantage, from a particular point of view." He added quickly, "Calvin, could you excuse us please. I have one last matter to discuss with our guest."

"Sure, Clem. No problem. I'll be out back." He meant the big porch at the back of the River House. For personal reasons, Calvin likes to spend time there.

After the younger man had gone, the elders walked in silence to the doorway. Just before they stepped outside, Clem said, "Calvin is unaware of your world fingerprint record, Vernon. You mentioned yesterday that you were interested in the list of matches. I'd like to know how you found out about that little adventure in the first place. Let's make a trade."

"I appreciate the offer, but I'd rather leave things the way they are."

"Why? I don't like things as they are. Loyalty is extremely important to me and whoever spilled the beans was damned disloyal."

"Loyalty is granted, Clem, not demanded, but it's extraordinarily easy to get in this day and age. If you're fair in your business dealings and honest with your people, they'll be so amazed and so appreciative that they'll give you all the loyalty you can handle. When you're not, you're likely to have a problem or two."

Clem harrumphed and said, "Am I likely to get another sermonette if I ask again?"

"It's a possibility." Mr. Moore put out his hand.

Clem shook it. "It's a pleasure doing business with you, Vernon. John will take you anywhere you want. Just make sure I have him back by Sunday night."

"Before I go, would you mind if . . . ?"

"Take all the time you want. It's the best view in southeast Nebraska. Always has been, always will be."

After the two men parted, Mr. Moore ventured out to the bluff directly behind the River House. Calvin came out the back porch and stood by his side, shoulder-to-shoulder, so that they were both facing the Missouri River.

Mr. Moore said, "I don't know when I'll be back, Calvin. I'd appreciate it if you could keep an eye on Loretta and Laverne while I'm gone."

"Of course, but you have to tell me the truth, man-to-man. Did you do it? Did you bring Loretta back from the dead?"

"I don't know."

"You don't know?"

Mr. Moore turned to face his old friend and replied, "Sometimes I get what I ask for; sometimes I don't."

Leftovers

IN A CLOSED COURTROOM on Monday afternoon, Matt stood before the bench and told the judge everything he knew about the attack on the Bold Cut, the O'Rourke brothers, and his association with the Divine Temple of the Everlasting God Almighty. He was given a ten-year sentence at a medium-security facility in Iowa, but he could be out in less than seven with good behavior.

The entire family was allowed to see Matt in a little meeting room afterward, Mark and Laverne included. It was more of a reunion than a going-away party but we all cried anyway, especially when Matt picked Laverne up and apologized for what he had done. Just before Deputy Giant led him away, his little brother gave him a brand-new iPod that had been programmed with his favorite songs. Mark didn't divulge that he had embedded a complete set of Tony Robbins lectures in the music. I hope they help.

As promised, I didn't tell Matt about the baseball card Mr. Moore left behind, which was a 1948 Jackie Robinson. He was a second baseman and the first black man to play in the Major Leagues. Mona looked the card up on the Internet and discovered that it's worth about nine thousand dollars. It should give Matt a nice nest egg after jail.

Hail Mary Wade offered the O'Rourkes the same plea deal Matt got if they would name the person or persons who ordered the attack on the Bold Cut and the torching of my tree. Dottie even offered them their favorite meals, but their lawyers stepped in and neither boy ever said a word. Matt was deposed at his new jail, but Loretta testified in a wheelchair and didn't leave a dry eye in the house. The jury took less than an hour to convict the boys of one count of attempted murder and one count of first-degree arson. They were sentenced to fifty years each.

Earl Gault was never charged with any crime or misdemeanor, but you can hardly say he came out smelling like a rose. The O'Rourke conviction and the call of his loans broke him, especially since Clem made sure that no other bank in the state would touch him with a ten-foot pole. A few days after the trial was over, the reverend and his flock disappeared into the dead of night. Every woman in Ebb has breathed easier since he left.

To considerable fanfare, Loretta and Mona reopened the Bold Cut on January second. Clem Tucker was their first customer. Like half the other men in town, he was long overdue for a haircut. Loretta is the next thing to fully recovered and back to doing hair and nails herself now. The pin in her forearm aches in the winter cold and her ears ring all the time, but she has no recollection of the attack except for what she has learned since Mr. Moore left town.

Laverne has been back home with Lo for several months, but she still calls her mama, Mona, and me, "Mee-maw." Down deep in my heart, I hope that never changes, but she still hasn't cried. We're all a bit worried about that. Last weekend, Loretta walked Laverne over to the Angles House, just like she promised Mr. Moore. She said that Calvin was a bit withdrawn but he invited them back again this coming Sunday, which surprised everybody.

After weeks of debate, the Circle elected to purchase 29 percent of Millet's Department Store but to pass on Clem's offer for 19 percent of the Hayes County Bank. Our reasoning was that the store was the real linchpin of the county. We wouldn't have had much of a say in the running of the bank anyway since it was a subsidiary. The board of governors also decided not to offer Clem a "chicken exception" membership. That was a mistake in my book, but nobody has asked me to choose between him and the Circle since.

Clem never received the list of Mr. Moore's fingerprint matches from the state patrol. He wasn't told why either, but he was too busy to have more than a day-long temper tantrum about it. That same week, he had the National Bank of the Plains file a jillion-dollar civil suit against Burt Nettles, the CEO he had just deposed. I guess he wasn't finished with the man.

He and I are still dating, even though he spends more time in Omaha than at home nowadays. We even talk about tying the knot from time to time but I have no desire to while away my autumn years in a city far from my friends. I'm not nearly ready to retire from the bed and breakfast business either, even though I secretly harbor a stray gray cat. That little critter is as cute as a dimple and as quiet as a breeze, but he comes and goes whenever he pleases. When he's gone, which is most of the time, I have no idea where he is or what he's up to. Naturally, I named him Vernon after you-know-who.

Marie Delacroix, John Smith, and Calvin Millet each told me who was behind the call of Reverend Gault's loans. Considering the lesson Mr. Moore taught my grandson, that was hardly the most charitable thing he could've done. I guess he's no angel after all.

On the other side of the coin, nearly everybody believes he gave Loretta her life back at least once, which means he gave Laverne her mama back, too. For sure, he gave Matt a second chance, he gave my daughter a new and improved son, he helped Dot and Mary solve their big case, he helped Clem buy a new number-two memory, and he helped Bebe and the Quilting Circle become part-owners in Millet's Department Store. He even gave an antique banjo to an inmate and sent the reverend off with a brand-new speakerphone.

Maybe he's one part angel, one part not.

One Part Angel

George Shaffner

A READER'S GUIDE

A Conversation with
George Shaffner

Jennifer Morgan Gray is a writer and editor
who lives near Washington, D.C.

Jennifer Morgan Gray: It's great to talk to you again, George! So here we are, back in Ebb, with the same colorful cast of characters. Was writing about these characters a bit like visiting old friends— some of whom had gotten into quite a bit of trouble? Did you ever stop thinking about them?

George Shaffner: I do stop thinking about them every so often, but sometimes I find myself quoting them! So they do take on a life of their own. That's very true. And in fact, from a novelist's perspective, they *have* to have a life of their own. The most significant thing about characters like these, and coming back to them, is that every one of them has a point of view. And you have to look at what they're doing, look at what they're saying, from that point of view.

This book was very much like revisiting old friends, although in this book I did have to create some new characters. In many ways, the setting is different this time, because we have a new malevolence that's moved to the outskirts of the county. A lot of what happens takes place in the courthouse and the county jail. So it's set in the same town [as the first book], but the scene overlap is not extraordinarily high.

JMG: Do you do an outline or a family tree?

GS: I have a real clear picture in my mind—and one time I charted it out—of what Ebb looks like. I've never done a detailed family map, but I've always known what the geography was like. Before I sit down and write a book, I'll probably have ten or twenty pages of notes that include primary and secondary plot lines. Tempo is a big issue in a book like this.

JMG: Was it easy to get back into Wilma's voice? It seems as though her eyes would be good prisms in which to see all the workings of Ebb unfold.

GS: It's a piece of cake. I can sit down and write Wilma anytime. I don't know what's wrong with me, why that's so easy! I'm sure that it's some kind of serious psychological problem, but it's really easy for me to look at things through her eyes.

JMG: I was shocked that a grandson of Wilma Porter's would be involved in what amounts to a hate crime. Given that, do you think that Ebb is still the last oasis of nice? Or is the outside world encroaching upon it? If there are problems in Ebb, it seems like the rest of the globe must be in dire straits.

GS: Well, it is still the last oasis of nice, but it's a struggle. What Matt has become is a garden-variety disaffected teenager, and one of the big points of this book is that kids like that are incredibly easy to manipulate. They don't have any self-esteem—or not enough. They don't have any direction. With no self-esteem, there is no confidence. There just isn't any keel there. And it makes it easy for someone who comes along and says, "You're great. We have a different kind of solution for you. All these different people are wrong and we're going to help you become the real you. And, by the way, all you have to do is become a suicide bomber."

That's the metaphor for this whole thing. Showing how easy it is for a teenager, particularly for a young male, to fall into a trap like that. There is a stratum of teenagers who are a lot more disaffected than others. They are underachievers. They don't have the type of self-esteem they'd like to have. They're not comfortable where they are. They want to go someplace else, although they don't have any idea what or where that is. A sweet-talking someone who comes along with that destination, and who basically flatters them, can fall in with them very quickly. And because teens are young, and because they're inexperienced, and because they're so incredibly naïve, they're very easy to manipulate. And because of their arrogance, they don't know it.

JMG: And that's why someone like Matt would take refuge in a religious sect.

GS: And that's why they all do! Or why they fall in with gangs. Or why they disappear into vicarious forms of self-gratification, like video games. Those are all ways of adapting badly to the problem, rather than facing it and solving it. And in this particular case, Vernon's challenge coming in—in his usual six days, a theme that carries on, by the way—is that he has to break Matt out of it. He has to find a way in a very short period of time first to get through to him, and then to give him a way to deal with all these issues.

And that's what this book is about. It's the "charity" book of faith, hope, and charity. But the real underlying theme of this book is: What do you give a teenager that will give him or her the ability to look at their situation skeptically and intelligently when they need to? That's where the trilogy comes in. In the first book, Vernon sold hope to Calvin Millet. In this book, he sells charity. It turns out, as he says, that charity is where being smart and being strong overlap. In the third book, he comes back to sell faith.

If you look at conventional religion, there are basically three parts that really matter to people. One is belief in life after life, which was book one—which was hope. Another is faith and the possibility that God can intervene, that he can answer my prayers. That's book three. Book two, this book, is a code of conduct. But if you take a look at the existing biblical code of conduct that we have, it's not very useful, especially when you're confronted with modern problems. And this is the ultimate question of the book.

JMG: How did all the tumult in today's world over long-held beliefs—and delusions—affect your writing of this book? Did you aim to make it topical and political, or was this a case where life imitated art?

GS: That's a huge part of this book, a huge part of this theme. It was that way all along. The issue here, because once I'm in the code of conduct, it allows me to philosophically explore some things that I couldn't explore in book one or book three. But it strikes me that one of the key parts of this book is that belief is the gray area between fact and delusion. When you think about what's going on in the world with religious fervor, these are all people who are killing and maiming each other. Terrorism. Closing borders. Kidnapping. Beheading. All of these horrible things—all based on belief. They're guessing. Since the get-go, we have murdered millions because we're guessing. Because we think that our guess is better than their guess. Isn't that the most appalling and stupid thing you've every heard of?

I might have entitled [this book], "Put Him on the Speakerphone." I get so tired of people like Pat Robertson saying that they talk to God. Let all of us hear it. And if you can't, you know what? I don't think He's talking to you. I think you're making it up.

These are not books about a small town that happen to have a philosophical foundation. These are philosophical books that happen to take place in a small town. That's the stage.

JMG: That was a conscious decision on your part, to present these philosophies in a way that people would not be intimidated by it?

GS: When I wrote the first book, I didn't know yet that there were three paradoxes. I knew there was one, but I didn't know I'd have to solve two more. But I was a business executive. I know that to solve difficult concepts, you need to make them understandable to people. And you want to make it entertaining. And from that perspective—even though I'd never written a novel before—it was Novel 101.

But look at somebody like Hesse. The difference between him and some of his Germanic counterparts is that a book like *Demian* is very easy to read. And my objective from the beginning was, how can I take Hesse and move him closer to Mark Twain?

I think that the best storyteller in the history of American literature was Mark Twain. He has to be updated, because at the time that he wrote, the pace was slow. Everything was slow. His books were slow. *Life on the Mississippi* was incredibly slow—but then, so was life on the Mississippi. In contemporary terms, you have to speed things up.

JMG: And talk about someone being able to weave in relevant, controversial themes with everyday life. Mark Twain was a master at that.

GS: And how did he do it? He did it in small towns. He did it with people who were street smart, but intellect never plays a role in his novels. Instead, it's about people exploring simple, common themes that require common sense.

JMG: Loretta is targeted because she's different in many ways. What about her differences make some people in Ebb uncomfortable? How does her color—and her status as a single mother—play into that?

GS: Well, gee. Let's take a bunch of low-self-esteem, weak white men and put them in a room with an intelligent, strong black woman, and tell them to go fly a kite. What would be worrisome about that? To me, she's the embodiment of what a lot of weak men fear. She's a business owner. She's articulate. She's one of the smartest women in town. She's very strong. She's nobody's fool.

JMG: And now she's an unwed mother.

GS: In the book she says, "It wasn't Vernon's fault. I seduced him." There's no way that she would cede that kind of control to a man, whether it was true or not.

JMG: What was the point you wanted to make in this book about the value of diversity?

GS: It's another one of those issues where the human race doesn't even approach intelligence. We take diversity so much for granted that we're constantly killing it off. And it is one of the great values of life. That's why Vernon goes through so much time showing Matt the value of diversity. It was handed to us on a platter, and as a species we treat it no better than a child.

Diversity is one of the keys to richness in life, and all we do as human beings is organize ourselves to stomp it out. It's simply unintelligent. If we are going to call ourselves an intelligent race, we need to be intelligent enough to understand that the richness of our life depends upon it.

JMG: We touched on this a little bit, but why do you think that someone like Matt would take refuge in a religion like the Divine Temple of the Everlasting God Almighty?

My son was a disaffected teenager also. A committed under-achiever. No direction whatsoever. He didn't know what he wanted—he just knew what he *didn't* want, which is what he had. He didn't want to be put into the box he was in. All he wanted was another box that was built for him, that would make him more comfortable. The world is full of kids who are looking for that other box. And you know what, they're not very smart about the next box they are looking for. All they know is that they want a box. And if the people in that box say, "We love you. You're fine. You're like us," that's the attraction of cults.

Vernon's answer to the code of conduct was two simple questions: Is it better to be smart or stupid? Is it better to be strong or weak? And that actually was a huge philosophical exercise underneath the book. As a former mathematician, it was me boiling down a lot of things into these two simple questions. Well, I wish I had been smart enough, when my son was growing up, to ask him a question. Gee, Carl, is it better to be stupid or is it better to be smart? When the options were plainly there, but I couldn't articulate the question.

And the same is true of strong or weak. One of the problems with our culture in particular is that we've changed the definition of strong. Strong is taking care of yourself. Strong, in this society, is doing what you want. And the reason is that it sells beer, it sells cars, it sells chewing gum. That's the new strong. But it's merely self-indulgent. And, in fact, that's weak when you look at it.

But strong means only one thing. It's the way Vernon treats it in the book. It's strong enough to help others. It's past the point that you can take care of yourself. That's the only definition that matters.

An awful lot of this book deals with very simple truths that have been lost, somehow. We can't even define words anymore! Strong versus weak. They're confused. They're upside down.

JMG: As in the first book, the Quilting Circle thinks it all comes back to Millet's Store as the linchpin of the town. Do you think they're right about that? What about the store is so integral to Ebb as an entity?

GS: It *is* the linchpin of the town. If you look at a mall, every mall has one or more anchor stores. If you look at the history of Nebraska and the plains states, even now, one or two towns in Nebraska disappear every year. They just evaporate and go away. They don't die from the outside in. They die from the inside out. The economy breaks down, there's no gathering place any more, there's no focal point.

Millet's is the economic focus of the town. It's the main thing that brings people to Main Street. It's analogous to the anchor store that sits on either side of a mall. If they lose it in a mall, they have to go out and get another one. If you're in a remote rural town of two thousand people, you're not going to get another store. What you're going to do is get a Wal-Mart out of town in a ravine somewhere, and the town is dead.

The store really is the linchpin of the town. The Circle decides to invest in the store rather than the bank because the store is a corporation unto itself; the bank is a subsidiary. There's no point to having a defensive position in a subsidiary, because the parent company can tell you to just take a hike.

JMG: Clem Tucker has had somewhat of a rebirth since In *the Land of Second Chances*. For example, he definitely seems to be thinking of life as more of a game these days. What's behind Clem's new attitude? How did Vernon Moore influence him and his actions?

GS: Vernon is *the* influence. Clem isn't doing all this for the hell of it. Clem has a strategy. In the first book, Clem tried to take a majority position in Millet's basically so that he could control the future of the town; Vernon prevented Clem from doing that. That taught Clem a lesson. So Clem is now in the process of changing his strategy. In fact, that strategy unfolds here in *One Part Angel*. Clem's reason for living is that he's a pure money man. All he wants to do is to make the trust as big as he can make it. And since he couldn't own the county, he has decided to change strategy—and that was the point of the Big Buyback. He got out of the farming business, so he sold all the farms. But then the local bank owned all the mortgages. So then he has this fantastic, high-valued loan portfolio, then he used that as leverage to take over a bigger bank—along with many other things.

So what's Clem done? Because he couldn't own the county, he took his investments out of the county. It's very much analogous to sending your jobs offshore.

JMG: The interplay between Clem and Vernon is really interesting.

GS: You know, I know a lot of Clem Tuckers. I used to be a business executive before I became a late-onset novelist. I've had six C-fill-in-the-blank-O titles. I have had a lot of those interchanges myself. So I know the kind of person extremely well.

And I don't want to portray Clem Tucker as one-sided or stereotyped. He's not. I may have thought that some of the executives I worked with were relatively black-hearted, and that they were too weak to realize that they could succeed and help people at the same time, rather than succeeding by *not* helping them, but they were also complex and smart people. I wanted Clem to be that way, too.

And Vernon has to be a strong character. You're only beginning to understand what Vernon really is. All I wanted from the interchange was for Clem to have a strategy and a vision, and for them both to be strong. The irony of this book is that Vernon sees what Clem is doing, and he actually helps him this time. And that should cause a question in the reader's mind.

JMG: Why would Vernon help Clem?

GS: And the answer to that is in the third book.

JMG: Whenever Vernon Moore appears, amazing things happen. What about him inspires trust—and a suspension in the typical rules of the day, an acceptance that certain odd, miraculous things may well happen?

GS: Vernon is just this guy who goes out and does good work. That's one reason why people like him. Another reason is that he looks successful, and he behaves that way, but he asks them questions and he listens to their answers. The real reason that people like him, and that he gets along with them, is that he's very good at what he does! He gets everything fixed. He's successful at it. By the time he leaves, it's becoming clearer and clearer to everyone—because he seems to be prescient—that Vernon just isn't like the rest of us.

Remember the "Lady Be Good" theory—the World War II bomber that went down in a failed mission over Naples? When Buford Pickett tried to find out who Vernon was, he could only find a

Vernon L. Moore that went down with it, who was also born in New Boston, Ohio. When Vernon is fingerprinted, they find nine fingerprint matches going back to 1954, for a guy who looks like he's in his mid-forties? How is that possible?

Even before we get to the point where Vernon may or may not have helped Loretta, it should be becoming clear that Vernon is not us.

JMG: In the third book, will we actually find out what Vernon is?

GS: All of this is explored in book three, which is divine-intervention theory. And that's when it becomes almost perfectly clear who or what Vernon is. But not quite.

JMG: Another way that Vernon Moore remains an enigma: If he's retired, why can't he just settle in Ebb permanently? Seems like everyone would be happy to have him—particularly his daughter Laverne.

GS: And the answer is, he just can't. He always has somewhere else to go, doesn't he?

JMG: Can you give a hint of whether Clem and Wilma will *ever* get married?

GS: No. Book Three!

JMG: When last we spoke, you outlined your plan for three books in Ebb: one where Vernon Moore sells hope (*In the Land of Second*

Chances); one, charity (*One Part Angel*), and one, faith. When can we expect this third book in the Ebb trilogy on bookshelves?

GS: The third book is finished. We're pretty deep into the edits. That book is the completion of the story. It is the philosophical examination of faith. It should be out in twelve to fifteen months; it's on the Algonquin fall list.

READING GROUP QUESTIONS AND TOPICS FOR DISCUSSION

1. What does the title *One Part Angel* mean to you? Which characters in this book could be aptly described by the book's title?

2. Why do you think that George Shaffner begins this book in media res—that is, in the middle of things? In your opinion, what was the most surprising thing that had happened in Ebb since Vernon Moore had left town? How is the town changed? How is it still an "oasis of nice"?

3. Why do you think Vernon returns to Ebb so unexpectedly? Do you think that the townspeople were awaiting his return? What do you think is Vernon's most admirable quality? How is he otherworldly? In which ways is he a typical man?

4. On page 87, Vernon says, "Between here and history, chance is all there is." What do you think he means by that assertion? How do the events that unfold in the book support that statement? How do you think this forms a theme of the book?

5. Why do you think that Wilma waits for her "perpetual fiancé," Clem Tucker? Why do you think Clem elects to sell off his holdings

in the town? What do you think his master plan for the town might be? Do you think the Quilting Circle's opinion of him changes from the beginning of this book to its conclusion? How about Wilma's attitude toward Clem?

6. Vernon sets out to teach Matt a code of conduct. How does he succeed in doing so? Can you give an example from your own life of how adherence to a code of conduct can make the world a better place?

7. Vernon Moore describes belief as the gray area between fact and delusion. Do you agree or disagree with this definition? How does reliance on belief spur problems in the town of Ebb? In the world today?

8. How do Matt's mother and grandmother cope with his actions toward Loretta? How are their coping mechanisms similar and different? How about Mark's reaction to his family's tumult? How are the two brothers different? What do you expect to see from them both in the future?

9. In which ways is Matt a typical teenager? What about Reverend Gault's religion might appeal to Matt? How is Reverend Gault himself an imposing figure? How is he easily ridiculed?

10. At first, Matt refuses to disclose his accomplices in the attack on the Bold Cut because he wants to protect "me and mine." How does this noble impulse have bad ramifications? What do you think you would do in a similar situation?

11. One of the questions Vernon asks Matt is whether life is an individual sport, a team sport, or both. How would you answer this

question? How does the answer to this question inform Matt's own actions—and more broadly, how does it inform world events?

12. When Loretta comes back from the dead, the town regards Vernon as a miracle worker. What is your opinion of how she is revived? Do you think that Vernon would ever come back to stay with her and Laverne? Why or why not?

13. Vernon says that strength requires selflessness (page 288). Describe how different characters in this novel display strength in the face of adversity. How do those who are strong also display courage and intellect?

14. Do you think that the Quilting Circle makes the right decision by buying part of the store, but not of the bank? What do you think prompts their choice? How does the Quilting Circle function as a business entity within the town? How does it form an informal governing body of Ebb?

15. At the end of the book, Vernon says that the "chickens are coming home to roost." In your opinion, does everyone get what he or she deserves at the novel's conclusion? Were you surprised by anything that transpired?

16. George Shaffner has said that this is the second in a three-book series. From the conclusion of this book, what do you imagine will be front and center in the next novel? Which characters do you most want to hear more about?